## "When di

Becki caught Josh's arm... note. "It was in the mailbox when I got here. Courtesy of my sister."

Josh frowned. "Why would she say you don't belong here?"

"Because if I sell, she thinks she'll get more money."

"Who else knew you were moving in today?"

"I don't know." Becki rubbed her worsening headache. "My boss, my roommate, my mom."

"No one from around here?"

"Not that I know of. Like I told my sister, I'm here to stay."

Josh sat beside Becki on the sofa, and her heart jumped at the touch of his knee. "Who else might have sent this note?"

"What do you mean?"

"I mean...who didn't want you moving here badly enough to attack you?"

She dug her fingers into the seat cushion. "You think the note and the incident in the barn are connected?"

Obviously he did. Which meant whoever was slinking around the property had been expecting her.

**Books by Sandra Orchard**

Love Inspired Suspense

\*_Deep Cover_
\*_Shades of Truth_
\*_Critical Condition_
  _Fatal Inheritance_

\*Undercover Cops

## SANDRA ORCHARD

hails from the beautiful countryside of Niagara, Ontario, where inspiration abounds for her romantic-suspense novels—not that she runs into any bad guys, but because her imagination is free to run as wild as her Iditarod-wannabe husky. Sandra lives with her real-life hero husband, who happily provides both romantic and suspense inspiration, as long as it doesn't involve poisons and his dinner. But her truest inspiration comes from the Lord, in the beauty of a sunrise over the field and the whisper of a breeze, in the antics of a killdeer determined to safeguard its nest and the faithfulness of the seasons. She enjoys writing stories that both keep the reader guessing and reveal God's love and faithfulness through the lives of her characters.

Sandra loves to hear from readers and can be reached through her website, or at www.Facebook.com/SandraOrchard or c/o Love Inspired Books, 233 Broadway, Suite 1001, New York, NY 10279.

# FATAL INHERITANCE

# SANDRA ORCHARD

HARLEQUIN® LOVE INSPIRED® SUSPENSE

Recycling programs
for this product may
not exist in your area.

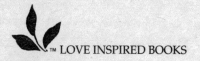

™ LOVE INSPIRED BOOKS

ISBN-13: 978-0-373-67572-2

FATAL INHERITANCE

Copyright © 2013 by Sandra van den Bogerd

www.LoveInspiredBooks.com

**Printed in U.S.A.**

You will be consoled when you see their conduct
and their actions, for you will know that
I have done nothing in it without cause.
—*Ezekiel* 14:23

To my stepsister, Rebecca-Becki-Bec,
for letting me borrow all her names.

With special thanks to Karen and Alf Acres for
giving me a ride in their "horseless carriage" and
answering all my antique car questions, along
with Albert Unrau. Also to my wonderful critique
buddies, Eileen, Laurie, Vicki and Wenda, who help
smooth all the story's rough edges. And to the NRP
officers who tirelessly answer my police questions.

# ONE

At the sight of her grandparents' old farmhouse, with its wide front porch and empty rocking chairs, Becki Graw blinked back bittersweet tears. All her life she'd longed to live in Serenity's beautiful countryside, but not like this. She stopped at the roadside mailbox and grabbed the mail—a single letter addressed to her. No return address.

*That's strange.* Who would know to write to her here? She slid her thumb under the flap and pulled out the single typewritten page.

You don't belong here.

Her heart jolted at the cold, black words. Who—
She crushed the note in her fist. *Sarah.* Becki floored the gas and veered into the driveway, then punched her sister's number on her cell phone.

Sarah answered on the first ring.

"You've sunk to new lows," Becki fumed.

"I warned you I'd go to the lawyer if you didn't

agree to sell and split everything fifty-fifty. You should've listened to me."

Becki ground to a stop in front of the white two-story willed to her by Gran and Gramps. It wasn't as if they hadn't left her sister anything. She'd gotten most of the liquid assets, not to mention all the financial help when her husband was in law school. Even if Becki sold the house, Sarah probably wouldn't come out that much further ahead.

While Becki would lose the only place that had ever felt like home.

She looked at the darkened windows and empty porch and swallowed a rush of grief. "I'm talking about the note."

"What note? I didn't send any note."

"Right. Because people are lining up to scare me out of here."

To think she'd once idolized her beautiful older sister. No more. At twenty-seven, Becki could finally see Sarah for who she really was—a spoiled trophy wife as materialistic and money-grubbing as her flashy lawyer husband. "Gran and Gramps wanted this house to stay in the family, and I'm here to stay whether you like it or not." Becki punched the power button and jumped from her packed-to-the-roof car.

Inhaling the sweet scent of summer in Ontario's farm country, she shoved Sarah's threats from her mind and turned to the home she loved so dearly.

If only the carbon-monoxide detector had worked

the way it was supposed to, Gran and Gramps would be bustling outside to wrap her in their arms this very moment.

Becki scrunched her eyes closed as memories flooded her mind. Swinging from the barn loft into a pile of hay. Fishing in the creek with Gramps. Collecting fragrant bouquets of bouncing bets for Gran. Her summers here had been her happiest. More than once she'd begged to be allowed to live here always.

But not like this—not without them. She pressed her arm against the ache in her chest.

The sun dipped behind the trees with a splash of brilliant reds and purples as if Gramps himself was painting a welcome-home banner across the sky.

*I can do this. I want to do this.*

Let Sarah call her crazy for quitting her admin job and giving up the lease on her apartment. So what if she'd never find a husband in the boonies? Maybe she didn't want one. If Sarah's and Mom's unhappy marriage experiences were anything to go by, she was better off single.

Besides, Sarah didn't really care whether Becki found a husband or a decent job in Serenity. All she cared about was squeezing more inheritance out of their grandparents' estate.

Indignant-sounding meows drifted from the weathered hipped-roof barn behind the house.

*Kittens!* Memories of laughter-filled afternoons playing with each summer's new litter propelled her feet toward the barn. The light was fading fast, but from the way Mama Cat carried on, Becki would have no trouble finding them.

The meowing stopped.

She hurried past the enormous sliding door and pushed through the regular door next to it.

A flight of barn swallows swooped out a hole in the roof.

She paused while her eyes adjusted to the dim light slanting through the gaps in the weathered boards.

A yowl sounded from the back of the barn, but instead of a cat, her gaze lit on Gramps's 1913 Cadillac. *Oh, wow!* How could she have forgotten about Gramps's antique in here?

She drew in a deep breath. Now it was hers, along with everything else at the farm.

Sadness gripped her. Riding in the old car wouldn't be the same without Gramps at the wheel. She just wanted her grandparents back.

She picked her way around the farm implements, her gaze tracking to the car every few seconds. How she'd loved riding with Gran and Gramps, all dressed up in old-fashioned clothes, to the church's anniversary Sunday celebration.

Becki danced her fingers over the hood and marveled at how little dust coated it even after all these weeks. Gramps had always taken such pride in keeping it polished.

A soft mew whispered from the shadows.

Grateful for the distraction, Becki rounded the car. "Here, kitty."

A thunk sounded behind her.

Heart pounding, she whirled on her heel.

A puff of dust floated up from around a block of wood on the floor.

She peered up at the hayloft, thinking a cat must have knocked it down. The dust and smell of moldy hay scratched her lungs.

Movement flashed in her peripheral vision. Something big. Much bigger than a cat.

She ducked behind an upturned wheelbarrow and squinted into the shadows. "Hello." She took a deep breath, forced her voice louder. "Anyone there?"

A faint echo taunted her.

She strained to listen for movement, but she couldn't hear anything over the roar of blood pulsing past her ears. She edged around the wheelbarrow and scanned the other direction.

Something shuffled behind her.

She spun toward the sound. "Who's there?"

A figure lunged out of the shadows, swinging a hunk of wood.

She thrust up her arms.

The wood glanced off and slammed into the side of her head.

White light exploded in her vision. She dropped to her knees, tasting blood. The ground rushed toward her.

Swishing whispered past her ears as blackness swallowed her.

\* \* \*

Becki gripped her pounding head. *What happened?*

She opened one eye. The sight of a strange, shadowy room jerked her fully awake. Unfamiliar smells assaulted her. Dirt. And…

She froze. Now she remembered. Gramps's barn. Someone had hit her.

She lifted her head a few inches and waited for the ringing in her ears to subside. She rolled onto her back and peered up at the loft. Was that where he'd been hiding?

Out of nowhere a beam of light flashed over the hood of the car.

She swallowed a scream.

The beam jigged across the barn wall, casting ghoulish shadows.

Hide. She had to hide. Pain rocketed through her head the instant she tried to rise. Gritting her teeth, she dragged herself away from the car—the first place he'd look. Only…why'd he leave, then come back?

She shrank behind an old tractor tire. The reason couldn't be good.

"Bec? You in here?" Joshua Rayne called into his neighbor's barn.

A gasp came from somewhere in the shadows.

He rushed forward. "Bec?"

"Over here."

Josh jerked his flashlight beam toward the tentative response. Bec sat huddled behind a tractor tire, her face chalky-white.

Lowering the beam, he hurried to her. "What happened? Why are you hiding back here?"

"You scared me."

His heart kicked at the crack in her voice. "I'm sorry." He clasped her hand. Her fingers were far more delicate than those of the freckled tomboy she'd been the last time he'd found her hiding in this barn. He tugged her to her feet. "I saw the barn door open and—"

She swayed and clutched her head.

"What's wrong?" He directed his flashlight beam toward her face.

Shielding her eyes, she leaned back against the tractor tire with a moan and soothed her swollen lower lip with the tip of her tongue. "Someone hit me."

"Hit you?" Apparently that car he'd seen hightail it out of the farmer's lane a minute ago hadn't been just a couple of teens looking for a place to park as he'd supposed. He scanned her head for signs of trauma. "Are you okay?"

She pushed his light away. "I will be when you get that out of my eyes."

Josh redirected his flashlight to the floor.

A four-foot length of timber lay on the ground a few feet away.

"Did you see who hit you?"

"I just saw a shadowy figure."

"Tall? Short? Fat? Skinny?"

"I don't know." Bec clutched her head again. "Your average-size shadow."

He needed to get her inside and check her over properly. Irritability could be a sign of a concussion. He quickly swept his flashlight in widening circles. "Why'd you come in here in the dark?"

"I heard cats meowing and hoped to find kittens."

*Of course. Same old Becki.*

She stepped past him and stroked the hood of her grandfather's old Cadillac. "Then I saw Gramps's car."

At the emotion in her voice, Josh's breath hitched. Her grandfather had had a way of making troubles seem not so bad. The hours he and Josh had spent together tinkering on the "old gal" had been a lifeline after his mother had up and left Serenity without so much as a backward glance. But he couldn't help Josh through this loss.

Josh forced his mind back to the present, to his police training. "Did you hear or see anything that could help us identify who hit you?"

She started to shake her head, then winced.

Josh resisted the urge to wrap an arm around her shoulders and instead directed his flashlight at the items a thief might have been after. Nothing appeared to be missing, but he couldn't be sure until daylight.

Misty twined herself around his legs, purring.

He lifted her into his arms and scratched her chin. "I guess you're looking for your supper, huh?" He turned to Bec, remembering how much she'd adored the cats as a kid. "I've been feeding them since your grandparents…" He lowered Misty to the ground and let the explanation trail off rather than dredge up her loss. He pointed his flashlight at a box beneath the car. "The kittens are under there."

Her delighted squeal tugged a grin to his lips—his first since finding her grandparents' lifeless bodies.

He tugged the box out from under the car.

Bec sat cross-legged on the floor and gathered the kittens into her arms.

Josh chuckled. She hadn't changed a bit. For all her tomboy ways, she was still a soft touch. He gave Misty fresh food and water and then looked around as best he could without leaving Bec in total darkness. If only the barn had overhead lighting, he might find some clue as to who she'd surprised. Most likely kids out for a lark. He hadn't recognized the car he'd spotted as belonging to any of their usual troublemakers. He wished he'd gotten the license plate number.

Josh let his gaze settle back on Bec. Seeing her delight in the wiggling kittens, he could almost feel the years strip away to when they were both kids and life was carefree.

She winced, her forehead creasing.

"Hey, we'd better get you inside. Take a look at that bump. You might need to see a doctor."

A frown curved her lips, but she returned the kittens to the box and pushed it back under the car, which told him more than words would how lousy she felt. When she was a kid, not even promises of chocolate cake and ice cream had been incentive enough to drag her away from the squirming fur balls.

He didn't miss the way she braced her hand on the car fender to pull herself up, either. He moved to her side and, lighting the floor ahead of them, guided her with a light touch to the small of her back. "Do you feel nauseous?"

"A little. But I haven't eaten since lunch."

Outside the barn, he steered her toward his place. "Did you lose consciousness after you were hit?"

"I'm not sure. I think, maybe. Everything went black for a second or two."

"You probably have a concussion. I can do a few tests to see if you should go to the hospital."

She walked a little taller. "I'm fine really. I just need a couple of painkillers. All the doctor's going to do is tell me to go home and take it easy."

"Humor me."

She squinted up at him, then at the tree line that separated their properties and abruptly stopped. "Hey, where are you taking me?"

"To my house. You said you hadn't eaten, right?"

"You don't have to feed me."

"You're in no condition to cook. Besides, it'll be

nice to have someone to eat with." Life had been too quiet around here since her grandparents' deaths.

"I don't want to put you out," she protested.

He nudged her forward. "It's no imposition."

She wavered a moment but soon started walking again. "Gramps told me you took over your parents' place after your dad died. Did you still tinker with Gramps on the old car?"

"Yup. Went with them on one of those organized tours they were always taking, too. Saw some cool places most tourists don't get to see."

"I wish I could've gone on one. Gramps said he'd take me when I turned thirteen, but that's when Mom left Dad, and I never got to come back for any more summers."

He steered her around his truck in the driveway. "Yeah, come to think of it, life got pretty quiet around here without you girls."

She swatted him.

He let out an *oomph* and clutched his gut.

"Very funny."

He smiled to himself and mentally ticked off two of his concussion tests. Nothing wrong with Bec's memory or her aim.

He led her to the side of the house and pulled out his key. "Feel like a steak?"

"Yuck."

"You're kidding? You still prefer a burger to steak?"

"Yup."

He pushed open the door, flicked on the light and

motioned her in ahead of him. "What a cheap date. Guys must love you."

She squirmed past him into the kitchen, then hesitated, her gaze flagging about, pausing briefly on his Home Is Where the Heart Is plaque, then stealing his way. She looked more uneasy than a suspect in custody.

But unlike with his suspects, he felt strangely sad seeing her this way. "Have a seat at the table while I light the barbecue." He returned a moment later to find her nuzzling his three-legged pooch.

She spluttered at its exuberant kisses and wiped off the slobber with the back of her hand. "What's his name?"

"Tripod."

"I should have guessed. He moves amazingly quick for having only three legs."

Josh filled Tripod's dish, and the pooch demonstrated just how quick. "While the barbecue heats up, let's take a look at this bump of yours."

She finger combed her hair as if only just realizing how messy it was.

He resisted the urge to tease. Her honey-brown corkscrew curls had always poked out every which way and been peppered with hay or leaves or twigs, depending on where she'd last played.

Dropping her hand, she fidgeted under his perusal. "That bad, huh?"

"I didn't say anything."

She rolled her eyes. "You didn't have to."

He didn't bother to hide his grin. "Show me where you got hit."

She leaned forward and pointed to the back of her head.

He palpated the area. Her hair was incredibly soft and smelled faintly like citrus. "That's some goose egg." He reached into his catchall drawer and pulled out a penlight. "Look at me."

Her shimmering brown eyes turned to him, framed by the longest lashes he'd ever seen. Natural, too.

Her head tilted. "You planning to do something with that light?"

*"Patience,"* he muttered at being caught staring. He flicked the penlight on and flashed it across each eye. "They look good. Equal and reactive."

"Why, thank you, Josh," she drawled, batting those long lashes. "That's the most romantic thing a man's ever said about my eyes."

"What?" He blinked, glimpsed her smirk and gave her a nudge. "You're cute, Bec." He tossed the penlight back into the drawer. "Now, stand up, arms out from your sides, and touch each hand to your nose."

She stood and obeyed his directions effortlessly.

"Okay, take a seat." He opened the cupboard next to the sink and grabbed a glass and the bottle of painkillers. He tipped two from the bottle, filled the glass with water and handed them to Bec. "Take these, and if you want, you can lie down on the sofa until supper's ready."

She planted her palms on the table and pushed to her feet. "I can't let you cook alone," she protested, then immediately clutched the side of her head.

"As stubborn as ever, I see." He scooped her into his arms and gently lowered her onto the sofa. "Rest. That's an order."

He turned on his heel and did his best to ignore the scent that lingered on his shirt, as it had after their embrace at the funeral home. "I'll get those burgers grilling."

She didn't argue, which worried him. She'd always been a tough kid. Unless she'd changed dramatically in the past fifteen years, whoever had walloped the back of her head had done a serious number on her. Maybe he should ask his sister to come by after her shift at the hospital and check Bec over. It'd be easier than convincing Bec to go there.

He texted Anne a request to stop by and then pulled out the fixings for a decent supper. Sliced potatoes and onions. Peppers, carrots and zucchini for grilling. He dug through the freezer and unburied a couple of burgers that looked more like frozen hockey pucks. Forget it. She could learn to appreciate the good stuff. He tossed the burgers back into the freezer and pulled out a couple of filet mignons.

An hour later, he'd just set the last dish on the

table when she meandered to the doorway, rubbing her eyes.

"Dinner is served." He pulled out a chair and waited for her to take a seat. To humor her, he'd put her steak on a hamburger bun and brought out the mustard and ketchup. If she noticed the ruse, she didn't comment.

He took the seat opposite her. "How do you feel now?"

"Hungry. This smells amazing."

He opted to let her nonanswer go. For now. His sister would be there soon enough. He reached across the table and clasped Bec's hand.

Her eyes widened.

"Let's pray," he said quickly, not sure what to make of her reaction. He bowed his head. "Lord, we pray for Your healing touch on Bec and that You'll comfort her in her grief. Thank You for giving her a safe journey here and for this food and time together. Amen." When Josh lifted his gaze, she was still staring at him, moisture pooling in her eyes.

"What's wrong?"

"No one's prayed for me like that since...Gran and Gramps. I...guess I'd forgotten how nice it felt."

His throat tightened. She'd still have them if only... He gave her hand a warm squeeze. "Let's eat."

They ate in silence for a few minutes, then Bec set

down her "burger" and reached for her fork. "What happened to the huge trailer Gramps usually kept the car in?"

"That's over at Pete's Garage. Your grandfather had some trouble with the car during the last tour he and your Gran took, so while we worked on finding the problem, he sent in the trailer to have the bearings repacked. I can give Pete a call. Ask him to bring it by."

"I'm just amazed how clean the car stayed sitting out like that. There wasn't a bird dropping on it."

A steak morsel lodged in Josh's throat. He coughed, swallowed hard. "You mean you didn't pull off the canvas cover?"

"No."

He set down his knife and fork. He'd just assumed... He clenched his fist. *A rookie mistake.* After the front-page article the newspaper had run last week about the Graws, every would-be thief in three counties would've pegged the whole place as easy pickings until the new owner arrived. But if her assailant had come for the car...

"Are you telling me that Gramps didn't leave it uncovered?"

Josh surged to his feet and paced to the window that overlooked the rear of the Graw property. Her arrival wouldn't deter a car thief. He'd have to keep a close watch on the place.

And pray this guy didn't return when Bec was home alone.

\* \* \*

Becki shrank into the corner of Josh's couch as he debated with his nurse sister whether she needed to see a doctor.

Even dressed in faded jeans and a black T-shirt, his furrowed brow radiating concern, he exuded a powerful presence. Not to mention he'd grown more handsome than ever. His dark hair no longer curled at his temple the way she remembered, but the trimmed look and broader shoulders reflected a strength and integrity that had clearly deepened in the past fifteen years.

How cruel could God be to let Joshua Rayne find her cowering in the barn as if she was still a twelve-year-old kid?

The kid who'd had a hopeless crush on him—a sixteen-year-old boy who'd had eyes only for her gorgeous older sister.

Not that she'd ever admit to having a crush. Bad enough that she'd tumbled into his arms at the funeral.

Never mind that she'd been a wreck and that when Josh had reached for her hand in the reception line, she'd known, without stopping to think, that *he* understood her sorrow.

She hugged a sofa pillow to her chest. He hadn't hesitated a second before wrapping her in his arms, which should've been her first clue that he was still playing the protective big brother. At the time, she'd barely registered his whispered reassurances. The grief had been too raw. But now…

She pushed the pillow away. She did not want him thinking she was a helpless female who couldn't take care of herself.

"Can you recite the months of the year in reverse order for me?" his sister asked.

Becki did, then turned back to Josh. "See. I'm fine."

"Concussions can suddenly take a turn for the worse," he argued, holding out his hand for her car keys. "Can't they, Anne?"

"She's agreed to stay already!" Anne snatched up Becki's car keys and slapped them into Josh's hand. "Go get her suitcase so we can finish the tests in peace." Her eyes were twinkling when she turned back to Becki. "Just humor him for me, okay? I'm getting a free oil change out of the deal."

"No way! He bribed you to stay the night?"

Anne giggled. "Not exactly. I offered…in exchange for the oil change. He would've done it anyway, but this way we set his mind at ease about your condition and I don't have to drive the car back until morning."

"What about your husband? Won't he mind if you don't come home?"

"Not married."

"But…" Becki pointed to the wedding band on Anne's finger.

Anne splayed her fingers and smirked. "That's to keep the doctors and patients from hitting on me."

"You're kidding."

"Nope. Now, stand on one foot, hands on hips, eyes closed, until I say stop."

Becki did as she was told. "I'm surprised Josh hasn't married yet. When I was here as a kid, there was no shortage of girls mooning over him." Her younger self included, but Anne didn't need to know that.

"Yeah, well. He never got over being rejected in favor of life in the big city."

Was Anne talking about Becki's sister? He'd had it bad for her that last summer they were here, and Sarah hadn't discouraged him, even though she was two years older.

"He escaped to the military after that," Anne went on. "Hasn't dated much since coming back. The pickings are slim around here, and he won't dare date a wannabe city girl."

Considering how the city had changed Sarah, Josh was probably smart to hold out for a country girl.

Anne jotted something on her notepad. "Now tell me all the words you can remember from that list I gave you earlier."

Becki repeated them all. "Now do you believe me?"

"How's your headache? Any worse? Feeling dizzy?"

"It still hurts, but no and no."

"All right, yes, I think you'll be fine, but don't tell Josh. It's nice to see him fretting over someone else for a change."

"What do you mean?"

"Um." She bit her lip and glanced toward the door as if he might burst through at any moment. "He'd kill me if I told you."

"We wouldn't want that," Becki drawled, remembering how often her own sister used to preface her secrets with a similar remark. How she missed those days.

"Maybe you could help him stop being so hard on himself," Anne whispered.

"Me?" Becki caught one of her curls, tugging it straight. "Why would he listen to me?"

Becki didn't know what to make of the expression that flitted across Anne's face. Perhaps if she knew her better, but she'd never really met her before today. She'd heard Josh had an older sister, but she'd never been around.

Anne leaned forward and clasped Becki's hand the same way she had when she'd first arrived and expressed her condolences. "Josh feels responsible for your grandparents' deaths."

Becki stiffened.

Anne must have felt it, because she quickly added, "He's not. But your grandfather had complained the day before he died about having a headache, and Josh thinks he should have suspected a carbon-monoxide leak. As if people never get head-aches for any other reason!"

Numbness crept over Becki's limbs. "Gramps never got headaches."

"Please don't remind Josh. He's already beating himself up enough over not questioning that. I mean, your grandparents had a carbon-monoxide detector. And it was the middle of summer. Whoever heard of a hot-water tank causing carbon monoxide?"

The screen door slammed shut, and Josh strode into the room.

Becki and Anne sprang apart, but Josh didn't seem to notice. He dropped her suitcase at her feet and waved a note in front of her face. "When did you get this?"

She caught his arm long enough to get a look at the paper. "It was in the mailbox when I got here." She squared her jaw and fought to keep her tone even. "Courtesy of my sister."

He frowned. "Why would she say you don't belong here?"

"Because if I sell, she thinks she'll get more money."

Anne picked up the envelope that had fluttered to the floor. "Where does your sister live?"

"Toronto."

Anne flapped the envelope against her palm. "The stamp on this envelope was never canceled. It looks like someone hand delivered it."

Josh took the envelope from her. "You're right." He passed it to Becki.

So Sarah hadn't been lying. Unless… "She could've asked someone to put it in the mailbox for her."

"Who else knew you were moving in today?"

"I don't know." Becki rubbed her worsening headache. "My boss, my roommate, my mom."

"No one from around here?"

"Not that I know of."

"Could be those developers," Anne chimed in.

"What developers?"

Josh blew out a breath and paced. "A conglomerate of investors who want to see our farmland turned into subdivisions and shopping malls." His scathing tone told her exactly what he thought about their plans. "Have they approached you with an offer to buy?"

"No!" Becki folded her arms over her chest. "Even if they had, I wouldn't sell to *them*."

Josh nodded, his expression grim. "The trouble is you couldn't trust anyone who offered to buy the place not to turn around and pass it on to the developers for a tidy commission."

"Well, like I told my sister, I'm here to stay." Sarah had hated being dumped here every summer. Unlike her big sister, Becki didn't have a life to speak of in the city, and she wouldn't miss it in the least. She happened to like the slower pace of rural living. Maybe she'd even start writing again in her spare time.

"Where will you work?" Anne asked.

"Huh?" Becki shook her sister's voice from her head and focused on Anne. "I haven't figured that out yet. But I'm sure I can find something before my savings run out."

Anne let out a sigh. "Not many new jobs around since the economic downturn."

"Never mind that for now." Josh sat beside Becki on the sofa, and her heart jumped at the touch of his knee. "Who else might have sent this note?"

"What do you mean?"

"I mean…who didn't want you moving here badly enough to attack you?"

She dug her fingers into the seat cushion. "You think the note and incident in the barn are connected?"

Obviously he did. Which meant whoever was slinking around the property had been *expecting* her.

# TWO

What would Sarah say if she saw her now, sleeping under Josh's roof?

Well, trying to sleep. Becki flopped over in the unfamiliar bed. Shafts of moonlight shone through the edges of the drapes, highlighting a pair of 4-H trophies perched on the bookcase of Josh's old bedroom.

Her sister would probably feel bad to learn that Josh never got over her. That is…if Sarah was who Anne had meant. Maybe not, since he'd still had a couple of years of high school left after their last summer visit. But he'd sure had it bad for her then.

Becki rolled over and punched the pillow. She didn't want to think of Josh mooning over her sister, especially considering how unreasonable Sarah had been acting lately. Despite her denials, she must've sent that note. Who else?

The two of them were the only living relatives.

Josh was blowing the whole situation way out of proportion. The note and prowler couldn't be connected. She'd probably just surprised a couple of teens who were afraid of getting caught fooling around in Gramps's car. As a cop Josh must see that sort of thing all the time.

But then why was he getting so worked up?

*Josh feels responsible for your grandparents' deaths.*

Becki's heart clenched. That had to be why Josh wasn't taking any chances.

If only he'd…

She squashed the wishful thinking. If she let her thoughts go there, she'd never get to sleep.

Closing her eyes, she tried not to think at all. An hour later, she was still awake.

A glass of milk might help. She listened for sounds of Anne and Josh still milling about. Hearing none, she pulled on her bathrobe and stole downstairs.

The computer and desk lamp were on in the otherwise darkened living room, but there was no sign of Josh.

She tiptoed to the desk to see what he'd been working on. His internet browser was open to a page about an antique-car theft. Did Josh really think some sort of theft ring had targeted Gramps's car?

She skimmed the article but couldn't see any similarities between that theft and her situation.

A beam of light flashed across the window.

She flicked off the desk lamp and peered past the curtain.

A tall figure disappeared around the corner of the house.

Was that Josh?

The kitchen door banged open.

She shrank deeper into the shadows. It had to be Josh. An intruder wouldn't be so noisy. The glow of the computer screen cast eerie shadows on the walls.

Tripod bounded into the room, tongue lolling, followed by Josh, his cell phone pressed to his ear. "Hey, Hunter, can I borrow your game cameras for a couple of weeks?" He walked to the desk and flicked on the lamp. His gaze abruptly veered her way. As his eyes landed on her bare toes, his eyes widened, then quickly traveled up to her flaming cheeks.

"Huh?" He half turned and lowered his voice.

"Yeah, the one with night vision and motion trigger," Josh muttered into the phone. "No, not animals." He pushed back a corner of the curtain and stared out into the deep blackness of the country night. "I'm looking to catch a human."

*A human!* Becki tugged her bathrobe together more tightly. Why hadn't she stayed in bed?

At least there she could have blissfully deluded herself into imagining there was nothing to be afraid of.

Becki woke early the next morning. She might have let Josh evade her questions last night, but today she intended to get answers. She dressed quickly and tiptoed to the stairs. Halfway down, the aroma of fresh-brewed coffee greeted her, reminding her that *early* had a whole other meaning in farm country. She should've paid more attention to that rooster crowing *before* the crack of dawn.

"Hey, sleepyhead," Anne chirped as Becki meandered into the sunbathed kitchen. Anne handed her a mug of coffee. "How's the head?"

"Good." If she didn't count the gazillion questions that had raced around it all night after overhearing Josh's plan to catch her prowler. "Josh doing chores?"

"They're long done. He only has chickens to feed these days. He's changing my oil. Probably almost done with that, too."

"Will he have to do anything in the fields today?"

"No, he doesn't farm." Anne set a covered platter on the table. "The farmer down the road rents the land."

"But I thought… Josh always talked about running the farm one day."

"Sometimes childhood dreams don't look so rosy when you grow up."

Becki sank into a chair. Her sister had said the same thing. She stiffened her spine. Gran and Gramps's farm was the only place she'd ever felt truly happy. Sure, it wouldn't be the same without them, but she couldn't bear to lose it, too.

"By the time Josh resigned from the military," Anne continued, "Dad had sold off too much of the farm for Josh to make it profitable again."

Becki envisioned him wrestling down a burly drug dealer instead of an ornery cow. "So that's why Josh became a cop?"

"He wanted—"

"To serve and protect," Josh finished for his sister as he strode into the kitchen and plopped a small cage on the counter.

The "criminal" he'd protected them from emitted a tiny peep, and Becki couldn't help but giggle.

"What have you rescued this time?" Anne peered around his shoulder.

He stepped aside, allowing them both to see. A tiny sparrow with a broken wing huddled in a corner of the hamster cage.

"Oh, the poor thing." Becki snagged a piece of toast from the breakfast Anne had spread on the table and sprinkled crumbs into the cage. "Where did you find it?"

Anne rolled her eyes. "The strays always seem to find him."

"What am I supposed to do? Ignore them?"

His sister tipped onto her toes and planted a kiss on Josh's cheek. "Nope, you'd never. That's why I love you."

Josh pulled Anne into a fierce hug, revealing a depth of feeling that caught at Becki's heart. His eyes lifted to hers. More brown than green this morning, they held a warm familial affection that Becki could only dream of now that Gran and Gramps were gone.

Anne ducked out of his arms and grabbed her purse from the counter. "If my car's done, I need to go. Enjoy your breakfast." Anne shook a finger at Becki. "And no heavy lifting. If you get dizzy or your headache persists, have a doctor check you over."

"I will. Thank you."

After seeing his sister out, Josh lifted the lid from a pan of bacon and eggs on the table. "Shall we?"

"Farm-fresh eggs. Mmm. I haven't had a breakfast like this since the last time I visited Gran and Gramps. Your sister outdid herself."

Josh spooned out a plateful of scrambled eggs and bacon. "She likes to stay on my good side so I'll keep her car running."

"I think you'd do it anyway. You always loved to work on cars."

"Shh, don't let her hear you say that." He raised a jug of OJ. "Juice?"

"Uh, sure." Suddenly Becki's insides felt as scrambled as her eggs. To think she was sharing breakfast with Joshua Rayne!

Not only was he more handsome than she remembered; he was as kind as ever. She bet the three-legged dog had been another rescue effort.

She fiddled with her silverware. Obviously the blow to her head had crippled her common sense for her to be thinking up more reasons to still have a crush on the guy. She stabbed at her eggs. It wasn't as if she would ever be anything more to him than another needy stray.

Her mind flailed about for another topic of conversation. "Funny that I don't remember you fussing over animals as a teen. That was more my domain." She struggled to restrain the smile that suddenly tugged at her lips. "Seems to me you were more interested in fussing over my sister."

He choked on his orange juice.

She batted her eyelashes ever so innocently. "Am I wrong?"

He tipped back his head and laughed. "Nothing got by you."

Becki shrugged. "If not for you, I doubt Sarah could have stood being away from the malls for two whole months."

"Not at all like you. You were a farm kid through and through." Amusement danced in Josh's green-brown eyes.

The color reminded her of the grassy meadows she'd loved to run through as a child. "No. Not like me." She shoveled a forkful of eggs into her mouth and then focused on buttering her toast and the non-Joshua reasons she loved being in Serenity. "If Sarah had her way, I wouldn't stay."

"These old houses can be a lot of work to upkeep."

Her butter knife halted midspread. "You don't think I should stay, either?"

"Not at all. The Becki Graw I remember could do anything she set her mind to."

"Thank you. That hasn't changed. So why don't you tell me about your plan to catch my prowler?"

"Finish up your breakfast, and I'll show you."

Becki finished before Josh and started on the dishes.

"Leave those," he said, tossing the dog his last piece of bacon. "I'll wash them later."

"Nonsense. I've put you out enough."

He reached around her and dropped his plate into the soapy water, his outdoorsy scent teasing her nostrils. "No imposition. I enjoyed the company." He picked up a tea towel and began drying. The graze of his hand as he reached for the mug she'd just rinsed unleashed a flutter of butterflies in her stomach.

*Oh, boy.* She seriously needed to get over this schoolgirl crush. She'd seen enough failed marriages to know they never lasted.

*Marriage?* She shook her head. Clearly, no worries there. In Josh's eyes, she was still *little* Becki. She let the water out of the sink and pictured her silly girlhood crush swirling down the drain.

Little Becki grew up a long time ago…the day her parents had announced their divorce.

"Okay, let's go." She dried her hands on the edge of his towel. "Show me what you plan to do with those cameras. I need to start unpacking."

He tossed the towel on the back of the chair and reached over her head to hold open the door. Tripod raced past and out ahead of them. "I'll carry your boxes into the house."

"No need. I can handle them."

"You heard what my sister said." Josh's stern tone dared her to argue. "No heavy lifting for a few days." He led the way to the barn, where he stopped and scanned the nearby trees. "I'm going to set up a couple of motion-triggered cameras so if your car thief comes back, we'll catch him in the act."

"Then what?"

"I'll arrest him for trespassing and attempted robbery and whatever else I can think of."

"Hmm." She grinned. "Pretty handy having a police officer for a neighbor."

His expression sobered. "No telling what time of day or night this guy might show up. If I'm not around, call nine-one-one and stay locked in the house. Don't try to confront him."

"Don't you think he'd run off if he realized he'd been spotted?"

"Some guys would just as soon shoot a witness as run away."

She planted her hands on her hips. "Are you *trying* to scare me?"

"*Prepare* you." Tripod bounded up to them, barking happily. "Maybe we should get you a dog."

Her heart leaped at the suggestion. "What a great idea. I've always wanted one. Maybe a big lovable golden retriever who—"

"The idea is to get a dog that will scare a robber off, not show him to the silver."

She laughed. "Oh, like Tripod here?"

"Yeah." Josh tousled the scruff on the dog's neck. "He's *not* what you want."

"I like him. He's sweet."

"*Sweet* won't scare away a prowler." Josh rolled open the barn's big sliding door. "And you definitely have one. I found a couple of footprints." He pointed to the dirt-crusted floor. "See those? Too big for your grandparents or you, and the tread pattern doesn't match anything I wear."

"You were already over here this morning?"

"The sun rises early." He winked.

For the first time she noticed dark shadows under his eyes. Had he even gone to sleep last night?

An hour after she'd headed back up to bed the night before, she'd heard the screen door clap shut and figured he was doing another scan of her grandparents' property. Her property. That trek probably hadn't been the only one.

A cat bolted from the corner of the barn, and Tripod took off after it.

"Won't see him for a while." Josh strode toward the car, which sparkled in the sunlight beaming through the gaps in the boarded walls. "It looks like the guy gave the car a thorough going-over. Both the gear stick and emergency brake lever had been shifted. The toolbox under the seat had been rifled through. Looking for a key, maybe. Best-case scenario, it was a kid playing around." His tone sounded grim.

"But you don't think so?"

He shook his head. "I dusted for fingerprints on the door handles, gear shift and steering wheel. They were clean."

"Clean? As in not even Gramps's prints were on them?" She failed to keep the wobble out of her voice. No prints meant someone had wiped them away.

"Your grandfather was pretty meticulous about keeping it polished. But kids don't usually think to wear gloves. Not in the middle of summer."

She swallowed, forcing calm into her voice this time. "So worst case?" She opened the passenger door, and memories of riding proudly around town with her gramps flooded her thoughts.

"If it's a professional, he's got to realize he wouldn't get far driving this thing out of here before being spotted. So I'm guessing next time, he'll stash a trailer nearby to drive it into."

"You really think someone would go to that much trouble?"

Josh raised an eyebrow. "The last Cadillac of this vintage I saw sell at auction went for eighty-five thousand dollars."

"Are you serious?"

"Trust me." He buffed a smudge from the hood with a fond smile. "If I could have afforded to buy this car from your grandfather, I would have made him an offer."

Becki bit her lip. If Sarah found out what the car was worth, she'd demand it be sold for sure.

Becki's heart lurched at the thought. She didn't care about the money. The car had been Gramps's pride and joy. How could she let it go?

She had sat for hours on the backseat with her notepad and pen as Gramps tinkered with something or the other and recounted adventures he'd had driving the car as a boy. She whirled toward Josh. "We can't let it be stolen!"

"I don't intend to."

His confident tone quelled her alarm. Embarrassed she'd let it get the better of her, she gave him a lopsided smile. "Would you show me how it works, too?"

"Be happy to. First, I'll need to figure out what's wrong with it. Your gramps and I never did get it running reliably again. I'll take a look at it this afternoon, after I get those cameras up. If I can get it working, we can take it out after church tomorrow, if you like."

Becki gave him an impulsive hug. "Thank you!"

Josh folded his arms around her. "My pleasure, Bec."

The tender sound of his pet name for her momentarily stayed her instinct to pull back. Since learning of her grandparents' deaths, she'd felt so alone. Josh was the only one to comfort her who really cared.

"Maybe you and I could work on it together, like your gramps did with me after my dad died."

Reluctantly, she eased her arms from around him, questioning the wisdom of jumping at reasons to spend *more* time with him. But one look at his red-rimmed eyes and she squeezed her own shut and laid her head against his chest. "You miss them as much as I do."

He rested his cheek against her hair. "Yes, I do."

Remembering the secret Anne had shared about how Josh blamed himself for her grandparents' deaths, Becki hugged him harder.

"Well, well, well," a familiar voice drawled from the direction of the door. "Settling right in, I see."

Becki sprang from Josh's arms. Smoothed her hair. "Neil? What are you doing here?"

"I thought you might need some help moving in." His muddy-blond hair was moussed back, his shirt and pants perfectly pressed, his polished shoes not the least bit appropriate for traipsing across the over-grown yard. His gaze drifted up Josh's full six feet and narrowed on his face. Neil pushed up his glasses with a single finger to the bridge. "But I see you're covered."

Was it her imagination or were the two of them puffing out their chests like rival birds fighting over a mate?

*Yeah, right.* She let out a choked snort. Definitely her imagination.

"How did you find me? I mean…" She hadn't given anyone from work her new address. The dusty barn air seemed to close in on her.

"Looked up the address on the internet. I remembered you mentioning your grandfather lived in Serenity." Neil stepped closer, arm outstretched toward Josh. "Neil Orner."

Josh gave Neil's hand a swift shake. "Joshua Rayne."

"Josh is my new neighbor and an old family friend," Becki rushed to explain. "He was just comforting me over my loss." She squirmed at how defensive that sounded. She didn't owe Neil an explanation. They hadn't dated for over three months. "Um, Neil is a colleague from work," she said to Josh.

A muscle in Neil's cheek ticked, but what did he expect her to say?

Josh hooked his thumbs in the front pockets of his jeans. "I don't think Bec ever told me. Where is it you work?"

Neil inhaled, appearing to grow another half inch. "We work at Holton Industries."

Josh's jaw dropped a fraction, his eyes widening as he turned his attention back to her. "Industry?" He sounded skeptical. "I always figured you'd go into something to do with writing or graphic arts."

He thought about her?

"You never went anywhere without a pad and paper." A far-off look flickered in his eyes and a smile whispered across his lips as if he was picturing her as that tagalong girl again.

"That's fine for a hobby," Neil interjected. "But one can hardly make a living—"

"I don't know. If you're doing something you love, the rest seems to take care of itself."

Becki's chest swelled at Josh's defense, but his quiet confidence didn't seem to convince Neil. Of course, Josh had never needed much to be content, whereas Neil always wanted whatever seemed just out of reach. He'd admitted to being a bit of a runt growing up and seemed determined to put the ridicule behind him by latching onto the latest status symbols, which before they broke up had started to include an obsessive interest in her career decisions. That thought made her jittery all over again.

She closed the Cadillac's door, willing steel into her backbone. "Well, with any luck I'll find a job I love right here in Serenity."

Josh rested his hand at her waist, and his touch calmed her instantly. He urged her toward the barn door. "No luck needed. We'll pray you do."

The confidence in Josh's voice raised goose bumps on her arms. Stepping outside, she turned her face to the sun, wishing she could believe prayer would make a difference.

She once had. All those summers here, God had seemed so real. Even when He didn't answer her prayer that she be allowed to stay with Gran and Gramps after the divorce, she'd clung to Gran's assurances that God worked all things together for good. But how could any good come from letting Gran and Gramps die of carbon-monoxide poisoning?

Clearly, from the sour look on Neil's face, he didn't believe prayer would make a difference, either.

A cell phone rang, and both men reached for their hips.

"It's mine," Josh said. He glanced at the screen, then caught Becki's gaze. "Excuse me a sec." He stepped away from them, his phone to his ear.

"Why don't I give you a hand with those boxes in your car?" Neil suggested.

"I can't believe you came all the way out here."

He shrugged. "What's a three-hour drive to help a *friend?*"

She winced, certain his emphasis on *friend* was a dig to her "colleague" reference. "Last time we talked you told me I was crazy to want to move here."

"Still think so. Figured I'd come see what the attraction was." His gaze strayed to Josh, and he snorted. "I talked to Peters. He's going to fill your job with a temp for a few months. Give you a chance to decide if this is really what you want."

"I've already made my decision." She fisted her hands. This was the kind of I-know-what's-best-for-you attitude that had made her break up with him in the first place. He was more controlling than her mother.

"Don't be mad." He tucked an errant curl behind her ear. "You know you don't belong here."

She jerked away from his touch and stalked to her car.

"Rebecca." He trailed after her. "I was just trying to help. Country living may not be as great as you remember."

She opened the back door of her car, tugged out a box and plopped it into his arms. "I appreciate that. Really I do." She grabbed another box and led the way to the front door. "But you shouldn't have interfered."

"You're still mad at me because I didn't make it to your grandparents' funeral, aren't you?"

"What? No!" She shifted her box onto one hip and shoved her key into the door lock. "I never expected you to."

"I should have been there for you." He covered her hand and turned the key, pushing open the door.

She snatched her hand back and plowed past him into the house. She set the box on the old deacon's bench in the front hall, averse to inviting Neil any farther.

"Hey, no matter what else happens, we *are* friends. Right?"

She stared at him, a tad uneasy about what exactly that meant to him.

"Where do you want these?" Josh's voice drifted through the door, wrapping around her ragged nerves like a soothing hug. He held a stack of boxes in his arms.

She rushed forward and grabbed the one teetering from the top. "The living room is fine. Thanks."

"This, too?" Neil asked.

"No. It can stay here. Could you grab the boxes from the trunk next?"

The instant Neil went back outside, Josh stepped up behind her. "Do you mind if I do a quick walk-through? Make sure everything's okay?"

"Yes, thank you." Her words came out breathlessly. From the possibility that the prowler had been inside, she told herself, *not* from Josh's proximity.

Becki hurried out after Neil, before he got too curious. One time she'd caught him peeking in her desk drawers while he waited for her to finish getting ready for a date. He'd said he'd been looking for scissors to clip off a loose thread, and maybe he had been, but he had no sense of boundaries. Clearly.

If he did, he wouldn't be there.

It was one thing to stop by her desk and chat for a few minutes every day. It was entirely another to drive three hours to do it.

She'd appreciated that he had the self-confidence not to let their breakup ruin their working relationship. And okay, it had been really thoughtful of him to bring over supper and flowers from everyone at the office after she'd gotten word about her grandparents' deaths and left work so suddenly.

But now that their professional relationship had ended, she really didn't want to deal with him anymore.

"What does your neighbor do for a living?" Neil asked, passing her with an armload stacked even higher than Josh's had been.

She grabbed the top two boxes. "He's a police officer."

Neil gave a start. "That's handy."

"What do you mean?"

"If you have any trouble."

She pressed her lips closed, loath to admit she'd already had some. That was just the kind of thing Neil would latch onto to try to change her mind about moving here. He and her sister should start a club.

Josh met them at the door. He waited for Neil to pass by, then pulled her aside. "I need to go. They've found a submerged car in the old quarry and need a diver to check for…anything suspicious."

She gasped, certain he'd been about to say *bodies*. "I didn't realize you were a diver."

"Trained in the military." His eyes were shadowed. "Will you be okay?"

"Of course. Go."

"There's no sign your prowler got into the house, and I don't think he'll come around in daylight, especially with a couple of cars in the driveway. But if you see anything suspicious, don't hesitate to call me. Okay?" He pressed a business card into her hand with a number scrawled on the back. "That's my cell number."

For some reason Josh's protective concern didn't feel so condescendingly suffocating as Neil's always had. Maybe because the concern didn't seem so irrational coming from a cop. "I'll be fine."

"I'll be back as soon as I can." He lifted a hand to Neil, who'd stepped back into the foyer from wherever his curiosity had taken him while she'd been distracted by Josh. "Nice meeting you, Neil. See you around."

Neil sidled up to her as she watched Josh jog across the driveway back to his house. "He sounds worried about you. Not on my account, I hope."

She let out a puff of air—half cough, half snort. "Uh, no."

"Then why?"

"It was a little unsettling being back here for the first time with Gran and Gramps gone," she said evasively.

"I'd be happy to stick around for a while. Keep you company."

"Actually, I'd rather be alone right now." She tilted her head and added softly, "You understand?"

He clasped her upper arms and pressed a kiss to her forehead. "Of course. Let me just grab the housewarming gift I brought you."

She stood in the doorway, her arms wrapped

around her waist, feeling like an ingrate, as he hurried to his flashy Mustang. He'd driven all this way to extend his help and friendship. The least she could do was offer him a cup of coffee before he left.

He opened his door and pulled out a hanging basket overflowing with fuchsia-colored dianthus. He strode toward her with a wide grin. "Do you like them?"

"They're beautiful. Thank you."

"I remembered you telling me how your gran used to have them hanging from the beams of the wraparound porch."

"You remembered that?" He'd never seemed to be listening.

"Of course." He patted the rails. "It's just like you described." He reached over her head and looped the basket onto a hook in the beam. "There."

"Would you like a glass of lemonade before you leave?" she blurted on impulse. Lemonade at least would be quicker than coffee. Gran always had a mix in the cupboard.

"That's okay. I know you have a lot to do. I just wanted to make sure you got here all right. And let you know that if you change your mind about staying…"

"I won't."

His eyes flicked around the yard, to the fields surrounding the two houses and to the thick stand of trees beyond. "It doesn't scare you to be out the back of nowhere? With next to no neighbors?"

"I won't change my mind," she said more adamantly.

He held his hands up in surrender. "Okay. I'm just saying if you did, no one would blame you. Not with who knows what kind of wild animals stalking those woods. Or creeps prowling for easy prey."

# THREE

Josh shone his waterproof flashlight in, under and around the submerged car, fanned the search out another ten yards in every direction, then kicked to the surface. Hailing the officer in charge of the recovery, Josh pulled the regulator from his mouth. "It's clear."

"Good." Walt passed Josh the tow cable. "Hook her up. Then check the rest of the pit."

Josh reinserted his mouthpiece, then dived to the bottom with the cable and secured the towline to the car's frame. It'd take him another hour at least to thoroughly search every corner of the former quarry. Most of it was under eight feet or less of water, but one of the guys had said it got as deep as forty in the northeast corner. He kicked out of the way of the vehicle and surfaced long enough to signal it was okay to start towing.

He didn't want to spend any more time out here than he had to. He couldn't get that Neil guy off his mind. Bec hadn't seemed all that comfortable with him, and Neil clearly hadn't been deterred.

Josh didn't like how fidgety the guy had made her. Thanks to her prowler, she'd been jittery enough already. She didn't need an unwelcome wannabe boyfriend insinuating himself into the situation. And any guy who traveled this far just to check up on her had to have been more than a colleague, *or wanted to be.*

Josh clawed through the water, scoping every rock crevice. Had he been too quick to take Bec's word that she was okay being left alone with Neil?

He was taking way too much interest in Bec's affairs. A carp jutted from behind the rock ahead of Josh, stirring up a cloud of silt. He treaded in one spot, waiting for the water to clear. At least he'd had the decency to let a woman go without argument when she turned him down. Maybe he should have run a background check on Neil, made sure the guy wasn't some sort of stalker.

He hadn't missed Neil's *You know you don't belong here,* which sounded too much like the note that had been waiting for Bec in her mailbox when she'd arrived.

Josh dived back under, swimming faster than ever. Broken beer bottles littered the bottom of the pit. The area had been a popular hangout for teens for as long as he could remember. Surprising there wasn't more graffiti on the rocks than the occasional heart framing lovers' initials.

His thoughts slipped back to Bec, or more precisely the strange feeling that had come over him when she'd given him that impulsive hug. It reminded him of the time she'd thanked him for rescuing her from the tree she'd gotten herself stuck in as a kid. Only, when he'd folded his arms around her, it hadn't felt the same at all. He probably should be relieved Neil had shown up when he had.

If she knew how he'd failed her grandparents, she wouldn't want him anywhere near her. She was too vulnerable right now, between coping with her loss and starting over in a new town, a new job. Moving into the house. And now this prowler. Josh needed to focus on keeping her safe. Not on how wonderful it had felt to hold a woman in his arms.

He gave a hard kick and propelled himself into the deeper water. A woman in his arms... He knew better than to let his thoughts wander into that territory. He supposed helping his old high-school pal bring in his hay yesterday had started it.

His friend's wife and young son had brought a picnic lunch to the field for them, the boy squealing with delight when Josh's friend tickled his sides as the wife looked on with a contented expression.

It was the kind of life Josh had always longed for.

He sliced his arms through the water, relying more heavily on the narrow beam of his flashlight as he pushed deeper. The same as he'd learned to do with God. The Lord had blessed him with a country home, a good job and plenty of friends, and had even brought his sister back to Serenity.

Wishing for more only led to a whole well of hurt.

Neil, on the other hand, didn't seem to be getting that message.

The vibration of the winding tow cable rippled through the water.

Josh beefed up his strokes. The sooner he covered the search area, the sooner he could get home.

A shadow fell over the water ahead of him. Glancing up, he spotted a signal buoy. He kicked to the surface.

"Over here," Walt shouted from a new position onshore.

Josh pulled the regulator from his mouth. "What's up?"

"You wanted me to let you know if your cell phone rang."

His pulse jerked. *Bec?* "What's the caller ID?"

"Hunter Madison."

Josh's heart settled back into a steady rhythm. "Okay, let it go to voice mail. I'll call him when I'm finished." Hunter probably just wanted to check on where to put the cameras.

Josh dived back under and swept his light in widening arcs. The fish had gone into hiding. Hopefully, Bec's prowler wouldn't do the same. The last thing Bec needed was weeks of worrying if and when the intruder would show up again.

He winged a prayer skyward that God would help him catch the guy quickly.

The water was crystal clear, tinted a nice aquamarine, thanks to the limestone. Maybe he'd bring

Bec here sometime with the dog. She might get a kick out of hunting for fossils in the rocks. It'd help take her mind off her troubles for a while. That and going out in her grandfather's old Cadillac.

Her eyes had lit up at the prospect, and he couldn't deny he was more than happy to fulfill that particular wish.

Overhead, the water grew choppy from the car breaking the surface.

Josh waited for the tow truck to haul the car out onto the flat rock overlooking the mini-lake and then did a final sweep of the area, his thoughts already back at the farm.

Finding nothing, he kicked to the surface and climbed out.

Walt handed him a towel. "There's nothing suspicious in the car. What do you make of it?"

Josh yanked off his regulator and mask and dragged his mind back to the investigation. "There's no body. Kids likely stole the car for a joyride, then ditched the evidence." More likely kids in this case than the incident in Bec's barn...unfortunately.

"Kids don't usually think to pull plates."

"True. Could've been used in a crime, then dumped." Josh scrubbed his hair dry with the towel. "Get any hits with the car's make and model?"

"Nope, not within Niagara anyway. No unrecovered Plymouths of any model reported stolen in the last two years."

"So not insurance fraud."

Walt shrugged. "Could be from another region."

"That car hasn't been down there more than a week." Josh walked around the car and then, stepping back, studied the distinctive rear taillights.

"You recognize something?" Walt asked.

"Yeah." Josh clenched the towel in his fist. "I think it's the same car I saw pull out of a farmer's field near my place last night...around the same time my new neighbor was attacked by a prowler."

Becki headed to the car to grab the last of her boxes and froze. A stone's throw away, a black SUV idled in Josh's driveway. The dark-haired guy behind the wheel squinted at her, then turned off his engine.

Her breath caught. Was he the prowler?

She glanced around. Where was Tripod?

The SUV's door opened, and the guy's enormous boots hit the gravel with a thud. Boots that could dispense with Josh's three-legged dog in one swift kick.

The guy peeled off a jacket and slapped a ball cap on his head, exposing tattooed, steely arms. He looked as if he hadn't shaved in two days. Army-olive fatigues completed the impression of a mercenary looking for action. The guy reached behind his seat.

Josh's words blasted through her mind. *Some guys would just as soon shoot a witness as run away.*

Becki whirled on her heel and ran for the house.

"Hey, hold up there. Are you Bec?"

*Bec?* She stopped two yards from the door. Josh

was the only one who called her that. This had to be
the friend he'd called about borrowing the cameras.
She turned slowly and backed up another couple of
steps just to be safe. "Who wants to know?"

A friendly grin—not in the least bit mercenary—
dented his cheeks. "I'm Hunter." He lifted his hand.
A couple of drab-colored boxes dangled from his
fingertips. "Josh asked me to hang these up for you."

"Thank you," she squeaked, then cleared her
throat and added, "I appreciate that. Follow me,
and I'll show—"

A sporty green car turned into her driveway.

"Oh." She looked from the car to the barn.

"You see to your visitor," Hunter said. "I can find
my way." He tipped his hat and devoured the distance to the barn in powerful strides.

Able to breathe again, she reasoned that if Josh
trusted the guy, she could, too. But the message
wasn't getting to her pounding heart. She turned to
the approaching car. The place was starting to feel
like Grand Central Station. She didn't recognize the
middle-aged man behind the wheel, but he looked a
whole lot safer than Rambo.

He parked behind her car and lowered his window. "You Graw's granddaughter?"

"Yes. May I help you?"

The man stepped out of his car. Unlike Rambo,
he was dressed conservatively, with his hair neatly
cut, and clean-shaven. Empathy shone from his
eyes when he extended his hand. "Name's Henry

Smith. Remember we talked on the phone a few days back?"

"Oh, yes. You're the friend of my grandfather's." On the phone, he'd sounded closer to Gramps's age.

He cupped her hand between his. "I wanted to drop by to give my condolences. Your grandfather was a dear friend."

She tilted her head. "You said you knew him through the antique-car club, is that right?"

"That's right." He released her hand and reached into the car. "I thought you might like this." He handed her an eight-by-ten photo of Gran and Gramps posing by their Cadillac in their period costumes.

"Oh, wow!" She savored her grandparents' smiling faces. "Thank you so much. It's lovely."

"Took that on our last tour together. Thought you'd like it."

Becki traced the hat her gran wore. "I used to love snapping Gramps's suspenders and trying on Gran's big floppy hats."

"Yup, those are great costumes. There'd be a lot of folks in the club who'd be happy to buy them from you if you wanted to sell. Might be interested in some myself if you have time for me to look them over."

"Oh." She fluttered her hand toward the barn. "I think they stored those with the car in the trailer, which isn't here right now. But I'm not ready to part with anything just yet."

"Of course not."

They stood in uncomfortable silence for a moment.

Becki hitched her thumb toward the house. "Would you like to come in for a cup of coffee?"

"Oh, no." He motioned toward her open trunk. "I can see you're busy. I just wanted to see you got the photo."

She grabbed the last two boxes from her car and closed the lid. "C'mon, I could use the break and I'd love to hear more about your trips with my grandparents."

"Well if you put it that way… There's nothing we car enthusiasts like to do more than talk about our cars. Except tour them, of course."

She chuckled, recalling countless Saturday afternoons sitting on the back porch, listening to Gramps and his buddies talk about cars. "What kind of car do you drive on the tours, Mr. Smith?" she asked, leading the way to the back porch.

"Call me Henry, please. Sure is a beautiful place your grandparents had here."

"I think so. Of course, my ex-boyfriend thinks I'm nuts to want to live out here. He thinks the seclusion and wild animals are way scarier than street crimes."

"Sounds like someone who's never spent a day in the country."

"You've got that right."

Henry's gaze drifted over her shoulder. "Not that fella, then?"

She glanced back at Hunter, who blended into the tree in his camouflage. "Uh, no. He's just a...neighbor." She motioned Henry to one of the porch chairs. "Just give me a minute to get the coffee."

Henry followed her as far as the open patio door. "Your grandfather had some car trouble on his last tour. If he didn't get the chance to fix it, I could take a look if you like."

Becki grabbed the coffee sweetener from the cupboard. "That's okay. My neighbor already offered." She poured their coffees and rejoined Henry outside. "So tell me about your last tour with Gran and Gramps."

"First, tell me about your plans. What will you do with the old Cadillac?"

"Um, not sure yet." Becki shoved away the guilty feeling that the car was too valuable to be lumped with "contents" in the will. She couldn't bear the thought of parting with the "old gal," knowing how much she'd meant to Gramps.

Henry sipped his coffee and shared a couple of touring yarns.

"Can you tell me about any more of my grandparents' adventures?" Becki asked.

He glanced at his watch. "I'm afraid they'll have to wait for another time. I need to get on the road." He patted his breast pocket, pulled out a pen and jotted a number on a scrap of paper. "Here's my number if you run into any trouble with the car that your neighbor can't handle."

"Thank you." She stood next to the driveway until he'd driven away, then returned inside and leaned against the closed door. For the first time since she'd arrived, she really absorbed the sight of her beloved grandparents' home. She inhaled, basking in the distinctive fragrance that was her grandparents'.

But the air smelled a bit stale. From being closed up so long, probably. She meandered from room to room, flinging open windows. The scraped paint on the bottom of the too-low window in the main-floor bathroom reminded her of the time she'd locked the window on her sister, who used to sneak in and out through it. Boy, did she get in trouble that night.

The house phone rang.

Becki hesitated. She didn't really want to talk to anyone else, especially someone who might not have heard that Gran and Gramps were gone.

She swallowed. More likely it was a telemarketer. Or maybe Mom checking in to make sure she'd arrived safely. Becki let out a puff of air. Yeah, in her dreams.

For most of her life, Mom had dictated what Becki could and couldn't do, who she could date, what extracurricular activities she could join, what college she should attend, but the instant Becki had the *gall* to defy her and move into an apartment, Mom had stopped showing *any* interest in what she did. Which was just one more way to control her.

Drawing in a deep breath, Becki snatched up the phone. "Hello."

No answer.

She listened for a moment, expecting an automated voice to kick in with a spiel about how she'd won a cruise to a Caribbean island.

"Hello?"

The line clicked off.

*How rude.* If someone dialed the wrong number, they should at least have the decency to say something. Then again...

The caller might have expected Gran or Gramps to answer and been thrown off by her much younger voice. Next time she'd have to identify herself.

Putting the call out of her mind, she grabbed a box marked Bedroom and meandered upstairs, letting memories whisper through her thoughts.

The same frilly pink curtains adorned the window of the bedroom that she and Sarah had shared the summers they'd visited. Gran's music box still sat on the nightstand, too.

Becki turned the mechanism, and the strains of "My Favorite Things" filled the room. As the last notes died away, Becki returned the music box to the nightstand and wiped the moisture from her eyes.

Thank goodness Josh wasn't there to see her sniffle over every knickknack. It was one thing to cry at a funeral. Everyone expected that. But almost a month had passed since her grandparents' deaths.

She glanced out the window. Across the yard, Hunter stood, scrutinizing the cameras he'd positioned. Josh wasn't taking any chances on missing her prowler the next time around.

If only he'd been as diligent investigating the cause of Gramps's headache.

She bit her lip, ashamed by the thought. Logically, she knew her grandparents' deaths weren't Josh's fault. She certainly didn't blame him. But...

Ever since Anne had told her about Gramps's headache, Becki couldn't stop thinking about how differently things could have turned out if only...

She shoved the pointless wish from her mind and unpacked the box she'd carried up. She set her jewelry box and hairbrush on the dresser next to the flip book of Bible promises that had been there for as long as she could remember. The visible page, yellowed and curled at the edges, read, "And we know that all things work together for good to them who love God..."

Becki tossed the book into the empty box and trudged downstairs. Passing the thermostat, she flicked it off.

If the weather hadn't been so humid the night her grandparents had died, Gran would have had the windows open instead of letting Gramps turn on the air conditioner. The carbon monoxide wouldn't have had a chance to build up and claim their lives. If God really cared, He would have worked things differently.

Josh's promise to pray for a new job whispered through her thoughts. How could he be so confident

God would answer that prayer when He hadn't protected Gran and Gramps?

The phone's ring fractured the silence. She drew in a deep breath, mentally prepared her greeting, then lifted the receiver. "Hello, Graw residence, their granddaughter Becki speaking."

Again silence greeted her.

"Hello, is anyone there?" She strained to hear any background noise. The faint whirr of traffic maybe. Was Josh calling from the quarry and unable to hear her? "Hello," she said more loudly.

The line clicked off.

She dialed star sixty-nine to find out who her caller was. The automated computer voice informed her the number was private.

Had the caller deliberately blocked his or her identity?

What if it was the prowler calling to see if anyone was home?

Now he knew who she was!

A knock sounded at the back door. She jumped, sending the phone toppling off the end table. She grabbed the phone and peered around the corner to try to catch a glimpse of who was there.

"Miss Graw? It's Hunter."

Her breath whooshed from her chest. *Of course. Idiot.* The phone call had scrambled her brain. She set down the phone and hurried to the back door. "Sorry, I was—" she waved toward the other room "—on the phone."

"No problem. I just wanted to let you know the cameras are up and I'm heading out. You can hang on to them as long as you need them."

"Will do. Thank you so much. Can I get you a coffee or something before you go?"

He tipped his cap, his mouth spreading into an amused grin. "That's okay. Maybe some other time when Josh is around." He winked, then strode across the yard back to his SUV.

Great, now he'd think his friend's new neighbor was a nervous Nellie. Of course, if he was in the habit of always dressing like Rambo, he probably got that reaction a lot. She flipped the dead bolt and returned to her unpacking.

A door upstairs slammed shut, making her jump yet again. *It's just the wind, you ninny.* She should probably shut the windows now that she was alone again.

She made quick work of the downstairs ones, then grabbed another box marked Bedroom and climbed the stairs. She wrestled the end room's window closed first. It opened to a meadow with a stand of trees beyond. Movement in the trees caught her attention. She squinted, hoping to spot a deer and her fawn. She'd have to find Gran's binoculars.

The phone rang as she reached her grandparents' bedroom. She snatched up their bedside extension, an old-fashioned rotary dial. "Hello."

Once again, an ominous silence greeted her.

"If you don't want to talk to me, stop calling." She

slammed the phone down with a satisfying thwack. If the creep called one more time, she'd have him blocked. There had to be a way for the phone company to do that, even if he was hiding his number. She shut the back windows and was about to move to the front bedrooms when the phone rang again.

If she had a whistle, she'd be tempted to let it blast. She smiled to herself, then puckered up and put her thumb and forefinger between her lips as she lifted the receiver. She didn't say a thing and when the person on the other end didn't either, she let loose for a full ten seconds.

After a second's pause, a voice came on the line. "Bec? Is that you?"

"Josh? Uh, sorry about that. Someone's been calling here and not saying anything and then hanging up. I figured I'd give him an earful."

"When? How many times?"

His staccato questions set her pulse racing all over again. "Three times in the last half hour or so. I tried star sixty-nine, but the guy blocked his information."

"I'm on my way now. That's why I called. If the phone rings again, don't answer it. When I get there, I'll get hold of the phone company and have them trace the call."

Outside, Tripod started barking.

Sure, where was the dog an hour ago when Rambo showed up? "Your dog's going nuts over something outside."

"Probably a cat again. Can you see him?"

Becki unwound the phone cord from behind the night table and moved to the window to try and see what had him riled. A noise sounded from downstairs. The dog?

She couldn't see him from the window. From his barking, it sounded as if he was prancing back and forth along the west wall. She moved toward the bedroom door, straining to hear if the sound had really come from inside.

Another thump sounded.

"Josh," she whispered, "I think someone's in the house."

"Where are you?"

"Upstairs."

A voice spoke in the background, and then Josh barked orders to send a cruiser to her address. "Help is on the way, Bec. I'm fifteen minutes out." Through the phone, a siren whirred to life, while at her end, silence reigned.

*The dog's not barking.* She clenched the phone to her ear. "Josh, the dog's not barking!"

"It's going to be okay. I want you to hide in the bathroom. Lock the door."

"But I'm on an old plug-in phone, I'd have to hang up."

"Listen to me. You need to hang up. If the intruder sees a light on the downstairs phone, he'll know someone's in the house."

Her fingers tightened around the receiver at the thought of breaking the connection.

A loud pop and whoosh cracked the silence.

She gasped.

"What is it? What's going on?" The urgency in Josh's voice sent her pulse careening.

"A… It sounded like a gunshot. Outside."

"Are you sure it wasn't one of the bangers that scare birds from the vineyards across the road?"

Her heart pummeled her ribs as she tugged the phone as far as it would reach and tried to see out the front windows from the hallway. "I don't know. Maybe."

A second shot sounded. And a puff of dirt kicked up in the yard.

She dropped to her belly. "No, it's real. Someone's shooting at the house!"

# FOUR

At the sound of dead air swallowing Bec's whispered "Hurry," Josh floored the gas pedal. What kind of car thief shot at a house?

Josh tightened his grip on the steering wheel. Was he reading the situation all wrong? Were the note, the incident in the barn and these shots really about scaring Bec off her grandparents' property?

He banked the corner too fast. His wheels bit into the graveled shoulder. He cranked the wheel hard to the left, then right, pulling the car straight, wishing he could get a grip as easily on what was going on.

The guy Bec had surprised in the barn had to believe she could identify him, or else why expose his proximity by shooting at the house?

Seven minutes out, his police radio blared to life. "We're on-site. No sign of an intruder outside. But no one's answering the door."

Josh snatched up the radio. "I told her to hide in the upstairs bathroom. Use the bullhorn."

Twenty long seconds later, an officer came back

on. "Okay, we see movement… The front door's opening… A lone woman, Caucasian, curly hair."

Relief washed through him. "Yeah, that's her. Rebecca Graw," he confirmed.

"She's fine," the officer assured him.

A second voice cut in. "Need first aid. West side of the house. Hurry."

"Hunter?" Josh careened onto his road, a whole other fear welling inside him. "What you got?"

"It's Tripod." The harsh rattle in his friend's voice clutched at his throat. "He's been hit."

Josh screeched to a stop behind the row of police cars and raced to the side of the house. The circle of uniformed officers opened, and the officer in charge ordered a search for the shooter.

Bec was kneeling in front of a whimpering Tripod. She stroked the pup's head. "What a brave boy you are. A real guard dog."

Josh stared at them, his heart pummeling his chest.

Hunter, dressed in street clothes—he must have picked up the call on his police scanner—glanced up from examining the dog's lone back leg. "He'll be okay. Just a graze. The force must have knocked his foot out from under him."

Josh let out a breath and nodded. Hunkering beside Bec, he squeezed her shoulder and ruffled Tripod's ears with his other hand. "You did good, bud. Real good."

He cleared the emotions clogging his throat and

rubbed slow circles on Bec's back. "You okay?" he whispered close to her ear.

She shook her head, moisture clinging to her eyelashes. "Why would someone do this?"

"I don't know. But I promise you we'll find him."

Hunter swabbed the dog's wound with antiseptic. "He should be as good as new in a day or two."

When Josh nodded his thanks, Hunter held his gaze. "We need Miss Graw to answer some questions." The unspoken question in his eyes asked if Josh could handle the job without becoming emotionally involved.

The answer was no, and Hunter clearly recognized as much. This was little Becki Graw, the girl he'd been getting out of scrapes since she was knee-high. Of course this was personal. "I'll take care of it," Josh said. "Can you run a trace on incoming calls over the past hour?"

With a brisk nod, Hunter disappeared around the house.

Josh gently scooped Tripod into his arms. "We'll talk inside."

As they approached the front door, Hunter came out. A squirming cat leaped from his arms. Tripod tried to jump after it, but Josh held him fast.

"How'd that get inside?" Bec asked.

"Not sure. Found it cowering in the basement when I came in. Probably squeezed under the root-cellar door to get away from the dog. Knocked a canning jar off one of your shelves by the looks of it."

"That must be what you heard in the basement," Josh said to Bec before turning his attention back to Hunter. "See if the cameras picked up anything useful, will you?"

Bec led the way inside and spread a thick blanket on the carpet for Tripod. "Maybe the shots were from a hunter. Someone might have mistaken Tripod's movements in the woods for game."

"You said the shots were directed toward the house."

She smoothed the edges of the blanket. "I was rattled from the phone calls and Tripod's barking. Maybe I was wrong. Maybe he got winged by a hunter in the woods and then ran to the house."

"On the phone, you said you heard the dog barking at the house before the shot."

"Do you think a hunter could have misjudged the distance his bullet would travel?" Bec asked, clearly grasping for any explanation that would put some much-needed distance between her and this latest incident. Her fingers worried the edge of the blanket.

Josh covered her hands with his to still them. "It's not hunting season."

"How about a farmer? Aren't they allowed to take down an animal that goes after their stock?"

"Sure, but they wouldn't be doing that on your property." He decided against mentioning his suspicions about the abandoned car they'd found at the quarry. She was upset enough.

By the time Josh had gleaned every detail she

could remember from the afternoon, Hunter had re-appeared at the door. "The cameras didn't pick up anything, but we got a couple of numbers for those phone calls. Last one was yours. The other three came from a cell phone, but the number couldn't be traced."

"A pay-as-you-go?" Criminals' phone of choice.

"Yeah."

Josh rubbed his chin. "Could they tell how long ago the phone was activated?"

"Yesterday."

Bec's face blanched.

Josh motioned for Hunter to give them some privacy. After the door closed behind his friend, Josh touched his finger under Bec's chin and tipped her face toward him. "Tell me what you're thinking."

"Someone's going to a lot of trouble to scare me off this property."

Josh searched her eyes. "Do you still think it's your sister? That she hired someone to do this?"

"It's the only thing that makes sense, but I just can't believe she'd go this far. I mean…those were real bullets!"

Josh rubbed his palms up and down her upper arms. "Tell me about Neil."

She croaked out a laugh. "It couldn't be him."

"From where I was standing, he looked like exactly the kind of guy who'd stoop to scare tactics to get what he wanted."

"We're not even dating."

Josh dropped his hands to his sides. "Looked to me like that wasn't his choice."

Her face flushed a bright red. "He accepted my decision."

"On the surface maybe. But deep down, I'm thinking he figured you'd eventually come to your senses. Only, now you've moved outside his sphere of influence, so to speak."

She shook her head vehemently. "He doesn't own a gun. At least...I can't imagine him owning one."

"They're easy enough to come by." Josh's hand skimmed his own holstered weapon as he tried to tamp down his irritation that she was defending the guy.

Her chin dropped to her chest. She reached out a trembling hand and ruffled Tripod's fur. "I can't believe he'd...He wouldn't shoot a dog."

So she conceded that he might shoot off a gun to scare her into fleeing back to the city?

Josh pressed his lips together to stop himself from saying it. He definitely needed to do a background check on the creep.

The more he thought about it, a guy like Neil was exactly the type who'd take an interest in a collector's item like the 1913 Cadillac parked in the barn, too. He'd probably snuck into town ahead of Bec and planted that note in the mailbox, then got caught nosing around the barn and panicked.

"I was thinking..." Bec pushed the hair from her face and stiffened her spine. "Whoever made those calls must have been phoning to see if the place was empty so they could come back and steal the car."

"If he'd called once, maybe. But three times so close together? Not likely."

Her gaze drifted to an old family picture on the mantel of Bec and her sister. The muscles in her jaw flexed. Then suddenly she snatched up the phone.

"Who are you calling?"

"Sarah."

"I'm not sure that's such a—"

Wes, the officer directing the search, poked his head around the door. "Josh, can I have a word with you outside?"

"Be right back," he said to Bec. He joined the other officer on the porch. "What'd you find?"

"Two possibilities. Seems your dog's been ripping through the neighbors' farmyards chasing cats. One of your neighbors said it wouldn't be the first time a farmer's taken a potshot at a roving dog."

"He say which farmer?"

"Nope, but we found these in the dirt around the house." Wes held out his palm.

Josh examined the small hunks of metal. "Air-rifle pellets."

"Yup. Looks like our shooter was a kid playing around or someone who just wanted to scare the pup off."

"Or Becki."

Wes clapped his hand closed around the pellets.

"My advice is that you keep your dog tied up and you won't have any more trouble."

Josh squared his jaw. "You said there were two possibilities?"

"Yeah." Wes glanced toward the barn. "Hunter said Miss Graw had an intruder last night messing with her grandfather's antique car."

"That's right."

"A few weeks back we got a call from a police officer in the Ottawa area, asking questions about Graw and his car."

"What kind of questions?"

Wes hesitated, his reluctance to say etched in his face.

"What kind of questions?" Josh repeated.

"Like if Graw was the kind of man who could pull off a jewelry heist."

"A jewelry heist?" Josh almost laughed at the absurdity of the idea.

"Seems they had some expensive pieces lifted from a museum that the antique-car club toured. A tour Graw was on. A tour he'd left two days early."

Josh shook his head. "You know Graw would never have been mixed up in anything like that."

"I know."

"So what did you tell the officer?"

"That Graw was dead."

"Are you nuts?" her sister screamed. "What kind of person do you think I am?"

Becki jerked the phone away from her ear. "The kind who'd go to any lengths to ensure I sell this house so that you get a bigger piece of the pie."

Sarah gasped. "I'd never threaten you. Never."

"You threatened to go to the lawyer if I didn't cave…and then did!"

Josh walked in the door, his expression grim.

"The police officer's back. I've got to go. But make no mistake, if they find proof it was you, I don't care if you are my sister, I will press charges." Becki disconnected before Sarah could respond.

Josh's mouth twisted to one side. "I take it she denied any involvement."

"Yup."

"Do you believe her?"

Becki hesitated. "I don't know. Her horrified gasp sounded real enough." Becki turned the phone over in her hands. "And she was home, so clearly she didn't pull the trigger. But maybe she just couldn't believe what her hired henchman would do. What did that officer have to say?"

Josh glanced away, and Becki recognized the tic in his cheek. He'd had the same reaction the time her favorite kitten had been hit by the hay wagon and he didn't want to tell her. He'd always gone above and beyond to try to protect her, even as a teenager. Given how insensitive her parents had been, Becki had always appreciated Josh's acute regard for her feelings.

"I'm a big girl now," she reminded him, setting the phone back on the table.

He took a seat. "It's good news, in a way." Leaning forward, he clasped his hands between his knees. "The shots came from an air rifle, which means they weren't intended to do more than frighten."

"Me or the dog?"

"I'm not sure." The concern in his gaze made her heart stutter. "Wes thinks the dog. One of the neighbors said as much."

"But you still think it's Neil?"

That muscle in his cheek twitched again. "I just don't like coincidences. Those phone calls are suspicious. I still want to check into his whereabouts. How soon did he leave here this morning?"

"Not long after you left."

Becki snatched up the phone again.

"Who are you calling?"

"Neil's house number. If he's home already, then there's no way he could be the one who fired those shots."

Neil picked up on the second ring.

Becki let out a breath of relief that her former relationship hadn't morphed into a *Fatal Attraction* remake. She quickly fabricated a story about feeling bad that she'd sent him off so quickly after he'd traveled so far to visit her, then thanked him again for the flowers.

"My pleasure, Rebecca. I'll try to make it down there again soon, and you can show me the sights."

Becki cringed at how he'd instantly mistaken her apology for interest. "Uh, there's not much to do but watch the grass grow here, remember? Not your idea of a good time."

"Any time with you is good."

She swallowed a gag, which wasn't fair. He sounded sincere…unfortunately. Becki threw Josh a desperate look, but he was absorbed in a conversation on his cell phone. "Uh, sorry, Neil, I've got to run. My neighbor just came to the door."

Neil's snort and terse goodbye left no doubt as to his opinion of Josh.

*Good.* Maybe that would stave off any more surprise visits.

"You're certain?" Josh clutched his phone with white-knuckled fingers, piquing Becki's curiosity. He glanced her way and quickly ended the call.

"Who was that?" she asked.

"It's not important."

"It sounded important."

He tucked his phone into his pocket. "Nothing for you to worry about. So what did Neil say?"

"Since he was home, I didn't want to mention what happened. Would only fuel his arguments against my moving here."

Josh nodded, but he looked as if he wanted to say more.

"Maybe that officer is right about the shots." Catching herself nervously twisting her necklace, she pressed her palms to her thighs. "I was so worked up with everything that happened yesterday and then the phone calls that I freaked. Obviously a car thief isn't going to start shooting at the house and draw attention to himself. He'd just wait until I'm out."

Josh squeezed her hand. "It's always better to call for help than regret it later. And don't forget one of those pellets winged Tripod."

The dog whimpered at his name.

Becki slipped her hand free from Josh's reassuring grasp and stood. She couldn't let herself start leaning on him. "I'd better finish unpacking."

Josh scraped his hand over his jaw. "How about I leave Tripod here with you tonight?"

She tilted her head and squinted at him, but she couldn't read his expression. "What aren't you telling me?"

"Bec, I don't want you to worry unnecessarily."

"O-kay…"

"Does Neil have call forwarding?"

"I don't know." A lump balled in her throat. "Why?"

"Because he's not answering his door."

*You don't belong here.*

Becki surged from her bed and paced the bedroom floor for the umpteenth time.

Tripod whined at being disturbed yet again. Josh had left him with her—for company, he'd said, but more likely so the dog would bark if anyone tried to break in.

Becki scratched his ears. "I'm sorry, boy, but your master has my stomach in knots. First he convinces me it's got to be Neil who's terrorizing me. Then he tells me not to worry even though Neil never showed up at his apartment tonight."

She inched aside the curtains and peered at the yard bathed in moonlight. Leafy shadows danced on the barn wall. *It doesn't scare you to be out the back of nowhere? With next to no neighbors? And who knows what kind of wild animals stalking those woods?*

She took a deep breath and slowly released it. Neil had just been trying to manipulate her. No one was out there.

She wasn't going to let Neil, or her sister, coerce her into leaving. First thing Monday morning, she'd call her old boss and tell him not to bother holding her job as Neil had suggested, and then she'd call Gramps's lawyer to find out if Sarah had any chance of challenging the will. Relieved to have a plan of action, she crawled back into bed and mashed her pillow into a new shape.

Something creaked.

Her eyes flew open. The wispy white sheers fluttered at the window, looking ghostlike with the moonlight shimmering through them. Becki slanted a peek at Tripod. Still sleeping.

She reined in her galloping heart. If the noise

had been an intruder, the dog would have been alerted. Surely.

The creak sounded again.

Only, it was more of a whistle. The wind sneaking through the eaves?

Fixing her gaze on the fluttering curtains, she listened more closely. How had she not noticed the peepers chirruping like a rock concert gone wild outside, punctuated by the bullfrog's occasional *owooga?*

She huffed onto her side and tried to ignore them. Then just as she'd gotten used to the "music," the critters invited a new voice to the party—the thrumming bass strings of some other amphibian.

"Aaaah!"

Tripod instantly lifted his head and gave her a worried look.

"Sorry, boy. Go back to sleep." One of them might as well. She snapped on the bedside lamp and shimmied up to lean against the headboard.

The phone rang.

She tensed. This couldn't be happening. Not again. Not at—she peered at the clock—three in the morning. What had Josh told her to do?

She scrubbed her head, trying to clear her foggy brain.

The phone blasted again.

She snatched it up.

"Bec, you okay?" Josh's sleep-roughened voice

wrapped around her heart and slowed it to an even gallop. "I saw your light come on."

She glanced back to the window. Through the sparse line of trees that separated her house from Josh's, she could just make out a light.

He sounded as if he'd just awakened, and the thought that he'd been watching her place so diligently that he'd noticed her light come on in the wee hours of the morning chased the chill that had gripped her.

"Bec?" he repeated, concern pitching the question up an octave.

She tried not to read more into his concern than there was. He was, after all, a police officer. Protecting people from intruders was his job. "I couldn't sleep for the frog noises. Do you have any idea how many different sounds they make?"

He chuckled. "And knowing your imagination, you sectioned them into orchestra parts."

"A rock band, actually," she admitted, heartened that he remembered their evenings sitting around the campfire with Gran and Gramps, making up stories about the night sounds.

Josh's laugh eased the last of her tension. "Tripod okay?"

"Sleeping like a baby. I'm sorry I woke you."

His snort suggested that he hadn't been able to sleep, either, despite the gravelly sound of his voice. She really should let him try. No reason both of them should be tossing all night.

"Have you tried counting sheep?" he asked.

"Just wolves."

He groaned. "We're going to catch this guy. I promise you." His earnestness wound around her heart the way his strong arms had protectively wrapped around her earlier. Oh, boy, she should so not be going there.

As noble as Josh was, sentry duty was bound to get old quick. "Um, I think I'll just read for a bit. Get my mind off…things."

"You sure?"

"Yes." Who was she kidding? She'd just traded one preoccupation for another. But thankfully, Josh took her at her word and said good-night. The last thing she wanted was for him to feel as if he had to constantly watch out for her like a big brother. She slipped the phone back onto the nightstand. "Or worse, like some rescued stray."

Tripod lifted his head and whimpered.

"No offense, bud. Josh loves you. I'm sure he'll never get tired of having you around." Not the way her dad had forced them to give up their one and only dog after less than three weeks.

Not wanting to remember other things Dad had quickly tired of—including her—Becki pulled one of Gran's photo albums onto her lap. Mom and Dad had never taken pictures of them, so Becki and her sister had relished posing for the camera whenever they visited Gran and Gramps.

Gran had written little notes beneath each one, too.

Becki traced her finger over a picture of Gramps carrying her on his shoulders in front of the house. She couldn't have been more than five or six. Beneath the picture Gran had written, "Our Becki says she wants to live here always, even when she's big."

Not like her daddy.

Gran would never have written the words that whispered through Becki's thoughts, but she knew that Dad's restlessness had always tugged at Gran's heart. Becki had never understood why her dad had loathed Serenity so much. He was the polar opposite of Josh.

She forced her mind away from Josh and back to her dad. He'd rarely stuck around for more than a day when they visited Gran and Gramps, leaving them time alone with Mom.

Before long, Gran had invited her and Sarah to visit without their parents, which had suited Becki just fine. Poor Gran must have grieved all over again when Mom moved halfway across the country and stopped sending them, too, with her default "it's for the best" excuse.

Becki traced Gramps's smiling face. *Becki wants to live here always.* Is that why they'd left her the place?

She'd loved everything about her grandparents' home, from sliding down the banister to swinging on the big oak tree out back. She'd loved that Gran never lamented how impossible it was to pull the comb through Becki's tangle of curls. She'd loved that Gramps never complained how many dishes she'd broken with her butterfingers.

When she would return from playing in the woods, covered from head to toe in mud, they would chuckle instead of scold. And she hadn't minded at all that Gran hosed her down outside with the icy well water before allowing her to step foot in the bathroom.

Becki smiled at the memory of Josh getting a blast of that same water a time or two.

*Stop thinking about him already!* She slammed the photo album shut and clicked off the light.

Somewhere between the frogs winding down their concert and her snuggling deeper under the comforter, thoughts of Josh must have turned to dreams, because the next thing she knew, a *ping* on the window jolted her awake.

She blinked at the bright sunlight beaming through the sheers.

"Hey, sleepyhead. You still in bed?" Josh's amused voice filtered through her fuzzy brain.

*Terrific.* He wasn't helping. How was she supposed to keep her mind off him if he showed up at her window, jolting her awake as if fifteen years had evaporated overnight and they'd sneak in an early-morning fishing trip before church?

Then again, maybe they could just skip church. She pulled on her bathrobe. He'd simply taken for granted that she'd attend. She swept aside the curtains. "Don't you know it's bad manners to—" The rest of Becki's thought flew from her head at the sight of Josh looking up at her second-story window wearing a handsome blazer, a crisply pressed shirt and tie, and a grin that turned her inside out.

# FIVE

Josh whistled as he waited for Bec to come downstairs with Tripod. He'd hated to wake her so early after the night she'd had, but if the dog didn't get outside soon, she'd hate him more.

Tossing pebbles at her bedroom window had felt like old times. Good times. Times when summers were carefree and the worst they could imagine happening was falling from a tree.

The instant her kitchen door opened and Tripod dashed out, Josh stepped up with the tray of coffee and bagels he'd brought with him. "Not as fancy as my sister's breakfast, but after the trouble you had sleeping, I figured you could use a jolt of caf—"

The sight of her soft, sleep-rumpled face swept the words clean out of his head.

She pushed the door wider and motioned him inside. "Thanks."

Struggling to ignore what the crackly, early-morning texture of her voice did to him, he carried the tray into the kitchen and helped himself to a mug of coffee. "Uh…" He hadn't been able to really see her up at the bedroom window, and now that he could…

He finished his coffee in three burning gulps and set it back on the tray. "I'd better wait for you outside."

Her brow creased. Then she swiped at the lines crisscrossing her cheeks from where she'd slept and scrunched together the neck flaps of her white terry robe.

He dropped his gaze to the floor, feeling bad that he'd made her self-conscious.

Her bare toes, with their hot-pink polish, wiggled.

The fact she painted her usually hidden toenails and yet didn't seem to wear makeup sparked even more curiosity about this utterly grown-up version of the cute kid he used to rescue from the old oak tree.

She cleared her throat, jerking his attention back to her face.

His own flamed. Okay, this was definitely *not* a good idea. "Uh…" He hitched his finger over his shoulder. "I need to feed the dog. Come get me when you're ready to leave for church. Okay?"

"Actually…" She stirred her coffee, her unsweetened, black coffee that didn't need stirring. "I was thinking maybe I'd skip church today. I'm not really up to facing—"

"We can take the Cadillac," he blurted on impulse. Anything to convince her not to stay home alone. He'd just have to call Hunter and alter their plan a bit.

Her eyes lit up. "You got it going?"

"Yup. Turns out it was just a bad connection. Finally found the problem this morning." He wasn't sure what had compelled him to work on the car again this morning. In the back of his mind, he must've known he'd need the carrot. He hadn't told her what Wes had said about the jewelry theft.

Not that he believed for a second that Bec's grandfather had anything to do with the robbery.

But the person who'd been poking around the place might. Might even have been poking around before Bec had arrived. Maybe even had tampered with the hot-water tank.

His stomach knotted. No, the service tech had insisted the squirrel nest blocking the chimney was to blame for the carbon monoxide.

"So…" he said, hoping his teasing tone didn't sound as forced to her ears as it did to his own. "Want to change your mind?"

She bobbed her head from side to side. "We could just go cruising after church like we'd planned."

"We could…. But do you really want me to worry about you being here alone all morning? I might get too stressed to drive this afternoon."

She rolled her eyes. "You're determined to guilt me into this, aren't you? Or scare me."

"Whatever works." He gave her a wicked grin.

"Okay, okay. I'll go. Just give me an hour to shower and dress. And wake up!"

"Perfect. That'll give me enough time to pull the

old gal out and dust her off." And contact Hunter to put a new plan in place. Maybe Wes could stake out the church parking lot once they parked the Caddy, and Hunter could still keep an eye on the house, in case Bec's prowler decided to take advantage of the time she'd be tied up in church.

With fifteen minutes to spare, Bec showed up on his doorstep dressed to turn every bachelor's head within a hundred miles. Wow. The instant he stepped through the church doors with Bec in that frothy vanilla sundress with her hair tamed by the doodad accessories that let the most becoming tendrils slip free to frame her face, he'd be the envy of every guy in the place.

She tugged at a wisp of hair, which sprang back to its curly Q shape the instant she released it. "That bad? It's impossible to do anything with it in the humidity."

"It looks fine," he said.

She frowned, and he winced at how gruff he'd sounded. It wasn't her fault he'd suddenly noticed how attractive she was.

*Oh, boy.* Maybe this wasn't such a good idea. Not to mention how carpooling together to church and then sharing a pew was bound to wind up the rumor mill, especially when the favorite pastime of the church's older ladies seemed to be trying to hook him up with a woman. As if he needed any more reminders of how big a failure he was at romance.

He gritted his teeth and reminded himself they

meant well. How were they to know that every woman he'd ever dated chose something better over him?

Bec flounced past him toward the car. Her exotic scent caught him by surprise. As a kid she'd always smelled like sunshine and flowers, except for the time...

He bit back a grin. "You sure smell better than the time you fell into that stagnant pond."

She stuck out her tongue. "Thanks for reminding me."

"No problem. What are friends for?"

"Neil actually gave me this perfume."

The grin slipped off Josh's face.

Bec waved her wrist in front of his nose. "Do you like it?"

*No.* "To tell you the truth," he hedged, "I always pictured you more of a sunshine-and-roses kind of girl."

She drew back her arm. "Well, in case you hadn't noticed, I'm not a girl anymore."

"Yeah, kind of noticed," he muttered under his breath and stopped alongside the car. "So Miss Grown-Up, does that mean you do or don't want the car's top down?"

"Oh, I almost forgot!" She rummaged through her purse and drew out a cowboy-style kerchief, which she draped over her head and tied under her chin. In an instant she went from runway worthy to schoolgirl.

Josh couldn't help it. He laughed.

"Oh, if you think this looks funny, you'd bust a gut over what the wind would do to my hair if I didn't wear it."

"I'll leave the top up."

"Doesn't help much when the car has no side windows!"

"Good point." He opened the passenger door, and Bec climbed in. He quirked an eyebrow. "You driving?"

She squinted up at him. "Not until you teach me how this thing works."

"Well, then…" He motioned to the driver's side—the right side of this particular car—where the would-be door was blocked by the stick shift and brake lever. "You going to let me in?"

"Oops." She scurried out. "I forgot."

He slid across the seat, and she climbed back in. "Okay. First lesson." He quickly showed her the positions of the gearshift, then moved it into Neutral and pushed the red ignition button on the dash.

The engine sputtered to life.

"That's it?" she asked.

"When all goes as it should, yes."

"And when it doesn't?"

He gunned the gas. "It's a lot more complicated than we have time for right now."

They settled into a rambling forty miles per hour, and Bec inhaled deeply. "I've missed the smell of country air."

"Cow manure?"

She swatted his arm. "I'm serious. As soon as the smell of hay and clean air and, yes, animals wafted through my car windows yesterday, I knew I'd found my way home."

The wistful way she said *home* made his heart skip a beat, but he couldn't help but wonder if her feelings would last. Lots of people fell in love with country living in the long, lazy days of summer, but their attitudes changed come February when winter entrenched itself in the community and showed no sign of releasing its grip for another two months.

"But I'm preaching to the choir. Right?"

"Yup," he confirmed and reminded himself that she was a city woman now. Not the girl who'd begged not to have to leave at the end of every summer and who'd always been humming one Sunday-school chorus or another.

She chattered on about various day trips she and her grandparents had taken in the car, but the closer they got to the church, the quieter she grew.

"You okay?" he asked finally.

"I'm not sure I can do this."

"It's okay to cry, Bec. I know I did at more than one service after my dad died."

"You did?" She suddenly sounded so lost.

"Yes," he said gently. He shifted the gear stick into First, so a kid couldn't accidentally start the car rolling, then pulled up the brake lever. "Trust me.

Everyone understands." He reached across the seat and squeezed her hand. "You'll be okay."

She dragged the scarf from her head, took a deep breath and released it slowly. "Okay, I'm ready."

As he waited for her to climb out ahead of him, he nodded to Wes, who'd positioned his truck near the exit where he could easily intercept a possible car thief.

When Josh looked back at Bec, Bill Netherby, a local farmer who had a knack for instantly turning strangers into friends, was pumping her hand.

"Becki, welcome back. We were so glad to hear that your grandparents' place is staying in the family, and—" he gestured toward the Cadillac "—I'm glad to see you didn't take that fella up on his offer to buy the old car."

Josh clambered out of the front seat to join Bec. "What fella?"

Bill looked from Josh to Bec's equally curious expression. "Didn't he find you? The night before last, I was out on my bicycle down your way, and this fella asked directions to your place. Said he saw your grandparents' death notice in the car-club magazine, alongside a picture of the car. I figured he wanted to make an offer."

Bec's gaze darted to Josh.

He nodded, silently acknowledging her suspicion that the guy might have been her attacker. "You catch the guy's name?" he asked Bill.

"Afraid not, sorry."

"Could you describe him?"

"Not much to describe. Average height, average build. Dark hair. Middle-aged. Can't think of anything about him that really stood out."

"A beard? A mustache? An accent, maybe?"

"Like I said, he was pretty average."

"What kind of car did he drive?"

"An old green Plymouth."

Josh's pulse spiked. The same color and make they'd pulled out of the quarry. Had the guy known Josh spotted the car and decided to dump it? "Thanks, Bill. We'll be sure to keep an eye out for him." Josh prodded Bec forward.

She dug in her heels and whirled on him. "What are we going to do?"

"Like I said, keep an eye out for him." Josh pulled out his cell phone and texted the new information to the officer investigating the abandoned car, then sent the suspect's description—for what it was worth—to Wes and Hunter.

"This helps, right?" Bec's voice hummed with nervous energy. "I mean, this has got to be the same guy who knocked me out and then made those phone calls and shot at the house. And it can't be Neil. No one would ever peg him as average."

Josh pictured the man's horn-rimmed glasses and pointy nose. "No, probably not." His background check on her ex hadn't turned up so much as a parking ticket, either, and no Plymouths registered to him. For the first time since failing to locate Neil after yesterday's visit, Josh could take a full breath. He'd rather deal with a thwarted car thief than an ex.

He turned to escort Bec inside, but the sight of Bart Winslow watching her with a predatory gleam from the front seat of his Maserati pitched his good mood into a tailspin.

If not for Netherby's encounter with the stranger interested in the Cadillac, Josh could imagine, only too well, Bart being behind the attacks on Bec.

The thirty-year-old son of the town's slimiest real-estate agent was the kind of jerk who would stoop to any tactics to help out his dad. And his dad's current pet interest was snatching up rural properties for development.

Properties like Bec's.

The rigid line of Josh's jaw sent Becki's pulse spiking. She tracked his gaze to a red car parked on the street. A casually dressed blond-haired guy sat inside. "Who's that?" she asked.

Anne swooped up from behind them and hooked her arm through Josh's. "The best-looking and most eligible bachelor in town."

Josh gave his sister a withering look. "If you prefer the partying, fast-driving type. C'mon, let's go inside and find a seat." He grazed his fingertips across Becki's back.

She started, caught off guard by the jitters his touch unleashed, and scrambled to gather her wits. She'd been so preoccupied with worrying about breaking down into a blubbering fool the moment she stepped inside the church that she hadn't been paying attention to her inconvenient reactions to Josh.

It wasn't as though the touch meant anything. Josh clearly didn't want Mr. Maserati messing with her and was just being his usual protective self, again.

And it wasn't as if she wanted it to mean anything.

Sure, she'd gotten all dolled up this morning, but *not* because she'd wanted Josh to notice her. Because the man had seen her with bedhead!

She had *some* pride.

She slanted a glance at his handsome profile. Okay, maybe she'd hoped he'd notice a smidgen.

As Anne led the way into the sanctuary, Becki remembered why she didn't want to be here. A cheery melody instantly transported her back to Gran's Sunday-school classes.

Becki drew in a fortifying breath. She blinked rapidly and tried to focus on something else. Anything else.

Sunshine gleamed through the windows, splashing rainbows about the room, nothing like the gray day when she'd buried her grandparents.

She avoided making eye contact with those who glanced her way, afraid she wouldn't be able to bear the sympathy in their eyes. She lifted her gaze to the stained-glass image, on the wall behind the pulpit, of Jesus cradling a lamb.

Josh gave her shoulder a reassuring squeeze. "You okay?"

The compassion in his whispered question threatened to undo her. She pulled her gaze away from the image and nodded, but she felt bereft the instant he withdrew his hand.

He motioned toward the back pew. "Let's sit here."

Grateful for his understanding, she quickly took a seat. When he slid in beside her, she snuck a glance at the others still filing in. Her gaze collided with Mr. Maserati.

He smiled, a dimple winking on his cheek.

Josh snorted, then leaned forward and reached for a hymnal, effectively blocking her view of the heartthrob.

*On purpose?* She shot him a glance.

Looking suspiciously innocent, Josh leaned back and rested his arm on the pew behind her.

He must've done it on purpose. Didn't Josh think she had enough sense not to get taken in by a guy like that?

Before she could decide if she was more irritated or amused, the worship team streamed onto the stage and invited the congregation to stand and sing.

Josh's deep baritone, so much like Gramps's beautiful singing voice, filled her senses, reminding her of the sweet harmonies Gramps and Gran used to sing during the car rides home from church.

A bittersweet ache squeezed her heart. She tried to join in on the chorus, but her voice cracked. Josh's sympathetic glance almost finished her. By sheer willpower, she shifted her mind into Neutral and joined her alto to the array of voices.

After a few songs, the pastor invited everyone to welcome those standing nearby.

Mrs. O'Reilly bustled across the aisle and gave Josh's hand a hearty shake. "Glad to see you're finally taking my advice."

Josh's lips flattened into the polite smile he used to don whenever his aunt Betsy visited, but the woman didn't seem to notice.

She scooped up Becki's hand with a smile as wide as the Mississippi. "Welcome, welcome!"

"Thank you," Becki responded automatically, tugging her gaze from Josh. *What was that all about?*

As the woman continued down the row, Becki glanced around, but she didn't see anything else that might explain Josh's peculiar reaction. "What advice was she talking about?" Becki whispered close to his ear.

He shifted in the pew. "Nothing."

She arched her brow. "Really, *nothing?*"

"Nothing important."

"Maybe you should just go with it," Anne suggested.

"Don't be ridiculous."

"Go with what?" Becki asked.

Ignoring the question, Anne squeezed Josh's arm. "It'd get those ladies off your back."

"It's only once a week. Pretty sure I can handle it, Anne."

"Handle *what?*" Becki interjected.

Bart turned her way and smiled again, diverting her attention.

He really was good-looking. Too bad he had that slick veneer.

At the feel of Josh's arm slipping around her shoulders, her heartbeat went wacky. And it didn't help that he met her puzzled look with that heart-stopping grin.

"On second thought…" He curled his arm a little more tightly around her and turned back to his sister. "That's a great idea."

"See, I told you."

Becki waved her hand in front of them. "*Hello?* What's a great idea?"

"You guys look good together," Anne added, still focused on Josh.

Heat rushed to Becki's face. Then Josh's warm-as-a-summer-meadow eyes captured her gaze, and her cheeks positively flamed.

"Oh, yeah." Anne chuckled. "You guys could totally pull this off."

"What are you two talking about?" Becki scrambled to catch up as her heart did crazy pirouettes.

"Just pretend to be his girlfriend," Anne whispered, motioning them to sit down again. "We'll explain later."

*Be his girlfriend?* "Seriously?"

Josh gave her a squeeze. "Mrs. O'Reilly drives me crazy with her matchmaking ploys. You'd be doing me a favor."

*A favor? A favor.*

Of course, because the speed with which he'd backed out of her house that morning should have been her first clue to his true feelings. "You're serious?"

He gave her a take-pity-on-me look.

The music swelled, saving her from responding. Only…the song—"The Old Rugged Cross"—was one of Gran's favorites.

Becki started to sing, but emotions clogged her throat. By the time they reached "Then He'll call me someday to my home far away, where His glory forever I'll share," tears stung her eyes. If only she could know it was true. That Gran and Gramps…

She tried to swallow, tried to forget that she still had the sermon to get through.

Josh reached over and squeezed her hand.

Blinking rapidly, she clung to it, grateful she didn't have to bear the loss alone.

If only the ruse was real.

# SIX

What had he been thinking? Josh glanced across the seat of the Cadillac at Bec's far-too-quiet profile. As bad as it sounded, he hoped she was quiet from being emotionally strung out by the service. Not because she was mortified that his sister had wangled her into pretending to be his girlfriend.

He never should have taken up Anne's suggestion—in church, no less—but when he'd seen Winslow tossing Bec that oily smile, he hadn't been able to help himself.

She needed protection from that creep.

Never mind that his heart had felt two sizes too big when she'd clung to his hand through the service or, Lord help him, that his heart sped up at the way her curls escaped her scarf to dance in the breeze. Josh dragged his attention back to the road. No wonder Winslow had tried to catch her eye. Not that he'd appreciate her other qualities—her faith and an appreciation for simple rural living that seemed so hard to find in a woman these days.

Josh tightened his grip on the steering wheel.

Maybe he should just put an end to the sham now. From her bewildered *You're serious?* back in the sanctuary, she'd clearly never thought of him as a potential boyfriend.

He'd always been a big brother. A big brother infatuated with her older sister. Which, as he recalled, had irritated Bec more than once when she'd wanted him to play in the woods with her and her menagerie of adopted animals. Then again, if he didn't mention it, the whole thing might be forgotten by next Sunday. It wasn't as if they had to pretend to be an item when no one was looking.

The car hit a bump and jostled Bec into his side.

"You okay?" he said.

She straightened. "Yeah. Just tired."

He gave her a sympathetic glance. She'd tried so hard to contain her grief during the service, but he'd felt her restrained sobs as she clung to his hand.

He was glad he could be there for her. At least some good had come of their ruse.

"The first time back is always the hardest," he said gently. "It'll get easier each week."

Her hands twisted in her lap, and suddenly he feared that she didn't plan on going back.

Hopefully, he could change that. "You still up for an afternoon outing?" He'd promised, and he'd keep that promise if she wanted, but he was also eager to follow up on Netherby's information. Maybe get a look inside the car from the quarry. See if he could find anything more to link it to its owner and Bec's prowler.

"I don't know." She sounded exhausted.

Or was she uncomfortable with the idea of spending time alone with him? "You weren't really interested in Bart Winslow, were you?" Josh pulled into the driveway. "Because I don't want this O'Reilly ruse to mess up any plans you might have to meet men."

She smirked. "Unless the man is Bart, right?"

"Yeah, except for him," Josh quipped, then instantly sobered. "He's the son of the most crooked real-estate broker in the county, and he will stoop to just about anything to help his dear old dad get what he wants."

"So he couldn't possibly be interested in *me*." She climbed from the car.

"I didn't say that." Josh shimmied across the seat to climb out, too. "You just need to know that his motives might not be what they seem."

She dragged her scarf from her hair and squinted at the sun. "It wasn't supposed to be like this."

"What wasn't?"

"Moving to Gran and Gramps's. I'd always felt happy here. Safe. But it's turning into a nightmare."

"We'll catch this guy, Bec. I promise you."

"It's not just that. My sister is doing everything she can to force me to sell. And now you think this real-estate guy's going to start harassing me, too."

"Let's not worry about any of that today, okay?

We'll change, grab the picnic basket and the dog, and go for a long ride—enjoy the countryside like your grandparents would have wanted you to."

"Yes," she said, a bit of her enthusiasm returning.

A patrol car pulled to the side of the road in front of the house, and the passenger window opened.

"Be right back," Josh said to Bec and then jogged down the driveway. "You see anyone?" he asked Hunter when he got to the car.

"Afraid I got called away. A camper jackknifed on the highway, caused a pileup."

Josh let out a sigh. "All right. Probably was a long shot anyway. But keep up the patrols if you can."

"Will do." Hunter drove off, and Josh turned back to the house.

The front door stood open. An instant later Bec backed out of the house, her hand splayed over her chest.

Josh raced toward her. "What is it? What's wrong?"

She half turned, her face ashen. "He's here."

Becki twisted her scarf between her fingers and searched the windows. "There's a smell. It's not right." The house was supposed to smell like the perfume Gran dotted on her wrists or her grandfather's Old Spice with maybe a hint of that muscle rub Gran used to massage into his shoulders.

Not the musky odor that had assaulted her senses.

Josh immediately positioned himself between her and the door. "You saw someone?"

"No. I could smell his cologne."

Josh whipped out his phone. "I need you back here now," he barked to the person on the other end. He clipped the phone back onto his belt and squeezed her shoulder. "We'll wait for Hunter."

Hunter's patrol car swung onto the street, its rear end swerving into the opposite lane before righting itself. He parked across the end of the driveway and killed his swirling lights, then jogged toward them. In his uniform, he looked more like a policeman than Rambo, but just as determined. He handed Josh his Taser.

Josh pulled the house key from the lock and tossed it to Hunter. "You take the back."

Becki teetered, but before she could ask what she was supposed to do, Josh grabbed her hand and tugged her behind him. "Stick close."

She welcomed his solid, confident grip and stayed right on his heels. In no time, he'd cleared the front of the house and Hunter the rear.

"Any sign he ran out the back?" Josh asked Hunter.

"Nothing."

"Okay, I'll take the upstairs. You take the basement."

The instant they stepped into the master bedroom, Becki froze. "He's here," she hissed.

Josh sniffed the air and nodded. He motioned her back then stepped to the side of the closet, his Taser raised.

Once again, his gaze connected with hers. *Stay back,* he mouthed, then flung open the closet door.

No one was inside.

No one was anywhere in the room or anywhere else upstairs.

"Are you sure it's not your grandfather's aftershave you're smelling? With the house closed up all morning, you could—"

"No, Gramps always wore Old Spice." She picked up the bottle from the highboy and spritzed the air, fighting tears. "I don't understand. Why'd this guy come in the house if he's after the car?"

Josh pried the bottle from her hand and set it back down. "Maybe you shouldn't touch anything just yet. Can you tell if anything is missing?"

"Not without touching anything."

"Okay, just try to stick to the edges."

She jerked into action, checked the drawers, the closet, Gran's jewelry box, inwardly fuming at the thought of some creep pawing through her grandparents' belongings. But nothing seemed disturbed, let alone missing.

She sank onto the edge of her bed and clasped her head. "Why is God letting this happen?"

Josh hunkered down in front of her. "It's going to be okay, Bec."

"My grandparents were good people."

"They were. But God doesn't promise to spare us from bad circumstances. He only promises to carry us through. You need to trust in Him."

She gave her head a violent shake. "How can I trust a God who let a squirrel build a nest in my grandparents' chimney?"

Josh smoothed her hair and held her gaze with a shared pain that chiseled cracks in the shell around her heart. "Because He loves you, Bec."

She lifted her eyes to the painting on the wall of Jesus cradling a lost lamb —a replica of the church's window. *God cares so much that He comes looking for you when you're lost,* her gran used to say.

In this house, when Gran and Gramps were alive, she used to be able to believe that.

"I didn't imagine that smell," she whispered, stuffing away thoughts of God. "Someone was here."

"Someone was here, all right." Hunter's massive frame filled the doorway.

Josh pushed to his feet. "What did you find?"

"The main-floor bathroom window was pried open."

Becki's anger exploded. "My sister always snuck into the house that way."

"Did you check the cameras?" Josh asked, dismissing her insinuation.

His teenage infatuation with her sister had obviously colored his judgment. Clearly she was behind this.

"Yeah," Hunter said flatly. "They're dead."

"What do you mean, they're dead?"

"Someone tampered with them."

Not her sister, then. Becki lurched to her feet. This was all too unbelievable. "If the guy knew about the cameras, why wouldn't he just rip them off?"

"My guess is that he didn't want you to know he was here." Hunter returned her house key. "If I hadn't checked the cameras closely, I might not have noticed. Would have just figured they weren't triggered."

Josh thrust his fingers through his hair and stared out the window. "So our intruder's no dummy."

Becki looked from Hunter to Josh, her head spinning. "This makes no sense. Yesterday, the guy's trying to scare me. Today, he doesn't want me to know he was here? What does he want?"

"Not sure if yesterday's incident is connected," Hunter said. "But this looks to me like someone's convinced your grandfather made off with those jewels."

"Jewels? What jewels?" Becki's gaze snapped to Josh.

Just in time to catch him flick his finger in a slicing motion across his throat.

"What's he talking about?" she demanded.

Josh lowered his hand. "Nothing."

"I'll…uh…grab the evidence kit." Hunter disappeared down the stairs.

"It's not *nothing*," she ground out, holding on to her patience by a thread. How much more could God possibly throw at her?

"Nothing you need to worry about," Josh said

in the soothing tones she'd heard him use on injured animals.

"Hunter just called my grandfather a *jewel thief!*" she said, hearing her own voice edge higher.

"Now, Becki, Hunter didn't—"

"Don't 'now, Becki' me like I'm five years old! And don't touch me!" She whirled from his grasp.


"Watch out!" Josh shouted as Bec's heel caught in the hem of her dress.

She teetered at the top of the stairs, her arms windmilling. He lunged for her but grasped only air.

Bec pitched down the stairs.

He vaulted after her.

Three steps from the bottom, she came to a thudding stop.

"Are you okay?" He dropped to his knees, his hands immediately roaming her limbs for injuries.

She swatted him away, a tear leaking from her eye. "This is your fault."

He sat back on his heels and let out a breath. She couldn't be that hurt if she was scolding him. "Bec, I'm sorry. I didn't believe the incidents could be connected. That's why I didn't tell you."

"Tell me what?" She pushed to her feet. *"Aaah!"*

He caught her by the waist and lifted her weight from her legs. "What is it?"

"My ankle." She made a disgusted noise. "It's okay. I can manage." She grabbed the handrail and, reaching around him, braced her other hand on the wall as if she intended to hop.

"Don't. You'll only make it worse." He scooped her into his arms.

"What do you think you're doing?" She twisted in his hold. "Put me down."

He set her on a kitchen chair. "You're down." He lifted her injured leg to rest on a second chair and slipped off her shoe. "I'll get you some ice."

"I don't want ice. I want an answer."

He poked around in the freezer, searching for answers as much as ice. The only thing he knew for sure was that with the daggers shooting from Bec's eyes, Mrs. O'Reilly wouldn't mistake them for a couple a second time. Not that he cared what Mrs. O'Reilly thought; he just wanted Bec to know she could trust him.

Josh pulled a bag of frozen peas from the freezer, wrapped it in a towel and gently laid it across her ankle.

Hunter reappeared with the evidence kit and peered over his shoulder. "What happened?"

"She fell down the stairs." Josh had never seen an ankle swell so fast.

"Looks like you're going to have to take her to the hospital."

Bec folded her arms over her chest. "I'm not going anywhere until I get answers. Why would anyone think my grandparents stole jewels?"

Hunter hitched his thumb over his shoulder. "I'll check that bathroom window for fingerprints."

"Yeah, thanks." *For nothing.* Josh sank into a chair opposite Bec. "Some valuable jewelry was stolen from a museum during your grandparents' last tour."

"You can't possibly think they'd have anything to do with that."

"No, I don't. But when the police learned that your grandparents had left the tour early, they became suspicious. Only—" A lump caught in his throat as he whispered, "It was too late to question them."

She went white. "You think they were murdered?"

"No." Josh stroked the hair from her face, needing to touch her, draw her back. "No, Bec. Your grandparents' deaths were an accident. Believe me, that's the first thing I triple-checked."

She dropped her hands to her lap, suddenly looking way too vulnerable for his peace of mind. "Do you think Hunter could be right about someone looking for the jewelry here?"

"I don't know. Someone might have heard about the police's suspicions. They didn't have enough evidence to secure a search warrant, so maybe your intruder figured he'd look himself."

Bec shook her head. "No would-be thief would go to all this trouble on a far-fetched hunch."

"That's why I didn't mention it yesterday. But now...I'm not so sure."

"No." She straightened. "You were right yesterday. It's probably Neil who's trying to scare me. That's got to be it." She sniffed. "This cologne kind of smells like something he'd wear."

Josh pushed open the kitchen window. As much as he'd like nothing better than to pin all of this on Neil, she was clearly grasping at anything that would divert suspicion from any connection to her grandparents and the jewelry. "We've already concluded that Neil wasn't the driver of the green Plymouth I spotted the night you were hit. He doesn't fit Netherby's description, remember?"

Hunter returned with the fingerprint kit. "Did you say her attacker drove a green Plymouth?"

"Yeah."

"He was here yesterday." Hunter turned to Bec. "That guy you had coffee with."

Josh jerked his gaze to Bec. "Why didn't you tell me?"

"I didn't know Henry's car was a Plymouth. Besides, he couldn't be my attacker. He was a friend of my grandparents'."

Josh expelled a breath. Why was he only finding out now that she'd had a visitor, let alone that he might be their man? "Does he match Netherby's description?"

"Sure, I guess. But it can't be Henry."

"Why not?"

"He gave me his phone number…." Her voice trailed off.

"Where is it?"

She pointed toward the phone.

Josh looked at the paper. Henry Smith. An alias if he'd ever heard one. "Dust this for fingerprints, will you, Hunter?" Except if this guy had been here yesterday, then his car wasn't the one they'd towed from the quarry.

Didn't matter. Josh wasn't about to take any chances where Bec's safety was concerned.

Bec smoothed her skirt, but he didn't miss the way she trembled.

Safety, *right*. He'd utterly failed to protect her already. The cameras hadn't worked. Someone had gotten into the house. What if she'd been home?

She was right. Her life had turned into a nightmare.

If he didn't catch this guy soon, she'd hightail it back to the city long before winter. He should probably encourage her to do just that. She'd be safer.

Except how could he be sure if she was fifty miles away?

# SEVEN

Monday afternoon, Becki scrolled through images on the library computer. Images of the jewelry her grandparents were suspected of stealing. Images of diamond-and-ruby earrings, monogrammed cuff links, cameo broaches and much more. She grabbed scratch paper from beside the computer and jotted down the names of the witnesses who'd been interviewed in the online article.

The bold lettering of the classified ads sitting next to her elbow drew her attention back to what she was supposed to be doing—finding a job. If not for her idea of coming to the library to search for one, Josh would probably have a cop babysitting her this very minute.

From the inquisitive glances Mrs. O'Reilly slanted her way every few minutes, Becki half wondered if the older woman was secretly on Josh's payroll, not a library volunteer as she claimed.

Her thoughts drifted back to the web article once more. She shook her head. How many times would she do this?

She had to focus, and not on the suspicions hanging over her grandparents' heads. She should be leaving that to the professionals…to Josh, who believed in her grandparents as much as she did.

She looked down at the scratch paper in her hands and worked to flatten the crumpled edges. Maybe her grandparents were friends with some of the witnesses.

*Stop it.* She turned again to the classified ads, but after skimming her finger over several without a word sinking in, she set the newspaper aside and pulled Gran's address book from her purse.

She searched for the names she'd jotted down from the article, but she didn't find a single match. *Now what?*

"Are you still using that computer?" the librarian asked.

"Yes." Becki launched an online search for the contact information of each witness.

Hopefully, these folks would be more helpful than the president of the antique-car club had been when she'd called him earlier. He'd asked more questions than he'd answered and had refused to give the name of a single friend of her grandparents' that she might call.

She would have tried Henry first if Josh hadn't taken his number. She couldn't believe he was a thief. He'd made no attempt to invite himself inside. Well, except for asking about Gran's costumes. But when she'd first invited him to stay for coffee, he'd declined. If he'd been looking for stolen jewelry, wouldn't he have jumped at her invitation?

The two people from Gran's address book she'd managed to connect with hadn't been touring friends, although they would have happily talked to her all day if she hadn't begged off.

If she could just talk to someone who'd been with her grandparents, she was sure she could figure out if there was anything to Josh's jewelry-theft theory. It made far more sense that someone would come after the Cadillac. Maybe when the prowler had seen the car was gone, he'd simply checked out the empty house on a whim.

She clicked back to the newspaper article and studied the photograph of one of the stolen pieces—a double-chained necklace with large gemstones embedded in elaborate filigree dangling from the lower chain. She sure hadn't seen anything like that in Gran's jewelry box.

What was she thinking?

Of course she hadn't. Gran and Gramps would never have stolen jewelry. Anyone who knew them would know that. So if whoever had been prowling around the place hoped to find the loot, he couldn't possibly know them.

In fact, the more she thought about it, the more ridiculous the whole theory seemed.

She shook her head. Would she rather believe her sister and brother-in-law had sent an intruder into the house?

She clicked back to the online directory and managed to track down numbers for three of the witnesses. Phone numbers in hand, she wedged the crutches they'd given her at the hospital last night under her armpits and hobbled outside to make the calls in private.

As she reached her car, another pulled to the curb behind her. "What do you think you're doing?" Josh called through his open window, sounding none too happy.

Becki opened her car door, tossed her purse inside, then repositioned the crutch under her arm so she could turn to face him without putting weight on her injured foot. "Can't a girl take a break?" She swallowed at the sight of him climbing out of a patrol car in his police uniform, looking so tall and handsome and protective. He'd been incredibly attentive at the hospital last night, keeping her company through the long hours they'd had to wait for the doctor to come in and confirm her injury was a sprain.

"Sure." He closed the distance between them in three long strides. "If you were *actually* job hunting."

"Of course I'm job hunting. If I hope to afford to stay in the house, I will need one."

"Uh-huh."

She teetered on her crutches. Did he have someone spying on her in the library?

He cupped her elbow, steadying her. "Your ankle won't get better if you don't rest it."

She tossed her crutches into the backseat, feeling way too much like another one of his broken-winged sparrows or three-legged dogs, even if it was kind of sweet that he worried about her.

Josh shook his head, looking utterly exasperated. "What?"

"We just got a call at the station from the detective investigating the museum theft."

"You did! What'd he say?"

Josh's stern expression shared none of her excitement. "Seems the president of the antique-car club that hosted the tour talked to a *person of interest*." Josh's gaze grew uncomfortably intense. "You wouldn't happen to know anything about that, would you?"

"Oh." She ducked her head. *Wait a minute.* "They think I had something to do with it?"

"They did until I explained the situation." The exasperation—yes, definitely exasperation—etched on Josh's face bit at her conscience.

"I couldn't just do nothing."

His gaze tracked up one side of the street and down the other. "Interfering with a police investigation isn't helping."

"I wasn't interfering. I just wanted to talk to someone who'd been on the tour with Gran and Gramps. Find out what they'd seen or heard."

"And if your prowler catches word that you're asking too many questions, what do you think he's going to do? Not call the station, you can be sure of that."

Becki couldn't help it. She grinned.

"What are you smiling about?" Josh growled. "This is serious."

"You're not really mad at me. You're *worried* about me."

"Of course I'm worried." He strode back to his car.

"Josh, don't be mad," she called after him, fearing he'd leave in a huff.

He didn't respond, just opened the back door and reached inside.

A floppy-eared dog soared to the sidewalk and bounded toward her, straining at the leash Josh held.

"Oh," she gasped. The tongue-lolling mixed breed, with his mismatched patches of brown-and-black fur and white belly and feet, looked just like the pooch she'd had for a short time as a child.

She knelt and offered him her hand.

The dog gave her a slobbery kiss instead.

Josh laughed. "I guess that answers that question."

"What question?" Becki scratched the dog's neck.

"Whether you want Bruiser."

Her heart leaped. "He's for me?"

"If you want him. He's had his basic obedience

training. One of the guys on the force needed to find him a new home after his daughter developed allergies."

"Oh, I'd love to give Bruiser a home." She threw her arms around the pooch and gave him a giant hug. "But such a tough-guy name won't do, will it?" she crooned. "I'll call you…Ruffles."

"Ruffles?" Josh tugged back on the leash. "You're not serious?"

Becki pursed her lips to try to maintain a straight face.

"C'mon, no self-respecting dog should have to endure being called Ruffles."

She laughed. "I knew you'd say that."

He offered her a hand up and held her gaze for a long moment.

She squirmed under the intensity, even as a thrill rushed through her chest.

"You can call him whatever you like. I want you to be happy here." His voice turned husky. "And safe."

*Oh. Safe. Right.* She tightened her fingers around the piece of paper containing the names and numbers she'd found. What would her prowler do if he learned she was asking questions?

Josh would be furious if she called the witnesses now. But if the news that she'd talked to the club president had gotten to Josh so quickly, maybe the idea that someone had heard of the cops' suspicions of her grandparents wasn't so far-fetched.

"Are you okay with me going home now?" she asked, since he'd been so sweet.

The muscles in his jaw flexed. "If you promise to call at the first sign of any trouble," he said finally, when he clearly wanted to say no. "Deal?"

"Deal." As she reached for the dog leash, Mrs. O'Reilly ambled out the library doors.

"Mighty fine day, isn't it?" the woman chimed, throwing Josh a meaningful look.

Becki struggled to contain the new grin that sprang to her lips. She gave Josh a sideways hug and leaned her head against his chest as she let the grin loose. "Oh, yes! Look at the dog Josh brought me."

Becki reached for the leash, but Josh caught her hand in his and held it fast as his other arm slipped around her waist.

Mrs. O'Reilly glanced from the dog to Josh, her eyes sparkling. "Yes, mighty fine," she repeated and moseyed on up the street.

Becki immediately tried to pull away, but Josh's arm cinched tighter around her waist.

His gaze dropped to hers, a dare flaring to life. "You set me up."

She slipped her hand from his clasp and splayed her fingers over her chest with wide-eyed innocence. "I was just trying to help your cause. Let her believe you're interested. Isn't that what you wanted?"

"My cause, huh?" Light danced in his eyes. "Like

the time you came up with the scheme to get your sister to notice me?"

"How was I supposed to know a family of skunks lived under that log? Besides, it worked, didn't it?"

He let her go and gave her a what-am-I-going-to-do-with-you shake of his head. "Oh, yeah, Sarah could smell me coming from a mile away." Josh opened the back door of her car and shooed the dog inside. "You haven't changed a bit, Bec. Still trouble with a capital *T*."

Becki glanced in the rearview mirror at Bruiser sprawled across her backseat. "Josh probably got you for me just so I'd go home and stay out of trouble."

Bruiser yowled.

Trouble with a capital *T*. Was that what Josh really thought of her?

Considering all that had happened around here since she'd arrived, she supposed she couldn't blame him. So she should just stop thinking about how handsome he looked in that police uniform, let alone how at home she'd felt in his arms.

Oh, yes, she definitely needed to forget about that.

Josh would never make a home with someone who didn't share his faith, and her outburst about the squirrels' nest had left little question about the shaky state of hers.

She pulled the car into her driveway and opened the back door to grab her crutches. "Here you go, Bruiser. Your new home. Hope you like it."

Bruiser bounded from the car without a second's hesitation and took off around the house.

So much for basic obedience. She supposed the phone calls would have to wait until after she got Bruiser settled. She grabbed her crutches. Before she reached the corner, Bruiser let out a low-pitched growl that sent a chill down her arms.

"Good dog" came a frightened male voice.

Becki ducked. There was only one reason why a strange man would sneak around her house. But he didn't sound like Henry. She edged closer to the corner as she fumbled for her phone. The hot sun glinted off a motorcycle parked behind the house. A big, shiny black bike. The kind of bike that scary-looking biker-gang dudes drove.

"Nice boy," the man repeated inanely between Bruiser's unrelenting growls.

Okay, maybe not a gang biker.

"Hello," he called out. "Anyone there? Name's Winslow, the real-estate agent." His voice pitched higher as if that should explain everything.

"Bart?" He didn't sound like Mr. Maserati.

"No, his father. Please call off your dog."

Becki's thumb hovered over the connect button for Josh's number. He was never going to see her as grown-up if she kept calling him to her rescue. "What are you doing here?" Becki asked without stepping into the man's line of sight.

"Albert Graw's granddaughter asked me to appraise the place."

Becki's fingers tightened around the handle of her crutch. She rounded the corner of the house. "You're lying."

The man took a step toward her, but Bruiser's growling immediately intensified.

*Way to go, Bruiser!*

The man's arms shot into the air. "I'm not. I swear." He wore a suit jacket, despite the heat and his apparent mode of transportation. Sweat beaded his forehead, pooling at his bushy eyebrows and dripping in tiny rivulets down his pudgy cheeks. "She called my office this morning. Asked me to meet her here at two."

Becki glanced at her watch. "Well, it's two. I'm here. And guess what? I didn't call you."

"You're Graw's granddaughter?"

"Yes."

His brows drew together. "Well, someone called me." He reached inside his jacket, and the dog lunged. The man's hand snapped back into view, a business card between his fingers.

Bruiser backed up, but he added a bark for good measure.

Becki hid a smile. She loved the dog already.

"Could you please call off your dog? If you don't want a valuation, I'll go, but I'm telling you the truth. Does Mr. Graw have another granddaughter, perhaps?"

Becki's heart dropped. Sarah wouldn't. Yes, she

would. Becki squinted at the man. "She said she'd meet you here?"

"Yes."

As if on cue, her sister's BMW rolled into the driveway.

Becki swung her crutches around and loped toward her sister's car.

"Hey, what about your dog?" the real-estate agent cried out after her.

"Bruiser, come here," Becki called over her shoulder, having no clue whether the dog would actually listen. "We have another culprit to corner," she muttered and braced herself as Sarah stepped from the car.

Bruiser raced around the corner, grazing his chin on the gravel as his legs went out from under him on the curve. But without losing a step he barreled right for Becki and took up sentry duty at her side.

Sarah arched a perfectly plucked eyebrow at the canine. Then, before Becki's eyes, Sarah's crusty facade crumbled. "He looks just like Max!" She squatted and ruffled the dog's ears. "Where did you find him?"

The wistful expression on her sister's face melted Becki's anger. They'd always been the best of friends as children, and never more so than the weeks after Dad gave away their beloved Max.

A man's voice jarred her back to the present. "You are the other granddaughter, I presume," the real-estate agent said, standing well back as he eyed Bruiser.

Sarah sprang to her feet, her gaze skittering past Becki to the agent. "Yes." Her face flushed.

"And she had no right to call you," Becki added. "I own this property, and I have no intention of selling."

"Most city folk say the same when they first move here, until they have to deal with the inevitable problems—annoying critters, leaky roofs, contaminated wells, not to mention the isolation. Then their idealistic view changes pretty quick." The man ventured closer, stiffening at Bruiser's growl, and handed Becki his card. "This is how to reach me if you change your mind. Summer is a better time to sell. These old places get drafty in winter. Expensive to heat, too." He strode toward his motorcycle.

"Wait," Sarah cried out. "I want to know how much the place could sell for."

"At least two hundred thousand," the man said, then kicked up his motorcycle stand and roared away.

"I guess now that you got what you came for, you'll be going." Becki turned toward the house and the phone calls she needed to make.

Sarah hurried after her. "Actually, I came to help you."

"Help me?"

"Yes. You can't clean and get settled in with that sore ankle. I can't believe you didn't call me."

Becki stopped. "That's right, I didn't. So how did you find out?"

A flower-delivery van pulled into the driveway.

At least, those were the words emblazoned across the side. Becki willed herself not to imagine gunmen pouring out the back of the van to mow her down. Stuff like that only happened in the movies.

The driver jumped down from the truck, carrying a colorful assortment of flowers. "One of you ladies Rebecca Graw?"

"Yes, that's me." Becki lifted her hand as she gaped at the spectacular bouquet. Who would send her flowers?

The man eyed her crutches and hesitated.

"I'll take them for her," Sarah volunteered, and the man handed them over.

Becki hopped closer to her sister to get a look at the card. "Who are they from?"

Sarah pulled out the card. "Neil. He wrote, 'Sorry to hear about your fall. Hope you get well soon.'"

Dread sank like a rock to the pit of Becki's stomach. "How'd he find out?"

She didn't realize she'd asked the question aloud until her sister answered.

"Probably the same way I did. From your former roommate. I can't believe you'd call her and not your own sister."

"I didn't call anyone. She happened to call while I was at the hospital." Becki left the *If you called once in a while...* unsaid. The only reason her sister called lately was to harass her into selling. Becki's glance snapped to Sarah. "What prompted you to call my roommate?"

"I didn't. She posted a prayer request for you on her Facebook page. Then when I tried to call the house, there was no answer."

"Oh." Becki wanted to believe genuine concern had prompted her sister's trip, but the real-estate agent's presence said otherwise. More likely she'd jumped at the excuse to scope out the place to compile more ammunition to give her lawyers, or lawyer husband, to force her out, which reminded Becki that she'd forgotten to call Gramps's lawyer today.

Sarah grabbed a small suitcase from her trunk. "Rowan said I could stay as long as you need me."

"As long as it takes to convince me to sell, you mean." Becki plowed toward the house on her crutches.

Sarah didn't respond.

Becki halted at the porch steps and faced her sister. "You don't deny it?"

"That's not why I'm here," she said quietly, her inability to look Becki in the eye denying every word. "But yes, it's why Rowan let me come."

"He *let* you, huh? As if you ever ask permission to do anything you want to." Becki let out a snort. But as she whirled to hop up the porch steps, she thought she saw tears in her sister's eyes.

Once inside, Sarah headed straight for the kitchen,

pulled a vase from the corner cupboard and arranged the flowers in it. "You were smart not to marry Neil."

"He never asked."

"Because you were smart enough to get out of the relationship before then."

Becki plugged in the kettle, then leaned against the counter and stared at her sister. "I thought you liked Neil. He's a lot like your Rowan."

An indefinable emotion flashed in Sarah's eyes before she glanced away, busying herself with the flowers. "But you're not like me. You were never obsessed with getting things."

Becki's grip on the crutches tightened. "I'm not giving up the house, Sarah."

"That's not what I meant."

"Isn't it?" Becki hated how petty she sounded. But Sarah had already admitted that Rowan had urged her to come here to convince Becki to sell. For all she knew, he was behind the attacks, too. "The value of this house to me can't be measured in dollars. So you might as well call off Rowan and his goons, because I'm not selling."

"Goons? What are you talking about?" Sarah set the vase on the center of the table and then tugged her long sleeves back to her wrists, gripping them with trembling fingers, as if she knew *exactly* what Becki was talking about.

And in that moment, Becki knew she wouldn't

need to make those phone calls, because Josh's jewelry-theft theory was wrong.

"I'm talking about the creep who broke into my house, who clobbered me with a two-by-four, who—" she snatched up the note she'd found in her mailbox the day she'd arrived and slapped it into Sarah's hand "—wants me out of this house."

Sarah gaped at the words. "I..." She shook her head. "You think Rowan did all that?"

"You're the only one who'd benefit from scaring me out of this place."

"But this isn't Rowan's writing. I can't believe..." Sarah's gaze shifted away.

"You can't believe what? That he'd stoop so low?"

# EIGHT

Outside the pet-food store, Josh tossed a bag of dog food and two dishes into the cab of his truck, grateful for an excuse to check on Bec. He yanked the truck door closed with a snort. If he was smart, he'd go home and keep a protective watch from afar.

She'd been all smiles and hugs after he sprang Bruiser on her. He'd gotten a kick out of watching her. She'd looked like an excited little kid as the dog slobbered over her face. But that hug—the one she'd given him for Mrs. O'Reilly's benefit—hadn't felt like a kid's hug at all.

Worse than that, he'd wanted it to be real.

Except he wasn't so sure anymore if she shared his faith. Never mind that another incident like yesterday's break-in was bound to drive her back to the city faster than he could say goodbye.

He peered through the windshield at the darkening sky. A gust of wind whipped the tree limbs into a frenzy. Looked as if they were in for a bad storm. Which made for the kind of night most people would hole up at home. Hopefully, Bec's prowler was one of them, because so far Josh hadn't tracked down a single Henry Smith that matched their suspect's description. Not that he'd had a lot of opportunity. As far as his captain was concerned, there was no case to investigate.

He stepped on the gas, hoping to beat the storm. Two miles from home—far too close for comfort—Josh spotted a green Plymouth.

He called dispatch. "Can you pull up the vehicle registration for…" He rattled off the license plate and a minute later had confirmation he'd found his man.

Now if only he were driving a patrol car, he could flash his lights, blip his siren and force the guy to pull over.

Instead he hung back to see if Smith would head for Bec's.

Sure enough, he turned onto their street and a moment later slowed in front of Bec's house.

*Yes.* If Smith pulled in, Josh would have him.

A second later, Smith sped off.

Josh sped up enough to keep Smith in sight and called Hunter. "You still in a black-and-white?"

"Yeah."

"I spotted Smith. Headed west on Elm. I'm—" Josh caught sight of a black BMW in Bec's driveway and hit the brakes. "Haul him in for me, will you? I'll be down as soon as I can." He clicked off and swerved into Bec's driveway, praying he wouldn't regret not taking time for reconnaissance first.

The Toronto dealer's logo on the trunk of the car

suggested the car's owner could be another one of her city friends come to lure her back or a developer trying to sweet-talk her into selling.

Both possibilities made him want to punch something, but at this point, either would be better than option three.

He shoved the bag of dog food under his arm and grabbed the pair of bowls. If she wouldn't even agree to move out for a few days while he tracked down her intruder, some flashy BMW driver wouldn't convince her to sell. She was too determined to hang on to the old place.

Thunder rumbled in the distance.

Josh strode to the back door, scanning the windows. Two figures moved about the kitchen. Both female. A friend, then. He let out his pent-up breath and knocked.

Sarah opened the door.

For a second he stood speechless. *You're the last person I expected to see here* didn't seem like a neighborly thing to say. She looked as perfectly put together as she had at the funeral, but from the amount of gunk caked around her eyes, clearly her vanity battled aging in daily combat.

Her gaze dropped to the bag under his arm, and she pushed the door wide. "Great timing. We were just wondering what we'd feed Bruiser."

A chair scraped the floor. Bec sank into the seat, a pained expression pinching her face.

Josh handed Sarah the dog dishes and squatted beside Bec. "Are you okay? Is the ankle worse?"

Her gaze slid to her sister. "No, I'm fine." She sounded defeated. Not fine at all.

Bruiser positioned himself between them as if Josh was the one she needed protection from.

Josh searched her face, but her expression had blanked.

How dare her sister come here and harangue her into giving up their grandparents' home?

Sarah filled one of the dog dishes with water. "Can I make you some coffee?"

"Thanks, but no. I can't stay," he said, not taking his eyes from Bec. "I've got a lead on Smith," he whispered for her ears only, then ruffled the dog's fur before standing.

A bouquet of flowers on the table snagged his attention. He tilted his head to peek at the card, then wished he hadn't.

"Oh, yuck. What is that smell?" Sarah wrinkled her nose.

Bec mimicked her sister's disgusted expression. "Gross. It smells like rotten eggs. Did it come from the fridge?"

Josh sniffed the air. "Could be sulfur in your water." He turned on the tap Sarah had just used, and the smell intensified. "Oh, yeah, you've got sulfur in your well, all right."

"Since when? I don't ever remembering smelling that when I visited."

Josh shook his head. "No, I can't remember your grandparents ever complaining about it. But last summer a few houses around here were suddenly struck with it. It's usually worse after a heavy rain." He glanced out the window at the storms piling up on the horizon. "Not before."

Sarah pinched her nostrils. "That must be what the real-estate agent meant about people moving back to the city. How could anyone stand living with that smell?"

Josh clenched his jaw. "Winslow?" He directed the question to Bec. He should've expected Bart and his dad wouldn't waste any time swooping in on the place.

"Yeah. He was here when I got home." Becki patted Bruiser's head. "But Bruiser let him know how we feel about real-estate agents. Didn't you, fella?"

A sentiment Sarah, no doubt, didn't share. "What brings you here, Sarah?" Josh asked.

She stopped holding her nose and cracked open the bag of dog food. "I came to help out my little sister until her ankle gets better."

Bec's lips pursed at the "little" modifier.

Josh wondered if she believed her sister's story. "I'm sure she'll appreciate the company. She tell you I'm a police officer now?"

Sarah set down the dish and turned abruptly toward him. "No, I thought you took over the farm."

"Yeah, I still live next door. It's given me a firsthand view of the trouble someone's been giving Bec. You know anything about that?"

"No. I already told Bec I don't."

"But you do want her to sell the place?" He wasn't sure what compelled him to push, considering Henry looked like their man.

Sarah folded her arms over her chest and pierced Josh with a glare. "That's between Bec and me. I don't see what business it is of yours."

*Whoa, talk about striking a nerve.* Josh's cell phone rang. He checked the screen. "Excuse me, I need to take this."

"You're going to want to get down here," Hunter said the instant Josh connected.

"Is Henry our man?"

"Yes and no."

"What do you mean?"

"Just get down here."

Josh darted through the pelting rain into the police station. The glare of fluorescents intensified the throb that had started in his head the second Hunter had called. He shook the water from his jacket.

"You're too late." Hunter's sour expression sent a chill through Josh that had nothing to do with the deluge outside. "The captain let Smith go. Wants to see you in his office."

"Let him go?" Josh stormed into the captain's office without knocking. "What's going on?"

Hunter leaned against the doorpost, arms crossed over his chest.

The captain stepped out from behind his desk and hitched his hip onto the corner, an action that made him seem a fraction more open-minded than the persona exuded by his severe crew cut, crisply pressed uniform and powerful build. "Hunter fill you in?"

"Said you let Smith go. Why? I can place this guy at the scene the night of the first attack."

"Calm down." The captain patted the air. "Smith is a P.I. The museum hired him to investigate the jewelry theft."

Josh jerked his gaze to Hunter. "That's his story?"

Hunter shrugged. "It checked out."

"Okay—" Josh swung back to the captain "—so he's a P.I. That doesn't give him license to trespass in the Graws' barn and clobber Miss Graw over the head with a two-by-four."

"Smith said another guy was in the barn. He saw him sneak across the field as he drove by. It's what made him pull into the farm lane."

"Sounds like a convenient alibi to me. He give you a description?"

The captain put on his reading glasses and pulled a paper from his desk. "Wore a dark hooded sweatshirt. Couldn't see any of his features."

"Lot of help that is."

"Look." The captain set down the paper and removed his glasses. "The fact is, we don't have enough resources to keep this up. Smith doesn't think the Graws had any connection to the heist, so there's no reason to think anyone else would."

"Someone's still terrorizing her." And despite Sarah's defensive reaction to his questions, Josh couldn't believe she was behind this. He paced to the window and squinted into the blackness.

"*Terrorizing?* She surprised someone in her barn. Now you think everything else is connected, like that car you fished out of the quarry. A car dumped by some guy cleaning out his back forty. Don't you think you might be letting your emotions cloud your judgment here?"

"No." Josh squashed the memory of his annoyance at those flowers from Neil. Bec was a neighbor who needed his help. Nothing more. "She's a citizen of Serenity who deserves our protection."

"She's got a police officer living next door." The captain pushed off the desk and returned to his seat. "That's going to have to do. She's not the only citizen in this town."

"But—"

The captain motioned to the door. "Go home. And don't call any more personnel in on this. Hunter and Wes are not your personal commando team."

Josh stalked out of the office with Hunter on his six. "Can you believe him?"

Hunter made a weird cluck and gave him a look like, yeah, he could.

Josh threw him a scowl.

"Hey, you've got to admit you get a little obsessed."

"Hardly."

"Man, you have a three-legged dog and a bird with a broken wing. If something or someone needs rescuing, you're the go-to guy."

Josh snorted. "Get real." If he'd been the least bit obsessive, the Graws wouldn't have died of carbon-monoxide poisoning.

He needed to get back to Bec. For all he knew, Smith could be on his way there now.

A scream. Her sister's scream yanked Becki out of a deep sleep—the deepest she'd had since arriving in Serenity, which was a little unnerving consider-ing that she was the only person that stood between her sister and more than half of their grandparents' estate.

"Becki!" Sarah shouted again, jolting Becki thor-oughly awake.

The dog barked and howled, prancing back and forth from Becki's bed to the closed bedroom door.

Becki grabbed her bathrobe and hopped to the door. The instant she opened it, Bruiser raced out. Becki squinted at the sudden change in light.

Sarah dashed from the bathroom to her bedroom, her arms loaded with bath towels. "The roof's leak-ing."

"I'll go down and get a bucket."

Sarah glanced at Becki's bandaged ankle and un-loaded the towels into her arms. "Better let me get the buckets." Sarah dashed down the stairs, turning every light on as she went. Bruiser raced after her.

Becki hobbled toward the bedroom, grateful her sister was there tonight even if Becki doubted her true motives for coming were as pure as she'd let on. Sarah had gotten too tight-lipped after Becki alleged Rowan was behind the trouble she'd been having.

Before she dared leave Sarah alone in the house, Becki needed to figure out why her sister was really here. Josh might think Henry was her attacker, but like he'd said, Sarah still wanted the house sold. And as much as Becki didn't want to believe her sister would stoop to any means to make that happen, she wasn't so sure anymore.

Becki turned into the bedroom, and the towels spilled from her arms. "No!"

Above the bed, the plaster bulged. Every couple of seconds, a giant water drop plopped onto the pillow below. Becki wedged herself between the head of the bed and the wall and shoved.

Sarah ran back into the room, carrying two big pots. "What are you doing?"

"Saving the bed."

"You're going to hurt yourself." Sarah moved in beside her, and they shoved the bed out of the way. "Okay, lay down some towels to catch the splash, and we'll set the pots on top."

Rain thrashed the window, and the drops from the

ceiling came faster. Becki positioned a pot beneath them. "I can't believe I slept through this storm."

"At the rate it's pouring, that plaster might not hold."

The concern in her sister's voice surprised Becki. She would have thought Sarah would latch onto this disaster as one more reason she should sell. Sarah certainly had continued to make a big deal about that horrid sulfur smell long after Josh had left.

Sarah passed her the second pot, and Becki gasped at the sight of her face.

Sarah's hand sprang to cover the bruise around her un-made-up eye.

"What happened?"

"I…I walked into the door, trying to find the light switch. Is it that bad?"

Becki squinted at the yellowing mark. "That didn't just happen." Her gaze skittered to similar marks on Sarah's arms.

Sarah must have noticed, because she immediately dropped her hand and tugged down the sleeves of her pajama top.

"How did you get those bruises?"

"I don't know what you're talking about."

"I'm talking about this." Becki grabbed Sarah's arm and shoved up her sleeve.

Sarah shrank back.

Becki stared at her sister, her beautiful sister, and felt sick and utterly ashamed. "Did Rowan…"

"I'm fine." Sarah fussed with the towels.

Becki threw her arms around her sister. "Oh, Sarah, I'm sorry. I didn't know. You should have told me." Here she'd been thinking such horrible thoughts about her sister when she'd really come here to escape her husband. Had Josh guessed?

Was that why he'd stared at Sarah so long when she'd first opened the door?

Becki had thought he was still infatuated…

Sarah remained stiff, sucking in air in short bursts. "It's not what you think. It was my fault."

Pounding erupted at the back door. Bruiser set off barking again and tore down the stairs.

"Bec, what's going on?" Josh's shout pierced the windowpane above the sound of the storm raging outside, which was nothing compared to the rage Becki felt toward her brother-in-law at the moment.

Sarah pulled away and tugged her sleeves back down. "You can't say anything. Please. Promise me." She grabbed her makeup bag and long-sleeved shirt and darted into the bathroom.

Downstairs, Josh sounded as if he might take down the door any second. And the dog's constant howling didn't help.

Gritting her teeth against the pain in her ankle, Becki raced down the stairs as fast as she could. "Quiet, Bruiser." She unlocked the dead bolt and, before she could twist the doorknob, Josh pushed through the door.

"What's going on? I saw all the lights come on and your phone's dead."

Becki took one look at the worry etched on his face and flung herself into his arms.

He drew her close, his heart hammering beneath her ear. "What's wrong? What happened?"

Coming to her senses, she reluctantly pushed away from him. "I can't tell you."

He caught her with a gentle hand at the back of her neck and whisked a tear from her cheek, the compassion in his eyes so heartfelt she yearned to step back into the shelter of his arms.

"The roof's leaking," Sarah said tersely from the kitchen doorway.

Becki jerked from Josh's grasp. Whoa, how had Sarah put herself together so quickly?

Josh's gaze ping-ponged between them, as if he'd sensed the underlying warning Sarah had sent Becki's way. His gaze stalled on her, waiting.

"The plaster's bulging. I'm afraid it might give way."

He nodded but looked far from satisfied. "I'll take a look. I might be able to throw up a tarp temporarily to ward off any more damage until the rain stops."

"I can't ask you to do that. It's pouring out there."

"You didn't. I offered. Which room is it?"

"I'll show you." Sarah led him upstairs.

Becki slipped into the downstairs bathroom and splashed water on her face. She never used to lose it so easily. But she'd been overwhelmed by the realization that Sarah's husband had beat her—she hadn't been able to help herself when she saw the concern in Josh's expression.

"Bec?" Josh called from the kitchen.

Becki dried her face and shook her head at the mess of curls in her reflection. Couldn't be helped. Rejoining Josh, she looked around. "Where's Sarah?"

"Upstairs changing the bedsheets." He stepped closer. "What did she say to upset you like that?"

Becki swallowed at the tenderness in his voice, at his concern for her, *not* her sister. But she held her emotions in check. "Nothing."

His head tilted. "*Nothing?* That sounds familiar."

She smiled at his teasing.

He caught a strand of her hair and twirled it around his finger. "Do you think she had that real-estate agent punch a few holes in the roof to convince you to sell?"

She chuckled. "Sounds like something I might've thought a few hours ago. But I was wrong about her."

Josh searched her eyes, and the change in his expression made Becki wonder if he could see right inside her head and read her thoughts. He'd learn the truth soon enough after she invited her sister to stay. He dropped his hand. "I'll see if I can jury-rig a temporary fix on the roof."

"Be careful, Josh, please. I don't want to see you get hurt on my account."

His lips quirked into a quick smile, and he pressed an equally quick kiss to her forehead. A kiss that made her feel like a kid who'd needed rescuing again.

Not the cared-about woman she'd felt like when she'd stepped into his arms. How was he ever going to believe she could take care of herself if she kept letting him run to her rescue every time anything remotely bad happened?

As he slipped out the door, Sarah rejoined her in the kitchen. "He's grown up to be a really nice guy."

Becki watched his flashlight bob in the darkness. "He was always someone you could count on." She drew in a deep breath and mentally rehearsed her invitation for Sarah to stay.

Sarah stepped closer to the door and watched Josh, too. "I guess I would've been better off waiting for *him* all those years ago."

Becki touched her forehead where Josh had kissed her. If Sarah stayed, would Josh...

Becki's invitation turned to paste in her mouth.

# NINE

Rain lashed Josh's back as he muscled the ladder through the barn door.

*You've got to admit you get a little obsessed.*

Dropping the ladder inside the pitch-black building, he shut out Hunter's voice. He wasn't obsessed. Any decent human being would have put up that tarp for Bec.

A rustle sounded from the far corner of the barn.

He swung his LED light that way. The beam picked up a light-colored trail of tiny pebbles. He bent to take a closer look. Not pebbles. Tiny yellow bits. He picked up a couple and brought them to his nose. Sulfur.

He should have guessed. He traced his light along the trail. Another rustle. He flicked his light toward the sound, but the light blinked out. He slapped it against his leg, toggled the switch. Nothing worked.

The door banged closed.

He ducked behind a bench.

"Whew, that's some wind." Bec's flashlight beam bounced around the walls. "Josh? Where are you?"

He hurried toward her. "Here. Can I borrow that? My light just gave out." He reached for hers and whispered, "Stick close."

He shone the light in the direction he'd heard the sound. A mouse scuffled across the floor and disappeared under a box.

Bec stifled a squeal.

Better a mouse than a prowler. Josh turned the light back to the yellow trail and traced it to a shelf where her grandfather had stored fertilizers.

"What is that?" Bec asked, staying close on his heels.

"You said a real-estate agent was here today? Winslow?"

"Yeah, he was already here when I got home."

"So he could have been here for some time?" Long enough to pour sulfur down her well.

"I guess. Why?"

"This is sulfur. My guess is he poured it down your well to help persuade you to sell. Leaky roofs and contaminated water supplies are just the kinds of things that prompt city folk to pack up and sell."

"You think Winslow contaminated my water?"

Something shifted behind them.

"Watch out!" Josh pushed Bec to the ground and threw himself over her. Tins and gardening tools rained down on his back. He shielded her head with his arms. Then a crushing weight slammed into him, and his breath escaped in a huff.

He shoved off the tipped-over shelves, and a puff of chemical-smelling dust bit at his throat.

Bec coughed.

Josh scrambled for the light he'd dropped. "You okay?"

"Yeah, I think so."

The barn door slammed against the wall, followed by a blast of wind and rain.

"I've got to go after him." Josh quickly lifted Bec out of the debris and set her on her feet.

"My crutches."

He flashed the light back to the mess on the floor and pulled out her crutches. "You going to be okay here?"

"Yes, go!"

Josh skirted around her and dashed for the door, pausing at the threshold to give her enough light to get out safely. "Go back to the house," he shouted over the wind and swept the beam over the yard. Visibility was near zero in the teeming rain.

Bec secured the barn door, then peered into the darkness with him, water sluicing down her yellow slicker onto bare calves. "Did you see which way he went?"

"No." Thunder rumbled. "We're never going to find him in this." Josh strained to listen for the sound of running feet, an engine, something. He tipped the light toward Bec's face. "Did you lock the house?"

Her eyes widened. "No."

He jogged across the lawn with Bec not far behind, swinging her crutches double time.

Sarah pulled open the door. "You two okay?"

"You see which way the guy went?" Josh motioned Bec inside ahead of him.

"What guy? I didn't see anyone." Sarah stepped back as Bec shrugged off her dripping coat.

No way could the guy have gotten inside without leaving a wet trail. "Okay, stay inside and lock the door." Josh turned his light back to the yard.

Lightning fractured the blackness, followed by a bone-shuddering crack.

The guy could have holed up anywhere, but he had to have gotten here somehow. Josh grabbed his keys from his pocket and jumped into his truck. He sped to the farm lane, where he'd spotted Smith's car the night Bec had first arrived, but there were no fresh tracks. He angled his truck so the headlights pointed in the direction Smith had claimed to have followed the guy he'd seen run out of her barn. Still nothing.

He circled the block. But in the pelting rain, he could scarcely see the road in front of his headlights, let alone a car that might be tucked in behind the hedgerow. He drove back to Bec's.

The instant his foot hit the porch step, she opened the door. She'd changed into dry clothes, but her hair hung in wet ropes around her face. "You didn't find him?"

"No."

"Do you think it was Winslow? Why would he come back?"

Josh checked the phone line coming into the house, then stepped inside. "I don't know. Where's Sarah?"

"She went up to bed."

Josh frowned. How could she sleep?

Bec handed him a towel. "Do you think this could have been Henry?"

"I doubt it. He's a P.I. investigating the jewelry theft. Claims he wasn't in the barn the night you were attacked."

"A P.I., for real? Do you believe him?"

"I don't know." He'd half expected to find the guy parked in Bec's driveway when he got back. "The P.I. part is true. The good news is he doesn't suspect your grandparents of involvement in the jewelry heist."

"Well, that's a relief anyway."

Josh glanced at the stairs. "Except it means we have no idea who we just chased out of the barn."

"Are you going to call this in?"

He imagined the captain's response if he did and shook his head. "No, I'm going to pay Winslow a visit. If he's just getting home, looking like something the dog dragged in, then I'll nail him." Josh picked up Bec's phone.

Still dead.

Had to be from the storm. The line wasn't cut.

He hated to leave her not knowing where this guy

had disappeared to, but if Winslow was their culprit, this might be their only chance to prove it. "I won't be long. Keep the doors locked and your cell phone handy." He ruffled the dog's ears. "And keep Bruiser nearby."

The shopkeeper gave Becki an apologetic look and pulled the help-wanted sign from the store window. "Sorry, the position's been filled."

She trudged out the door to Serenity's main street. What was this? Some kind of conspiracy?

She'd never been turned away by so many employers in her life, let alone in one day. So much for job hunting taking her mind off last night's prowler.

Josh's sister had warned her the job market was tight. But to be turned down for a waitressing job?

Becki shoved her crutches into the backseat of the car. Yeah, who wanted a waitress on crutches? She should have listened to Josh and waited a few more days. But now she had a roof repair to pay for. If she didn't find a job, she'd never be able to afford the upkeep and taxes on the house, let alone eat!

*Do unto others as you would have them do unto you.*

Becki cringed at the memory of the morning's verse in the devotional booklet Gran kept next to the coffeepot. Was God trying to tell her that she needed to sell the house?

Is that why she couldn't find a job?

Becki slumped into the driver's seat. Most of the

time she managed to ignore all the little God things Gran had scattered about the house. She'd always considered herself a believer, even if she didn't go to church as regularly as she had during the summers spent with Gran and Gramps. But had she ever really owned a faith of her own?

If she had, she wouldn't have ranted about God letting the squirrel build a nest in the chimney. Would she? Or hesitate to help Sarah?

Except, as much as seeing Sarah's bruises had broken her heart, she couldn't see how giving her sister more money would resolve anything. Inviting Sarah to move in with her might, but she still hadn't been able to voice that particular offer. Not after waking to find Sarah bringing a cup of coffee out to Josh's truck this morning.

Apparently, after he'd returned from Winslow's last night, he'd camped out in Gran and Gramps's driveway to keep watch.

Becki couldn't believe that she'd fallen asleep before he returned. Except that she'd felt safe, knowing he was out there hunting down her prowler.

The hair on the back of her neck prickled.

Her gaze shot to the street, the sidewalk, the shop windows. Josh had warned her to stay alert. Was it merely the power of suggestion that prompted the eerie sensation she was being watched?

Her gaze slammed to a halt at the barbershop window. Or, more precisely, at Bart Winslow standing at the window, looking her way.

His dad had been snug and dry in his home when Josh had paid him an unexpected visit last night. But Bart hadn't.

Josh had found him at the bar on the edge of town, drenched from the rain. Problem was, the puddles under Bart's feet didn't prove he'd been at her place. Half the people in the bar had been soaked from their dash for the door from the parking lot.

Bart disappeared from the barbershop window and an instant later emerged on the street.

Becki stuffed her key in the ignition, but she couldn't bring herself to turn it. Without evidence, Josh hadn't been able to do anything more than warn Bart to stay away from her. She didn't feel like sticking around to see if Bart intended to oblige, but she sure wasn't going to give him the satisfaction of thinking he'd scared her.

He paused outside the barbershop door, his gaze zeroed in on her windshield, although she wasn't sure he could see her with the sun glaring off the glass. His lips curved into a slow smile. Then he winked and headed in the opposite direction.

*Okay. That was creepy.*

Part of her wanted to swerve in front of him and tell him that he and his father should forget about ever getting their hands on her property. But the remote possibility he was just—well—a creep kept her foot off the gas.

She needed to get home anyway, make sure her sister wasn't getting into mischief. Sarah had offered to pick up groceries and cook them a nice supper, but maybe that glimpse of Sarah's bruises last night had made Becki too trusting.

When she pulled into the driveway a few minutes later, Bruiser and Tripod ran from the backyard together to greet her. "Well, hello. Glad to see you've made friends with the neighbor." Becki gave them each a thorough rub, noting that Josh's truck was back in his own driveway, then headed inside through the front door.

The aroma of fresh-baked chocolate-chip cookies greeted her.

"Mmm, those smell delicious." Becki tossed her purse on the bench in the entrance and clomped on her crutches to the kitchen. "If you're going to bake, you can stay as long as you want!"

The kitchen was empty.

Sarah's laughter floated through the back screen, followed by hammering.

Becki grabbed a couple of cookies and joined her sister on the porch. "What's so funny?"

Sarah motioned toward the roof. "Something Josh said."

Becki gaped up at Josh, shirtless, on her roof. "What are you doing?" She instantly clapped her mouth shut, hoping that didn't come out sounding as insanely jealous as it had sounded to her own ears. Her sister was a married woman, and…and… Becki wasn't interested in Josh that way. Not anymore. Not really. She shouldn't be.

"Patching your roof."

"But...shouldn't you be at work?"

"It's my day off. Other than that court appearance I had this morning."

"Oh."

He hammered on another shingle, then climbed down the ladder and pulled on his shirt. "All done." He plucked the second chocolate-chip cookie from her hand and took a giant bite.

"Hey!"

"This wasn't for me?" His expression turned all innocent, but she didn't miss the grin tugging the corner of his lips.

Becki rolled her eyes. "What kind of man steals from a cripple?"

Laughter danced in his eyes as he popped the other half into his mouth. "A hungry one."

Sarah scurried to the door. "I'll bring out a plate with more."

Becki squinted up at the roof. "I really appreciate your taking care of that for me." She sank into a chair. "I don't think I could have afforded to hire a roofer."

"No job prospects yet?"

"Not a one."

Sarah flounced back outside carrying a tall glass of lemonade and a plate loaded with cookies. "I thought you'd appreciate a cool drink, too."

Becki squirmed in her seat. Since when had Sarah turned into Suzie Homemaker?

Sarah took the chair opposite Becki and motioned Josh toward the one beside her.

Josh rested his hip on the arm and leaned toward Becki. "What if I told you that I got a gig for you?"

"A gig?"

"A freelance writing gig. If the editor likes what you produce, he'll give you more assignments."

"Are you serious? With what publication? On what topic?"

"For the region's tourism magazine, on touring in an antique car. The editor wants you to go on an upcoming weekend tour and write about the experience."

"That's awesome. Oh, wow. I can't believe it." Her heart felt like a helium balloon floating skyward. Light and carefree, soaring above the clouds. Then suddenly it popped. "But how will I get the car there? I've never towed a trailer."

"That's where I come in."

"Really? You'll come with me?"

"Yeah. It's kind of a condition of the assignment." Josh caught Becki's hand. "You okay with that?"

"Abso—" Meeting his gaze, Becki's answer stalled in her drying throat.

The phone rang, but Sarah popped from her seat and said she'd get it almost before Becki registered the sound. The instant Sarah disappeared inside, Becki yanked her hand from Josh's hold. "What are you doing? My sister's going to think we're dating or something."

"Yeah, that was the idea."

Her jaw dropped. He wanted to make Sarah jealous?

Josh hooked his finger beneath her chin and nudged it closed. "I figured your sister would be more likely to stop pressuring you to sell if she saw you had someone on your side." He slanted a glance toward the door. "All afternoon, she's prattled on over how concerned she is about you living out here alone."

Becki's goodwill toward her sister evaporated at the realization that she'd been working Josh to support her cause.

"For the record, I'm still uneasy about your being here, too, but I wasn't about to lend support to *her* agenda."

"Thanks." Becki tucked her hands under her legs. "What about this writing gig? Please tell me that wasn't an act."

His grin whisked away her worry. "Nope, that's a go. I guess I'll need to pick up the trailer." He glanced at his watch. "Anne's coming for supper, but I have time to do that first." Josh stood. Then he suddenly caught Becki's hand again. "Your sister's coming back."

Becki tried to ignore the butterflies that fluttered through her middle as his arm came around her waist, bringing her face within inches of his. He was enjoying this game way too much.

"Do you want to come with me?" he said huskily.

Her gaze dropped to his lips, which spread into an I-know-what-you're-thinking smile. Mortified, she placed her palm on his chest to push him away, only his heart was beating as crazily as hers. Not an act?

He covered her hand with his. "Maybe it's better if you stay here. I'll be back soon."

# TEN

Josh backed the box trailer up to Bec's barn as the girls made their way from the house.

The breeze teased Bec's honey-brown curls, and reflexively, his fingers curled.

Every time he saw her, he had this crazy compulsion to tug her into his arms. A compulsion that was getting more difficult to chalk up to wanting to get Mrs. O'Reilly off his case or to putting Bec's sister in her place.

She filled his thoughts when they were apart. And—Lord, help him—he liked that she needed him. When she'd tumbled into his arms during last night's storm, he'd been ready to do whatever he could to soothe away her tears.

It had taken every ounce of his self-control not to flatten Bart when he'd found him last night. He might not have been able to prove it, but he'd been positive Bart had just come from Bec's barn, no doubt scheming more ways to *persuade* Bec to sell if the sulfur in the well didn't do the trick.

Josh had to thank the guy for one thing, though. He'd sure proved Bec's determination to stay in the old place. If the freelance job Josh lined up for her panned out, maybe he could start believing that she'd stick around, work through her grief.

Sarah circled the trailer, looking stunned. "I had no idea Gramps had gotten so serious about touring."

Bec handed Josh the keys he'd asked her to find. "Maybe this wasn't such a good idea," she murmured.

He reassuringly curved his arm around her waist. "I think that's curiosity, not dollar signs, you see in her eyes." He thumbed through the keys. "These aren't for the trailer door."

"Those were all I could find. Are you sure Pete didn't have them?"

"No reason why he should. He only worked on the outside."

Sarah twisted the knob on the side door. "You're in luck. It isn't locked."

"It's not?" Josh skirted past Bec. "Your grandfather always kept it locked. He kept all his tools inside."

Sarah opened the door and gasped.

Josh's gut clenched. The Graws' touring costumes and duster jackets were strewn across the floor. The drawers of the cabinet their grandfather had built to hold his tools and clothing accessories were ripped out and overturned. Hatboxes were stomped. And the walls were pitted with dents.

Bec appeared at the doorway and let out a pained sound.

"I'm sorry, Bec. I should have checked on the trailer days ago."

"This isn't your fault," she said so softly he barely heard her over the roar in his ears.

Sarah lifted a dress from the floor and fitted it back onto the hanger.

Josh clasped her elbow. "Leave it. I'll want to take photos and dust for prints before anything's moved."

Nodding, she handed him the hanger. Without a word, she jumped down from the trailer and headed inside, while Bec remained frozen in the doorway.

Josh pulled out his cell phone and called in Hunter to help with evidence collection. The captain could hardly protest this time. Phone call made, he rejoined Bec. "I'm afraid this changes everything."

"What do you mean?"

"Winslow may have poured sulfur down your well, but I don't think he did this. This doesn't look like the work of someone trying to scare you into selling."

"Who, then?"

"Whoever did this was looking for something. And it wasn't the Cadillac."

The color drained from Bec's face. "The jewelry?"

"Possibly."

She stared through the open door at the destruction. "That P.I. knew about the trailer. He asked about Gran's costumes, acted like he'd be interested in buying them. I told him they were stored in the trailer."

"Did you tell him where it was?"

"No, but…now that I think about it, after he heard that I didn't have them he turned down my invitation to come in for coffee. You'd think he would have jumped at the chance to ask more questions."

"Yeah, unless he hoped to pocket the jewelry himself." Josh shook his head. "I can just imagine what my captain will say if I throw that theory at him. But whoever's behind this is clearly losing his patience. And that makes him dangerous."

Bec's fingers curled into fists. "Clobbering me with a two-by-four seemed plenty dangerous to me!" She had fire in her eyes, but the quiver in her lip pierced his heart.

Josh drew her into his arms. "We'll get this guy."

Hunter pulled into the driveway in a patrol car and joined them, carrying a camera and an evidence kit. "What do we have?"

Bec slipped from Josh's arms and readjusted her grip on her crutches. "I'll wait inside with Sarah."

Hunter poked Josh with his elbow. "So the scuttlebutt is true?"

"What?" Josh snapped his gaze from watching Bec's retreating back. "There's another lead on the case?"

Hunter laughed. "I'm talking about you and Bec."

"What about us?"

"That you finally found someone you're willing to hang up your bachelorhood for."

"Don't be ridiculous. She's my neighbor and in trouble. I'm just trying to catch a bad guy here."

Hunter shrugged. "If you say so."

"It is so."

"That's not how it looked a minute ago."

"That's an act for her sister's benefit," Josh said automatically, even though Sarah had been the last person on his mind. He raked his fingers through his hair. Hunter *would* have to arrive just as he was giving Bec a reassuring hug. He'd acted on instinct, but Hunter didn't need to know that.

Hunter looked over his shoulder and every which way. "What sister would that be?"

Josh jerked his hand toward the house. "She just went inside."

Hunter cocked his head and studied Josh with one squinty eye. "You missed your calling."

"What calling?" Josh shot back, losing his patience.

"Undercover, man. Any cop who can act that good should be working undercover."

Josh motioned to the trailer. "Just get in there and take your pictures."

Hunter whistled as he stepped in view of the devastation. "You might want to reconsider that car tour you'd planned." He jumped the foot and a half onto the trailer and snapped a picture. As he focused the camera on one of the dents in the wall, he added, "From the looks of it, this guy's ready to blow a gasket."

"Yeah, Bec's not going to be happy when I break the news that we can't go."

"Then again..." Hunter opened the trailer's back doors, letting in more light. "If we're looking for a jewel thief after all, you might pick up on a suspect if you hit the car tour."

"I can't put Bec at risk."

Hunter photographed the large wrench the guy had likely used to smash the walls. "I have the weekend off. I could go along, if you like. Watch your back."

"A single guy in the backseat?" Josh commandeered the evidence kit. "That'd be a sure tip-off."

"I could drive an old car, too. My uncle has a Model T I could borrow. Your sister's a good sport. She'd probably agree to come along and ride shotgun."

"I'm not bringing my sister into this." Josh brushed powder across the wrench handle, cringing at the thought of what else this creep might do with such a weapon.

"She was tough enough to work the E.R. in Detroit for three years. Do you really think this guy's going to scare her?"

"Probably not. And that's enough reason to not ask her to come along."

"Ask who to come along where?" Anne's voice came from behind him. "Whoa, what happened?"

"Someone got into the trailer," Josh said, but Hunter lowered his camera and opted to answer her first question instead.

"I suggested you and I could join Josh and Bec on a double date."

"Really?" Anne's face lit up.

"It's not a date," Josh growled. "He's talking about the car tour I told you about."

"I'd love to come."

Josh ground his teeth until his jaw hurt. "We can't go now. It's too dangerous."

Anne motioned toward the destruction. "Any more dangerous than staying here?"

"Why do you think? Everything in the trailer was strewn all over. The walls were bashed."

Becki's hand froze on the porch door handle. Who was her sister talking to?

Becki edged toward the open kitchen window. Normally, eavesdropping was not her modus operandi, but when some jerk destroyed Gran's special clothes and her sister sounded as if she knew who, normal no longer applied.

"I'm sorry." Sarah's voice suddenly sounded as small as a five-year-old's. "I didn't mean to..."

At the sudden silence, Becki inched forward another step and peeked inside.

Sarah cowered on the floor, her back pressed to the cupboard, her knees tight to her chest, trembling. "No, I'm sorry. I wouldn't. You know I wouldn't. I don't know what came over me. I...I was just upset over seeing—"

If Becki wasn't seeing her sister with her own eyes, she'd never believe it. Sarah had never kowtowed to anyone. Who had this kind of power over—

The question balled in Becki's throat as her gaze dropped to Sarah's bruises. When Josh had wrapped Becki in his arms and promised her they'd get this guy, she'd scarcely been able to believe that she was in any real danger. Had Sarah ever felt that safe in her husband's embrace?

"Of course," Sarah said into the phone. "I love you, too."

Becki jerked back from the window as Sarah rose and hung up the phone.

*What's going on? What do I do?*

*Love your enemy.*

The thought boomed through Becki's mind.

Was that what her sister had become? An enemy?

The patio door slid open, and Becki sprang to attention. "Hi."

Sarah glanced from Becki to the open window and flinched.

"You okay?" Becki asked gently.

"Sure, why wouldn't I be?"

"Who were you talking to?"

"No one." She gathered the empty glasses and plate from the patio table. "Probably chattering to myself. I do that a lot." Sarah turned back toward the door with the dirty dishes.

Becki touched her arm. "Talk to me."

"I don't know what you mean."

"Sarah, you're my big sister and I love you."

Sarah gulped. "I love you, too." She rushed inside.

By the time Becki maneuvered through the door after her, Sarah was squirting dish soap into the sink. She didn't look Becki's way. "You should get off that foot. It's never going to get better if you don't rest it."

Becki sank into a kitchen chair. Her ankle throbbed worse than the day she'd twisted it, but she wasn't about to admit it. "Do you think Rowan tore apart the trailer?"

"*No!* Of course not."

"Look, Sarah, I'm not going to lie to you, even if you're bent on lying to me. I heard you on the phone. It sure sounded to me as if you thought whoever was on the other end had ransacked the trailer."

Sarah set a dish in the drying rack and answered without turning. "I called Rowan because I was upset. I was just telling him what happened. He didn't like hearing me so upset. That's all."

"Is Rowan having trouble at work?"

"No, they love him at the law firm. In another year they'll probably make him a partner."

"If he's doing so well, why does he care about scraping a few more dollars out of our grandparents' estate? He has to know that with what you've already received, even if I got top price for this house, you wouldn't get much more than another fifty thousand. He must make that in less than half a year."

Sarah dropped the dish she'd been washing and sudsy water splashed over the lip of the counter. She grabbed a tea towel and sopped it up, then turned her panicked gaze to Becki. "You can't tell him you're thinking of selling."

"I'm *not* thinking of selling!"

Sarah's shoulders sagged with what seemed like relief, which was bizarre, because she'd spent the last how many weeks begging Becki to sell?

Becki squinted at her, and suddenly the puzzle pieces dropped into place. "You want more money, but you don't want him to know?"

Sarah balled up the tea towel and tossed it onto the counter. "I want to leave him, okay?" She stormed out of the kitchen.

"Sar-aaahhh," Becki called after her. "Come back here. Talk to me." She reached for her crutches, knocked one gliding across the floor and hopped to the doorway instead.

Sarah sank into Gran's favorite armchair, her elbows on her knees, her hands over her face. "I can't believe I said that. You can't ever tell him."

With Sarah's sleeves pushed up to her elbows, allowing a full view of her yellowing bruises, Becki didn't need to ask why. "Move in with me. You can live here." Peace washed over her the instant she said the words. That sense of family, of being with someone she could count on no matter what, that was what she'd been yearning for all along. What Gran and Gramps had always surrounded them with. "I know you never used to like living in the country. But Serenity might grow on you."

She shook her head. "I can't. This would be the first place he'd look for me."

"So you tell him you're through putting up with his abuse. If he refuses to get counseling and act like a civilized human being, demand a divorce. I don't care how good a lawyer he is. You'll still be entitled to half his estate and to alimony."

Sarah lifted her head and looked at Becki as if she'd just dropped off the turnip truck. "It's not that easy. Rowan doesn't believe in divorce."

"Neither do you. But, Sarah, your vows didn't say anything about being his personal punching bag."

"He's under a lot of pressure at work. I shouldn't have brought up the credit card being denied."

"Don't you dare justify what he did to you."

Sarah burrowed her face against the armrest. A moment later she turned her head and met Becki's gaze. "I can smell Gran's perfume."

"On the armrests." Becki loved to sit there to read for that very reason. "Gran always dabbed it on her wrists."

"I wish she was here. She always knew what was best."

"Stay with me, Sarah."

She shook her head. "I can't. I won't put you in any more danger."

# ELEVEN

Josh waited for his sister to drive away, and then, as promised, he headed over to Bec's to discuss what they'd do next. She stood at the rail of her back porch, watching the sunset, and didn't seem to hear him approach.

He quickened his steps, trying not to notice how beautiful she looked against the crimson sky. He'd let his empathy get the better of him earlier when he'd wrapped her in his arms. Or maybe on some level, he'd feared the vandalized trailer would be the final straw to drive her away.

She shivered.

He shrugged out of his flannel jacket and dropped it over her shoulders, resisting the urge to let his hands linger. "Better?" he said as he lifted her hair free of the collar and inhaled its fresh scent.

She burrowed into the jacket with a grateful smile. "Much. Thank you."

He forced himself to put another foot between them. "Would you rather talk inside?"

Bec glanced at Sarah through the patio door. She

sat at the kitchen table working on a crossword puzzle. "No, out here is better."

Bec seemed to want to say more, but she turned back to the sinking sun and curled her fingers around the porch rail.

Josh rested his forearms on the rail next to her. "This was your gran's favorite time of day."

"I remember."

"She once told me that sunsets reminded her how God works behind the scenes in ways we can't always see. The colors are there in the light the whole time, but we don't see the amazing picture He's painting until the light is fractured."

"Kind of ironic that happens just before night, huh?"

Maybe it was the coming darkness or maybe the despair in Bec's voice, but Josh couldn't help himself. He enfolded her in his arms and pressed a kiss to the top of her head. "We'll get this guy, Bec. I promise. We didn't pull any prints, but Hunter's running a more extensive background check on that P.I., and we'll canvas the neighbors around Pete's Garage." His heart ached at the way she melted against him, as if she'd grown too weary of fighting. "I'm afraid we should bow out of this car tour, though," he murmured.

She sprang from his arms. "What? We can't. It's the only job offer I have."

"Your safety is more important."

She bristled at his brusque tone.

He softened his voice. "Bec, we have no idea who this guy is or why he's targeted you. If he's connected to the jewelry theft and hears you're on the tour, there's no telling what he might try."

Bec shook her head. "He's not."

"What do you mean? Do you know who ransacked the trailer?"

Her gaze slanted to the kitchen door. "I think it was my brother-in-law."

"The attorney? For a bigger cut of the inheritance? It's one thing to launch a legal challenge, but a guy like that isn't going to risk a criminal charge and tanking his career for a few extra grand."

"You're forgetting that I'm the only person that stands between him and the *entire* estate."

A kick of fear swiped Josh's breath. Would her brother-in-law murder her for the money?

Hadn't the notion crossed his own mind last night?

Her brother-in-law had the strongest motive of anyone. But… "If Sarah's husband wanted you dead, he would have taken you out that first night in the barn."

"Maybe that wasn't him. You think Bart Winslow poured sulfur down the well. Maybe he left the note, too. Or…" Bec clutched his arm, her eyes widening. "Maybe Rowan staged the attacks to make it look like I had a stalker. He had to know that if he didn't divert suspicion and I turned up dead, he and Sarah would be the prime suspects."

Josh's heart thundered. As unlikely as the theory sounded, it was just the kind of elaborate scheme a crooked lawyer might pull. "Do you think Sarah knows? If you're right, I mean."

"She suspects." Bec wrapped her arms around her waist. "I think I overheard her call him on it. I doubt he's stupid enough to try anything more now."

Josh turned to the door. "I want to talk to her."

"No, please." Bec grabbed his arm. "She'll deny it. She's embarrassed and ashamed. But she's my sister. I trust her."

"What if you're wrong?"

"I'm not." Her voice was firm, but even in the deepening shadows, Josh didn't miss how her gaze blanked, betraying no hint of what she was thinking.

"What aren't you telling me?"

Her fingers tightened around his arm. "I need you to trust me. Okay?"

His mind flashed to the last woman he'd trusted, then the string of them, right back to his mother. Bec had no idea what she was asking of him. "I need evidence to put this guy away."

"I don't have any. Believe me, I'd give it to you if I did."

He let out a sigh, not sure what to believe. He'd run a background check on Sarah's husband the same time he'd run Neil's. Nothing had come up to suggest Rowan would turn psycho on his sister-in-law.

Josh squinted at the darkening fields. "I don't like you and Sarah being alone in the house."

"We're not alone. We have Bruiser." Bec handed him back his jacket. "And as for the car tour, I know that I'll be perfectly safe with you."

There was no use arguing with her. Truth be told, her sincerity swept any words from his lips. So he simply nodded, knowing somewhere down the road she'd change her mind about him, and he'd be right back in the middle of heartache.

Becki nestled in the passenger seat of her sister's BMW and laughed at Sarah's imitation of the heroine in the movie they'd just watched. After a week with no more incidents, she finally felt able to relax. Maybe Sarah had brought Rowan to his senses or Josh had spooked the guy off—whoever the guy was. Becki was just glad that the trouble seemed to be past. Of course, it helped that her ankle finally felt better, too. "This feels like old times. Remember when Gran and Gramps used to take us out on Tuesday nights to watch the latest movie?"

Sarah chuckled. "The movies were never exactly the latest. I think Serenity brought films in only days before they released on DVD."

"I never cared. I just loved going out like a family." Becki turned in her seat to face her sister. "I wish you'd reconsider moving in with me. Maybe if you separate from Rowan for a while it will smarten him up, make him figure out what he stands to lose."

Sarah threw her a wry look. "Let's not spoil the evening by talking about Rowan, okay?"

Becki released a sigh. The more she'd tried to coax her sister into facing her marital problems, the more Sarah had closed off. She'd even denied that Rowan had ever hit her or that her cryptic *I don't want to put you in any more danger* had been a reference to what he might do to Becki if she interfered.

Becki turned her attention to the side window and the black night beyond. She couldn't understand her sister's loyalty to the man. Becki would rather live the rest of her life alone than stay married to a man who hurt her.

Her thoughts skittered to Josh. How *not* alone he'd made her feel since moving here. How safe she felt in his arms. How that would change if he ever up and married.

Piercing blue headlights skirted across the side mirror.

Becki squinted against the blinding light. "Learn to drive," she muttered under her breath. Nothing irked her more than people who drove on her bumper, especially with their high beams glaring into her mirrors.

At least they'd be turning off on the next road.

Sarah made the left. But a moment later, their tailgater did, too.

Becki spun in her seat to look out the rear window. The car had an unusual shape. Nothing like those of any of her neighbors.

A hundred yards from their driveway, Sarah started to slow.

"Keep going. Don't turn in," Becki ordered.

"What? Why?" Sarah shot back. Thankfully she pressed the gas anyway.

"There's someone following us, and the last thing I want is to give him the chance to corner us in our own driveway." She whipped out her phone and punched Josh's name.

He answered on the first ring. "Hey, Bec, what's up?"

"Someone's following my sister's car."

His tone instantly turned urgent. "Where are you?"

"We just passed the house. It could be nothing, but he's riding our bumper and I don't recognize the car."

"I'm on my way. Turn right at Spiece Road. If you see lights on in the Spieces' house, pull in there. If not, keep driving. I'll—"

"Josh? Josh, are you there?" Becki glanced at her screen. "Lost reception."

"Is he coming?" Sarah demanded.

"Yes. He said to turn right on Spiece."

Sarah's attention jerked to the rearview mirror. "Oh, no!"

Becki whipped around as blinding headlights swept the car. An instant later, the car pulled alongside theirs.

"He's trying to push us off the road!" Sarah screamed, fighting to hold the wheel steady.

The car kept pace with theirs, edging dangerously close.

Sarah eased off the gas.

Becki grabbed the dash. "Don't stop!"

The guy in the other car motioned for them to pull over.

Sarah gasped. Touched the brake.

Becki braced for impact. "Don't stop, Sarah!"

Her cell phone rang.

Becki snapped it on. "Josh, he's trying to push us off the road."

"I'm on Spiece. Where are you?"

"Still on Elm." Becki glanced over her shoulder. "We missed the turn. Hurry!" To Sarah she yelled, "Why are you slowing down?"

"It's Rowan," Sarah whispered.

Her husband whipped his car ahead of theirs and touched his brakes.

"Go around him," Becki ordered, terrified he'd kill them both.

"I can't." Sarah jerked the car to a stop.

Ahead of them, Rowan burst from his car.

Becki reached across her sister and slammed the door-lock button.

"What are you doing?" Sarah hit the button again. "That'll only make him more angry."

Becki slapped the button a second time. "Better out there than in here. Josh will be here any minute."

"Oh, that'll go over real well—bringing a cop to the scene." Sarah unlocked the door and pushed it open before Becki could stop her.

Rowan yanked the door wide. "Did you think I wouldn't find out that you lied to me?"

Sarah shrank against the side of the car. "What are you talking about? I told you I was coming to help my sister."

Becki burst out the passenger side. "Don't you dare touch her!"

"This is none of your business," Rowan seethed.

"Stay out of this, Becki, please," Sarah pleaded.

"I won't." Becki rounded the front of the car, wishing she still had her crutches to take a swing at him if he laid a hand on Sarah.

Josh's patrol car swung onto the road and barreled toward them.

"What lies has she told you, huh?" Rowan ranted. "She told me she was coming here to find out what was taking so long for the inheritance to come through."

"But—" Becki stopped. He wasn't after her share? She shot her sister a questioning look.

"Yeah." Rowan leaned his face into Sarah's and sneered. "Why do you think my pretty little wife let me think she didn't have it?"

"Freeze!" Josh crouched behind his car door, gun—no Taser—aimed at Rowan.

The red-and-blue lights strobed over Rowan's

face, turning his sneer into something uglier. "You called the cops on me?"

"Hands in the air," Josh ordered, stepping from behind his door and taking a cautious step forward.

Becki's breath caught at the sight of a red dot painted on Rowan's chest.

He looked down at his chest, and his hands instantly shot into the air. "This is a misunderstanding, Officer. My wife didn't realize I was looking for her and got scared when I drove up behind her."

Josh drew closer. "Step away, Sarah."

"You know this cop?" Rowan hissed, his hands still in the air, but looking as if he wanted to give her a good shake.

"From childhood." Sarah's voice came out small and scared.

"Sarah, step away," Josh repeated more forcefully.

She inhaled, regaining a couple of inches, and after an apologetic glance in Becki's direction, she turned toward Josh. "I'm sorry. Becki called you for nothing, Officer Rayne. Like my husband said, it was a misunderstanding."

Josh's gaze narrowed. "Did he lay a hand on you?"

"No! What do you think I am?" Rowan took a deep breath and exhaled slowly. "Look, Officer... Rayne, was it? I've done nothing wrong. I'm a lawyer and am fully aware of my rights."

"Well, I suggest you use your right to remain silent." Now that Sarah had stepped out of Rowan's reach, Josh holstered his gun. "Sarah?"

"What?" Sarah's gaze skittered from Rowan to Becki before returning to Josh. "No, he didn't touch me. This was nothing."

Becki started toward her sister. "Sarah, those bruises weren't nothing. Maybe—"

"It was nothing," Sarah repeated more adamantly. "My husband was understandably worried about me." She offered Josh an apologetic smile. "I'm sorry we troubled you."

Josh's concerned gaze shifted to Becki. "Did you see anything different?"

Becki almost wished Rowan had grabbed Sarah's arm. Josh was obviously looking for a reason to haul him in. But she couldn't lie.

They'd clearly overreacted when they thought he wanted to push them off the road. Not to mention it'd be his word against theirs, and she suspected Sarah would side with him.

After hearing that Rowan didn't know the estate had already been settled, Becki wasn't so sure he was even her prowler.

She shook her head. "He didn't touch her."

"On the phone you said he tried to push you off the road."

"I just pulled alongside them," Rowan said, lowering his hands. "So she could see it was me." He turned to Sarah and brought her hand to his lips. "Babe, I'm sorry I scared you. You know I love you."

Josh returned his attention to Becki. "Is that the way it looked to you?"

She let out a sigh. "Yes."

"It's probably best I head home," Sarah said.

"No, you can't. I mean, I'm sure Rowan won't mind your staying longer."

"Your ankle's better. You don't need me any longer. I'll drop you off and pick up my suitcase."

Becki gaped at her sister. How could she agree to go home with this man, knowing how furious he was over his discovery about the inheritance?

Becki threw Josh a wordless plea. *Can't you do something?*

# TWELVE

Josh opened the car door as Bec hurried from the house. She'd captured her hair into a ponytail, and that, along with her ruffled skirt and tie-dyed shirt, made her look as if they should be driving a 1970s Chevy instead of a 1913 Cadillac.

"Any word on Rowan?" she asked.

Last night it'd been all Josh could do to get her to calm down long enough to relay everything she knew about her brother-in-law. When she'd poured out her suspicions about the bruises she'd seen on her sister's face and arms, Josh had felt sick. If only she'd told him sooner, he might have come up with a legitimate reason to detain the jerk.

"There was one domestic call to their address eighteen months ago. A neighbor complained of shouting. No charges were filed."

"Nothing since?"

"Not on record, but my friend promised to dig deeper. In the meantime…" He motioned for her to climb in. "What do you say you try to relax and enjoy the ride?"

He'd hoped a drive to the old quarry would distract her from fretting over her sister all day.

"Sorry. I've just been so worried."

"Yeah." He knew the feeling. He'd pulled a couple of favors just to get the day off so he could watch over her. Taking the car for a test run before the tour had been the perfect excuse to get her out of the house. He slid in beside her and showed her again how to start the car.

She pulled on the choke and pushed the ignition button, but nothing happened.

"Try pushing the button at the base of the steering column. The flood bowl might have dried out." It hadn't been sitting long enough for that to be likely. The car had run fine last week.

She tried again. Still nothing. "We got gas?"

"Oops." He'd been so preoccupied, he'd forgotten to check. He grabbed the gasoline can from the corner of the barn, thinking he might've picked a more picturesque spot to run out of gas.

"Why, Josh…" Bec leaned out the car window and fluttered those impossibly long eyelashes of hers. "If I'd known you just wanted to go parking, I'd have worn something more becoming."

He chuckled, but that didn't stop the heat from climbing to his face. He unscrewed the gas cap. "We've got plenty of gas." He topped it up anyway.

"I guess you'll have to crank her."

He groaned. Last time he'd done that, the thing had backfired and ripped the crank out of his hand, almost breaking his wrist. He set the gas can aside and gave the crank three and a half quick turns, being careful to keep his thumb off to the side just in case. "Try it now."

The engine sputtered to life.

"We're good." She laughed as he climbed back in. "It always sounds like a sewing machine to me." Struggling to master the clutch, she clunked it into a stall.

"Try again," he urged.

This time she turned smoothly onto the road and flashed him a victorious smile that gave him a kick of pleasure.

As Bec experimented with changing gears on the hilly gravel roads, he sat back and enjoyed the view. Her sun-kissed cheeks glowed in the morning light, and her mouth quirked in the cutest way whenever she had to step on the clutch.

She stopped at a stop sign on a steep hill, and when she managed to start again, he gave her an approving elbow nudge. "You're a natural."

"I know why Sarah's been after me to sell," Bec said, her mind apparently on a different road than his altogether. "I think she wants to disappear."

He instantly sobered. "You think she's *that* scared of her husband?"

"She practically said as much when I invited her to stay with me."

"Do you really think he'd risk his career to maintain control over her?"

"I think he'd risk everything. Why else keep secret that she already had her inheritance payout?"

Josh focused on the winding road and braced himself for where this conversation was headed. Bec was being utterly unselfish, but he didn't want her to sell the house and leave Serenity.

Bec shot him an apologetic glance with those gorgeous brown eyes, and hard as he tried to withstand the impact, his heart ached. He'd miss her more than he wanted to admit.

"I've decided I need to sell the car."

He blinked. "The car?"

"I'm sorry. I know how much you love it, but I just don't feel right holding on to something so valuable when I could use the money to help my sister."

"You're a pretty great sister."

Her cheeks were tinged pink. "You're not mad?"

"How could I be mad?" His heart practically soared. He'd rather have Bec around than an old car any day.

A few strands of hair broke free of her ponytail and whipped across her cheek. She tipped back her head and laughed.

Josh reached across the seat and tucked the strands behind her ear.

The laughter in her eyes turned to panic as the car barreled down the hill.

"The brakes! I have no brakes." Bec white-knuckled the steering wheel.

"Pull the emergency."

"Where is it?" Her gaze darted from the winding road to the center of the car, where she'd expect it if the driver's seat were on the left.

"By the door!" Josh reached across her lap and pulled the lever.

The car didn't slow.

Bec veered around a corner. "What do I do? It's picking up speed."

"It's okay. Gear down."

She played the clutch and shifted to a lower gear.

The engine whined higher, but the car slowed only a fraction.

Trees blurred by.

"Take it down another gear. Ride it out until we reach the bottom of the hill. You're doing great."

Except with two hairpin turns before the road leveled, great might not cut it.

What idiot designed a car with a blocked driver's door?

"We're going too fast!" she screamed. "I can't make the curve!"

"Yes, you can." With no seat belts, if she didn't make it, they'd be airborne whether they wanted to be or not. "Lean into the curve."

Halfway around the bend, the outside tires caught loose gravel. He grabbed the steering wheel and cranked hard to the left.

The car kept going straight. Straight to the ravine.

Trees raced toward them.

Josh kicked open the passenger door, clamped his

arm around Bec's waist and hauled her across the seat. Her screams reverberated through his chest.

"Jump!" He sprang through the opening, dragging her with him. *Oh, God, please don't let her die.*

Becki opened her eyes and slowly lifted her head. Her fingers squished through muddy leaves, and for a terrifying instant, she imagined she was feeling Josh's bloodied body. She pushed to her knees. "Josh?"

A groan rose from a few yards away.

She scrabbled toward the sound, her breath frozen in her lungs.

His face was scraped and bruised and ghostly pale.

Her heart fisted into her ribs. "Oh, God," she whispered, unable to finish her desperate prayer as she clasped his arms. "Josh?"

Glassy eyes met hers, looked at her as if he'd been given a precious gift. "Bec," he whispered, real tears in his eyes.

She brought his hand to her cheek. "You saved us."

"You're…okay?" The question came out pained, breathless.

"Yes."

He slid his fingers through her hair, looking as if his entire world had nearly careened off that cliff with the car. Then he pulled her to his chest and held tight. "Thank God."

She wasn't sure how long she stayed wrapped in his arms, listening to his pounding heart begin to slow, feeling his warmth melt away the terror. But it was too long.

So long that she let herself start to imagine what it might be like to be wrapped in his protective arms every night. So long that she let herself imagine that she could have a relationship like Gran's, not like her mom's or her sister's. So long that she let herself forget that Josh didn't think of her that way.

She eased out of his embrace. "We need to call for help."

His hand trailed down her arm as if he didn't want to let her go. Then he reached for his hip. "I must have lost my phone when we jumped."

She scanned the ground, but neither his phone nor her purse were anywhere in sight. She eased sideways down the embankment toward her mangled car.

The roof had been sheered. The front end bashed. The driver's side crushed.

"Gramps's car," she whispered.

Josh drew to her side. "I'm sorry, Bec. I should have checked—"

"No, this isn't your fault."

"Someone's been terrorizing you from the day you got here. I should have been more diligent."

She froze in her tracks. "You think Rowan—" She cupped her hand over her mouth, unable to form the words. He could have killed her. "I've got to call Sarah. Warn her to get away from him."

Josh caught her arm. "Wait. We don't know if *anyone* is behind this yet."

Surging from his grasp, she scanned every which way for her purse. If there was the slightest chance Rowan had done this, Sarah needed to be warned.

"There." Josh pointed to a filthy mound wedged like a squashed melon beneath the driver's side of the car.

She gulped. That could have been her head.

Josh pressed his shoulder into the upturned car and heaved.

She yanked the purse free and fished out her phone.

Josh stayed her hand before she could connect. "You'll only incite her husband more if you start making allegations. If he's behind it, we don't want to alert him until we have proof." He pried the phone from her hand. "Let me call Hunter." A moment later he spoke into the phone. "It's Josh. The brakes went on the Cadillac…No, we're fine. But can you send a tow truck to Deadman's Hill?"

Becki took back the phone the instant Josh disconnected. "Why didn't you tell him your suspicions?"

"Trust me. It's better if we have proof first." Josh examined the underside of the car, which sat perpendicular to the rocky ground.

"See anything?"

"The cotter pin is missing. But I'll need more proof than that."

Becki turned the phone over and over in her hand. She hated waiting, not knowing, not being able to do anything. "She wants to leave him anyway. If she doesn't, who knows how badly he might hurt her the next time he loses his temper? And now I can't even help by selling the car."

Josh's hands shook as they touched the mangled metal. "I'll make out a police report. The insurance company will pay you something."

"But…" Oh, why didn't she pay more attention to all the paperwork the lawyer had given her? "I didn't contact the insurance company after Gramps died. What if they canceled the policy?" She walked around the upturned car. "There's no glove box. Where—"

"Careful." Clasping her shoulders, Josh pulled her away from the wreckage. He reached into a pocket on the door and produced the insurance slip. "Why don't you call them while we're waiting?"

He went back to examining the car's underside as she explained the situation to the insurance company. The rep grilled her with a gazillion questions, and even after she answered them all, he couldn't give her an answer.

She gave the car a swift kick.

"Whoa." Josh braced his hand on the car as if she'd kicked hard enough to topple it. "What'd they say?"

"They have to investigate, but it doesn't sound

hopeful. They kept asking me why I didn't notify them when I took possession." She kicked the car again, because it was either that or burst into tears, and she did *not* want to cry on Josh's shoulder. He might have held on to her after the crash as if there was no tomorrow, but—she gave the car another hard kick—there wouldn't be any tomorrows. Not when it looked as if the only way to help her sister now was to sell the house.

Josh caught her from behind in a bear hug and yanked her away from the car. "It's okay. Everything will work out."

"It's not okay. It's never going to be okay. They're dead."

# THIRTEEN

Josh turned Bec away from her grandfather's mangled car and tucked her head against his shoulder. Bits of grass and twigs fluttered from her hair, over his hands, inflaming the shame burning in his chest.

"I'm so sorry," he whispered. More sorry than she could ever know.

"I don't know what to do." Her tears dampened his shirt. "Sarah needs my help, but I don't want to give up the house. It's all I have left of them." Bec lifted her head and swiped at her eyes. "Why couldn't she have married you?"

He stiffened. *Sarah?*

"You would never have hit her," Bec mumbled against his shirt

His arms tightened around her. His gaze drifted to the wreckage, a glaring reminder of how utterly he'd failed her. "No," he whispered. "A wife should be cherished."

"Josh? Bec?" Hunter shouted from the crest of the ravine.

Josh eased Bec out of his arms. "Down here."

Hunter and a guy in blue coveralls, with Ted's Towing embroidered on the chest pocket, picked their way down the embankment. Hunter gave the scene a sweeping glance, his expression grim. "Are you sure you two are all right?"

Josh rubbed the shoulder he'd bruised taking the brunt of the fall to shield Bec from injury. But the shoulder didn't hurt half as much as the punch to the gut that came from Bec pairing him with her sister.

"I can call an ambulance."

"We're fine." Bec swiped at her damp cheeks. "I just want to get home and talk to my sister."

Josh winced. He needed to figure out what really happened before she said anything to Sarah.

The tow-truck driver circled the car and made a face. "Gonna take a while to haul this puppy out of here. I'll have to call in help to get it up that cliff."

Hunter took out his notepad.

Josh pointed to the rods. "The cotter pin that links these is missing."

"You think this was another attack?"

"Yeah. A cotter pin doesn't just slip out."

"You'd be surprised," the tow-truck driver said. "If it wasn't seated right, these rough roads could shake it loose, easy."

Some of the fear left Bec's eyes.

As much as he'd like to believe the theory might be true, Josh shook his head. "I don't think so. The emergency brake was tampered with, too."

The tow-truck driver scrutinized the cables. "Nothing wrong with the emergency brake. But it would've been useless on that steep incline."

"Sounds to me like we're looking at an accident," Hunter said.

Josh let out a pent-up breath. *Or the guy wanted it to look like an accident.*

Hunter filled out the police report the insurance company would require. "I guess you and Bec will have to join me and Anne in my uncle's Model T for the car tour now."

"Until I'm convinced this wasn't sabotage, the last place I want to take Bec is the car tour."

"Then I'll go on my own." Bec hiked up her purse strap, fire in her eyes. "I have to write that article. I won't let him win."

Hunter tapped his pen on the notepad. "She's got a point."

"Are you nuts? Even if this wasn't sabotage, I knew she was a target and I didn't catch this. I can't risk—"

"Blaming yourself for this is as ridiculous as blaming yourself for not checking the Graws' chimney for squirrels' nests."

Josh couldn't draw a breath into his drying throat. *Please tell me you didn't just say that.*

Bec's strangled gasp confirmed the worst. She gaped at him. "You *saw* squirrels go into the chimney?" The question came out as a whisper, but there was no masking the utter betrayal that coated her words.

"No. I—" Josh cut off the explanation. Nothing could bring back her grandparents. No excuse could absolve him of responsibility.

He'd never registered her grandfather's bright red cheeks—the trademark sign that carbon monoxide was replacing oxygen in his blood.

Hunter looked as if he wanted to crawl into a hole.

Josh would've been happy to dig it for him, too. Not because he didn't deserve her derision. Because she needed protection more than ever, and now she'd want nothing to do with him.

Bec backed farther and farther away from him until she came up against a tree, her arms wrapped around her waist.

Josh swallowed, but he couldn't dislodge the wad of regret blocking his throat. He'd been to countless accident scenes. Held victims as they died. He'd even had to break the news to their loved ones. But not a single case had haunted him like the Graws' deaths.

Nightmares still woke him. If he managed to sleep at all.

"About the car…" Hunter mercifully interjected. "If it was sabotaged like you think, maybe keeping Bec away from the tour was what the guy wanted."

Josh shook his head. Strained to wrap his mind around Hunter's detour.

"Think about it. The first day she got here, the

note in her mailbox said she didn't belong. Sounds like he doesn't want her in the house. And if she doesn't write the article, she won't get the job."

Bec straightened. "And if I don't get the job—" her voice pitched higher "—I can't afford to stay in the house."

Josh ground his fists deep into his pockets and stared at the wreckage—another connection to her grandparents that she'd lost. If she couldn't keep the house, she'd be devastated.

Following the crash, his only thought had been to thank God he hadn't lost her. Except he couldn't lose something he never had.

"C'mon." Hunter flipped closed his notepad. "I'll give you both a lift home. You can hash this out there and let me know what you decide about the tour."

"You're forgetting that besides Anne and us, her sister is the only one who knew about the writing job."

Bec's face paled. "Sarah wouldn't have done this."

Josh didn't know what to think anymore. He needed to put his emotions aside and look at the facts. Figure out who did this and why. And whether he *or she* would try again.

The next morning, frantic barking yanked Becki from her sleep. Bruiser clawed at the bedroom window, looking as if he might sail through any second.

Becki sprang to her feet and grabbed his collar.

"Easy, boy." Staying low so she couldn't be seen, she peered outside.

At the sight of the barn's open bay door, her breath caught. They'd had the tow-truck driver unload the wrecked car inside, but who would want it now?

She reached for her cell phone to call Josh.

Her stomach tightened. Josh was the last person she wanted to face right now. She snuck another peek out the window. Okay, maybe the second last.

Tripod scampered out of the barn.

*Tripod?* Becki let Bruiser's collar go. If Tripod was outside, then Josh had to be up. She squinted at the clock: 5:30 a.m. Didn't the man ever sleep?

No, he'd probably stood guard all night despite her protests. *And he calls me stubborn.*

Bruiser whimpered at her bedroom door.

"Yeah, okay. I'm coming." She quickly threw on a pair of jeans and a T-shirt and opened the door.

Bruiser soared down the stairs, skidded to the kitchen door and started barking again.

"Hold your horses. I need my shoes."

Bruiser snatched up one of her sneakers and pranced in a feverish circle as Becki dropped onto a kitchen chair. The dog deposited the shoe at her feet.

Becki swiped the slobber off the laces. "Thanks."

Ten seconds later, she pushed open the door, and Bruiser took off for the barn, barking loud enough to wake the town three miles away. He raced straight for Tripod at full speed, and they tumbled in a ball of yipping fur. A prowler didn't stand a chance.

Becki wavered at the kitchen door. Josh must be going over the car again—one more thing he felt he owed her for. She didn't even blame him for her grandparents' deaths. It was just hard to face him, knowing how differently things might've turned out. She'd never thought that she'd rather be considered a needy stray, but it beat being his penance.

She drew in a deep breath and ambled to the barn. She couldn't avoid him forever.

"You don't have to do this," she said loud enough for Josh to hear...wherever he'd disappeared to.

His head popped out from beneath the car. "Sorry, I didn't mean to wake you."

"Should've thought of that before you opened the big door and set off my dog siren."

He rolled out from under the car and onto his feet. "At least one of us is doing our job." He snatched up a rag and wiped the grease from his hands.

So she was a job. Well, that was better than penance. "I thought you gave up trying to prove the brakes were sabotaged."

"Wanted to see what it would take to salvage her for you."

"But the insurance adjuster said she'd be a write-off even if they honor Gramps's policy."

"Doesn't mean she can't be fixed. Just means they think it'd cost more to repair than it's worth."

"Well, if they pay me, the money's going to Sarah. I already told you that."

He tossed the rag onto his tool chest and picked up a ratchet. "My labor's free."

For the first time since she'd moved there, she felt as though Josh was the one who needed her, instead of the other way around. Needed to know she didn't blame him for not preventing her grandparents' deaths. "You don't owe me anything," she whispered.

He bent over the engine and ratcheted a part. "I like to tinker. Remember?"

She wedged open the crumpled rear door and slid onto the backseat, the way she used to when Josh and Gramps would tinker together. She scratched at the chipped paint on the door frame, and Gramps's deep baritone whispered through her mind. *God wouldn't settle for just slapping on a coat of paint to fix that, would He? He wants to change us from the inside out. Not just change what people see on the outside, because—*

"God's in the business of restoration," she said aloud. She sensed Josh studying her, but she focused on the chipped paint. "How do you do it?"

"What's that?"

"Keep believing when…God doesn't seem to care."

"I focus on the things that show me He does."

"My grandparents are dead. My sister's husband is beating her. I almost got killed—"

"*We* didn't get killed." He put down his ratchet, leaned over the door. "Your grandparents passed peacefully in their sleep to a new life. You've reconnected with your sister, grown to understand her better. You have a home in the country like you've always wanted."

Bruiser raced into the barn and planted his giant paws on the door beside Josh.

Josh ruffled his fur. "And we can't forget your fiercely protective dog."

"Or my even more protective big *brother*." She winced. She hadn't meant to emphasize the last word. Fortunately, Josh didn't seem to notice.

"See how easy it is to notice God's blessings when you start looking?" A dimple dented his cheek, but his smile didn't reach his eyes.

"My grandparents were good at that. They never doubted God's love even when my dad rejected them. I want to know God the way they did."

He covered her fingers, which had been chipping away at the paint. "You can."

"Josh," she said softly, "I don't blame you for what happened." Their eyes met, and…he looked so tormented, she wished… She looked away, dug her fingers into the gap between the seat cushion and the back of the seat.

"Hey, I think I've found something." She wiggled her fingers, straining to catch hold of whatever it was. "Maybe it's what the thief was after." She twisted onto her knees. "My fingers aren't long enough."

"Here, let me have a go." Josh climbed in beside

her, and the air filled with the homey scents of clean soap and pine. His hair, still damp from his morning shower, grazed her arm as he leaned over to reach between the cushions.

Trying to savor the moment despite herself, she withdrew her hand to give him more room. "It's right in the middle there."

"It feels like paper. Got it." He pulled a small notebook free from the cushion.

"Oh, that's mine!" Nostalgia bubbled up inside her at the sight of the long-forgotten book. "That's what I used to write my stories in." She reached for it, but he moved it out of her reach.

"Your stories, huh?" He flipped through the pages.

She tried to grab it from him, but he stretched his arm so she'd have to climb over him if she wanted it.

"Let's read one. See if they're as good as I remember."

She lowered her hands. "Really? You thought they were good?"

"Sure." He brought the book to his lap and thumbed through a few pages before suddenly stopping. "This one sounds like it'll be interesting. 'When I grow up,'" he read.

Becki gasped and snatched the book from his hand. Now she remembered how the notebook got between the cushions…and why.

"C'mon, Bec. It'll be fun. You always had a great imagination."

Oh, she had imagination all right.

He reached around behind her and recaptured the notebook.

"No!" She flailed her arms after it. "Please give it back," she said firmly. "I don't want you to read it."

His grin fell. "I thought you'd get a kick out of hearing the stories again. You were always reading them to your Gramps and me when we worked on the car."

"I know, but—" She grabbed back the notebook. There was a good reason she'd stuffed this particular notebook deep between the seat cushions the instant Gramps and Josh had returned from their trip to the scrap yard all those years ago.

"Is it a diary or something?" he asked. "About your parents?"

"No, nothing like that."

"Then what's the big deal?"

She shimmied across the seat and climbed out. "It just is. Okay?" It was bad enough she'd started to imagine that he'd finally noticed her after all these years when he'd only had a guilty conscience.

He scooted out after her. "Now you've just made me all the more curious."

"Well, you know what they say about curiosity."

"Yeah, it's a good trait."

"No, it killed the cat!"

He leaned back against the car and casually crossed one leg over the other. "'When I grow up, I'm going to marry Joshua Rayne,'" he recited as if he had X-ray vision and could read the pages through her hand.

"You saw that?"

He grinned wickedly.

"Argh!" She turned away and buried her face in her hands.

His strong, muscular arms encircled her. His scent enveloped her. "Hey," he whispered, his breath lifting the hair from her neck. "Why are you embarrassed? I'm flattered. I want to read the rest. Find out what happens."

She leaned back, and her head collided with the solid wall of his chest. "I was twelve."

"I'll keep that in mind." Amusement flickered in his voice.

But what was the point in making a big deal about it if he'd already seen the worst?

"Fine." She slapped the notebook against his chest. "Read to your heart's content."

She climbed back into the car and continued digging between the cushions for real clues.

"'We'll live in a big farmhouse like Gran and Gramps,'" Josh read, resting his forearms on the edge of the car window. "I like that." He grinned.

She ignored him.

"'We'll have lots of animals, because we'll take in all the injured ones God brings our way,'" he read on. As he turned the page, he added, "You and I rescued our share of animals over the years, didn't we?"

Becki chuckled. Josh had never stopped—rescuing animals or damsels in distress.

"'Josh wants to be a farmer. I like that, because I don't want him to be away from home all the time like Daddy is.'" Josh's voice quieted, and she wondered if it was from the reminder of his lost dream or the mention of her father. "'We'll have lots of kids. At least two of each. Jeffrey, Josh Junior, Jessica and Jenny.'"

His meadow-green eyes captured hers. "You named our kids," he whispered.

"I was twelve."

"I love those names."

Her heart skipped a beat. "You do?"

He closed the notebook. "Except if we have a Josh Junior, we'd need to have a little Becki, too."

"But of course." She played along. It was just like old times, sitting around the campfire as kids, weaving far-fetched stories.

"We already have a three-legged dog, a bird with a broken wing and Bruiser."

She laughed. "Yup, a steady supply of needy animals won't be a problem with your reputation."

His grin snagged her breath. He grazed his fingers along her cheek, the color in his eyes darkening, his expression growing intense.

He was *serious!*

His gaze dropped to her lips, and he slowly stroked his thumb across them.

She held her breath, certain she must be dreaming. Certain any second she'd wake up to Bruiser licking her face.

He cradled her face in his hands, his fingers curling beneath her hair, and looked at her as if he couldn't believe she was real. Had she been wrong? It wasn't guilt that had him being so protective... so near so often?

He traced her lips with whisper-soft butterfly kisses. No, definitely not guilt.

She slipped her arms around his waist and kissed him back. He tasted of sweet meadows and babbling streams and an abandon that took her breath away.

# FOURTEEN

Josh waited for Hunter to drive his uncle's Model T into the box trailer, then helped secure the holding straps. "You're sure your uncle won't mind my taking the car for tonight's reception?"

"What's to mind? You're just transporting it. Anne and I will meet you there tomorrow." Hunter double-checked the straps. "How'd Bec talk you into going on the tour anyway?"

"Let's just say she can be very persuasive." Josh strained to contain the smile tugging at his lips. He could still taste her kisses, feel the warmth of her arms encircling him. He hadn't wanted to let her go. Ever. He sure wasn't about to let her go on the tour without him.

Not that Hunter needed to know any of that.

Hunter laughed. "Man, you've got it bad."

"What are you talking about?"

Hunter slapped him on the back. "She's already got you henpecked."

Josh shrugged off Hunter's hand. "I happen to admire her determination not to give in to this creep's tactics. *And* I want her to nail this writing job as much as she does."

"So she can afford to stick around, huh?"

This time Josh didn't bother to rein in his smile. "You've got to admit she's better than any neighbor you've ever had."

Hunter hopped down from the box trailer. "Why don't you just marry her?"

"What?" Josh stubbed his toe and grasped at the car's fender. He missed and stumbled off the end of the trailer.

Hunter roared with laughter. "Oh, man, you should see your face."

Josh turned his attention to shoving away the ramp. It wasn't as if he hadn't entertained the idea of marrying Bec. Entertained it a hundred times over since reading her journal. He'd even imagined what their children would look like with Bec's adorable curls.

"I knew from the minute you called to borrow the cameras that she'd gotten to you."

Josh slammed shut the trailer's back doors. "Yeah, right."

"I'm serious. After the shooting, all the guys noticed that she wasn't *just* a neighbor."

"I was concerned about her safety."

"And that Winslow might ask her out. And that she might not find a job here and would have to sell." Hunter leaned against the trailer, his expression smug. "Marrying her would solve all your worries."

"That's crazy. She's only been here a couple of weeks." And already he couldn't imagine his life without her.

"Sure, but you've known her all her life. Didn't you say Graw told you he proposed to her grandmother after only three weeks? Look how well that turned out."

True. And from what Bec had written in her journal, they'd always wanted the same things. If all this trouble didn't scare her into running back to the city, maybe… He shook the crazy notion from his head. "It's too soon. She hasn't even found a job here yet."

"Wouldn't matter if you married her."

"Don't go blurting that to her this weekend. Your mouth has already gotten me into enough trouble." Then again…Josh tossed his truck keys in the air and caught them. Maybe this time Hunter would be doing him a favor. "I've got to run. She'll be waiting for me."

"Give me a sec to grab a wrap," Becki called out the front door as Josh drove into her driveway, his truck window open. Her insides bubbled at his lopsided smile and the anticipation of feeling that smile on her lips again. The way he looked at her warmed her clear down to her toes.

She lifted the long skirt of her gown and turned back to the foyer. What was she after?

Oh, yes, a wrap. Now, where did she see some? She flipped up the lid on the bench where Gran had always kept a supply of winter hats and mitts. Her eyes lit on a silk scarf. Ooh, that would make a gorgeous wrap. She snatched it up, and an evening glove tumbled out. Something pinged across the tile.

Bending to take a look, she stopped short at the sight of a gold-and-ruby earring. She turned it between her fingers. The design was old, older than anything she'd ever seen in Gran's jewelry box. Old enough to be a museum piece.

Her stomach pinched. It couldn't be. She quickly searched the scarf. No other pieces were wrapped inside, not even the matching earring.

She breathed a relieved sigh. Gran must've worn the earring during one of the car rides and didn't realize it caught on her scarf. The match was probably sitting in Gran's jewelry box upstairs.

Becki studied the piece again, ignoring the churning in her stomach. Okay, she was 99 percent sure that she hadn't seen anything like this the last time she'd checked Gran's jewelry box, but that didn't mean the earring was a museum piece. A visitor who'd borrowed one of Gran's scarves for a ride could have lost the earring.

Becki set it on the hall table so she'd remember to look for its mate when she got back and, spotting a long white glove that had also tumbled from the scarf, scooped that up.

A necklace spilled out.

Her breath caught in her throat.

This couldn't be what it looked like. Becki slumped

to the floor. Gran must've taken the necklace and earrings off while away and stored them in her gloves for safekeeping, then forgot about them.

Except…Becki held the glove by two of its fingers and gave it a shake.

Cuff links, a pair of earrings and a matching necklace and bracelet tumbled to the floor.

*No!* Becki lifted one of the black onyx cuff links. An *M* was monogrammed on it in tiny diamonds. *Montague.* The name blazed through her mind along with the image of this very piece—the image she'd seen in the newspaper article about the jewelry theft.

The sound of Josh's truck door slamming cut through the air.

Her heart hammered. She couldn't let Josh see these before she figured out what to do. She stuffed the cuff links back into the glove, then scrambled to scoop up the other items.

The front door burst open. "I grabbed your mail. Are you just about—"

Becki's gaze snapped to Josh, her fingers tightening around the fistful of stolen jewelry.

"Are those—"

She sprang to her feet and backed away from him. "I was going to tell you."

He slapped the mail onto the hall table and halved the distance between them. "Where did you find these?"

"This can't be what it looks like."

"Where did you find them?" he repeated.

She pointed mutely to the deacon's bench. Before she could stammer out a word, he started pulling out hats and mitts and scarves.

"They were inside the evening glove."

"Where's the other glove?"

She scanned the pile he'd emptied from the bench, shook out the scarf. "I don't know. Gran usually kept the gloves with her costumes in the trailer or in the cedar chest in her room."

Josh commandeered the single glove and jewelry and motioned her to the kitchen. He laid the items out on the table. "Why would you hesitate a second to tell me you found these?" He sounded like a father scolding a six-year-old, but apparently the question was rhetorical, because without waiting for an answer, he pulled out his cell phone and scrolled through his contact list.

"We can't turn them in yet," she blurted.

"Why on earth not? Don't you realize what this means? Your attacker must have been after the jewelry all along and may be more desperate than ever to recover it." He put the phone to his ear. "We turn them in. The media reports they've been recovered, and he'll have no more reason to bother you."

"No." She snatched away his phone and hit the power button. "If we turn them in before we figure out how they got here, the police will blame Gran and Gramps for the robbery."

"Bec, I'm a police officer. I can't *not* turn them in!" He pried the phone from her fingers.

Okay, she was upset and, yeah, probably being unreasonable, but… "How can you let Gran's and Gramps's reputations be destroyed?"

Josh stroked his thumb across her knuckles. "I promise we'll figure out a way to clear their names. I'll ask the investigating officer to keep the source of the recovery quiet. Chances are no one around here would ever learn of your grandparents' connection anyway."

"They're not connected! See, even you're talking as if they stole them."

"Bec, you know I don't want to believe that, but how do you explain their being in the house?"

"Maybe the guy who broke in planted them."

Josh cocked an eyebrow. "*Planted* them?"

"Okay, that doesn't make sense, but he searched the car first, right? So he must've put them in there, and when he couldn't find them, he figured Gramps had taken them inside. Gramps probably found the scarf in one of the door pockets and figured Gran had just forgotten to bring it in."

"Sounds reasonable. I'll suggest as much to the investigating officer, and he'll look into it."

"No, he won't. He'll pin this on Gran and Gramps because it saves him work. It lets him close the case in a neat and tidy package." The twitch in Josh's jaw confirmed her fear. Budgets were stretched to the snapping point these days. If they could close a case, they would.

"I doubt the detective will keep quiet about the

source, either." Becki twisted the necklace between her fingers. "The robbery made network news. The recovery will, too. They always sensationalize everything."

"We'll make sure the truth gets reported."

"When? Three weeks later when the news stations have moved on to the next major story? No one will hear that Gran and Gramps have been cleared of any wrongdoing unless we prove it before we turn in the jewelry."

Josh shook his head. "We can't hold on to stolen goods. I understand your fear, Bec, but it's illegal."

"I don't care!" Why did he have to be so...responsible?

"You could go to jail. Is that the kind of legacy you want for your grandparents?"

"Are you going to arrest me?"

"No, of course not."

"Then if I figure out who stole these before I turn them in, it won't matter what they do to me."

"You're being reckless. This is not some elaborate childhood scenario we've concocted around a campfire. These are real stolen goods. There's a real thief out there looking for them. You have no concept of the risk you'd be taking."

"I am not a child!"

He clasped her hands. "Your grandparents wouldn't want you to put your life at risk to clear their names."

The tenderness of his touch, the pleading in his

eyes, clutched at her heart, but she couldn't let him change her mind. "I need to do this," she whispered. "Don't you see? They were the only people who ever accepted me just as I am."

His grip on her hands tightened, his expression pained. "Not the only ones, Bec."

She gave her head a violent shake and yanked her hands free. "You don't understand."

"I do. I want to clear their names as much as you, but I care more about keeping you safe."

She surged to her feet. "I am not some bird with a broken wing that you can lock away in a cage for my own good."

"That's not what I'm doing."

"Yes, it is. It's what people have done to me my whole life. I'm tired of everyone else deciding what's best for me. I'm doing this."

Josh caught her arm. "I can't let you."

She lifted her chin defiantly. "Can't or won't? Because I thought you were someone I could count on."

After a long pause, he shook his head. "Has anyone ever told you how obstinate you are?"

She quirked a half smile, certain the resignation in his voice meant he'd play this her way.

"It wasn't a compliment," he huffed.

"But you'll help me?"

"Yes, just not the way you're asking." He snatched a Baggie from the kitchen drawer and swept the jewelry into it.

"What are you doing?"

"Turning in the recovered property. I'm a police officer. That's what police officers do."

For a moment, she couldn't utter a word, just stared at him in disbelief. "If you do this, I'll never speak to you again."

"Real mature," Josh said, as if Bec were still the kid she was behaving like. She'd used the same I'll-never-speak-to-you-again line on him dozens of times, usually just before he tossed her into the swimming hole.

She planted her hands on her hips. "I mean it."

Yeah, she used to say that, too. He never should have argued with her this long. "I'll be back as soon as I can. Stay inside and keep the dog with you." He turned away and forced himself to open the door and keep walking. There was no reasoning with her when she got like this.

As he unhitched the trailer from the truck, he second-guessed his decision a dozen times. He climbed into the truck and slammed the door. He had no choice. Hopefully, by the time he returned, she'd be cooled down enough to keep the truck cab from overheating for their trip. Then they could discuss how they might go about clearing her grandparents of any suspicion.

Not the conversation he'd hoped to have during their drive this evening.

Her rant about being tired of everyone else deciding what was best for her roared through his mind as he sped off.

He had a bad feeling she wouldn't get over this as easily as being thrown into the swimming hole.

What was she supposed to do now?

From the living-room window, Becki frowned at the trail of dust still swirling from Josh's hasty departure. The man was downright infuriating.

She snatched up the mail he'd tossed onto the table. At the sight of the insurance company's return address on the top envelope, she sucked in a breath. Her hands shook as she slid a thumb under the flap. She unfolded the paper and her gaze stopped on the second word—*regret*.

"No!" She slumped onto the bottom step.

Bruiser rested his head in her lap and nosed her hand with an apologetic whine.

"It's okay, boy. You didn't do anything wrong. It's…" She crumpled the letter in her fist. "Why, Lord? I don't want the money for me. I want to help my sister."

Bruiser retreated to the doormat.

Becki stared up at the ceiling as if God might actually answer, but no answer came.

After a long while, she lifted the skirt of her gown and trudged upstairs. The last thing she felt like doing now was attending the evening reception. She hung the gown back in Gran's closet and pulled on jeans and a T-shirt.

Her cell phone jangled.

*He changed his mind!* She grabbed the phone. "I knew you wouldn't let Gran and Gramps down."

"What are you talking about?" her sister asked. She sounded as if she'd been crying.

"Sarah, what's wrong?"

Sarah sniffled. "I left him."

Clutching the phone to her ear, Becki dropped to a chair. "What happened?"

"It doesn't matter. I just needed to warn you."

"Warn me?" Becki's thoughts whirled to the gunshots, the car accident, the bruises on her sister's face. "Where are you? I'll come get you."

"No, your house will be the first place he'll look for me."

Her heart clenched at the tremor in Sarah's voice. "Do you have money?"

"Becki, I didn't call to ask for money. I'm sorry I ever asked you to sell the house. You shouldn't have to pay for my mistakes."

The regret in Sarah's voice stripped away the last of Becki's irritation with her. She'd misjudged her sister terribly. How had they drifted so far apart?

"Maybe one day, when it's safe," Sarah went on quietly, "I can come back."

"Come *now*. I can't bear to lose you, too." Becki swallowed a sob. She'd made such a mess of everything.

"I can't, Becki. I just can't. I have to get far away.

Go somewhere that Rowan wouldn't think to look for me. I'm sorry."

The real-estate agent's card stared up at Becki from where she'd tossed it next to the phone all those days ago. She picked it up, set it down, picked it up again. "I'll sell the house," she heard herself whisper into the phone.

"What? No, you can't do that. You love that house. And what about Josh?"

Crushing Winslow's card in her hand, Becki stifled a sob.

"What's wrong? What did he do?"

"He betrayed me." Becki pressed her bunched hand to her mouth. She hadn't meant to say that. Sarah had enough problems without getting into hers.

"How?" Disbelief laced Sarah's voice.

"Oh, Sarah." The pressure building in Becki's chest erupted like a volcano. "There was a jewelry theft. At the last tour Gran and Gramps were on."

"Gran and Gramps would never be involved in anything like that."

Becki stuffed Winslow's card into her pocket and swiped at the tears leaking from her eyes. "We found the jewelry here in the house, in one of Gran's gloves in the hall bench."

Sarah gasped. "A glove?" she said faintly.

"I begged Josh to help me find the real thief before he turned in the jewelry. But he refused. Gran's and Gramps's reputations are ruined."

"The police think they stole the jewelry?" Sarah's voice cracked.

"That's how it looks! Josh said he'd tell the police they didn't, but... Oh, Sarah, I know he's a cop, and he has to do the right thing, but..."

"Why couldn't *you* come first for once?" Sarah finished softly.

*Yes.* Becki traced the image of her father standing with Gran and Gramps in a photo sitting nearby. "Maybe we could've lured the thief to reveal himself at the car tour somehow. Now I don't know how we'll ever prove their innocence."

"I have an idea."

Becki's heart leaped. "What?"

"You'll see! This tour starts with a reception at the Grand Hotel, right?"

"Yes." Becki tipped aside the curtain on the window facing Josh's house. "We were about to leave for it when I found the jewelry."

"Okay, I'll meet you at the hotel."

"But what about Rowan?"

"He'll never think to look for me there."

"Josh isn't back yet." Becki surged to her feet. After his "real mature" quip, she wasn't all that anxious to ask for his help, but she'd eat crow a hundred times over if it would help clear their grandparents' names.

"All the better. Come alone."

"I can't tow that monstrous trailer!"

"Don't bother with it. You can ride along with other drivers. It'll be all the better for your article. Give you a chance to experience a bunch of different cars and gather the owners' stories."

Her article! She'd been so concerned about clearing her grandparents' names she'd completely forgotten about the freelance opportunity. Not that she'd need to win over the editor once she sold the house. Her heart hitched at that thought.

Outside, gravel crunched and the purr of a car engine went silent.

She jogged down the stairs. "He's back."

"Is he coming to the house?"

A head bobbed past the living-room window.

Becki sucked in a breath. "It's not Josh. It's Neil."

"That's perfect. Ask him to drive you. Didn't you say he was a car fanatic, always going to car-club shows?"

"Yeah, 1960s sports cars, not horseless carriages."

"Still, you know he'd jump at the chance to spend the weekend with you."

The doorbell rang, and Bruiser went ballistic.

Her heart thudded against her rib cage. "I don't want to give him the wrong idea," she whispered frantically even though Neil couldn't possibly hear her.

"Leaving your car in the driveway will throw Rowan off my trail. Besides, might be good for Josh to see you out with someone else. Make him jealous."

Becki's jaw dropped. *That* would be immature. "All I care about is protecting our grandparents' reputations."

"Then head out now with Neil, or alone. It's getting late. If you don't hurry, we'll miss the reception."

The doorbell rang again.

"I'll see you in two hours." Sarah clicked off.

"Quiet," Becki ordered Bruiser and grabbed his collar before pulling open the door.

"Whoa." Neil backed up a step.

"It's okay." She released Bruiser's collar and patted his behind. "Go on out, boy."

Neil stepped inside without waiting for an invitation.

Becki pasted on a smile. "Neil, what a surprise." She hitched her thumb over her shoulder. "I'm afraid I was heading out. I have to meet my sister for a car-tour reception."

His gaze traveled up from her ratty jeans to her wrinkled T-shirt and stopped on her face, probably splotchy from crying. "Like that?"

"I was about to change." She backed up a step, feeling oddly uneasy. She wrote it off to Sarah's jealousy comment about Josh and drew in a deep breath. After the way Josh had ignored her pleas and walked out on her, she shouldn't be the one feeling guilty. "Was there something you wanted?"

Neil took in the foyer, front room and eating area

in one sweeping glance. "Doesn't look like you've changed the place much."

"No, I like it the way it is."

"Was the dog your grandparents'?"

"No, he's new."

Neil nodded, looking as discomfited by their stilted conversation as she felt. His gaze drifted around the room again, then settled on the hall table. "Wow, this is an impressive piece." He picked up an earring—the stolen earring she'd found in the scarf!

In all the rigmarole, she'd forgotten to add it to the rest. Funny that its match hadn't turned up, either.

"Your grandmother's?" Neil asked, holding it out.

"Yes," Becki said automatically, then bit her lip at how easily the lie had slipped past.

Neil rolled the earring between his fingers. "Looks like it could be worth a bit. You shouldn't leave it lying around."

"You're right." She scooped it from his hand. "I'll put it back now." She took another step backward toward the base of the stairs, even though she knew she couldn't go up until she got rid of Neil.

"Were you heading to the reception alone?"

"Uh…" The mantel clock dinged the hour. *Hurry, hurry,* her thoughts whispered. How long would Josh be? Dare she wait? Did she even want to?

"Yes, actually, I am going alone. Would—" The invitation lodged in her throat.

"Would you like an escort?" he offered with an old-fashioned bow.

She recalled how Gran would giggle when Gramps greeted her that way, and she wished she could feel that giddiness, too. Becki had to admit she didn't relish the idea of a two-hour drive alone in the encroaching darkness. "If you'd like to join me," she heard herself respond.

"What are friends for?"

His expression was friendly, undemanding, but the uneasy feeling crept down her spine again. She shook it off. It was just the way the evening had been going that made her so unrealistic. "Give me a few minutes to get dressed."

Neil glanced at his dark dress slacks and crisp white shirt. "Am I okay?"

"You'll be fine." She hurried up the stairs to her grandparents' bedroom, where she dropped the earring into Gran's jewelry box and then went to the closet.

Her fingers glanced over the emerald satin gown that Josh had wanted her to wear. She lifted out the red one next to it and frowned at the low neckline.

"That one's very nice."

Becki startled at Neil's voice behind her. She clutched the dress to her chest and whirled toward the door. "What are you doing up here?"

"Thought you might need some help." He leaned casually against the door frame. "Those earrings would look stunning with that dress. Did your Gran have a matching necklace?"

"Uh, I'm not sure." She should have known the

earring would pique Neil's curiosity. He prided himself on his expensive tastes, a trait that had taken her far too long to notice.

"Let's look." He strode toward the dresser.

"What? No. There's no time." She shooed him out. "You need to let me get dressed or we'll be late." She'd forgotten about his habit of making himself right at home, whether invited or not. Josh would never do that.

She locked the door behind him before peeling off her shirt and jeans. Winslow's business card tumbled from the pocket. *Do you care more about your sister than a house?* it taunted.

*I do.* If she wanted to help her sister, she needed to make the call.

Before she could change her mind, she dialed Winslow's number and gave him the go-ahead to list the house. Josh would be furious that she'd asked Winslow of all people, but if she put off the decision until she could find someone better, she'd talk herself out of it. Or…Josh might. She dressed quickly, then wavered at the bedroom door.

She couldn't just leave without telling Josh. What if he'd still planned to take her on the tour despite their fight?

Part of her—the part that could never stay mad at him—wished she had the courage to call and ask. But it was too late now. She jotted a quick note to tape to his door. She'd call his sister once they were on their way.

By the time Becki descended the stairs, Neil was checking out Gran's antique tea trolley in the living room. She pulled on a pair of long, white evening gloves she'd found in Gran's room. "I'm ready."

Neil's gaze widened, and he let out a low whistle. "You look stunning."

"Thank you, kind sir."

"Didn't find a necklace to go with the dress?"

Her hand splayed over her bare throat. "No. It's okay without, isn't it?"

"Exquisite."

Her face warmed. He could be very charming when he wanted to be. So why did his flattery make her feel so edgy tonight?

She shrugged off the sensation. Between finding the jewelry and fighting with Josh, not to mention learning Sarah had left her husband and deciding to put the house up for sale, anyone would be edgy.

He lifted the wrap she'd draped over her arm and dropped it on her shoulders. "This is a beautiful place. I can see now why you're so fond of it." He tapped the ornate paneled wood beneath the stairs. "Any trapdoors or secret passages like you see in the old movies?" he asked conspiratorially.

"Not that I know of." She opened the front door and let the dog in.

Neil took the hint.

Outside, Becki breathed a sigh of relief that Josh still wasn't home. She sent Neil over to tape the note to Josh's door while she called Sarah's cell phone to let her know they were on their way.

An automated message said, "The number you are trying to reach is no longer in service."

Returning to the car, Neil caught her arm. "What's wrong? You look like you've seen a ghost."

"I don't know. We need to hurry."

# FIFTEEN

Only one thing could've made Josh feel worse than Bec feeling as if she couldn't count on him. Winslow was hammering it into her front lawn.

The man gave the for-sale sign one last whack and then scuttled back to his motorbike as Josh pulled into the driveway.

Josh rammed his truck into Park. He got that she was mad at him. Got it loud and clear. But mad enough to leave?

She loved this place. This place. Not him. He shoved the thought away.

He strode past her car and pounded on the back door.

Bruiser slammed his paws into the door with a howl, then sat back on his haunches and wagged his tail, tongue lolling.

"C'mon, open up. We're neighbors, Bec. You can't not talk to me forever."

Josh crossed his arms and watched for movement through the window. Figured she'd pick today to actually stick to her no-talking promise.

He shouldn't have walked out the way he did. When two more minutes passed and she still hadn't come to the door, he stalked to his house.

Deep down he'd known this day would come. With all the trouble she'd had, it was a wonder it hadn't come sooner. But for how desperate she'd been to clear her grandparents' names, the last thing he'd have expected her to blow off was tonight's reception.

If she still wanted to go on tomorrow's car tour, he supposed she'd let him know. In the meantime, he might as well take care of the animals so there'd be less for his pet-sitter to bother about. He stripped out of his old-fashioned getup, put on a pair of jeans, then got to work cleaning the birdcage. When he'd finished, he laid a fresh sheet of newspaper in the bottom and coaxed the lame bird back inside, wishing he could have won Bec's cooperation as readily.

"At least *you* understand that I just want to help you. Don't you?" he cooed to the tiny sparrow. "A woman with any sense would appreciate a guy who wants to protect her."

A chuckle rose behind him. *Anne.*

"They say talking to yourself is the first sign of senility."

Josh snapped the cage door shut. "What are you doing here?" He whistled for Tripod and lifted him into the laundry tub.

"Becki called and told me that Hunter and I were off the hook for the car tour."

Josh's heart jerked. So she was bailing on the tour, too. Not just tonight's reception. He schooled his expression and lathered the shampoo into the dog's fur. "I'm surprised she gave that up so easily."

"It wasn't your idea?" Anne sounded surprised.

Apparently Bec hadn't shared the rest of their discussion. "No. I was looking forward to the tour." Now that the jewelry had been recovered, he'd figured they could dig up evidence to clear her grandparents' names without the risk.

"But you were so worried she'd be in danger, I just assumed—"

"You assumed wrong." He focused on scrubbing the dog's coat, doing his best not to betray how irked he was that Bec didn't talk with him before canceling the tour. Never mind that she wasn't talking to him. He supposed now that she'd decided to hightail it back to the city, she didn't need the freelance job. She was just like Mom and every other woman he'd ever tried to get close to.

"Stop it."

"Stop what?" He turned on the short hose he'd rigged to the tap and rinsed the dog's fur.

"Your infernal—" She waved her hand at the sink. "You always do this."

"Do what?"

"Fuss with your pets when you have people problems."

"I do not." Josh rubbed Tripod down with a towel and then lifted him to the floor. If Bec wanted to be childish and not speak to him, let her. He'd insisted the detective on the jewelry-theft case keep the Graws' name out of the paper. He was ready to turn over every rock to find the guy. What more did she want?

"How did you get Becki so mad at you?"

"Why should you care?"

Anne looked at him as if he'd just landed from another planet. "Because I've never seen you as happy as you've been these last couple weeks."

"You've got to be kidding. I've been a basket case worrying about Bec's stalker."

Anne's eyes sparkled. "And you've loved every minute of it."

Josh pushed past his sister and snatched up the kettle to fill. "That was an act for O'Reilly, remember? It didn't mean anything."

"Yeah right, that's why you've been doodling potential names for your future kids on the scratch pad by the phone."

"Get real." He glanced at the pad on the counter, then nudged it under the electricity bill. "I was trying out potential bird names."

Anne caught the edge of the pad with her index finger and drew it back into view. "Little Becki? Think she'd like having a bird named after her?"

"It was a joke." His thoughts drifted to the day he'd found her old journal, how right she'd felt in his arms, how his heart had soared to discover that she'd dreamed of them as a couple, a family.

"Right. Do you want to be single for the rest of your life?"

He set the kettle on the stove and snapped on the burner. "Is there a point to this conversation?"

"Do you know what Mom said after your high-school sweetheart ran off for the city?"

"Was that before or after Mom headed in the same direction?" Bitterness dripped from his words. He winced. He thought he'd gotten over his resentment. Anne was pushing all of his buttons today.

Anne lounged in a kitchen chair as if utterly oblivious to the thorn she'd twisted in his side. "She said it was for the best. That you didn't love the girl enough to marry her."

"How would she know?" And what did a high-school flame have to do with any of this? She was ancient history.

"Because I told Mom that the afternoon Charlotte left, you took apart that old Cadillac with Mr. Graw instead of chasing after her."

"She'd made her position clear. I wasn't enough to keep her in Serenity." Not for his mom, either, for that matter.

Anne leaned forward and pierced him with a hard stare. "When you really love someone, you'll fight for them no matter how far or fast they run."

Josh unhooked a couple of mugs, a spark of hope warming his heart. "Did Bec tell you that?"

"No. Mom did when Dad didn't chase after her and beg her to come home."

Josh pinched the bridge of his nose. But the pressure inside his head only escalated. "Maybe he was respecting her choice. Maybe he didn't want to make her feel worse for leaving. Maybe he figured if she really loved him she wouldn't have left in the first place."

"Are we talking about Dad or you?"

The kettle screamed.

He snapped off the heat. "Isn't there someone else you can irritate?"

"What's the worst thing that would have happened if you'd chased after your high-school sweetheart and she turned you down again?"

"I would have been humiliated."

"And you didn't love her enough to take that risk?"

"I—" He clamped his mouth shut. Poured the water into a teapot. "I was young."

"You do it with every woman you date. You pull back the instant you discover they don't value something the same as you."

"Because relationships need to be built on shared values. If Mom had loved living in the country, she wouldn't have run off for the glitz of the city."

"Maybe, but you don't fall in love with a checklist of ideals. You fall in love with a person, with all her faults and differing opinions—the way God made her. And you trust God to help you make it work, because relationships get messy no matter how many boxes on your checklist you've ticked."

"This from the woman who wears a wedding band to avoid being picked up by guys."

Her gaze dropped. She twisted the gold band.

"I'm sorry. I—"

"No, you're right. I have no business giving advice. But I still think you should go after her."

"She won't even open the door. What would you suggest? I ram it down?"

"What are you talking about? She's not home. Didn't you get the note she left?"

"Of course she's home. Her car's still in the driveway."

"That's because Neil drove her to the reception."

Josh's heart felt as if it'd been ripped from his chest. "Neil?"

Anne opened the front door and untaped a folded paper. "I'm sure she explained everything in this."

Josh glanced at his watch. Bec must've called Neil the second he'd left. "How could she go back to that creep after one little fight?"

"Why don't you go after her and find out?"

Josh unfolded the letter. His heart did a funny flip at the sight of a couple of tear-size wrinkles on the paper.

Dear Josh,

I wasn't sure if you'd still want to go on the tour with me so when Neil stopped by and offered to escort me, I agreed. We'll hitch rides on a few of the other cars tomorrow. Might add some diversity to my article.

"Might give her more opportunities to ferret out what people know about the jewelry theft," Josh muttered under his breath. She was too obstinate for her own good. He flipped through his address book and dialed the number for the tour's director.

"What are you doing?"

"Making sure word of the stolen jewelry's recovery gets spread. At least then Bec will be safe."

"You could go make sure of that yourself, you know."

"I think I can do without your advice. It was your ridiculous idea that got me entangled with Bec in the first place. I was perfectly happy being single."

"Liar."

Bec's betrayed expression flashed through his thoughts. Her crackly *I thought you were someone I could count on* echoed painfully in his ears. He'd let her down.

Sure, her idea had been irrational, but he could've discussed options with her. Maybe they could have found a way to use the jewelry to catch the guy.

"May I help you?" the tour director asked over the phone, jerking Josh from his thoughts.

"Uh, sorry, no. Wrong number."

Anne lifted an eyebrow as he hung up the phone.

"Don't gloat."

"I wouldn't dream of it."

"Being humiliated in front of a room full of strangers can't be any worse than spending the rest of my life wondering if I could have won her back."

"Let alone living without her."

"Yeah, that, too." Josh dashed to the bedroom and quickly changed back into his old-fashioned getup, then snatched up the keys to his truck. "Lock up, will you?" He jogged across the driveway to hook his truck back up to the trailer.

He stopped short at the sound of Bruiser barking.

Sarah's husband stood on the back porch, his hands cupped around his eyes, peering through the kitchen window.

"What are you doing?"

The man jolted back. "Looking for my wife. Have you seen her?"

Josh bristled at the thought of what he might've done to make her leave this time. "Not since the night she went home with you."

Rowan smoothed his expensive-looking suit and gave Josh's outfit a cursory once-over. "Do you know where Becki is?"

"Not at the moment. But I can let her know you're looking for her next time I see her."

Rowan gave one last glance over his shoulder at the kitchen window. "Don't worry about it, thanks." The man climbed into his car and hightailed it out of the driveway before Josh finished hooking on the trailer.

A few minutes later two police cruisers pulled in,

followed by Smith's Plymouth. Hunter jumped out of the first cruiser and strode toward Josh, a sober look on his face.

"What's wrong? Did something happen to Bec?"

Hunter flashed him the paper he was carrying. "We have a warrant to search the premises."

"For the other glove? I already told you she'll turn it in if she finds it." Josh snatched the warrant from Hunter's hand. "Please tell me you're not trying to pin this on the Graws."

A thump sounded at the porch door—Bruiser throwing himself at it, barking frantically.

"Can you tie the dog up at your house until we're done?" Hunter asked, confirming Josh's fear.

Henry Smith—the insurance company's private investigator—studied Josh for a full thirty seconds before speaking. "Where is Miss Graw?"

"Why? She has nothing to do with this."

"A missing fifty-thousand-dollar necklace and earring set say otherwise."

The instant Neil drew close to the parking lot of the Grand Hotel, Becki scanned the rows of cars for her sister's. She had no idea what Sarah's idea for catching the jewel thief was, but at this point she'd be happy just to find her sister was safe.

"You okay?" Neil turned his car into the lot. "You're trembling."

Becki curled her fingers into the small satin clutch

she'd grabbed to go with the outfit. "I don't see my sister's car. She was supposed to meet me here."

"What kind of car?"

"A BMW, if..." Becki twisted in her seat and scrutinized each car they passed. Would Sarah have taken the BMW? With the built-in GPS, she'd be too easy to locate. "Um, actually, she probably came in a different car. Let's just go inside and see if we can find her."

Neil parked in a dark corner. "Stay put until I get your door."

She hung her camera strap over her shoulder and then placed her hand in his. She couldn't help but be impressed by his chivalry. "I appreciate your escorting me to this, Neil."

"It's my pleasure. Like old times."

Becki nodded, but as he cupped her elbow to guide her to the entrance, her insides didn't bubble as they did whenever Josh touched her. She shoved the thought from her mind. Her sister had just run away from an abusive husband. Did she need any more proof that a few momentary flutters weren't worth the inevitable heartache?

She breathed in the cool evening air. Once she saw Sarah for herself—safe—she'd be able to relax. They reached the sidewalk, and a car door slammed behind them. High heels click-clacked toward them.

Becki whirled toward the sound. "Sarah!" She pulled her sister into a fierce hug. "Are you okay? I couldn't get you on your cell phone."

Sarah gave Neil a surreptitious glance and whispered, "I had to ditch it so Rowan couldn't track me. I left the car parked at the bus station and put the phone on a bus headed for Thunder Bay."

Becki laughed and hugged her sister harder. "Brilliant. That will keep him busy."

"Shall we go in?" Neil put an arm around each of them and ushered them inside.

"Mmm." Sarah inhaled. "Enraptured for Him, isn't it?"

"That's what's different," Becki said. "I knew there was something."

"It's the male version of the perfume I gave you," he said, sounding smug.

Just inside the door, they stopped at the coat check and Neil lifted the wrap from Becki's shoulder, then helped Sarah with her coat. He caught the scarf along with the coat, revealing a stunning necklace.

"Whoa," Becki exclaimed. That must have set Rowan back a fortune.

Sarah snatched back the scarf and wrapped it around her neck, darting a furtive look at Becki.

*She must plan to hock the piece to finance her escape.* Becki squeezed Sarah's hand to assure her she understood. As Neil handed in the coats in exchange for coat-check stubs, Becki drew Sarah aside. "Are you okay?"

"I didn't steal it from you." Sarah sounded worried.

"Steal what?"

Big-band music drifted from the ballroom as couples jostled past them.

Sarah tugged Becki into a shadowed alcove, where she unwound her scarf and touched the teardrop pendant hanging from the center of a diamond-studded chain. "You don't recognize this?"

"Should I?"

Sarah blew out a breath. "It was in Gran's glove."

"What?" Her mind scrolled through the images in the jewelry-theft article.

"I didn't know it was there when I took the glove," Sarah said defensively. "I just...I... The glove smelled like Gran."

A lump rose to Becki's throat. Sarah missed Gran and Gramps as much as she did.

"When I left so quickly that night Rowan came, I just wanted to grab something that would remind me of her. I should have told you when I got home and found the necklace inside. I thought it was Gran's and I hoped you wouldn't miss it. Can you ever forgive me?"

"Yes, but—" Becki pulled the edges of the scarf back together and lowered her voice. "It's got to be one of the stolen pieces."

"Yes. I thought if I wore it, the thief might reveal himself."

"That's your idea?" With sudden, terrifying clarity, Becki realized why Josh had so adamantly nixed *her* idea to do basically the same thing.

Hadn't the trashed trailer been proof enough the

guy had lost patience? Not to mention maybe even tampered with her brakes. Once he set eyes on the necklace, he'd go after it no matter the cost.

Neil approached with a smile. "Finished your powwow?"

"Could you give us one more minute?" Becki asked, appreciative of his sensitivity.

Women in evening gowns sauntered past, scarcely paying them any attention, but the gaze of every man seemed drawn to her beautiful sister.

"Why don't I get everyone some punch?" Neil suggested.

"That would be wonderful. Thank you," Sarah said.

Once Neil disappeared through the ballroom doors, Becki said, "I can't let you do this, Sarah. It's too dangerous."

"What are you talking about? How did you think you'd draw out the thief?"

"I don't know. I was frantic over finding those jewels in Gran's glove and desperate to prove she didn't take them. But I won't risk your safety to do that."

"But you'll risk yours?"

Becki let out a sigh.

Sarah's fingers gripped her scarf. "I want to do this for Gran and Gramps just as much as you do. This can work."

Becki envisioned the last time they'd conspired together—to get a puppy—and the disaster that had turned into. "I don't even know what we'd do if we came up with a suspect."

"You're here to do an article. Take photos of everyone who shows an interest in the jewelry, especially if they seem to watch my every move."

"That's half the guys here."

"So take down names on the pretense of it being for the article. If they don't want you to use their pictures or names, that'd be all the more suspicious."

"But if this guy is here, he's going to look for any opportunity to steal the necklace."

"So we let him." Sarah hooked her arm through Becki's and led her into the ballroom.

Tables laden with cakes and pastries lined the walls. Couples milled about them.

"If the guy steals the necklace, we don't have to prove anything," Sarah went on. "Just call the police and they'll catch him in possession of the stolen goods."

*Like you are now?* Becki silenced the voice in her head. The voice that sounded too much like Josh. This could work. It had to work.

Sarah unwound the scarf and draped it across her shoulders. The lights from the chandeliers made the attached pendant glitter.

Lifting her camera, Becki took a few steps back. "That necklace is stunning," she gushed loud enough for others to hear, and then she snapped a couple of photos of Sarah hamming it up for the camera.

The ploy attracted the attention they'd hoped. Several couples meandered over and admired the pendant. Becki took their photos, too. Told them she was writing an article. She glanced around, wondering what had happened to Neil. She spotted him chatting with an older lady by the punch bowl.

He gave Becki a warm smile and, with a slight lift of his chin, mouthed, *Be right there.*

She tightened her grip on her camera. He was being so nice, but she didn't want him to think this changed her mind about *them*.

Sarah's sudden gasp snapped Becki's attention back to her sister. Sarah clutched her scarf at her throat, her panicked gaze colliding with Becki's. Lifting her camera, Becki whirled to capture the source of Sarah's panic.

*Josh.*

Becki's heart slammed into her ribs. He didn't look like a policeman in his breeches and suspenders and crisp white shirt topped with a cravat. He looked noble, honorable, almost like someone she might be able to reason with. But that didn't change the fact he was first and foremost a cop, and if he'd seen the stolen necklace, she was finished.

# SIXTEEN

Josh couldn't take his eyes off Bec as she lowered her camera and offered him an awkward smile. Okay, so she wasn't wearing the dress he liked, but she looked stunning in red. At the sight of her bare neck, relief filled him that she hadn't come with the stolen necklace to hatch some harebrained plan to nab the real thief.

She scanned the ballroom, and her creamy shoulders relaxed when her gaze met Neil's over the punch bowl.

She couldn't be serious about Neil. Could she?

Josh forced his fingers to unclench. He'd seen the way she'd flinched the day Neil had shown up uninvited.

He frowned. But if she didn't come to catch the thief, why was she here with Neil and not him?

Neil weaved through the crowd toward her, carrying two glasses of punch. Apparently he was someone she could count on.

Maybe coming here had been a mistake.

Couples dotted the room, heads inclined toward

each other, whispering, laughing, sharing secret smiles. The way Bec's grandparents had always been. How many times had he noticed their eyes meeting across a crowded room as they shared a smile?

He wanted that with Bec.

He wanted the house in the country, full of rescued strays and four kids whose names all started with *J* and a little Becki.

His heart squeezed as he closed the distance between them.

He'd already defied his captain's orders by coming here. If he was going to crash and burn, he might as well go all out.

"You came," she said with a hint of uncertainty, but had he imagined the hint of pleasure, too?

He let his gaze caress her skin. "The red looks good on you."

"Doesn't it?" Neil said smugly, handing Bec a glass of punch. "It's my favorite color."

Josh stiffened.

Apology washed through Bec's eyes, but Josh didn't know how to interpret it.

Neil handed the second glass to another woman.

Josh did a double take. "Sarah? I didn't expect to find you here."

She clenched a scarf about her neck with a white-knuckled grip, but he didn't miss the bruise under her left jaw.

A surge of anger gripped him. "Have you finally left him?"

The grip on her scarf relaxed a little. "Yes."

"That explains why he was at Bec's house looking for you."

"Who? Your husband?" Neil interjected.

"Yes."

Sarah set her glass on a table and fussed with the scarf at the back of her neck, then caught Bec's hand between hers.

Bec's eyes widened as they seemed to telegraph silent messages as only siblings could.

"I need to go," Sarah whispered. "Rowan might have followed Josh here."

Seeing Bec's gaze drop to the scarf hiding her sister's bruises, Josh interjected, "Where will you go? We could help you find a safe place."

"I have one lined up. Thank you." She squeezed Bec's fisted hand for a long moment. "I'll call you soon."

Neil produced a coat-check stub from his pocket. "I'll walk you to your car." He touched Bec's shoulder. "I'll just be a minute."

Josh watched them leave. Begrudgingly, he had to concede that Neil seemed like a decent guy, but that didn't stop Josh from hoping that Sarah kept Neil chatting outside for a good long time.

As Josh turned back to Bec, she fumbled with her purse, sloshing punch over her gloved hand.

He lifted the glass from her hold. "It's stained."

"That's okay. It'll wash." She hurriedly snapped shut her tiny purse.

At the sight of a diamond-studded chain dangling from it, Josh's planned speech died on his lips.

Bec reached for her punch glass, but Josh caught her wrist. "Why did you come?"

"What do you mean? I'm here to write an article."

He set down the punch glass, opened her purse, nudged the chain inside—against his better judgment—and snapped the purse shut again. "I mean, you better let me in on whatever plan you've concocted."

"I didn't keep the necklace from you, Josh." He steeled himself against her defensive expression. "You have to believe me. Sarah had it. She didn't tell me until I got here."

"That's why you scrambled to hide it in your purse when I wasn't looking? When did I become the enemy?"

Her expression crumbled.

His anger seeped away. "I'm sorry, Bec." He stroked her cheek. "Trust me, if I didn't believe in you, I wouldn't be here. The police know about the missing jewelry."

Her face paled, and everything in him wanted her to believe he could help her, but he couldn't sugarcoat the truth. "You're their prime suspect."

"They think I stole it?" Clutching her purse, Becki searched Josh's eyes. He didn't think that, too, did he?

No, he'd said he believed in her.

Josh steered her away from the crowds into a quiet corner. "They think you *found* the jewelry, but *with-held* the necklace and earring set."

"But you know I wouldn't steal them. You told them. Didn't you?"

He looked pointedly at her purse.

"Sarah had the necklace. I didn't know."

"Bec, they found one of the earrings in your jew-elry box, not to mention they know that Sarah threat-ened to oust you out of your house if you didn't give her a bigger cut of the inheritance."

"Fine, don't believe me. Take it."

Josh covered her hand and closed the clasp an instant before Neil's arm curled around her waist.

"Ready to hobnob?" Neil murmured close to her ear. "Get that story you're after?"

Josh's hand dropped to his side. Something flick-ered in his eyes. His expression went blank. "I need to make a phone call." Josh walked a few steps, then pivoted on his heel. "By the way, I towed the Model T here. We could ask Hunter's uncle if it'd be okay for you and Neil…"

He'd towed the car? Really?

"That'd be great. Don't you think?" Neil piped up.

"Yes." Becki turned back to her date and mus-tered a smile.

He'd towed the car? He didn't just come to recover the jewelry? How sweet was that? Had he hoped to join her, too?

"I thought your article might sound better from a front-seat view."

Her article. Right. He'd been rescuing her again.

If only her heart wouldn't somersault in her chest every time Josh acted like some fairy-tale prince. She knew better than to believe in fairy tales.

What had she expected? That he'd turn into a green-eyed monster like her sister had supposed?

You actually had to love someone to be jealous.

Josh slammed his fist into the side of the trailer. God help him, when he saw Neil slink his arm around Bec's waist, and Bec not so much as lean away, his chest had felt as if she'd dug that old-fashioned boot heel square into the center.

He pulled out his phone and clicked Hunter's number.

"You got it?" Hunter asked the instant the phone connected.

"Soon." Josh sucked in the night air, but the heavy dampness did nothing to relieve the fire in his chest. "I'll need you to bring it in, though. I need to stay and watch Bec's back."

"Already on my way. Got Anne with me."

Josh stuffed the phone back in his pocket and sucked in a couple more deep breaths. He'd quietly corner Bec one last time, recover the necklace and then back off. Scan the crowd. Make sure no one was watching her.

He turned back to the hotel, but a faint whimper stopped him. He glanced around, expecting to find an abandoned kitten or pup. This end of the parking lot backed onto the cliff above the ravine and wasn't well lit—just the kind of place someone might choose to dump an unwanted pet.

The whimper sounded again—from the direction of the ravine. Josh reached into his truck and grabbed his flashlight. He swept the light over the steep embankment and caught sight of a blond head.

He scrambled toward the victim. "I'm coming. Hang on."

Six feet from the gagged, prone body, his heart slammed into his ribs. "Sarah?" *Oh, God, please let her be okay.*

A purple splotch colored her cheek. Her dress was torn and muddy. Leaves and twigs tangled her hair.

"Sarah? Sarah, can you hear me?"

Her eyes remained closed. Her face twisted in pain.

He skidded to his knees and untied the scarf binding her mouth. Guilt cut off his breath. He must have led Rowan straight to her. Josh checked her breathing, her pulse. "Sarah, talk to me." He unbound her hands; they'd been tied behind her back with the belt of her dress. It was a miracle she'd been conscious enough to make any sound after being pushed over the ravine with no hands to brace her fall.

He checked her arms and legs for fractures. They'd need a spinal board just to be safe. He pulled out his cell phone and dialed 9-1-1.

The phone flashed No Service. "Sarah, can you hear me? I need to climb up the ravine to get a signal so we can get you an ambulance."

Her eyelids fluttered open.

"Did you hear me? I'll be right back."

"Becki?" she whispered.

"In the hotel. I'll call her, too."

"No!" She struggled to get to a sitting position.

He gently urged her back down. "You need to lie still until the paramedics get here."

She lashed at his arms, her eyes flaring. "You have to protect her."

Josh cupped her shoulders. "It's okay. Rowan's not going to bother Bec in a ballroom full of people." His calm tone belied the frantic scramble in his chest. "Neil will watch out for her."

Sarah flailed out of his grasp. "No, not—" She pushed herself up and immediately blacked out.

"Sarah?" Josh shook her gently, terrified to move her.

Her breathing remained steady.

"I'll be right back." He raced up the steep incline, his gaze glued to his cell-phone screen. The instant a signal appeared, he called in an ambulance and police, then rushed back to Sarah's side.

She drifted in and out of consciousness, mumbling gibberish.

At the top of the ravine, a car door slammed.

"Hello, up there!" he shouted. "I need help."

"Josh?" Hunter's voice floated down the ravine.

Josh pointed his flashlight toward the ridge. "Down here. Bec's sister is injured."

Hunter and Anne plowed down the ravine toward them. Anne immediately began assessing Sarah's injuries. "What happened?"

"Her husband found her," Josh said flatly. He'd never forgive himself for leading the brute straight to her. "We need to put out a BOLO alert for him."

At the mention of a be-on-the-lookout, Sarah's eyes flew open. "No." She grabbed his arm when he reached to hold her still. "Not Rowan."

"What?" Josh turned the light to her face.

Her hand went to her throat. "He thought I still had the necklace."

"Who?" Josh surged to his feet, praying he wasn't too late to get to Bec.

Tears filled Sarah's eyes. "Neil."

# SEVENTEEN

Josh raced back inside the hotel and then forced himself to slow his steps as he reached the entrance to the ballroom. He wanted to storm in, knock Neil's lights out for terrorizing Bec these past weeks and pull her safe into his arms. Instead, he stood in the doorway and methodically scanned the room.

If he played it cool, Neil wouldn't know he'd found Sarah and was onto him. Just like he hadn't known the jewelry had already been turned in.

Josh toed off the worst of the mud caked to his shoes.

A gray-haired lady looked over her glasses at him as she walked past.

A minute later, a hotel employee touched his shoulder, the nosy woman at the employee's flank. "May I help you, sir?"

Josh flashed his police ID. "I'm looking for Becki Graw. She was wearing a long red gown."

"The woman with the camera?" the gray-haired lady piped up.

"Yes. Have you seen her?"

"She and her husband left about half an hour ago. Probably went up to their rooms. I noticed because—"

"Can you give me her room number?" Josh asked the hotel employee. "We have reason to believe she might be in danger from the man she was with."

"Of course. Follow me." The employee hurried to the desk and typed on the computer. "No, we have no one registered under that name."

"What about Neil Orner?"

The employee tapped a few more keys as unwelcome feelings crammed Josh's throat.

"No, sorry."

Josh peeled a business card out of his wallet. "Check the security cameras, bathrooms, everywhere. If you see the woman, call me immediately."

His cell phone rang before he made it out the door. Josh checked the screen. Hunter.

"Anne went to the hospital with Sarah. Neil ransacked her car, too."

Josh hit the door at a run. "We're looking for a red Mustang. Someone saw Bec leave with Neil a half hour ago."

"On it."

Josh raced up one row of cars and down the other. If only he hadn't walked out on Bec back at the house, she never would have gone off with Neil. Josh reached the back corner of the lot at the same time as Hunter.

"It's not here!" Dread cut off his breath.

"I put out a BOLO alert with both the local and highway police," Hunter said. "Sarah said Neil was ranting that he'd lost his job and his house because of them."

"That's crazy. How's he figure?"

"Don't know about the job, but sounds like he was investing on margin and got caught short. Must've been counting on selling the jewelry to cover the margin call."

Josh climbed into his truck. "Then he's got to be headed for Serenity to get the rest of the jewelry."

"She would have told him he's too late."

"Not Bec. She'd know she had to buy time." Josh prayed he was right. He smacked his portable light onto his roof. Neil must've showed up at the house ready to demand the jewelry, only Bec surprised him by inviting him on the tour. Maybe gave him hope that he could win her back, or at least that he could get the jewelry without her learning the truth about him.

Hunter jogged to his truck. "I'll call the captain. Tell him to have someone watch the house."

Josh barreled out of the parking lot and floored the gas with Hunter on his tail. *Please, Lord, let our guess be right.* Neil had already lost his job, his house and his girl. He had nothing left to lose. If he couldn't get away with the jewelry, there was no telling what he'd do.

\* \* \*

Eyes closed, Becki smacked her tongue against the roof of her mouth, trying to draw moisture to take away the strange taste. Her seat bounced, jostling her. Where was she?

She tried to open her eyes, but she couldn't seem to make her eyelids cooperate. The whir of an engine filtered through her thoughts. She was in a car?

She couldn't remember leaving the reception.

She turned her face toward the driver and this time managed to pry open her eyes.

Neil glanced from the road to her and smiled. "Have a good sleep?"

She blinked, straining to make sense of how she'd gotten here. Her mind flailed back over the evening. She remembered Josh leaving the reception to make a phone call. After that, things got fuzzy.

"I knew if I was patient you'd realize we were meant to be together."

*What?* If he thought they were a couple again, he'd totally misinterpreted her invitation to the reception.

Wait. Her sister. He'd said they had to hurry, that her sister needed her. Only... She pressed her fingers to her temples, straining to remember what he'd said.

Images flashed through her mind. She'd been about to climb into his car when she'd heard Josh shout from the direction of the ravine.

"You don't want him," Neil had snarled into her

ear as he clamped a cloth over her mouth and nose, and her mind drifted into oblivion.

"After we pick up the rest of the jewelry, I was thinking we could fly to the Caribbean," Neil said. "What do you think?"

*The jewelry?* He knew about that? She felt in her lap for her purse.

He patted his pocket. "Don't worry. The necklace is safe and sound."

"That's all there is. My gran never had—"

Neil cackled. "You and I both know that necklace wasn't your grandmother's."

"But…how do you know that?"

His grin chilled her to the bone. "Because I took them."

"You?"

"Is that so hard to believe? I have many talents. I could have made you a wealthy woman."

"I—" She caught herself before saying she didn't care about money. "I've always wanted to go to the Caribbean," she mumbled instead, hoping that playing along with his delusion would buy her time.

He turned his car onto her road, cruising slowly past her house.

"Where are you going? You passed—"

He pulled into the rutted farm lane behind her property. "My parking spot." He threw her another creepy grin.

It was now or never. She quietly unfastened her

seat belt and sprang out the door. Hiking up her long gown, she sprinted for the trees, remembering too late that her ankle couldn't handle the strain.

He tackled her, and she pitched face-first into the dirt.

"I should have known you were lying." He wrenched her arms behind her back and cinched them with a zip tie until the plastic dug into her wrists. She'd never be able to outrun him now.

She rolled onto her back and struggled to get up, refusing to ask for help. She wouldn't give him the satisfaction.

He hauled her to her feet. Snatched her purse from the front seat of the car, extracted her key and jabbed it at her face. "We can do this the easy way or the hard way."

"I don't know where the rest of the jewelry is," Becki yelled, hoping against hope that someone would hear her and send help.

"Don't lie to me. I saw the earring, remember?" Neil's grip tightened painfully around her arm. "I don't want to hurt you, Rebecca, but if you don't start telling me what I want to know, you'll be joining your sister."

"What did you do to her?" Sarah couldn't be dead. *Please, Lord, I won't believe it.*

Neil shoved her ahead of him through the damp meadow that backed onto her house. Josh's yard light scarcely cut through the thick darkness of the moonless night. But Neil moved confidently, as if he'd been that way before.

Just as Josh had first suspected. Why hadn't she listened?

As they got closer, the familiar shape of her grandparents' house emerged. A smidgen of hope surged through her.

Somehow she had to stall Neil, buy time until Josh figured out where she'd been taken.

Thank God she didn't tell Neil that the rest of the jewelry had already been turned in. If he killed her sister—*please, Lord, don't let that be true*—he wouldn't hesitate to finish her off, too.

A car rolled slowly up the road. Neil slapped his clammy hand over her mouth and clamped his other arm around her waist, drawing her tight against his chest, and hauled her to a stop.

As the car drew close, Becki could just make out the outline of something on its roof. *A patrol car!*

She struggled against Neil's grip, praying the officer would spot her. Had Josh sent him? She knew she could count on him.

The patrol car turned into her driveway and two officers got out.

Neil's arm snaked from her waist to her neck and squeezed. The air stalled in her chest, flaming through her throat. Searing pain shot to her head, and what little she could see began to fade. "I don't need you alive to search that house, Rebecca," Neil hissed into her ear.

She stopped fighting, and his hold loosened a fraction.

She sucked in a lungful of air. *Oh, God, he's going to kill me.*

The officers shone their flashlights around the yard, peered through the windows, checked the barn.

Neil drew her deeper into the shadows.

"Let's go," one of the officers said, turning back to the car. "There's nobody here."

Becki lurched forward and tried to shout, but with Neil's hand clamped over her mouth, she barely managed a squeak and a scuffle.

The second officer turned his flashlight in their direction.

Neil pinned her against his chest.

The light beam scraped the ground yards from their feet, then abruptly spiraled toward the driveway.

The officers climbed back into the car and slammed the doors.

"Serenity's finest at work," Neil said with a sneer. "Your new boyfriend won't come to your rescue this time. Trust me. Guys don't like to be snubbed for another man."

"Why are you doing this?" she mumbled through his fingers.

"I need the money. Why else?"

The patrol car backed slowly down the driveway and kept on going.

*No! Come back!* the voice in her head screamed.

"Move," Neil snarled, shoving her forward again. "This is your fault. If you hadn't broken up with me when I got back from the car tour, we would have paid your grandparents a nice friendly visit. I would have recovered my jewelry from the hiding place in your grandfather's car. And no one would have been the wiser."

"You were on that tour?"

He laughed. "It would've been perfect. If they hadn't croaked." Another set of headlights turned onto the road.

Neil dragged her into the shadow of the barn and crouched low.

She couldn't see the car, but its headlights draped the far-off trees in a ghostly light.

Neil's back teeth clicked in the familiar rat-a-tat that meant he was growing impatient.

Finally the car passed and disappeared down the road.

"C'mon." Neil pushed her toward the house.

She dug in her heels. "But you said the jewelry was in the car."

"Nice try. I already checked."

"You're the one that clobbered me over the head my first night here?"

"I couldn't afford to let you see me." His foot kicked something, sent it rattling against the barn wall. "What the—" He flicked his flashlight toward the sound.

The gasoline can. Josh must've left it out after he topped up the car.

Neil picked up the can and shook it. Gasoline sloshed. "This could come in handy. Maybe you'll start talking if I threaten to burn down your beloved house, room by room, eh?"

"No, please."

"Begging doesn't become you." He shoved her up the back steps.

She stepped on the hem of her gown and pitched to her knees.

He grabbed her arm and lifted her back to her feet, causing the bottom of her gown to rip. "Move." He jostled the can of gasoline tauntingly.

Her legs moved woodenly. *Think.* She had to stall him. "So you put that note in my mailbox, too," she asked loudly, hoping to alert Bruiser.

"Yup."

"And the sulfur in my well?"

"Sulfur? No, can't take credit for that."

"But you made those phone calls and tampered with the brakes and shot at the house?"

"The potshots were inspired, don't you think? Made it look like an incompetent hunter to show you how dangerous country living was. Too bad you didn't take the hint."

"So I'd come back to you?"

"I figured you'd see the light sooner or later. How long could a neighbor-farmer boy keep a sophisticated woman like you entertained?" Neil peered through the window on the kitchen door. "Where's your dog?"

Becki looked, too. There was no sign of him. "I don't know."

Neil tapped the door.

Still no barking.

Becki's hope drained. Josh had said the police had searched her house. He must've taken Bruiser away.

Neil unlocked the kitchen door and pushed her inside.

Automatically she hitched up her elbow to flick on the light switch.

He slapped it off. "Nice try." The dead bolt clicked with a sickening ping. Then he caught her by the chin and pushed her up until she was standing on her tiptoes, back pressed to the wall. "Try anything like that again and you'll regret it." In the dim light seeping through the windows, he studied her face for a long moment, pressing her head harder against the wall. His thumb licked across her bottom lip.

Closing her eyes, she sucked in a breath. *Please, Lord, don't let him hurt me.*

As suddenly as he'd grabbed her, he flung her away. "We could have been good together."

She scanned the room for a weapon, struggling to regain her balance. There were plenty of knives, but with her hands tied behind her back, how would she use one?

Neil snapped down the kitchen blinds, then stalked

into the living room and drew the drapes. Utter darkness swallowed her.

*Darkness is as light to God.* Her Gran's words whispered through her mind. She began to make out shapes in the room. She knew every inch of this house in the dark or light. If she could just free her hands...

Neil disappeared down the hallway, followed by the sound of more blinds snapped shut. Did he plan to turn on the lights?

Or was he afraid she would?

She twisted her hands within her binds, straining to pull free. But she could scarcely move, let alone manipulate the tie with her numb fingers. She plowed backward until she slammed into the wall, then felt her way toward the door. Her fingers contacted the cool metal of the doorknob, and she inched them higher toward the dead bolt.

A light suddenly flashed into her eyes. "Where do you think you're going?" Neil's long strides swallowed the distance between them. He grabbed a hunk of her hair.

Pain screamed through her scalp.

He pushed her toward the living room. "You love this house. Isn't that what you told me?"

He let out an icy chuckle, punctuated by the slosh of gasoline.

A chill shivered down her arms.

"If you don't produce the rest of my jewelry, your stay will be permanent."

# EIGHTEEN

Josh pulled up to the makeshift command post behind Bec's house, where Serenity police had found Neil's car. "See anything?" He yanked off his white shirt and tugged on a spare black T-shirt.

Wes handed him a Kevlar vest, then held up a stained white glove. "Found this on the floor of the car. Recognize it?"

"Yeah." Heart racing, Josh thumbed through his keys for the one to the lockbox bolted to his truck floor.

"There are no lights on in the house. How do you want to play this?"

*Play this?* This wasn't a war game. This was Bec's life. "We'll scout the situation first."

"The tactical team's on its way."

Yeah, he wouldn't be waiting. He pulled out his gun and loaded a clip.

Hunter strode up, already outfitted in full tactical gear. He handed Josh a black paint pot and night-vision goggles. "Just saw a flash of light in the second-story window, west wall, second from the back."

"Does this guy own a gun?" Wes asked.

"I don't know." Josh fitted an earpiece and mic and lowered his goggles. "Let's go."

He and Hunter stole across the field in silence, an exercise they'd done countless times during night ops the three years they'd served together in the military. But Josh's gut had never felt as strangled as it did tonight.

At the edge of the yard, he motioned for Hunter to take the front. Within minutes, Hunter's whispered voice sounded through the earpiece.

"Can't get a visual."

"Same here. Doors and windows are locked."

A scrap of fabric fluttered past his foot.

Josh stooped to pick it up, recognized the silky feel of the dress Bec had worn tonight. *She's here.*

"A light just went on in a second-story window, back of house, west end," an officer's voice said over the mic.

Josh glanced at the barn. "Get a sniper in the hayloft."

"I'll go." Hunter said. "Think you can get in through the basement without him hearing you?"

"I can do better than that." Josh pulled out the spare key Bec had given him. "You in position?"

"Just about."

Josh listened at the door, then fit in the key. "Command post, on Hunter's mark, make the call. Patch it to our comms. I want to know what this guy's saying." Josh inched open the door, scanned the area. The green, filmy image through his goggles betrayed no movement. He entered. "I'm in," he whispered.

The smell of gasoline assaulted him. "Get the fire department here," he growled into his mic. "He's gonna torch the place!"

"In position," Hunter said.

"Backup standing by," command post announced. "Putting in the call now."

Josh quickly checked the main-floor rooms. Strewn clothes and books littered the floor.

The house phone rang once. Twice.

*Come on, pick up.* Josh stole up the stairs.

The ringing stopped. Josh inched toward the bedroom door. What was going on? He tapped his earpiece. Had Neil picked up or not?

"This is Officer Wade of the Serenity Police Department" Josh heard through the comm.

No response.

Back pressed to the wall outside the occupied room, Josh drew in a breath and shot a glance inside.

His heart lurched. Bec stood at the window, gasoline dripping from her hair, down her neck and over her gown in black, angry rivulets.

Josh jerked back out of sight. "You don't have a clear shot," he hissed into the mic. "I repeat—"

"Copy that," Hunter responded, and Josh's breath left him in a rush.

"Mr. Orner, we know you're holding Miss Graw

against her will. Let her go and come out with your hands up."

"Rebecca is exactly where she wants to be. In her beloved home," Neil said in an icy voice and slammed down the phone.

Josh took another peek, and Bec's gaze shot in his direction.

Her eyes went soft, brimming with emotion he'd thought he'd never see again.

He touched a silencing finger to his lips.

She shifted her eyes to the left and back.

He nodded and moved to the other side of the door to get into a position where he could see Neil. He jerked back at the sight of his own reflection in the dresser mirror.

Neil caught Bec by the hair. "So your boyfriend found you after all."

Josh's hands went slick with sweat. He was 99 percent sure Neil hadn't seen him, that he was referring to the phone call.

Neil lifted an old silver lighter to Bec's face. "Think he'll still want you after the flames are through with you?" His thumb flipped back the lid and caressed the lighter's igniter.

The terror in Bec's eyes shredded Josh's heart. Somehow he had to distract Neil enough to ease his grip.

Fire engine sirens split the air.

Neil's thumb turned jerky on the lighter. "I'm not going to jail. I'd sooner burn with you in hell."

"Kill the sirens," Josh hissed into his mic. "He's antsy enough."

As if Bec knew exactly what Josh needed her to do, she edged out of his line of fire.

Neil yanked her to his chest. "What are you doing?"

Her gaze lifted to the opposite wall, and the terror slipped from her eyes. "I was trying to see the picture of Jesus better."

"He's not going to save you." Neil clamped his arm around Bec's waist, holding her like a shield. "Neither is that boyfriend of yours. You want out of this alive—" Neil swiveled her away from the painting "—you do exactly as I say."

Bec dug in her heels. "Wait. I don't want you hurt, either."

"Call him again," Josh whispered into his mic. "Hunter, get ready to take the shot on my signal."

The phone rang.

Neil ignored it. "You don't love me," he growled. "So don't bother pretending."

"I may not love you the way you'd hoped," Bec said, her voice surprisingly calm. "But I care about you. And Jesus—"

"*Care* about me?" Neil roared and took a wild swing at the blaring phone.

Josh barreled into the room, scooped Bec from Neil's arm and dived into a roll. "Now. Now. *Now*," he yelled.

Three shots cracked through the glass and blinds.

"No!" Bec screamed.

Neil clapped a hand to his chest, shock glazing his eyes.

Josh hoisted Bec to her feet and pushed her toward the door, wrists still bound. "Get out."

His backup charged up the stairs as Neil lifted the lighter. "Get her out of here," Josh ordered.

Neil's gaze fixed on Josh, pure hatred blazing from his eyes.

"Let me help you," Josh soothed, taking a cautious step forward.

Neil flicked on the lighter, an ugly sneer curling his lips.

The lighter tumbled to the floor.

A roar shook the house. Flames shot out the bedroom door, blasting Josh's backup off their feet.

"Josh!" Becki screamed from the base of the stairs.

Hunter hoisted her over his shoulder and hustled her out the front door.

Firemen dragging hoses streamed toward the house.

"We have two men down at the top of the stairs. Two men in the second bedroom on the right," Hunter reported to the chief, setting her down on the back of the ambulance.

The paramedic snipped the binds cinching her wrists. Becki sprang from the ambulance.

Hunter caught her.

She thrashed her arms. "Let me go. Josh is in there. This is my fault."

Hunter tightened his hold, lifting her off the ground.

She kicked wildly.

He gave her a hard shake. "Racing back in there isn't going to help. Stay here and let the firefighters do their job."

Two firefighters came out the front door, each helping a hacking, smoke-blackened tactical officer.

She strained against Hunter's hold, needing to go to Josh the second he appeared.

But he didn't.

She watched in horror as flames melted through the second-story window blinds and yellow-brown smoke puffed from the eaves. A couple of firefighters hauled a chain saw up a ladder.

"What are they doing? Why aren't they going after Josh?" She clutched Hunter's arm. "They can't let him die."

"They're cutting a ventilation hole to lift the smoke off the guys inside." He set her back on the end of the ambulance. "Wait here," he ordered and strode to the rescued officers. Hunter spoke in low whispers.

The other officer shook his head.

*No! Lord, please, You can't let him die.*

Her lungs felt raw from the smoke filling the air. Neil's taunts echoed in her mind. His sick pleasure in dousing her precious home with gasoline, in telling her how it would burn.

Yet, in that moment, all she'd cared about was believing her sister was still alive and seeing Josh again, telling him she was sorry.

Then when he found her and looked at her with such, such...*love,* she couldn't remember why she'd ever gotten angry with him. She loved him so much it hurt.

He hadn't returned the jewelry because he was a control freak like her brother-in-law or because he cared more about his job than her. He did it because he wanted her safe, because he was honorable, trustworthy, because he could be counted on. And she never got the chance to tell him.

Tears coursed down her cheeks.

"Hey," Hunter said. "We're going to get him out."

She nodded, willing herself to believe it, feeling a little of the peace seep back into her soul that she'd felt when she'd looked at that painting in the bedroom of Jesus cradling the lamb. She swiped at her cheeks with the back of her hand. "What about my sister? Neil said—" She choked on the memory.

"She's okay." Hunter squeezed her shoulder. "Neil beat her up pretty bad, but your sister is one tough lady. She'll be okay."

Two paramedics raced to the back of the house, pushing a gurney.

Becki cupped a hand over her mouth, afraid to

hope. What if Josh…died? Could she still believe God cared then?

Josh's words whispered through her mind. *I focus on the things that show me He does.*

She closed her eyes, shutting out the image of her grandparents' home burning. *He saved my sister. He brought Josh in time to save me. He showed me what real love looks like. "Greater love has no man than this, that he lay down his life for his friends."*

The Bible verse she'd memorized as a little girl in Sunday School, and never really understood until today, scrolled through her mind. *I'll believe, Lord. No matter what.*

She sensed Hunter moving away and opened her eyes.

He had a finger pressed to his ear, listening intently. "Copy that," he said, his expression grim.

The paramedics reappeared, pushing the gurney more slowly this time.

Becki's throat thickened, her feet glued to the ground, her heartbeat reeling. A blanket covered the body on the gurney, including…his face. "Please, God, no." Tremors overtook her.

Hunter's warm hand came to rest on her shoulder. "Neil's choices led to his death, Bec. Not yours."

"Neil?" Becki swallowed the sudden relief that bubbled up from her chest. She didn't want Neil's life to end this way, either. But if that wasn't Josh…

Too scared to ask after him, she mutely watched

the paramedics load Neil's body onto an ambulance and drive away. No sirens. No hurry. It was too late.

Hunter nudged her arm and pointed to the house. Firemen surrounded it, anchored by hoses aimed at the upper story. The front door still sat open.

Then, at the side of the house, she saw him.

She picked up her skirt and ran into his arms.

He caught her in a bear hug. "Glad to see you, too," his voice rumbled close to her ear, husky with emotion or maybe from the smoke.

She wrapped her arms around his waist and hugged him as if there was no tomorrow. "I'm sorry. I—"

Josh nudged her head up from his chest and stroked the hair from her face.

She swallowed, her heart tumbling into the depths of his tender gaze. Soot and black paint smeared his face, but he'd never looked better.

He kissed her forehead, her temple, the tip of her nose, her cheek and finally her lips.

Savoring the sweet taste of reunion, she returned his kiss, pouring out her love for him. Finally, she touched her forehead to his. "I came here hoping to find peace in the home I'd once loved so dear. I never—"

Josh released a ragged sigh. "I'm sorry we couldn't save it, Bec. I know how much—"

She touched a finger to his lips. "You didn't let me finish." She nestled into his arms. "This is home."

# EPILOGUE

On a sunny May evening, standing in a tux at the front of the church, Josh clasped Bec's hands in his and said the words he'd been longing to pronounce for ten long months. "I do."

Bec's smile widened, and his heart expanded with sheer joy.

He swept the filmy white veil from her shoulders and cradled her face in his hands, soaking in the promise of forever beaming from Bec's eyes. He lowered his head and...

"Ahem." The pastor cleared his throat. "I haven't gotten to that part yet."

The congregation tittered, and Josh looked up with a sheepish grin.

The pastor winked and resumed, "I now pronounce you man and wife." He paused dramatically. "You may *now* kiss the bride."

"Finally," Josh said, and he did just that, smiling against his bride's lips as thunderous applause mingled with laughter broke out.

Josh eased back with a contented sigh. "I love you, Mrs. Rayne."

"I love you, too," she whispered.

Josh curled her hand through the crook of his arm and turned her to the still-applauding guests. And sitting beside his sister, with tears streaming down her face, his mom applauded loudest of all.

As he led Bec up the aisle, his heart raced with anticipation, and a little trepidation, over the surprise waiting for her outside—her grandfather's Cadillac restored.

Of course, the surprise paled in comparison to the gift she'd given him last night—suggesting that, instead of rebuilding the farmhouse and selling one of their places, they combine the land...if he still wanted to farm. And maybe use the house settlement to buy back what his dad had sold off, too.

Standing at the back of the church, Mrs. O'Reilly winked at him.

The church doors opened to an honor guard of saluting officers.

Taken up by the display, Bec didn't seem to notice the officer at the curb opening the Cadillac's back door.

Josh gave her a nudge and tilted his head toward the street.

Her look of absolute delight calmed his runaway heartbeat. "Oh, Josh. It's just like Gramps and Gran's. Wherever did you hire it?" Sudden moisture glistened in her eyes.

He squeezed her hand, certain she was wishing they could have shared this day.

"Hire it?" Hunter razzed from directly behind them, already tugging at his bow tie. "He worked us like slaves. Didn't pay us a penny."

"Worked you?" Bec's forehead crinkled adorably. "That's…Gramps's car?"

Josh nodded.

"But…I don't understand. The lawyer said the insurance company wrote it off after he convinced them to pay a settlement. Did—" Bec's gaze jerked to her matron-of-honor sister. "Did you put the money I gave you into the car?"

"No, I'm as surprised as you."

No doubt Sarah had been too preoccupied with the intensive counseling she and her husband had recently started after their lengthy separation. "It's your wedding present from me," Josh explained. "I bought it at scrap value and wangled the guys into helping me repair it."

"Oh, Josh!" Bec threw her arms around his neck. "I love it. Thank you."

Curling his arms around her waist and inhaling her sweet scent, his heart soared. "And how does a cross-country tour sound for our honeymoon?"

She pulled away just enough to meet his gaze, her expression suddenly serious. "Do you promise to check the cotter pins before we set out each day?"

"Without fail."

Her lips spread into a smile more radiant than the

deepening colors of the setting sun. "Then I say it sounds like a wonderful adventure."

Josh dipped his head and whispered against her lips, "Every day with you is sure to be an adventure."

"Are you saying I'm trouble, Joshua Rayne?" she said teasingly.

"With a capital *T,* Mrs. Rayne. With a capital *T.*"

* * * * *

Dear Reader,

Writing this story turned into an unforeseen challenge as the characters veered into uncharted detours and threw roadblocks in my path. I hope you enjoyed a few surprises yourself. I had a lot of fun researching antique cars and car clubs for this story, but, regrettably, could include only a few of the many fascinating details I learned. "Horseless carriage" tours sound like wonderful adventures—worth exploring if you ever have the chance.

I'd love to hear about your own exploits. You can reach me via email at SandraOrchard@ymail.com or on Facebook at http://www.facebook.com/SandraOrchard. To learn about upcoming books and read interesting bonus features, please visit me online at www.SandraOrchard.com and sign up for my newsletter for exclusive subscriber giveaways.

Sincerely,
*Sandra Orchard*

## Questions for Discussion

1. Josh gave up his dream of becoming a farmer, but he wasn't willing to give up making his home on the family farm, even for the love of a woman. What dreams would you give up for love?

2. After losing her grandparents, Becki grows to realize that she'd never owned her grandparents' faith for herself. Are you living on borrowed faith?

3. Josh believes that not chasing after a woman who leaves shows respect for her choice, whereas his sister suggests that the woman might really want him to come after her. Have you ever kept to yourself what you'd like a loved one to do to show his or her love? Did you hope he or she would just figure it out?

4. Becki begins to feel that God is asking her to give up her grandparents' home so she can help her sister. Have you ever felt God nudging you to give something up for another? What did you do?

5. Josh's faith is strong, yet he struggles to trust God in his relationships. Instead he's established a mental checklist of criteria a woman

must meet, a checklist that keeps him from risking his heart. Is there an area of your life that you're resistant to surrender to God?

6. Becki's sister didn't want Becki to know that her husband was abusive. Do you think she was prompted by shame, embarrassment, pride or a desire to protect Becki? What might prompt you to keep something from a loved one?

7. To Josh's dismay, his friend Hunter has a tendency to speak before thinking. Does this happen to you? How might you curb the problem?

8. When Becki first arrives at her grandparents' house, happy memories flood her mind. What kind of memories are you creating with your loved ones?

9. Seeing Becki in Josh's arms fuels Neil's jealousy. He resists accepting her decision to leave him, the city, her job. Becki blames his controlling nature on his being bullied as a youth. Do you unconsciously try to overcome a deep-rooted wound in ways that might have unwelcome consequences?

10. Sunsets reminded Becki's grandmother that God is working behind the scenes even when we can't always see how. Similarly, when Becki

asks Josh how he can keep believing God cares when things go bad, he responds that he looks for the good in his circumstances. Are you facing difficult circumstances? What good might come from them?

11. As welcoming as Joshua's protective arms feel, it's important to Becki that Josh see her as a woman who can take care of herself. Are you the kind of person who prefers to look out for yourself, or do you appreciate someone looking out for you?

12. Scents are powerful memory triggers for Becki. Are there any scents that stir strong memories in you?

# LARGER-PRINT BOOKS!

## GET 2 FREE LARGER-PRINT NOVELS PLUS 2 FREE MYSTERY GIFTS

*Love Inspired*

## SUSPENSE

RIVETING INSPIRATIONAL ROMANCE

### Larger-print novels are now available...

# *ReaderService*.com

## Manage your account online!

- Review your order history
- Manage your payments
- Update your address

---

*We've designed
the Harlequin® Reader Service
website just for you.*

---

## Enjoy all the features!

- Reader excerpts from any series
- Respond to mailings and
  special monthly offers
- Discover new series available to you
- Browse the Bonus Bucks catalog
- Share your feedback

*Visit us at:*
## ReaderService.com

# The Acts

# of the Apostles

**VOLUME III**
(Chapters 15—20)

$5.00

by
**Oliver B. Greene**

The Gospel Hour, Inc., Oliver B. Greene, Director
Box 2024, Greenville, South Carolina 29602

*First printing, February 1969 — 15,000 copies*

## FOREWORD

In this third volume in our Commentary on *The Acts of the Apostles* we have covered chapters 15 through 20, beginning with the meeting of the Council in Jerusalem, covering Paul's second missionary journey and ending with that apostle's meeting with the Ephesian elders at Miletus where he gave instructions for the welfare of the churches God had used him to establish.

We note the amazing growth of the New Testament Church, the indomitable courage and absolute devotion of the early Christians.

These six chapters are rich in spiritual truth which we have tried to present with clarity and understanding, in prayerful hope that present-day Christians may find encouragement and renewed zeal in serving God amid the apostasy and modernism of this age in which we live.

Only when Christians conform to God's design will sinners be won to Christ.

The Author

# CONTENTS

# THE ACTS OF THE APOSTLES

# THE ACTS OF THE APOSTLES

## CHAPTER XV

1. And certain men which came down from Judaea taught the brethren, and said, Except ye be circumcised after the manner of Moses, ye cannot be saved.

2. When therefore Paul and Barnabas had no small dissension and disputation with them, they determined that Paul and Barnabas, and certain other of them, should go up to Jerusalem unto the apostles and elders about this question.

3. And being brought on their way by the church, they passed through Phenice and Samaria, declaring the conversion of the Gentiles: and they caused great joy unto all the brethren.

4. And when they were come to Jerusalem, they were received of the church, and of the apostles and elders, and they declared all things that God had done with them.

5. But there rose up certain of the sect of the Pharisees which believed, saying, That it was needful to circumcise them, and to command them to keep the law of Moses.

6. And the apostles and elders came together for to consider of this matter.

7. And when there had been much disputing, Peter rose up, and said unto them, Men and brethren, ye know how that a good while ago God made choice among us, that the Gentiles by my mouth should hear the word of the Gospel, and believe.

8. And God, which knoweth the hearts, bare them witness, giving them the Holy Ghost, even as he did unto us;

9. And put no difference between us and them, purifying their hearts by faith.

10. Now therefore why tempt ye God, to put a yoke upon the neck of the disciples, which neither our fathers nor we were able to bear?

11. But we believe that through the grace of the Lord Jesus Christ we shall be saved, even as they.

12. Then all the multitude kept silence, and gave audience to Barnabas and Paul, declaring what miracles and wonders God had wrought among the Gentiles by them.

13. And after they had held their peace, James answered, saying, Men and brethren, hearken unto me:

14. Simeon hath declared how God at the first did visit the Gentiles, to take out of them a people for his name.

15. And to this agree the words of the prophets; as it is written,

16. After this I will return, and will build again the tabernacle of David, which is fallen down; and I will build again the ruins thereof, and I will set it up:

17. That the residue of men might seek after the Lord, and all the Gentiles, upon whom my name is called, saith the Lord, who doeth all these things.

18. Known unto God are all his works from the beginning of the world.

19. Wherefore my sentence is, that we trouble not them, which from among the Gentiles are turned to God:

20. But that we write unto them, that they abstain from pollutions of idols, and from fornication, and from things strangled, and from blood.

21. For Moses of old time hath in every city them that preach him, being read in the synagogues every sabbath day.

22. Then pleased it the apostles and elders with the whole church, to send chosen men of their own company to Antioch with Paul and Barnabas; namely, Judas surnamed Barsabas, and Silas, chief men among the brethren:

23. And they wrote letters by them after this manner; The apostles and elders and brethren send greeting unto the brethren which are of the Gentiles in Antioch and Syria and Cilicia:

24. Forasmuch as we have heard, that certain which went out from us have troubled you with words, subverting your souls, saying, Ye must be circumcised, and keep the law: to whom we gave no such commandment:

25. It seemed good unto us, being assembled with one accord, to send chosen men unto you with our beloved Barnabas and Paul,

26. Men that have hazarded their lives for the name of our Lord Jesus Christ.

27. We have sent therefore Judas and Silas, who shall also tell you the same things by mouth.

28. For it seemed good to the Holy Ghost, and to us, to lay upon you no greater burden than these necessary things;

29. That ye abstain from meats offered to idols, and from blood, and from things strangled, and from fornication: from which if ye keep yourselves, ye shall do well. Fare ye well.

30. So when they were dismissed, they came to Antioch: and when they had gathered the multitude together, they delivered the epistle:

31. Which when they had read, they rejoiced for the consolation.

32. And Judas and Silas, being prophets also themselves, exhorted the brethren with many words, and confirmed them.

33. And after they had tarried there a space, they were let go in peace from the brethren unto the apostles.

34. Notwithstanding it pleased Silas to abide there still.

35. Paul also and Barnabas continued in Antioch, teaching and preaching the word of the Lord, with many others also.

36. And some days after Paul said unto Barnabas, Let us go again and visit our brethren in every city where we have preached the word of the Lord, and see how they do.

37. And Barnabas determined to take with them John, whose surname was Mark.

38. But Paul thought not good to take him with them, who departed from them from Pamphylia, and went not with them to the work.

39. And the contention was so sharp between them, that they departed asunder one from the other: and so Barnabas took Mark, and sailed unto Cyprus;

40. And Paul chose Silas, and departed, being recommended by the brethren unto the grace of God.

41. And he went through Syria and Cilicia, confirming the churches.

## The Council At Jerusalem

This chapter of Acts records the account of the first church council that met after the founding of the Church on the Day of Pentecost. The city of Antioch had become the new center of Christian activity, the fountainhead of the missionary ministry of the New Testament Church, and a grave problem had developed in that assembly. It was to discuss this situation that the council met in Jerusalem. Certain men from Judaea had gone to Antioch and sought to put the Gentile converts under the Law of Moses as pertaining to circumcision, maintaining that men who were not circumcised were not saved. It was deemed necessary, therefore, for representatives from the church in Antioch to meet with the church in Jerusalem to consider the serious problem thus brought about.

In order to better understand this council and what occurred there we should study Paul's letter to the Galatian church. It contains many things not given here in our present study, and for fear that many who study this commentary will not turn in their Bibles and *read* Paul's account in Galatians, I quote the entire text of chapters 1 and 2 of that epistle, so that they can be read in preparation for our studies in this chapter of Acts:

## GALATIANS

### CHAPTER 1

#### *Salutation*

1. Paul, an apostle, (not of men, neither by man, but by Jesus Christ, and God the Father, who raised him from the dead;)

2. And all the brethren which are with me, unto the churches of Galatia:

3. Grace be to you and peace from God the Father, and from our Lord Jesus Christ,

4. Who gave Himself for our sins, that He might deliver us from this present evil world, according to the will of God and our Father:

5. To whom be glory for ever and ever. Amen.

#### *The Theme and Occasion of the Epistle*

6. I marvel that ye are so soon removed from Him that called you into the grace of Christ unto another gospel:

7. Which is not another; but there be some that trouble you, and would pervert the Gospel of Christ.

8. But though we, or an angel from heaven, preach any other gospel unto you than that which we have preached unto you, let him be accursed.

9. As we said before, so say I now again, If any man preach any other gospel unto you than that ye have received, let him be accursed.

*Paul's Gospel A Revelation, Not A Tradition*

10. For do I now persuade men, or God? or do I seek to please men? for if I yet pleased men, I should not be the servant of Christ.

11. But I certify you, brethren, that the Gospel which was preached of me is not after man.

12. For I neither received it of man, neither was I taught it, but by the revelation of Jesus Christ.

13. For ye have heard of my conversation in time past in the Jews' religion, how that beyond measure I persecuted the Church of God, and wasted it:

14. And profited in the Jews' religion above many my equals in mine own nation, being more exceedingly zealous of the traditions of my fathers.

15. But when it pleased God, who separated me from my mother's womb, and called me by His grace,

16. To reveal His Son in me, that I might preach Him among the heathen; immediately I conferred not with flesh and blood:

17. Neither went I up to Jerusalem to them which were apostles before me; but I went into Arabia, and returned again unto Damascus.

18. Then after three years I went up to Jerusalem to see Peter, and abode with him fifteen days.

19. But other of the apostles saw I none, save James the Lord's brother.

20. Now the things which I write unto you, behold, before God, I lie not.

21. Afterwards I came into the regions of Syria and Cilicia;

22. And was unknown by face unto the churches of Judaea which were in Christ:

23. But they had heard only, That he which persecuted us in times past now preacheth the faith which once he destroyed.

24. And they glorified God in me.

## CHAPTER 2

1. Then fourteen years after I went up again to Jerusalem with

Barnabas, and took Titus with me also.

2. And I went up by revelation, and communicated unto them that Gospel which I preach among the Gentiles, but privately to them which were of reputation, lest by any means I should run, or had run, in vain.

3. But neither Titus, who was with me, being a Greek, was compelled to be circumcised:

4. And that because of false brethren unawares brought in, who came in privily to spy out our liberty which we have in Christ Jesus, that they might bring us into bondage:

5. To whom we gave place by subjection, no, not for an hour; that the truth of the Gospel might continue with you.

6. But of these who seemed to be somewhat, (whatsoever they were, it maketh no matter to me: God accepteth no man's person:) for they who seemed to be somewhat in conference added nothing to me:

7. But contrariwise, when they saw that the Gospel of the uncircumcision was committed unto me, as the Gospel of the circumcision was unto Peter;

8. (For He that wrought effectually in Peter to the apostleship of the circumcision, the same was mighty in me toward the Gentiles:)

9. And when James, Cephas, and John, who seemed to be pillars, perceived the grace that was given unto me, they gave to me and Barnabas the right hands of fellowship; that we should go unto the heathen, and they unto the circumcision.

10. Only they would that we should remember the poor; the same which I also was forward to do.

11. But when Peter was come to Antioch, I withstood him to the face, because he was to be blamed.

12. For before that certain came from James, he did eat with the Gentiles: but when they were come, he withdrew and separated himself, fearing them which were of the circumcision.

13. And the other Jews dissembled likewise with him; insomuch that Barnabas also was carried away with their dissimulation.

14. But when I saw that they walked not uprightly according to the truth of the Gospel, I said unto Peter before them all, If thou,

being a Jew, livest after the manner of Gentiles, and not as do
the Jews, why compellest thou the Gentiles to live as do the Jews?

*Justification Is by Faith Without Law*

15. We who are Jews by nature, and not sinners of the Gentiles,

16. Knowing that a man is not justified by the works of the
law, but by the faith of Jesus Christ, even we have believed in
Jesus Christ, that we might be justified by the faith of Christ, and
not by the works of the law: for by the works of the law shall
no flesh be justified.

17. But if, while we seek to be justified by Christ, we ourselves
also are found sinners, is therefore Christ the minister of sin? God
forbid.

18. For if I build again the things which I destroyed, I make
myself a transgressor.

19. For I through the law am dead to the law, that I might
live unto God.

20. I am crucified with Christ: nevertheless I live; yet not I,
but Christ liveth in me: and the life which I now live in the
flesh I live by the faith of the Son of God, who loved me, and
gave Himself for me.

21. I do not frustrate the grace of God: for if righteousness
come by the law, then Christ is dead in vain.

In Paul's account of the council and the necessity for
it—as recorded in these chapters from his epistle to the
Galatians—we see evidence of a great deal of dissension
and argument before an agreement was finally reached;
but in the account recorded by Luke in our present chapter in Acts we see not so much the details of the differences of opinion, but rather the harmony of the decision
to which the council finally came. In spite of the fact
that there were many grave differences—some of which
undoubtedly led to bitter words which are not recorded
here—there came a holy and marvelous fellowship as
this assembly of born again believers held forth in a
discussion based upon a master principle, and they were

able to say, "It seemed good to the Holy Spirit, and to us!"

## Legalizers From Judaea—
## The Question of Circumcision

Verse 1:    *"And certain men which came down from Judaea taught the brethren, and said, Except ye be circumcised after the manner of Moses, ye cannot be saved."*

It is interesting that these *"certain men"* are not named.    They were teachers of Judaism, contending that the Gentiles must become Jewish proselytes, embrace Jewish vows, be circumcised, and keep the Law of Moses. They said, *"Except ye be circumcised after the manner of Moses, YE CANNOT BE SAVED."* This was a grave declaration.    These men from Judaea were dogmatically declaring that salvation is not by grace through faith, but by grace through faith *PLUS circumcision.*    Such teaching among the Gentiles brought about confusion in the assembly at Antioch.

This was the beginning of the battle between law and grace—and that battle continues today.    There are many ministers who cry "Grace—*only* grace!" and in the very next breath those same ministers put Christians under law.    Such teaching will be with us until that glorious morning when the Church is called to meet Jesus in the clouds in the air!

It was because of the issue of mixing law and grace that Paul was led of the Spirit to pen his epistle to the Galatian Christians, setting forth the *truth* concerning law and grace.    In Galatians 3:1—3 he wrote, "O foolish Galatians, who hath bewitched you, that ye should not obey the truth, before whose eyes Jesus Christ hath been evidently set forth, crucified among you?    This only would I learn of you:    Received ye the Spirit by the works of the *law,* or by the hearing of *faith?*    Are ye so foolish? having begun in the *Spirit,* are ye now made

perfect by the *flesh?*"

In Galatians 5:1−6 Paul further declared that those who sought to be justified by the law "made Christ of none effect" and were fallen from grace. In other words, there is no such thing as being saved by grace *plus LAW*. If we are saved by law there is no grace, and if we are saved by grace then law does not enter into it at all. Furthermore, those who attempt to mix law and grace, teaching that we are justified by law *and* grace, are debtors to keep *the whole law* (Gal. 5:3) because the law of God given through Moses is not satisfied through partial obedience. James 2:10 declares, "Whosoever shall keep the whole law, and yet *offend in ONE point, he is guilty of ALL!*"

If we teach that men are justified by keeping the Law of Moses, we must also teach that they must keep *all* of the law. There must be perfect obedience, perfect holiness, and righteousness of character—requirements that only the Lord Jesus Christ could meet. Therefore *"Christ is the END of the law for righteousness to every one that believeth"* (Rom. 10:4).

If mortal man could give perfect obedience to God's law, if by nature he had within him the ability to live *a perfect life* by that law, then he would have no need of a Saviour, no need of the blood of Jesus or the regenerating power of the Holy Spirit. If righteousness could come by the law *"then Christ is dead in vain"* (Gal. 2:21).

But quite the contrary is true! No man has ever kept the law, no man ever *could* keep it—"for there is no difference: *for all have sinned,* and come short of the glory of God" (Rom. 3:22, 23). Therefore it was a divine necessity that Christ die to satisfy God's law and meet the demands of God's righteousness and holiness. "Christ died for our sins according to the Scriptures" (I Cor. 15:3), He was "raised again for our justification" (Rom. 4:25), and because of this we have *perfect salvation:* "By

Him all that believe are justified from *all things*, from which ye *could not* be justified by *the Law of Moses"* (Acts 13:39).

Jesus made it plain that perfect love to God is the greatest commandment, the first requirement of the law (Matt. 22:36—40). Perfect love produces perfect obedience. Perfect love manifested in perfect obedience produces sinlessness in life—and *apart from divine nature* that is impossible! Perfect *obedience* cannot be produced by law any more than perfect *love* can be produced by law. All the law in the world cannot make a mother love her child, nor can any law or combination of laws force a child to love its mother. Love is born in the breast of the child by the attitude of the mother in their relationship to each other. By like token, all the thunder of Sinai cannot make the natural man love God. The natural man is depraved, dead in sins, alienated from God through the disobedience of Adam. "Herein is love, not that we loved God, but that *He* loved *us*, and sent His Son to be the propitiation for our sins. . . . *We love Him because HE FIRST LOVED US"* (I John 4:10, 19).

When we are born again, when we have life through faith in the shed blood of Jesus, we do not need law to command us to love God! We love Him because we have His life within our hearts, and that life will bring us into loving fellowship with God and with His Son.

To Timothy Paul declared, "The law is not made for a *righteous* man, but for the lawless and disobedient, for the ungodly and for sinners, for unholy and profane, for murderers of fathers and murderers of mothers, for manslayers, for whoremongers, for them that defile themselves with mankind, for menstealers, for liars, for perjured persons, *and if there be ANY OTHER THING that is contrary to sound doctrine, according to the glorious Gospel of the blessed God*, which was committed to my trust" (I Tim. 1:9—11).

Born again believers possess imputed righteousness—

the righteousness of God in Christ (II Cor. 5:21). The born again believer is not under law; he is under *grace,* and the law has no claim on him (Rom. 6:14). In Romans 2:14 the Apostle Paul declared, *"When the Gentiles, WHICH HAVE NOT THE LAW, do by nature the things contained in the law, these, having not the law, are a law unto themselves."* The law was never given to Gentiles, it was given to only one nation—*Israel.* In Deuteronomy 33:1, 2 we read, "This is the blessing, wherewith Moses the man of God blessed the children of Israel before his death. And he said, The Lord came from Sinai, and rose up from Seir unto them; He shined forth from mount Paran, and He came with ten thousands of saints: *from His right hand went a fiery LAW for them."*

Nehemiah 9:13, 14 declares, *"Thou camest down also upon mount Sinai, and spakest with them from heaven, and gavest them right JUDGMENTS, and true LAWS, good STATUTES and COMMANDMENTS: and madest known unto them thy holy sabbath, and commandedst them PRECEPTS, STATUTES, AND LAWS, by the hand of Moses thy servant."*

The law was given that every mouth might be stopped and the whole world stand guilty before God, "for *by the law* is the knowledge of sin" (Rom. 3:19, 20). God gave the law to Israel (knowing that they could not keep it) in order to show them the exceeding sinfulness of man and bring out the transgression in even the elect of God. *"Wherefore then serveth the law?* It was added *because of transgressions,* till the Seed should come to whom the promise was made; and it was ordained by angels in the hand of a mediator"* (Gal. 3:19).

If the children of Israel failed to keep the law and are shown *by the law* to be guilty sinners, then surely the Gentiles (who were never brought nigh to God *ceremonially*) are lost and without hope! But Jesus brought grace for Jew and Gentile. As John the Beloved explains,

*"The law* was given by Moses, but *grace and truth came BY JESUS CHRIST"* (John 1:17).

Through pure, unmeasured, undeserved grace God brought the children of Israel out of Egyptian bondage and led them to Sinai under the conditionless government of this covenant with father Abraham. Then at Sinai He tested Israel and inquired whether they would continue *in grace, dependent upon HIM,* or if they would endeavor to earn their way into the promised land by faithfulness and obedience. The people responded to God's inquiry, "All that the Lord hath spoken we will do!" (Please read Exodus 19:1—8.)

So the Lord drew a line around Mount Sinai and put the people back from the line, back from Himself (Ex. 19:9—13). Then He came down upon Mount Sinai and called Moses up to the top of the mount. There the law was given. "Moses was in the mount forty days and forty nights" (Ex. 24:18), "and *(God) gave unto Moses, when He had made an end of communing with him upon mount Sinai, two tables of testimony, tables of stone, WRITTEN WITH THE FINGER OF GOD"* (Ex. 31:18). Please read Exodus chapters 20 through 31 for full details of God's dealing with His people in the giving of the law.

Now note this, beloved: Before Moses *returned* to the people they had already broken the very heart of God's law! They repudiated the one true and living God and fell down in worship before a golden calf:

"And when the people saw that Moses delayed to come down out of the mount, the people gathered themselves together unto Aaron, and said unto him, Up, make us gods, which shall go before us; for as for this Moses, the man that brought us up out of the land of Egypt, we wot not what is become of him.

"And Aaron said unto them, Break off the golden earrings, which are in the ears of your wives, of your sons, and of your daughters, and bring them unto me.

And all the people brake off the golden earrings which were in their ears, and brought them unto Aaron. And he received them at their hand, and fashioned it with a graving tool, after he had made it a molten calf: and they said, These be thy gods, O Israel, which brought thee up out of the land of Egypt" (Ex. 32:1—4).

When Moses came down from the mount he heard the sounds of music and laughter. As he drew near the camp he saw the golden calf, and the people dancing. "And Moses' anger waxed hot, and he cast the tables out of his hands, and brake them beneath the mount" (Ex. 32:15—19).

Moses returned to Mount Sinai and the tables of stone were rewritten, that he might place them in the ark under the mercy seat and thereby typically obtain atonement for the rebellious people of Israel (Ex. 34:1—4; 40:20).

The law God gave Moses for His people was intended as a ruler is to a crooked line. If we place a yardstick by the side of a crooked line, the straight edge of the yardstick will reveal the crookedness of the line. By like token, the law showed how evil and sinful Israel was. As a mirror is to our face, so the law reveals the total depravity of man; and it was given to show for a time (even in this day) the helplessness of the natural man as pertaining to the holiness of God.

Paul expressed it this way: "Wherefore the law was our schoolmaster to bring us unto Christ, that we might be justified by faith. But after that faith is come, we are no longer under a schoolmaster" (Gal. 3:24, 25). "Schoolmaster" (or pedagogue) speaks of the servant or slave who conducted the children to school; but the authority of the servant ceased when the children became adult. Thus the law was God's schoolmaster, taking His people to school to learn their total depravity, teaching them that salvation must come from without.

This was accomplished in two ways: (1) morally,

(2) ceremonially. From the *moral* aspect the law revealed the absolute helplessness of the natural man—that is, apart from God's miracle in the heart, man cannot meet the *moral* demands of the law. From the *ceremonial* aspect, the law established the sacrifices which were a type of the promised Lamb of God who *fulfilled* all types and shadows. In Galatians 4:4, 5 we read, "When the fulness of the time was come, *God sent forth His Son,* made of a woman, made under the law, to redeem them that were under the law, that we might receive the adoption of sons."

In their moral helplessness Israel was like all other nations. Jesus on the cross was the only ground of approach to a holy God, the indication to them that only by the faith that claimed and offered Him as a substitute could they be saved. Every sacrifice, ceremony, feast, and holy day pointed to the coming of Christ. Therefore Jews and Gentiles alike are saved through faith in the finished work of the Lamb of God—*MINUS the works of the law.*

After faith is come we are no longer under a "school-master" because we are "children of God by faith in Christ Jesus" (Gal. 3:25, 26). *Jesus IS that faith:* "In the beginning was *the WORD,* and the Word was with God, and the Word was God. . . . And the Word was made flesh, and dwelt among us, (and we beheld His glory, the glory as of the only begotten of the Father,) full of grace and truth" (John 1:1, 14). "So then faith cometh by hearing, and hearing by *the Word of God*" (Rom. 10:17).

In Galatians 2:20 Paul testified, "I am crucified with Christ: nevertheless I live; yet not I, but Christ liveth in me: *and the life which I now live in the flesh I live by THE FAITH OF THE SON OF GOD,* who loved me, and gave Himself for me."

We are *saved* by faith (Eph. 2:8), we *live* by faith (Rom. 1:17), we *overcome* by faith (I John 5:4), we *walk*

by faith (II Cor. 5:7), *and whatsoever is NOT of faith is SIN* (Rom. 14:23).

The Law of Moses, moral or ceremonial, has nothing to do with salvation. The law was never *intended* as the grounds of salvation—"by the deeds of the law there shall no flesh be justified in (God's) sight . . . a man is justified by faith *without* the deeds of the law" (Rom. 3:20, 28). The law has nothing to do with saving us, keeping us saved, or making us holy. We are saved by God's grace, we are justified by God's grace minus the works of the law. *"We are HIS workmanship,* created in Christ Jesus *unto* good works, which God hath before ordained that we should walk in them" (Eph. 2:10). *"NOT by works of righteousness which we have done, but according to His mercy He saved us,* by the washing of regeneration, and renewing of the Holy Ghost" (Tit. 3:5).

### Paul, Barnabas, and Other Believers
### From Antioch Go to Jerusalem

Verse 2: *"When therefore Paul and Barnabas had no small dissension and disputation with them, they determined that Paul and Barnabas, and certain other of them, should go up to Jerusalem unto the apostles and elders about this question."*

*"Dissension"* sometimes denotes very hot controversy, as in Acts 23:7, 10 where between the Pharisees and Sadducees there arose a dissension so violent that had the chief captain not rescued Paul he would have been "pulled in pieces."

However, the original language in our present verse indicates that while there was earnest and warm discussion, there was no display of hot tempers or unchristian behavior. Important principles were at stake. The Judaizers demanded circumcision after the Law of Moses as part of the doctrine of salvation, while Paul and

Barnabas preached grace minus the rites of the Mosaic law.    Therefore it is understandable that when these ministers of grace, led of the Spirit, refused to give ground to the legalizers, the discussion was marked by sternness and determination from both factions.    But it was not a church "fuss."    It was an orderly conference where heated discussion was carried on in a Christian manner.

After all, it is the solemn duty of God's ministers to defend the truth, and a preacher is not worth two cents if he cannot speak with some "heat" in defense of the Gospel.    The only effective way to oppose error is to advance the truth, and Paul and Barnabas did exactly that.    In Philippians 1:17 Paul gave personal testimony that he was "set for the defence of the Gospel."

God's Word gives solemn warning—not only against *preaching or teaching* error, but also against *supporting* those who do teach it.  In II John 7—11 we read, *"Many deceivers are entered into the world, who confess not that Jesus Christ is come in the flesh.  This is a deceiver and an antichrist.*  Look to yourselves, that we lose not those things which we have wrought, but that we receive a full reward.    Whosoever transgresseth, and abideth not in the doctrine of Christ, hath not God.  He that abideth in the doctrine of Christ, he hath both the Father and the Son. *If there come any unto you, and bring not this doctrine, RECEIVE HIM NOT INTO YOUR HOUSE, neither bid him God speed:  FOR HE THAT BIDDETH HIM GOD SPEED IS PARTAKER OF HIS EVIL DEEDS!"*

When it became evident that there was no hope of settling the question of law and grace in the assembly at Antioch, it was decided that Paul and Barnabas "and certain other of them" from that assembly should go to Jerusalem *"unto the apostles and elders about this question."*  This was not for the purpose of debating further among themselves, but to lay the matter before the

apostles and elders in the church in Jerusalem.

Then too, some of the apostles were in Jerusalem. From Galatians 1:18,19 and 2:9 we know that Peter, James, and John—together with the elders—appear now as the governing body of the infant Church. The church in Jerusalem was also an *older* church and would be regarded by the Judaizers as a source of authority since its membership included many Jews who were experienced in the law as well as having heard the words of Jesus when He tabernacled among men. They would therefore be better acquainted with the pure doctrine of salvation by grace through faith.

There is also a possibility that the Judaizers thought the Jews in the church in Jerusalem would decide in their favor, and this made them perfectly willing to take the question to Jerusalem and place it before the believers there. (The Scripture does not tell us whether or not these men were born again believers. I think they *could* have been believers who had simply not come to fully understand that since they were saved by grace through faith there was no longer any need for them to observe the rituals of the law such as the rite of circumcision. Force of habit could have made them feel that circumcision should be added to grace, or they could be the false teachers Paul spoke of in Galatians 2:4. At any rate, they were not of the violent opposition groups such as had opposed and persecuted the believers to the extent of stoning them or driving them out of town.)

Most Bible scholars agree that this journey to Jerusalem is the same as that spoken of by Paul in Galatians 2:10, which he mentions as having occurred fourteen years after his conversion. Also in Galatians 2:3 he names *Titus* as having been with him on that trip, and of course Titus traveled extensively with Paul in the later years of his ministry. Titus was a *Greek*, and the question to be settled in Jerusalem was whether or not the ceremonial laws of Moses were binding on Gentile believers.

Verse 3: *"And being brought on their way by the church, they passed through Phenice and Samaria, declaring the conversion of the Gentiles: and they caused great joy unto all the brethren."*

*"Being brought on their way by the church"* means that they were attended and conducted by believers in the various cities and villages through which they passed. This was the custom in that day, as set forth by Paul in I Corinthians 16:5—11:

"Now I will come unto you, when I shall pass through Macedonia: for I do pass through Macedonia. And it may be that I will abide, yea, and winter with you, that ye may bring me on my journey whithersoever I go. For I will not see you now by the way; but I trust to tarry a while with you, if the Lord permit. But I will tarry at Ephesus until Pentecost. For a great door and effectual is opened unto me, and there are many adversaries.

"Now if Timotheus come, see that he may be with you without fear: for he worketh the work of the Lord, as I also do. Let no man therefore despise him: but conduct him forth in peace, that he may come unto me: for I look for him with the brethren."

John the Beloved also wrote, "Beloved, thou doest faithfully whatsoever thou doest to the brethren, and to strangers; which have borne witness of thy charity before the church: whom if thou bring forward on their journey after a godly sort, thou shalt do well: because that for His name's sake they went forth, taking nothing of the Gentiles. We therefore ought to receive such, that we might be fellowhelpers to the truth" (III John 5—8).

Phenice (or Phoenecia) and Samaria were directly on the road to Jerusalem, but notice: As the group from Antioch passed through those cities they declared *"the conversion of the Gentiles."* Thus they brought *"great joy"* to other believers along the way. Jesus declared that there is rejoicing in the presence of the angels over

the salvation of one sinner (Luke 15:10). If there is *rejoicing in heaven* when a soul is saved, certainly *Christians in this life should rejoice* when we hear the good news of revival where sinners are being converted and becoming members of the New Testament Church!

Verses 4 and 5: *"And when they were come to Jerusalem, they were received of the church, and of the apostles and elders, and they declared all things that God had done with them. But there rose up certain of the sect of the Pharisees which believed, saying, That it was needful to circumcise them, and to command them to keep the law of Moses."*

When this little group from Antioch arrived in Jerusalem the church there received them in a friendly manner, hospitality was extended to them, they were shown every Christian courtesy and kindness. Paul explained, "When James, Cephas, and John, who seemed to be pillars, perceived the grace that was given unto me, *they gave to me and Barnabas the right hands of fellowship;* that we should go unto the heathen, and they unto the circumcision" (Gal. 2:9).

*"And they declared all things that God had done with them."* They testified to the remarkable conversions they had seen among the Gentiles and the evidence of fruit-bearing they had witnessed. They had firsthand information that these Gentiles loved and served the Lord just as the Jewish believers did.

*"But there rose up certain of the sect of the Pharisees which believed."* It is generally believed by Bible authorities that this statement does not refer to the men who caused dissension in the church at Antioch. We note that these were Pharisees *"which believed,"* and no such statement is made of the Judaizers who caused the trouble in Antioch. It seems evident that the statement refers to a group of Pharisees in Jerusalem who, though believing, also resolved to abide by the Law of

Moses and to demand that all other Christian converts do the same. Therefore they maintained that it was needful to circumcise the Gentiles and require them to keep the Law of Moses.

In the religious atmosphere of that day this was only natural. To the believing Jews, Christianity was the fulfillment and continuation of the old economy. Thus was the Jew, in his mental attitude, definitely distinguished from the new converts. He did not think of the Gospel message as the new converts thought—those who were converted in Antioch, Iconium, Lystra, and Derbe. The salvation Jesus brought to the hearts of *these people* was real and wonderful. It filled them with joy and zeal. But to the mind of the Hebrew believers the religion of Jesus was not something that *destroyed* the religion of their fathers, but was rather the *fulfillment* of that religion. To the believing Jew, Christianity had grown out of the religion of the Hebrew fathers, it was the continuation of one divine movement. The Jew did not fully understand—and therefore could not accept—the fact that Christianity was not a continuation of *anything*. It was a completely new economy, and *through Christ* men became new creations.

When the Apostle Paul preached in the synagogue in Antioch of Pisidia he dealt with the great doctrines of the unity of God. He did this in order to capture the minds of the Gentiles and get their attention so that he could present *the grace of God;* but he also declared that *the entire Hebrew movement* saw its fulfillment in Christ. However, in Antioch of Syria there was no synagogue; and since Paul did not preach in a synagogue there his message in that city was not influenced by the tradition of the Jews as related to the religion of the Hebrew fathers. The movement in the city of Antioch of Syria had not even an *apostolic condition* behind it—it began with the message of Christ's finished work, and the men of Antioch were therefore quite careless as to the things

*preceding* that finished work. They had come in contact with the message of life, liberty, and joy and they had no interest in the rite of circumcision nor in any other ceremony of the old economy.

With a bit of reasoning we can see the differences between the born again Jew and the born again Greek (Gentile). The believing Jews looked upon Christianity as the direct outcome, continuation, and fulfillment of the religion of their fathers, and when the Jews from Judaea came to Antioch and other cities and found *Gentiles* who testified to the saving grace of God, such discovery *upset* the believing Jew. These Gentiles had no relationship with Hebrew religion or tradition. For *them,* Christianity began with their knowledge of Christ, and even the *converted* Jew found this hard to accept immediately. Thus we see the naturalness of the difficulty between the believing Jews and the believing Greeks.

Very probably these believing Jews were perfectly sincere in declaring that the Gentile Christians could not be saved by beginning in the *middle* of a process. The Jews had followed the religion of their fathers step by step, they had faithfully observed the ceremonies of the law, the rituals and holy days, whereas the Greeks knew nothing of the law, they were aliens from the commonwealth of Israel and strangers to the covenants. Yet they claimed to be saved *in an instant* simply by trusting in the death, burial, and resurrection of Jesus! The Jews simply could not understand this, and therefore they declared that the Gentiles *must* be brought into and prepared for salvation by conforming to the Law of Moses and the rites of the old economy.

Of course the fact of their *sincerity* did not make them right, but from infancy they had been trained in their traditions and rituals, and it was not easy for them to discard the old way of life in a moment. Even *today,* when children are brought up in homes where they are consistently trained in a religion that majors on works

instead of grace, it is extremely difficult to win those children to Jesus by simple faith. It is much easier to win a drunkard to Christ, it is much easier to win someone who has never professed religion at all, than it is to win a religionist who since babyhood has been trained in error.

The old Jewish economy set forth denial and sacrifice; but the new economy declared liberty, life, and joy through the free gift of God—the death of His Son on the cross. When Saul of Tarsus met Jesus on the road to Damascus and believed in Him, he found that through the bondage of Christ he had liberty, and through the death of Christ he had life. Therefore he testified, *"I am crucified with Christ:* nevertheless I live—yet *not I,* but *Christ liveth in me:* and the life which I now live in the flesh I live by the faith of the Son of God, who loved me, and gave Himself for me"* (Gal. 2:20).

Circumcision was ordained of God as an outward and visible sign that Israel was separated unto God, a people dependent upon Him. All that they were and all they were able to accomplish in this world was because of God, through His power and His government over them. This was the original purpose of circumcision, but through the years the Hebrew people had entirely missed its meaning. That for which they were now prepared to fight was an act of *self-righteousness.* In its original meaning circumcision had nothing to do with salvation, and in the days of the infant Church, when the apostles were preaching *salvation by grace through faith plus nothing,* circumcision (and all other rites and ceremonies of the old economy) had become an evasion of the true purpose of God.

Verse 6: *"And the apostles and elders came together for to consider of this matter."*

This gathering was in accordance with the authority Jesus gave in Matthew 18:19, 20: "If two of you shall

agree on earth as touching any thing that they shall ask, it shall be done for them of my Father which is in heaven. For where two or three are gathered together in my name, there am I in the midst of them.''

From verses 12, 22, and 23 of this chapter we conclude that the entire church in Jerusalem gathered for this occasion; therefore the entire church took part in deciding the case. The tone of the language here also leads us to believe that they did not meet to quarrel, or to decide the matter arbitrarily, but that they came together to deliberate, to hold open discussion, and to hear the views of the elders and the apostles. The final result of the council would then be submitted to the church in Antioch.

### Peter's Argument For Christian Liberty

Verse 7: *"And when there had been much disputing, Peter rose up, and said unto them, Men and brethren, ye know how that a good while ago God made choice among us, that the Gentiles by my mouth should hear the Word of the Gospel, and believe.''*

That there was *"much disputing"* does not necessarily mean that these people were arguing in anger. They were deliberating, inquiring, discussing the matter under consideration.

*"Peter rose up, and said unto them . . . ."* Peter could have been the oldest of the apostles, and other Scriptures indicate that he was accustomed to acting as spokesman for the group. This was true at Pentecost (Acts 2:14), it was true when Peter and John encountered the lame man at the temple gate (Acts 3:1—11). Peter also had firsthand evidence that God saved Gentiles without Mosaic rites (Acts chapter 10) and he knew it would be unscriptural and contrary to the will of God to impose such rites on these Gentiles who had been converted and received the Holy Spirit as demonstrated in the household of Cor-

nelius. It is to his experience there that he refers in the last part of this verse.

*"God made choice among us."* Of all the apostles who *could* have gone to the home of Cornelius, God chose Peter and sent him into a Gentile household that through his message Gentiles *"should hear the Word of the Gospel and believe."* This was the first instance of Gentiles' being converted and accepted into the New Testament Church and it was important that the council be reminded of the conversion of Cornelius and all who were in his house.

Verses 8 and 9: *"And God, which knoweth the hearts, bare them witness, giving them the Holy Ghost, even as He did unto us; and put no difference between us and them, purifying their hearts by faith."*

God knows the hearts of all men (Acts 1:24). He knew whether these Gentiles were true converts or not. He *"bare them witness, giving them the Holy Ghost"* just as He had given the Holy Ghost to the Jews in the upper room at Pentecost. Thus did He testify that the Gentiles were true converts:

"While Peter yet spake these words, the Holy Ghost fell on all them which heard the Word. And they of the circumcision which believed were astonished, as many as came with Peter, because that on the Gentiles also was poured out the gift of the Holy Ghost. For they heard them speak with tongues, and magnify God. Then answered Peter, Can any man forbid water, that these should not be baptized, which have received the Holy Ghost as well as we? And he commanded them to be baptized in the name of the Lord . . ." (Acts 10:44—48). Most assuredly God would not have poured out the Holy Ghost upon people who were not truly born again!

*". . . and put no difference between us and them."* Peter made a bold declaration here. These Gentiles had not been circumcised, he did not command them *to be*

*circumcised;* but even though they did not conform to the Law of Moses God gave them the Holy Spirit, thus showing (contrary to what the men from Judaea taught in Antioch) that observance of the Law of Moses was *not* essential to salvation. In other words, Peter stood up in the council and declared that he personally witnessed the conversion of Gentiles who were *not* circumcised, and that God had purified their hearts by faith just as He justified and purified the hearts of the *Jews* who were saved by faith. Peter clearly sets forth the Gospel truth that God purifies the heart and saves the soul—not through external rites or ceremonies, but by simple faith in the finished work of the Lamb of God.

Verse 10: *"Now therefore why tempt ye God, to put a yoke upon the neck of the disciples, which neither our fathers nor we were able to bear?"*

Peter's message was not the message of a trained theologian. He was not arguing a doctrine, he was not entering into a delicate and difficult discussion concerning rites and ceremonies; but we must give credit where credit is due. Peter contributed two things to the discussion: (1) He stated a definite fact; (2) he stated a deduction. It was a fact that God had sent him to the Gentiles, he had delivered God's message, and God had given His Spirit to the Gentiles exactly as He had given the Spirit to believing Jews on the Day of Pentecost, "making no distinction." Peter therefore drew the deduction that these men who demanded circumcision as essential to salvation *should not tempt God.*

What does it mean to tempt God? To tempt God is to know the *will* of God, know what He says, and refuse to follow His will, obey His Word, or accept His guidance. When Jesus met the devil on the Mount of Temptation Satan said, *"IF thou be the Son of God,* cast thyself down: for it is written, He shall give His angels charge concerning thee: and in their hands they shall

bear thee up, lest at any time thou dash thy foot against a stone." Jesus replied, "It is written again, Thou shalt not *tempt* the Lord thy God" (Matt. 4:6, 7).

Jesus did not need to leap from the pinnacle of the temple and reach the ground unharmed in order to decide whether or not He was the Son of God! *He KNEW who He was.* He knew His Father's will, and it was *not* God's will that He heed Satan's suggestion.

Peter's application of that truth was simply that since God had given the Gentiles grace without ceremony, since He had given them the Holy Spirit without ceremony and without observance of the Law of Moses, the Jews must not tempt God by refusing to obey His will and follow His clear guidance. Peter's assertion was, "God has put His stamp of approval upon the ministry of those who had preached to the Gentiles, God has bestowed the Holy Ghost upon the Gentiles without circumcision or ceremony, and we dare not forbid or reject that which God has accepted."

"... *to put a YOKE upon the neck of the disciples.*" A yoke signifies anything burdensome or oppressive. For example, in I Timothy 6:1 it is a symbol of slavery: "Let as many servants as are *under the yoke* count their own masters worthy of all honour, that the name of God and His doctrine be not blasphemed."

In Lamentations 1:14 the yoke was a symbol of punishment: "*The yoke of my transgressions* is bound by His hand: they are wreathed, and come up upon my neck: He hath made my strength to fall, the Lord hath delivered me into their hands, from whom I am not able to rise up."

In Lamentations 3:27 the yoke symbolizes affliction: "It is good for a man that he should *bear the yoke* in his youth."

In Galatians 5:1 Paul admonished the Galatian believers, "*Stand fast* therefore in the liberty wherewith Christ hath made us *free,* and *be not entangled again*

*with the YOKE OF BONDAGE!"*

In our present verse a yoke refers to the burdensome Mosaic ceremonies which would infringe on—or rob the people of—their freedom and Christian liberty as sons of God, in direct contradiction to Christ's invitation, "Come unto me, all ye that labour and are heavy laden, and I will give you rest. *Take MY yoke upon you,* and learn of me; for I am meek and lowly in heart: and ye shall find rest unto your souls. For *MY YOKE is easy,* and my burden is light" (Matt. 11:28—30).

". . . *which neither our fathers nor we were able to bear."* Peter reminded the council that the Israelite fathers had not been able to bear these burdens of the law, they had broken every detail of the law; and since they had found the law so oppressive and painful, why attempt to impose the same yoke upon Gentile believers? They should be rejoicing that Jesus had fulfilled every jot and tittle of the law and had set believers *free* from the curse of the law. Jesus Himself said, "Think not that I am come to *destroy* the law, or the prophets: I am not come to destroy, *but to FULFIL"* (Matt. 5:17).

Then in Romans 10:4 the apostle to the Gentiles declared, *"Christ* is the *end of the law* for righteousness to every one that believeth!"

Verse 11: *"But we believe that through the grace of the Lord Jesus Christ we shall be saved, even as they."*

*"Through the grace of the Lord Jesus Christ"* is the only way for either *Jew OR Gentile* to be saved. Since Christ fulfilled every jot and tittle of the law and became the end of the law for righteousness to all who believe, these ceremonies are no longer necessary because we are complete in Him (Col. 2:9, 10). Since we are saved by the mercies of God through Jesus Christ our Saviour—not by ceremony—why attempt to impose the burden of

such ceremonies upon those whom God has set free through His mercy and grace?

## Testimony of Paul and Barnabas

Verse 12:   *"Then all the multitude kept silence, and gave audience to Barnabas and Paul, declaring what miracles and wonders God had wrought among the Gentiles by them."*

*"All the multitude"* is indicative that the entire assembly of believers in Jerusalem had gathered to hear the discussion of the council.   When Peter had finished speaking there was silence in the assembly as Paul and Barnabas also declared *"what miracles and wonders God had wrought among the Gentiles BY THEM."*   In other words, Paul and Barnabas said "Amen!" to Peter's testimony.   They had witnessed those same things many times over in the cities where they had preached the Gospel of grace.   They had witnessed miracle after miracle—all apart from ceremony, ritual, or any part of the old economy.   Wherever these two men had gone in their missionary work God had given grace and the gift of the Holy Spirit, and had gloriously saved the Gentiles upon whom some men would now put the yoke of bondage to the Law of Moses!

The legalizers had made the religion of the most high God a religion subservient to the observance of external rites.   Paul, Hebrew of the Hebrews, himself once in bondage under the law, saw the peril of grafting a ritual onto the New Testament Church.   He saw the danger of putting a rite or ceremony in the place of essential spiritual life through the miracle of the new birth and the power of the Word of God.   God is a jealous God (Ex. 20:5), and Paul displayed godly jealousy for the pure Gospel of God's grace.   He could not bear the thought of substituting ritual for the Holy Spirit and the miracle of the new birth.   It was this jealousy that later inspired

his stern and pointed denunciation of Peter as set forth in Galatians 2:11, 12.    To Paul this was a grave matter having to do with the cardinal truths of Christianity, the very fundamentals of the New Testament faith.

### James Testifies Before the Council:
### The Outcalling of the Gentiles
### Agrees With God's Promises to Israel

Verses 13 and 14:    *"And after they had held their peace, James answered, saying, Men and brethren, hearken unto me:    Simeon hath declared how God at the first did visit the Gentiles, to take out of them a people for His name."*

The speaker here is James "the less," son of Alphaeus, mentioned several times in the book of Acts along with the other apostles.    We find reference to him in Acts 12:17 and 21:18, also in Galatians 1:19 and 2:9—12.    Most Bible authorities believe that James was perhaps next to Peter in age, and that he had spent most of his life in Jerusalem.

The words he spoke here constitute one of the most important dispensational passages in the entire New Testament.    He states the divine purpose of Almighty God for this Church Age in His eternal program—*the taking out from among the Gentiles "a people for His name."*    This process has been going on since the day when the Holy Ghost came upon the one hundred and twenty in the upper room.    The Church was not put here to convert the world, and the preaching of the Gospel has never converted everyone who heard it; but it always reaches some.

*"Simeon hath declared how God at the first did visit the Gentiles."*    The first visit of God to the Gentiles was in the house of Cornelius when Simon Peter delivered the Gospel message and all in that household were saved. Since that day Gentiles have been saved by millions.

Verse 15:   *"And to this agree the words of the prophets; as it is written."*

It was a very material point with the Jews to inquire whether this that had occurred among the Gentiles was in accord with the prophecies contained in their Scriptures.    It should be the habit of Christians today to take the message they hear from the pulpit on Sunday morning and compare it with the Word of God.    Liberals and modernists have added to and taken from the Scriptures until many times it is difficult to recognize what they read as a passage from the Bible.    The prophet Isaiah said of such, "If they speak not according to this Word, it is because there is *no light in them"* (Isa. 8:20).    Whatever is not in accord with the Word of God should not be supported by God's people.

However James declared that *"the words of the prophets" agree* with the calling out of the Gentiles.    The prophecies were penned under inspiration of the Holy Spirit and they set forth what would occur among the Gentiles before the glorious period promised to the Jews— the Millennium when King Jesus would sit on the throne of David and the knowledge of the Lord would cover the earth as the waters now cover the sea.

Verse 16:    *"After this I will return, and will build again the tabernacle of David, which is fallen down; and I will build again the ruins thereof, and I will set it up."*

Although the prophets did not fully understand what they prophesied, they declared that God would visit the Gentiles and take out of them a people for His name. Then after the Gentile bride, the New Testament Church, is complete and is taken out of the world, Jesus will return and will *"build again the tabernacle of David."* Amos prophesied, "In that day will I raise up the tabernacle of David that is fallen, and close up the breaches thereof; and I will raise up his ruins, and I will build

it as in the days of old: that they may possess the remnant of Edom, and of all the heathen, which are called by my name, saith the Lord that doeth this" (Amos 9:11, 12).

The Hebrew language of Amos differs widely here, but the Spirit enabled James to give the full interpretation of the prophetic words—i. e., that according to the words of the prophets God had included the Gentiles in this glorious salvation, thereby making them His children even as the Jews.

God's prophet Amos minutely described the calamities that would come upon the nation Israel because of their sins. They would be scattered and driven out of their land, and this implied that the Holy City—even the temple itself—would be destroyed. But there would come a day when Jesus would return to recover them from desolation, dispersion, and destruction. He would rebuild the Holy City and the temple, He would restore the blessings—and the blessings would descend not only upon Israel, but upon others also. *"The remnant of Edom,"* the heathen upon whom God's name is called, would also be partakers of the blessings, the mercies, and the glorious peace that God would bestow upon His people Israel.

Then after that glorious period, *prosperity and permanent blessings* would be upon them and upon all the righteous, as prophesied in Amos 9:13—15:

"Behold, the days come, saith the Lord, that the plowman shall overtake the reaper, and the treader of grapes him that soweth seed; and the mountains shall drop sweet wine, and all the hills shall melt. And I will bring again the captivity of my people of Israel, and they shall build the waste cities, and inhabit them; and they shall plant vineyards, and drink the wine thereof; they shall also make gardens, and eat the fruit of them. And I will plant them upon their land, and they shall no more be pulled up out of their land which I

have given them, saith the Lord thy God."

*"The tabernacle of David . . . ."* The promise to Israel
is that God will restore their former glory and splendor.
The reference to the temple speaks of all of the magnificence, splendor, and blessings God had showered
upon His people under the reign of Solomon and David
as long as they served Him wholeheartedly. God was
compelled to judge His people because of their sin, they
had been driven to the four corners of the earth and to
every island of the sea; but after the Church Age comes
to a close and the Church, the bride of Christ, is caught
out of the world, Jesus will return as King of kings and
Lord of lords, and He will restore the splendor and
blessings Israel once knew.

The tabernacle of David *"is fallen down."* In Matthew 24:2 Jesus declared to His disciples, "There shall
not be left here one stone upon another, that shall not
be thrown down." This was fulfilled in 70 A. D. when
Titus the Roman destroyed the temple and leveled the
city of Jerusalem. Today the city itself has been rebuilt,
but the magnificent temple has *not* been restored and
the Mosque of Omar now stands on the ground where
the temple once stood. But when Jesus comes to reign
He will rebuild the temple, restore its magnificence, and
all of the spiritual blessings of Jehovah God will be
poured out upon Israel.

The Prophet Isaiah tells about the glorious kingdom
which will be established here on earth when Jesus comes
to reign as King of kings and Lord of lords:

"And there shall come forth a rod out of the stem of
Jesse, and a Branch shall grow out of his roots: . . . The
wolf also shall dwell with the lamb, and the leopard
shall lie down with the kid; and the calf and the young
lion and the fatling together; and a little child shall lead
them. And the cow and the bear shall feed; their young
ones shall lie down together: and the lion shall eat
straw like the ox. And the sucking child shall play on

the hole of the asp, and the weaned child shall put his hand on the cockatrice' den. They shall not hurt nor destroy in all my holy mountain: for the earth shall be full of the knowledge of the Lord, as the waters cover the sea.

"And in that day there shall be a root of Jesse, which shall stand for an ensign of the people; to it shall the Gentiles seek: and His rest shall be glorious. And it shall come to pass in that day, that the Lord shall set His hand again the second time to recover the remnant of His people, which shall be left, from Assyria, and from Egypt, and from Pathros, and from Cush, and from Elam, and from Shinar, and from Hamath, and from the islands of the sea. And He shall set up an ensign for the nations, and shall assemble the outcasts of Israel, and gather together the dispersed of Judah from the four corners of the earth.

"The envy also of Ephraim shall depart, and the adversaries of Judah shall be cut off: Ephraim shall not envy Judah, and Judah shall not vex Ephraim. But they shall fly upon the shoulders of the Philistines toward the west; they shall spoil them of the east together: they shall lay their hand upon Edom and Moab; and the children of Ammon shall obey them. And the Lord shall utterly destroy the tongue of the Egyptian sea; and with His mighty wind shall He shake His hand over the river, and shall smite it in the seven streams, and make men go over dryshod. And there shall be an highway for the remnant of His people, which shall be left, from Assyria; like as it was to Israel in the day that he came up out of the land of Egypt.

"And in that day thou shalt say, O Lord, I will praise thee: though thou wast angry with me, thine anger is turned away, and thou comfortedst me. Behold, God is my salvation; I will trust, and not be afraid: for the Lord JEHOVAH is my strength and my song; He also is become my salvation. Therefore with joy shall ye

draw water out of the wells of salvation. And in that day shall ye say, Praise the Lord, call upon His name, declare His doings among the people, make mention that His name is exalted. Sing unto the Lord; for He hath done excellent things: this is known in all the earth. Cry out and shout, thou inhabitant of Zion: for great is the Holy One of Israel in the midst of thee" (Isa. 11:1, 6–16; 12:1–6).

That glorious kingdom is just ahead for the people Israel. There are preachers and teachers who declare that God is finished with Israel, and that the promises to Abraham have been extended to the Church. But God has not forgotten His people, and in His own time He will graft into the olive tree those natural branches which were broken off *that the Gentiles might be grafted in.* (Study Romans chapter 11.)

Verse 17: *"That the residue of men might seek after the Lord, and all the Gentiles, upon whom my name is called, saith the Lord, who doeth all these things."*

*"The residue of men . . . ."* This phrase differs slightly from the Hebrew, which reads, "That they may possess the remnant of Edom." It is evidently understood by the Prophet Amos and by James to mean men other than Jews—Gentile nations who will hear the message of salvation, receive it, and be saved. In that day, even in *the transition period,* people who were not of the house of Israel were counted as heathen, but James makes clear the fact that God in His great salvation, His grace and favor, included people other than the Jews—and He included them without requiring them to conform to the Jewish rites, laws, and ceremonies.

Verse 18: *"Known unto God are all His works from the beginning of the world."*

Here James makes reference to the omniscience of God and the fact that He knows the end in the beginning,

and everything between the beginning and the end.  He sees everything in the future, He knows what He will do, He knows when and how He will do it.  He has a blueprint of the ages, a plan that was already perfected before He made this earth, before He created the dust from which He made Adam.  There is nothing God does not know.  God had no beginning—He has always *been.* He will have no ending—*from everlasting to everlasting He is GOD* (Psalm 90:1, 2).

James was trying to get his brethren to see that salvation for the Gentiles was part of God's eternal plan. The prophets declared it, God knew it would come to pass, and since it was included in God's plan they should not oppose it nor attempt to add to it by placing upon the Gentile believers a yoke which neither they nor their fathers had been able to bear.

### Gentile Believers Are Not Under Law

Verse 19:  *"Wherefore my sentence is, that we trouble not them, which from among the Gentiles are turned to God."*

*"Wherefore"* means "because of the preceding, the following is true."  The prophets had foretold what had occurred among the Gentiles.  God had put His stamp of approval upon it, and the conclusion reached was that this was of God and the Jews should not *"trouble"* (oppress or harass) *"them which from among the Gentiles are turned to God."*  Since God had extended His salvation to the Gentiles without observance of Jewish rites and ceremonies, the Jews *must not* impose those burdens upon them.

Verse 20:  *"But that we write unto them, that they abstain from pollutions of idols, and from fornication, and from things strangled, and from blood."*

James suggested that a letter be written to the Gentile believers in the various churches so recently set up, and

in that letter they would make known what had been discussed in the council in Jerusalem, as well as stating the decision reached concerning those things under discussion. They would also admonish the Gentiles to abstain from indulging in unchristian practices or any action that might bring offense to the Jewish believers.

They would request the Gentiles to *"abstain from pollutions of idols."* The Greek word here translated "pollutions" applies to anything that defiles, or to any kind of defilement. As used here it refers to the flesh of animals which had been offered in sacrifice to idols (see verse 29). Idol worship was prevalent among the Gentiles, but idolatry in any form was forbidden among the Jews. They were not to partake of the sacrifices nor participate in the feasts and ceremonies. They dared not even go near one of the festivals where idol worship was being carried on.

The flesh of animals sacrificed to idols was often sold in the market places and served at feasts, and the Jewish believers maintained that it was just as sinful to eat the meat which had been offered to idols as it was to participate in the actual idol worship. The Gentile believers argued that even though the meat had first been offered to an idol, that fact had nothing to do with whether or not a Christian should then partake of the meat. It was not contaminated, it was just as wholesome and nourishing as meat that had not been offered to idols, and therefore they saw nothing wrong in eating it.

This became a very important question in the early Church. Paul spoke at length on this subject in his first letter to the Corinthian believers:

"As concerning therefore the eating of those things that are offered in sacrifice unto idols, we know that an idol is nothing in the world, and that *there is none other God but one.* For though there be that are *called* gods, whether in heaven or in earth, (as there be gods many,

and lords many,) but to us there is but one God, the
Father, of whom are all things, and we in Him; and one
Lord Jesus Christ, by whom are all things, and we by
Him.

"Howbeit there is not in every man that knowledge:
for some with conscience of the idol unto this hour eat
it as a thing offered unto an idol; and their conscience
being weak is defiled. But *meat commendeth us not to
God: for neither, if we eat, are we the better; neither,
if we eat not, are we the worse. But take heed lest by
any means this liberty of your's become a stumblingblock
to them that are weak.* For if any man see thee which
hast knowledge sit at meat in the idol's temple, shall
not the conscience of him which is weak be emboldened
to eat those things which are offered to idols; and through
thy knowledge shall the weak brother perish, for whom
Christ died? But when ye sin so against the brethren,
and wound their weak conscience, ye sin against Christ.

"*WHEREFORE, IF MEAT MAKE MY BROTHER
TO OFFEND, I WILL EAT NO FLESH WHILE THE
WORLD STANDETH, LEST I MAKE MY BROTHER
TO OFFEND*" (I Cor. 8:4—13).

In I Corinthians 10:25—33 Paul wrote, "Whatsoever
is sold in the shambles, that eat, asking no question for
conscience sake: For the earth is the Lord's, and the
fulness thereof. If any of them that believe not bid you
to a feast, and ye be disposed to go; whatsoever is set
before you, eat, asking no question for conscience sake.
But if any man say unto you, This is offered in sacrifice
unto idols, eat not for his sake that shewed it, and for
conscience sake: for the earth is the Lord's, and the
fulness thereof: Conscience, I say, not thine own, but
of the other: for why is my liberty judged of another
man's conscience?

"For if I by grace be a partaker, why am I evil spoken
of for that for which I give thanks? *Whether therefore
ye eat, or drink, or whatsoever ye do, DO ALL TO THE*

*GLORY OF GOD.   Give none offence, neither to the
Jews, nor to the Gentiles, nor to the Church of God:
Even as I please all men in all things, not seeking mine
own profit, but the profit of many, that they may be
saved."*

There are many things which believers could do which
would not hurt them as individuals, but which might
prove harmful to others.   There are, for instance, some
places where Christians could go without harming their
own spirituality, yet if a weaker Christian saw them
entering that particular place, that weaker brother could
be hurt, caused to stumble, and perhaps be influenced
to do something that would bring the guilt of sin upon
his conscience.   Therefore, for the sake of weaker Christians we must be careful where we go, what we do, the
language we use, and the attitude we display.

You will notice Paul said that when we wound a fellow believer, the injury is actually to Christ Himself.
The Church is one body made up of many members,
and when one member suffers, the whole body suffers.
Christ is the head of that body, and when a weak Christian is hurt, the head of the Church is hurt.   Paul is not
setting forth the idea that we are to try to please all
people—it would be impossible to accomplish such a feat,
even if we tried.   He was simply stressing the fact that
Christian liberty should not be used in a way that would
give offense "to the Jews, nor to the Gentiles, nor to
the Church of God."

This is the principle James is suggesting in our present
verse.   For the sake of peace and unity in the Church,
lest the stronger Christians offend the weak, the Gentile
believers would be asked to abstain from meat which
had been offered to idols and to eat meat which would
not be counted morally wrong by Jewish believers.   Thus
would they avoid an occasion for division and offense
between Jewish and Gentile believers.

They would also be asked to abstain *"from fornica-*

*tion."* The word used here is applicable to any and all illicit sex practice. The question is often asked, "Why is this inserted in the middle of admonition to abstain from practices having to do with the *ceremonial* laws, since fornication has to do with *moral* law?" I believe it is mentioned here because of the fact that in those days illicit sex practice was prevalent among the Gentiles. The cities where Paul and Barnabas had traveled and preached the Gospel, and where many Gentiles were converted, were cities of sin and lust. Since fornication was practiced in those cities—and practiced without shame or remorse—the Gentiles did not regard it as being disgraceful and sinful. But to the Jews, such indulgence was strictly forbidden.

Fornication was connected with heathen religion, and as a part of many of their temple rites it was practiced in some of the heathen temples. Females devoted themselves to the service of the temples, and were used in connection with the order of pagan worship. Historians have penned down sickening and sordid records of that which went on in the name of "religion" in some of the heathen temples between the priests and priestesses who were leaders in idolatrous worship.

Many of the Gentiles now knew salvation through the finished work of Jesus; but they had been accustomed to the practice of fornication without guilt of conscience, they would be surrounded by and exposed to the unsaved people who would *still* indulge in such practice, and James believed it necessary and extremely important to impress upon these new converts their obligation to abstain from fornication and to oppose it as sinful and degrading.

This subject, too, was discussed by the Apostle Paul in dealing with the Corinthian church. Corinth was an idolatrous city and the Corinthian believers were still carnally minded. Therefore Paul found it necessary to admonish them about some of their worldliness. In

I Corinthians 6:13—18 he wrote, ". . . Now the body is not for fornication, but for the Lord; and the Lord for the body. . . . Know ye not that your bodies are the members of Christ? Shall I then take the members of Christ, and make them *the members of an harlot? GOD FORBID!*

"What? Know ye not that he which is joined to an harlot is one body? for two, saith He, shall be one flesh. *BUT HE THAT IS JOINED UNTO THE LORD IS ONE SPIRIT.*

*"Flee fornication.* Every sin that a man doeth is without the body; but he that committeth *fornication* sinneth against his own body."

In Galatians 5:19—21 Paul lists fornication as among *"the works of the flesh* . . . adultery, fornication, uncleanness, lasciviousness, idolatry, witchcraft, hatred, variance, emulations, wrath, strife, seditions, heresies, envyings, murders, drunkenness, revellings, and such like . . . *THEY WHICH DO SUCH THINGS SHALL NOT INHERIT THE KINGDOM OF GOD!"*

In Ephesians 5:3 Paul warns, *"Fornication,* and *all uncleanness,* or *covetousness, let it not be once NAMED among you, as becometh saints."*

He also admonished the Thessalonian believers, "This is the will of God, even your sanctification, *that ye should ABSTAIN FROM FORNICATION"* (I Thess. 4:3).

So you see, while fornication was accepted among the Gentiles without too much disturbance being made over it, it was quite unacceptable to the Jews and therefore the Gentile Christians were not to fall back into a sin which their previous lives had taught them to regard in a very different light.

The letter from the council was also to contain the admonition to abstain *"from things strangled, and from blood."* Any animal or fowl killed without shedding of blood was not to be eaten by the Jews. Leviticus 22:8 commanded, "That which *dieth of itself,* or is *torn with*

*beasts,* he shall not eat to defile himself therewith: I am the Lord." If a Jew ate meat from an animal or fowl that had been strangled and from which the blood had not been drained, he would be guilty of eating *blood,* which was strictly forbidden by the law.

In Leviticus 17:10−14 the law declared, "Whatsoever man there be of the house of Israel, or of the strangers that sojourn among you, that eateth *any manner of blood;* I will even set my face against that soul that eateth blood, and will cut him off from among his people. *FOR THE LIFE OF THE FLESH IS IN THE BLOOD; and I have given it to you upon the altar to make an atonement for your souls: FOR IT IS THE BLOOD THAT MAKETH AN ATONEMENT FOR THE SOUL.* There-fore I said unto the children of Israel, *No soul of you shall eat blood, neither shall any stranger that sojourneth among you eat blood.*

"And whatsoever man there be of the children of Is-rael, or of the strangers that sojourn among you, which hunteth and catcheth any beast or fowl that may be eaten; *he shall even POUR OUT THE BLOOD thereof, and cover it with dust. For it is THE LIFE OF ALL FLESH; THE BLOOD OF IT IS FOR THE LIFE THEREOF:* Therefore I said unto the children of Israel, *YE SHALL EAT THE BLOOD OF NO MANNER OF FLESH: FOR THE LIFE OF ALL FLESH IS THE BLOOD THEREOF:* whosoever eateth it shall be cut off."

The life of the flesh is in the blood, therefore it should not be eaten. Also, the heathen often used blood in their religious ceremonies. They drank blood in some of their rituals, and when they made a covenant or contract with each other they sealed the contract with blood. Israel was a separated nation and to set the Jews apart from the Gentiles, they had been forbidden by law to eat anything containing blood.

It adds tremendously to the force of these remarks

when we keep in mind that the same principle was settled by Almighty God before the Law of Moses was ever given.    The life of the flesh is in the blood, and God regarded this fact as of such grave importance that He declared the shedding of blood to be worthy of death. In Genesis 9:4–6 He decreed, "Flesh with the life thereof, *which is the blood thereof,* shall ye not eat.    And surely your blood of your lives will I require; at the hand of every beast will I require it, and at the hand of man; at the hand of every man's brother will I require the life of man.    *Whoso sheddeth man's blood, BY MAN SHALL HIS BLOOD BE SHED:*    for in the image of God made He man."

It was not unreasonable, therefore, to include these admonitions in the letter to the believers at Antioch and in other Gentile areas.

Verse 21:    *"For Moses of old time hath in every city them that preach him, being read in the synagogues every sabbath day."*

James now reminds the brethren that the Law of Moses—the law which expressly prohibited the practices he had just named—was read in the synagogues Sabbath after Sabbath, constantly reminding the people that these things were forbidden by God's law.    Christ is the end of the law for righteousness to all who believe, and we are complete in Him; but the Jewish converts would not soon learn that their ceremonial law had ceased to be binding and it was therefore wise to warn the Gentile believers to abstain from these things in order not to offend their Jewish brethren.

*"Of old time"* means from ancient generations.    The ceremonial laws had been read so often and were so firmly established in the minds of the people that they would not soon be forgotten.    They were read *"in every city"* where there were Jews, and they were read *every Sabbath.*    Small wonder that they were so deeply instilled

in the lives of the Jews.

*"Them that preach him"* means that not only was the Law of Moses *read* in the synagogues, but in addition to the *reading* it was customary for someone to explain the meaning of what was read. Therefore these Jewish converts had been so thoroughly trained in the ceremonial law that it was the Christian duty of the Gentile believers to respect their feelings and abstain from the things that offended them — not in order *to be saved,* but because they were saved and did not wish to offend the Jewish Christians.

Verse 22: *"Then pleased it the apostles and elders with the whole church, to send chosen men of their own company to Antioch with Paul and Barnabas; namely, Judas surnamed Barsabas, and Silas, chief men among the brethren."*

*"Then pleased it the apostles and elders with the whole church . . . ."* It does not stand to reason that the entire church would volunteer an opinion on what should be contained in the letter if they had not been consulted about its contents. It seems probable that the elders and apostles discussed the matter and then submitted their recommendations to the assembly for approval. So the decree was the voice of the whole church. The same would be true of the decision to send *"chosen men of their own company to Antioch."*

Believers from the church in Jerusalem were chosen to bear the letter to Antioch and other cities where Gentile converts lived and where the question of law versus grace had presented a problem. If some of their own number carried the letter to churches in other cities it would show more personal interest from the assembly in Jerusalem and would make a deeper impression on the Gentile believers.

They chose *"Judas surnamed Barsabas, and Silas."* Some Bible scholars believe this "Judas" to be the same

man mentioned in Acts 1:23, along with Matthias, when the apostles were choosing someone to replace Judas Iscariot in their number.    Others believe him to have been the *brother* of that "Joseph called Barsabas."    We have no detailed history of him other than the fact given here—that he and Silas were *"chief men among the brethren."*

*Silas* of course is more familiar to us as the traveling companion of the Apostle Paul in his missionary journeys. In verse 40 of this chapter, Paul chose Silas as his partner on his second missionary endeavor.    In Acts 16:25—29 Silas was Paul's companion in the Philippian jail, and in connection with his ministry with Paul he is mentioned again in Acts 17:4, 10, and 15.    Silas is also called *"Silvanus"* in II Corinthians 1:19, and in II Thessalonians 1:1 where "Paul, and Silvanus, and Timotheus" sent greetings to the assembly at Thessalonica.    Peter also mentions him as "Silvanus, a faithful brother" (I Pet. 5:12).    Nowhere is Silas called an apostle, but it is evident that he was capable, devoted, and tireless in his service to the New Testament Church.    Verse 32 of our present chapter declares that *both Judas and Silas* were prophets, men of influence and experience who held positions of authority in the church in Jerusalem.

Verse 23:    *"And they wrote letters by them after this manner:    The apostles and elders and brethren send greeting unto the brethren which are of the Gentiles in Antioch and Syria and Cilicia."*

The literal Greek reads, "having written by their hand letters or epistles."    This does not mean that they wrote more than one letter, but that they made *more than one copy* of the one letter and sent a copy to each of the churches.

They wrote *"after this manner."*    It was a letter of greeting, a *kind* letter—not of rebuke, but rather of admonition and instruction.    The fact that they addressed

the Gentiles as "brethren" is an expression of their happiness because of the salvation of the Gentiles. Before Jesus came, Gentiles had been "dogs," unworthy of even associating with a Jew. Now they are called "brethren" —brothers in Christ, *"in Antioch and Syria and Cilicia."*

Antioch was the city where the difficulty over circumcision had had its inception. Since Antioch was the capital of Syria it did not take the teaching of the Judaizers long to spread to other parts of the country, and it seems reasonable to suppose that it had even traveled into Cilicia since that country was adjacent to Syria. Paul and Barnabas had traveled through these areas, they had preached the Gospel and Gentiles had been saved there. It is not unlikely therefore that all of these places needed the instruction given in the letter sent out by the church in Jerusalem.

Verse 24: *"Forasmuch as we have heard, that certain which went out from us have troubled you with words, subverting your souls, saying, Ye must be circumcised, and keep the law: to whom we gave no such commandment."*

To paraphrase the first part of this verse, the meaning is, "Since we have heard that some of our own number have *troubled you with words* (or doctrine) . . . ." The trouble and confusion had come from the men from Judaea teaching doctrine concerning observance of ceremonial law as being essential to salvation. They had gone out on their own—they *sent themselves.* The new messengers bearing the letter were the choice of the church.

*". . . subverting your souls."* The Greek word here translated "subverting" is not used anywhere else in the New Testament. This particular word means, primarily, "to pack up baggage (*ana* - up; *skeuos* - vessel), hence from a military point of view to dismantle a town, to plunder." It is used metaphorically here in the sense of

destroying or disturbing the peace of mind of the Gentile believers and causing them to become anxious and distressed because of the doctrines of ceremonial law in relation to salvation by grace through faith.

*". . . to whom we gave no such commandment!"* The men from Judaea had gone to Antioch without either authority or sanction from the church in Jerusalem. The tone of the letter suggests that had the apostles and the believers in Jerusalem been consulted in the matter, they would never have allowed the men to go out and dogmatically declare that the Gentile Christians must be circumcised after the manner of Moses in order to be saved. Thus were the Gentile believers assured that the church in Jerusalem did not approve of what the men from Judaea had done, nor did they endorse their teaching of ceremonial law as essential to salvation.

Verses 25 and 26: *"It seemed good unto us, being assembled with one accord, to send chosen men unto you with our beloved Barnabas and Paul, men that have hazarded their lives for the name of our Lord Jesus Christ."*

*"It seemed good to us"*—i. e., in the interest of Christian unity and keeping peace among the brethren—*"being assembled with one accord."* Christian unity is demonstrated here, as well as interest being shown in the new churches and the welfare of the Gentile converts. The church in Jerusalem was *assembled* because of concern for other believers, and that they assembled *with one accord* showed unity of purpose—the purpose of discussing the difficulty and finding a solution to it.

*". . . to send chosen men unto you"*—men carefully chosen for their experience and dependability—*"with our beloved Barnabas and Paul."* Note the affection expressed here for these two men. It was well known that these missionaries had truly *"hazarded their lives"* in the interest of the Gospel. Not only had they carried

the message into pioneer territory, so to speak; but after their journey was ended they chose to return to Antioch over the same perilous route, facing the same dangers— perhaps facing death itself—in order to strengthen and encourage the new converts and help the churches so newly established. This was a noble testimony to the sincerity and character of Paul and Barnabas. They had not faced danger and death for personal glory or for a fine parsonage and fat paycheck. They did it in the name of the Lord Jesus Christ and for the glory of God. No wonder they were called "beloved" by their fellow Christians.

Verse 27: *"We have sent therefore Judas and Silas, who shall also tell you the same things by mouth."*

Paul and Barnabas were already acquainted in these churches and they could have carried the letter, presenting it in assemblies where they had been before and where they were known. But the sincerity and concern of the believers in Jerusalem prompted them to send two of their own number—two of their *"chief men"*—to deliver the letter and also tell the churches in person what the church in Jerusalem had *inscribed in the letter.*

Also, we recall that according to the Law of Moses the truth must be established by two or more witnesses (Deut. 17:6; 19:15). Therefore the church in Jerusalem gave *written testimony* and then sent Judas and Silas to give *personal* testimony to the Gentile converts, assuring them that this unfortunate incident had not occurred with the good will of the Jerusalem assembly.

## Gentile Believers Must Not Give Offense to Godly Jews

Verses 28 and 29: *"For it seemed good to the Holy Ghost, and to us, to lay upon you no greater burden than these necessary things: That ye abstain from meats offered to idols, and from blood, and from things strangled, and from fornication: from which if ye keep your-*

*selves, ye shall do well. Fare ye well."*

*"It seemed good to the HOLY GHOST and to us."* Here is definite indication that this council was under the direction of the Holy Ghost. It was with special reference to the organization of the New Testament Church that the Holy Ghost was promised (John 16:13), and just as He led Peter, Paul, James, and others in the council in Jerusalem, so would He lead all men in the business of the Church today if they would allow Him to do so. It is a sad fact that in most church meetings today the Holy Spirit is not invited and has no part in the plans and programs of modern religion.

*". . . to lay upon you no greater burden than these necessary things."* This does not mean that the things specified as "necessary" were to be added to the grace of God as essentials of salvation—indeed not. The things named (already listed in verse 20 and repeated in this verse) were necessary to preservation of unity and peace in the church and to bring Jew and Gentile into the love and fellowship whereunto God ordained them. Very simply we might say that the letter imposed no more restriction than was absolutely necessary to keep peace between the Jewish believers and the Gentile converts.

Therefore, in order that the Gentiles in their Christian liberty give no offense to believing Jews, they were to abstain from *"meats offered to idols . . . from blood . . . from things strangled . . . from fornication."*

*"From which, if ye keep yourselves, ye shall do well."* That is, to abstain from these things would be the Christian thing to do. Peace and unity *should* be preserved in the Church, and every believer should be willing to refrain from doing anything that might offend weaker Christians or have an adverse effect on unbelievers, perhaps hindering their coming to Christ for salvation. There are many things which we, as individuals, could do and still reach heaven; but while we are doing those things we may influence someone else to spend eternity in hell!

Believers are the only Bible some sinners will ever read, and we need to remember that unbelievers are prone to judge *all* Christians by the poorest example of Christianity they can find. So for the sake of those outside the Church, as well as to encourage other believers, we should be careful what we do and where we go. This is not in order *to be saved* nor is it that we might be *better* saved, but *because we ARE saved;* and as Christians we are living epistles read of men (II Cor. 3:2).

Verses 30 and 31: *"So when they were dismissed, they came to Antioch: and when they had gathered the multitude together, they delivered the epistle: which when they had read, they rejoiced for the consolation."*

When a decision was reached as to how the matter should be handled, the letter was written, the assembly in Jerusalem was dismissed, and the appointed brethren made the trip to Antioch. Arriving there, they called the multitude (the assembly) together and delivered the letter—*"which when they had read, they rejoiced for the consolation."*

We are not told just *how* these people rejoiced—which is, to me, another assurance that the Bible is verbally inspired. If *man* had been solely responsible for this account I am sure he would have gone to great length to describe how the congregation at Antioch reacted to the message from the church in Jerusalem. But the Word simply tells us that they *rejoiced.* People rejoice in different ways. Some folks *laugh* when they are happy, others *weep.* Some clap their hands, others sit in silence. There is no cut-and-dried formula for rejoicing. All people are *saved* alike—through faith in the finished work of the Lord Jesus Christ. All believers are *kept* alike—by the power of God. But we do not all demonstrate joy or sorrow in the same way. When the letter from the church in Jerusalem was read to the assembly in Antioch, the believers there rejoiced because of the

decision of the apostles and elders in Jerusalem. They
rejoiced that they were not to be subjected to the rites
and ceremonies of the Jewish religion.

Now what do we find in this first Church council that
can be applied to this day and hour? First of all, it is
worthy of our consideration that the whole procedure
*"seemed good to the Holy Spirit."* The operation of
the Holy Spirit is the heart and soul of the New Testament Church, and that operation is carried on through
dedicated servants of God. If we are to do the desig-
nated work of the Church, there must be leaders who
are fully surrendered to the will and purpose of God,
for He works through human instruments by the power
of the Holy Spirit who dwells within the born again
believer.

We hear and read of the meetings of great denominations today, where a decree or decision was carried "by
an overwhelming majority"—but that is quite different
from the report, *"It seemed good to the Holy Spirit, and
to US."* When an "overwhelming *majority*" carries the
vote you may rest assured that there is a *minority* to
furnish an element of opposition; and that dissatisfied
minority, no matter how small, can become frustrated,
unhappy, and lacking in co-operation. Such discord can
hinder the work of the assembly as a whole, and may
even bring shame and reproach upon the name of Christ.

If the council in Jerusalem had not been handled under
the full direction of the Holy Spirit, it could easily have
resulted in *two* churches—a Jewish church and a Gentile
church. But that would not have accomplished what
the Church is in the world to accomplish. Therefore it
was a divine necessity that there be no dissension among
them as to the decision reached.

This, then is the second outstanding characteristic of
that council—the *absolute UNITY of the believers,* and
unity *between believers and the Holy Spirit.* If the
Church is to go forward to the glory of God there must

be union between Christians and the living Lord who is *head* of the Church. This can be realized only by the Holy Spirit's having full sway in the life of believers in the assemblies. The council in Jerusalem was made up of a company of men and women who were sharing the life of Christ through faith in His finished work, and because they knew Him in full forgiveness of sin they also wanted to know the *mind* of Christ. Therefore they put away all selfish views and allowed the Holy Spirit to lead them into perfect unity, that they might reach a decision to the glory of God and to the edification of the Church.

There was no "politicking" in the first council at Jerusalem, but I judge not when I say that there is entirely too much of it in religion today. Too often great denominational groups come together with minds made up as to what they intend to accomplish. They are determined to pass certain rules and regulations, or to change those already in existence. They do not come together asking what the Lord's will may be in the matter. They know their own will and they have plans already made by which their aims may be accomplished. Thus the Holy Spirit has no opportunity to lead or direct, and whatever is accomplished is to the credit of man, not to the glory of God. Today, religious leaders have become "lords over God's heritage," and this is in direct disobedience to the instructions of the Holy Spirit.

In I Peter 5:1−4 we read, "The elders which are among you I exhort, who am also an elder, and a witness of the sufferings of Christ, and also a partaker of the glory that shall be revealed: *Feed the flock of God which is among you, taking the oversight thereof, not by constraint, but willingly; not for filthy lucre, but of a ready mind; NEITHER AS BEING LORDS OVER GOD'S HERITAGE, but being ensamples to the flock.* And when the Chief Shepherd shall appear, ye shall receive a crown

of glory that fadeth not away."

Verse 32: *"And Judas and Silas, being prophets also themselves, exhorted the brethren with many words, and confirmed them."*

The nature of the office of a prophet in the early Church is not clear. Possibly these men were teachers who, being gifted above their fellows, taught the deeper things of God. We know that in that day God gave revelations to certain men in order that they, in turn, might strengthen and encourage the brethren through teaching and exhortation. This was necessary during the days when the Church was in its infancy, because the perfect law of liberty had not yet come, the complete Word of God had not been given as we have it today. Therefore the Holy Spirit spoke to and through certain men in a very special way in order to meet the needs of believers. We do not need this operation today because we have the complete, written Word of God and as Paul declared to Timothy, we know that *"all* Scripture is given by inspiration of God, and is profitable for doctrine, for reproof, for correction, for instruction in righteousness: *That the man of God may be perfect, throughly furnished unto all good works"* (II Tim. 3:16, 17).

So Judas and Silas, as representatives from the church in Jerusalem, *"exhorted the brethren . . . and confirmed them."* They instructed, encouraged, and strengthened the Gentile believers in the faith, and assured them that the church in Jerusalem had done exactly what the letter stated.

Verses 33 and 34: *"And after they had tarried there a space, they were let go in peace from the brethren unto the apostles. Notwithstanding it pleased Silas to abide there still."*

How long *"a space"* Judas and Silas remained in Antioch on that particular mission we are not told. They

were "let go in peace," which means that the believers
in Antioch gave them the customary farewell, with Christian love and all good wishes for their prosperity.  Paul
instructed the church in Corinth concerning young Timothy, *"Conduct him forth in peace"* (I Cor. 16:11).  No
doubt the believers in Antioch assured Judas and Silas
of their prayers, and that they would be with them in
spirit as they ministered elsewhere.

Evidently they were expected to return to Jerusalem,
for the assembly in Antioch let them "go in peace . . .
*unto the apostles."* However, *"it pleased Silas to abide
there still."* Undoubtedly the Holy Spirit impressed
Silas to remain in Antioch, and in the verses that follow
we will see this more clearly.

Verse 35:  *"Paul also and Barnabas continued in Antioch, teaching and preaching the Word of the Lord, with
many others also."*

Perhaps this was a time of rest for Paul and Barnabas
—not rest from *"teaching and preaching the Word of
the Lord,"* but rest from the rigors of traveling from
place to place in their missionary work.  It is evident
that there is a lapse of time between this and the following verses, during which time these men continued to
teach and preach in Antioch—and only eternity will reveal how many souls were added to the Church during
those days, weeks, or months.

From chapter 2 of Paul's letter to the Galatians (quoted at the beginning of this study in Acts 15) we learn
that it was during this time that Peter came to Antioch
and Paul found it necessary to rebuke him for his attitude
toward the Gentiles.  When Peter first arrived in that
city he conducted himself in the true spirit of the decision of the council in Jerusalem and "did eat with the
Gentiles."  But a little later, some Jews arrived from
Jerusalem who were not in sympathy with such fellowship, and in deference to them Peter "withdrew and

separated himself, fearing them which were of the circumcision." In other words, Peter did not want to be criticized by these Judaizers, and so he withdrew from the Gentiles and *refused* to eat with them.

Of course this influenced still other Jews—even Barnabas was "carried away with their dissimulation," and when Paul observed these Jewish believers behaving in such an unchristian manner he said to Peter, before them all, "If thou, being a Jew, livest after the manner of Gentiles, and not as do the Jews, why compellest thou the Gentiles to live as do the Jews?"

Peter's conduct here is reminiscent of some preachers today. When he was with the Jews he followed the conduct of the Jews. When he was with the Gentiles he took the place of a Gentile under grace. He was under law one day and under grace the next. Certainly he was living a very inconsistent life, and Paul knew it. Therefore—since Peter sinned publicly, Paul publicly rebuked him.

Paul was standing alone here. Other Jews had followed Peter; even Barnabas, his bosom friend and former missionary companion had turned away. But the Apostle Paul feared no one but God and it was not unusual for him to stand alone, declaring the liberty wherewith Christ has made us free. He publicly asked Peter, "If you are a Jew, living after the manner of the Gentiles, why do you try to compel the Gentiles to live as do the Jews?" The record does not record that Peter answered Paul, or that he spoke up in defense of his authority for such action. He had made a sad mistake in his behavior, and it is at this point that Peter vanishes from inspired history. It is true that his epistles, I and II Peter, appeared much later, but this is the last *recorded act* of that apostle in connection with the New Testament Church.

It may seem strange that after being so definitely and singularly used and honored after Pentecost, in Caesarea

and at the council in Jerusalem, Peter should so suddenly
drop out of Church history; but the fear of man was a
snare to him. This was not the first time he had been
guilty of shrinking from the practical consequences of the
truth of the Gospel in this world. We must face the
fact that Peter was a spiritual giant in one sense, but
on the other hand he was extremely weak—and one moment off guard can be unbelievably costly to a minister!

### Paul's Second Missionary Journey:  Silas Chosen

Verse 36: *"And some days after Paul said unto Barnabas, Let us go again and visit our brethren in every city
where we have preached the Word of the Lord, and see
how they do."*

*"Some days after . . . ."* At some time—we cannot
estimate how long—after Paul and Barnabas, with Silas
and others, returned to Antioch from Jerusalem and tarried there to teach and preach the Word, Paul suggested
to Barnabas that they make another visit to the young
churches *"in every city where we have preached the Word
of the Lord, and see how they do."* This was so characteristic of this minister to the Gentiles, this man to
whom the revelation of the New Testament Church was
given. He loved his converts, he watched over them,
taught them, encouraged them, rebuked them when they
needed it. The burden of the churches rested heavily
upon him, these particular converts had been dearly won
—almost at the cost of his life—and he felt the expediency of visiting them again lest perchance some difficulty
had arisen for them for which they might need his help.

Verses 37 and 38: *"And Barnabas determined to take
with them John, whose surname was Mark. But Paul
thought not good to take him with them, who departed
from them from Pamphylia, and went not with them
to the work."*

Mark was the nephew of Barnabas (Col. 4:10), he had come to Antioch when Paul and Barnabas had returned there after taking alms to the saints in Jerusalem (Acts 12:25), and he had accompanied them on their first missionary journey (Acts 13:5).   However, for reasons not stated in the Scriptures he left them at Perga in Pamphylia and returned to his home in Jerusalem (Acts 13:13).

Barnabas now determined to take John Mark out with them on this second missionary journey.  No doubt he loved the young man because of their kinship, and it was probably his love for his nephew rather than the leadership of the Holy Spirit that disposed him to want his company on this trip.

*"But Paul thought not good to take him."*   Since Mark had left them early in the first journey, Paul was not disposed to take him a second time.  He could not depend upon the young man's perseverance, he had previously deserted them when the road became hard and their lives were threatened, and Paul had no assurance that he would not do the same thing again.  Whatever John Mark's reason (or reasons) for turning back, it is evident that Paul was displeased with him for so doing. There was undoubtedly some underlying cause which that apostle did not consider legitimate reason for such desertion, and because of this he refused to start out again with young Mark as a missionary partner.

Verses 39—41:  *"And the contention was so sharp between them, that they departed asunder one from the other:  and so Barnabas took Mark, and sailed unto Cyprus; and Paul chose Silas, and departed, being recommended by the brethren unto the grace of God.  And he went through Syria and Cilicia, confirming the churches."*

*"Contention"* in the Greek in this verse denotes excitement of the mind.  However, it is used in a better sense in Hebrews 10:24 where it is translated *"provoke."*  The contention between Paul and Barnabas resulted in an

argument between them, a disagreement so sharp *"that they departed asunder one from the other."* These two men, after great success in their combined ministry, now part company and enter into different spheres of ministry. Barnabas is mentioned no more in Acts after this chapter; however it is difficult to believe that this man was laid aside—or as Paul expressed it in I Corinthians 9:27, that he should become "a castaway"—disapproved and unfruitful as a missionary because of his disagreement with Paul. Barnabas had been one of the first believers to lay everything on the altar, presenting all that he was and all that he had to be used in the spread of the Gospel (Acts 4:37), and his ministry had been successful, although he now let personal feelings enter in and perhaps cloud his better judgment. However, his association with and training of John Mark turned out greatly to that young man's benefit and he was eventually restored to the confidence and fellowship of the Apostle Paul.

This is evident in Paul's epistles. In Colossians 4:10, 11 he speaks of "Marcus, sister's son to Barnabas" as his fellowworker "unto the kingdom of God." In II Timothy 4:11, as Paul wrote farewell to his earthly ministry in his second epistle to his beloved son in the faith, he said, "Only Luke is with me. *Take Mark, and bring him with thee: for he is profitable to me for the ministry."* Then in Philemon 24 he again speaks of Mark as being among his "fellowlabourers."

"So Barnabas took Mark, *and sailed unto Cyprus,"* which was the country from which Barnabas originally came (Acts 4:36). *Paul* chose Silas as his new traveling companion, and they left Antioch to revisit the young churches where Paul and Barnabas had ministered earlier.

That these two men were *"recommended by the brethren unto the grace of God"* indicates that they had a season of prayer, and as when Paul and Barnabas had gone out from the believers in Antioch (Acts 13:3) bade

them God speed as they started out on this new missionary undertaking.

As we continue our study in the following chapters
of the book of Acts we will learn a great deal about how
God honored the ministry of Paul and Silas with many
souls and great success.

# CHAPTER XVI

1. Then came he to Derbe and Lystra: and, behold, a certain disciple was there, named Timotheus, the son of a certain woman, which was a Jewess, and believed; but his father was a Greek:

2. Which was well reported of by the brethren that were at Lystra and Iconium.

3. Him would Paul have to go forth with him; and took and circumcised him because of the Jews which were in those quarters: for they knew all that his father was a Greek.

4. And as they went through the cities, they delivered them the decrees for to keep, that were ordained of the apostles and elders which were at Jerusalem.

5. And so were the churches established in the faith, and increased in number daily.

6. Now when they had gone throughout Phrygia and the region of Galatia, and were forbidden of the Holy Ghost to preach the word in Asia,

7. After they were come to Mysia, they assayed to go into Bithynia: but the Spirit suffered them not.

8. And they passing by Mysia came down to Troas.

9. And a vision appeared to Paul in the night; There stood a man of Macedonia, and prayed him, saying, Come over into Macedonia, and help us.

10. And after he had seen the vision, immediately we endeavoured to go into Macedonia, assuredly gathering that the Lord had called us for to preach the gospel unto them.

11. Therefore loosing from Troas, we came with a straight course to Samothracia, and the next day to Neapolis;

12. And from thence to Philippi, which is the chief city of that part of Macedonia, and a colony: and we were in that city abiding certain days.

13. And on the sabbath we went out of the city by a river side, where prayer was wont to be made; and we sat down, and spake unto the women which resorted thither.

14. And a certain woman named Lydia, a seller of purple, of the city of Thyatira, which worshipped God, heard us: whose heart the Lord opened, that she attended unto the things which

were spoken of Paul.

15. And when she was baptized, and her household, she besought us, saying, If ye have judged me to be faithful to the Lord, come into my house, and abide there. And she constrained us.

16. And it came to pass, as we went to prayer, a certain damsel possessed with a spirit of divination met us, which brought her masters much gain by soothsaying:

17. The same followed Paul and us, and cried, saying, These men are the servants of the most high God, which shew unto us the way of salvation.

18. And this did she many days. But Paul, being grieved, turned and said to the spirit, I command thee in the name of Jesus Christ to come out of her. And he came out the same hour.

19. And when her masters saw that the hope of their gains was gone, they caught Paul and Silas, and drew them into the marketplace unto the rulers,

20. And brought them to the magistrates, saying, These men, being Jews, do exceedingly trouble our city,

21. And teach customs, which are not lawful for us to receive, neither to observe, being Romans.

22. And the multitude rose up together against them: and the magistrates rent off their clothes, and commanded to beat them.

23. And when they had laid many stripes upon them, they cast them into prison, charging the jailor to keep them safely:

24. Who, having received such a charge, thrust them into the inner prison, and made their feet fast in the stocks.

25. And at midnight Paul and Silas prayed, and sang praises unto God: and the prisoners heard them.

26. And suddenly there was a great earthquake, so that the foundations of the prison were shaken: and immediately all the doors were opened, and every one's bands were loosed.

27. And the keeper of the prison awaking out of his sleep, and seeing the prison doors open, he drew out his sword, and would have killed himself, supposing that the prisoners had been fled.

28. But Paul cried with a loud voice, saying, Do thyself no harm: for we are all here.

29. Then he called for a light, and sprang in, and came trembling, and fell down before Paul and Silas,

30. And brought them out, and said, Sirs, what must I do to be saved?

31. And they said, Believe on the Lord Jesus Christ, and thou shalt be saved, and thy house.

32. And they spake unto him the word of the Lord, and to all that were in his house.

33. And he took them the same hour of the night, and washed their stripes; and was baptized, he and all his, straightway.

34. And when he had brought them into his house, he set meat before them, and rejoiced, believing in God with all his house.

35. And when it was day, the magistrates sent the serjeants, saying, Let those men go.

36. And the keeper of the prison told this saying to Paul, The magistrates have sent to let you go: now therefore depart, and go in peace.

37. But Paul said unto them, They have beaten us openly uncondemned, being Romans, and have cast us into prison; and now do they thrust us out privily? nay verily; but let them come themselves and fetch us out.

38. And the serjeants told these words unto the magistrates: and they feared, when they heard that they were Romans.

39. And they came and besought them, and brought them out, and desired them to depart out of the city.

40. And they went out of the prison, and entered into the house of Lydia: and when they had seen the brethren, they comforted them, and departed.

In this chapter the Apostle Paul fully and freely enters upon his second missionary journey. He again visits the churches already established, and moves on into new fields of evangelism.

You will recall that Paul and Barnabas parted company in the last part of the preceding chapter, and Silas is now Paul's missionary partner. Luke does not give an account of what happened to Barnabas and John Mark in their ministry together, but confines his account to the journeys and activities of Paul.

It is also in this chapter that young Timothy enters the record and becomes one of Paul's traveling companions.

The Macedonian call takes the missionaries eventually to Philippi where Lydia, the first convert in Europe, hears and receives the Gospel. Here is formed the nucleus of the church to which Paul later penned his epistle to the Philippians.

In verses 16 through 24, the salvation of a fortune-teller results in the beating and imprisonment of Paul

and Silas, and that imprisonment is climaxed by the conversion of the jailer and his entire household.

Exciting and inspiring events are recorded by Luke in the passages just ahead in our study.

## Paul Finds Timothy

Verses 1 and 2: *"Then came he to Derbe and Lystra: and, behold, a certain disciple was there, named Timotheus, the son of a certain woman, which was a Jewess, and believed; but his father was a Greek: which was well reported of by the brethren that were at Lystra and Iconium."*

Derbe and Lystra—especially the latter town—were places already familiar to Paul. His first ministry in Derbe had been peaceful and apparently unhampered by the enemies of the Gospel, but his first visit to *Lystra* had ended in his being stoned and dragged outside the city, where he was left for dead. It is entirely possible that this *"certain disciple . . . named Timotheus"* was present on that occasion, although that is not part of the sacred record here. Nor are we told which of these cities—Derbe or Lystra—was the home of this young man. There is ample Scripture however, for us to know that the Apostle Paul came to consider Timothy as his son in the ministry, and to him the apostle addressed two of the fourteen epistles which God has given us through his inspired pen.

Timothy's mother was a Jewess and a believer. In II Timothy 1:5 Paul speaks of "the unfeigned faith . . . which dwelt first in thy grandmother Lois, and thy mother Eunice." So we know that both Timothy's mother and grandmother were Christians. These two women had also been faithful in instructing him in the Christian faith, for in II Timothy 3:15 we read, *"From a child thou hast known the holy Scriptures,* which are able to make thee wise unto salvation through faith which is in Christ

Jesus."

*"But his father was a Greek."* It was not lawful for
a Jew to marry a person from another nation, nor was
it lawful for a Jew to *give his daughter* in marriage to
a man of another nation. In Ezra 9:12 we read, "Now
therefore give not your daughters unto their sons, neither
take their daughters unto your sons, nor seek their peace
or their wealth for ever: that ye may be strong, and
eat the good of the land, and leave it for an inheritance
to your children for ever." But this law was disregarded
by many of the Jews who lived in the midst of Gentile
nations, and this was the case with Timothy's parents.

*"Which was well reported of by the brethren . . . ."*
The connection requires us to understand that *Timothy*
was the one who was "well reported of" by other Christians who lived at Lystra and Iconium. (We have no
record of the character of the father of this young believer.) Timothy was highly esteemed by all who knew
him in his home area. As we have already seen, he had
been religiously educated, carefully trained in the knowledge of the Scriptures, and we might conclude that he
had been saved at an early age.

Verse 3: *"Him would Paul have to go forth with
him; and took and circumcised him because of the Jews
which were in those quarters: for they knew all that
his father was a Greek."*

*"Him would Paul have to go forth with him."* No
specific age is given for Timothy at this time but we
know he was very young. When Paul left him in charge
of the church at Ephesus he advised, *"Let no man despise thy YOUTH, but be thou an example of the believers, in word, in conversation, in charity, in spirit,
in faith, in purity"* (I Tim. 4:12).

In I Timothy 3:7 Paul said of a bishop, "He must
have a good report of them which are without . . . ."
Paul's choice of Timothy as his partner in the ministry

and in the labors of spreading the Gospel proved that he had utmost confidence in him in spite of his extreme youth. He esteemed Timothy as dedicated, consecrated, prudent, and evidently possessing some talents which could be used to the glory of God. He appreciated the fact that this young man was "well reported of" by all who knew him, and that appreciation was expressed in his choice of Timothy as one of his co-workers and fellow travelers. He was not disappointed in his choice, and the deepening of the apostle's love for Timothy is clearly seen in the epistles later written to him. For example, in the opening verses of II Timothy we find these words:

"Paul, an apostle of Jesus Christ by the will of God, according to the promise of life which is in Christ Jesus, *to Timothy, my dearly beloved son:* Grace, mercy, and peace, from God the Father and Christ Jesus our Lord. I thank God, whom I serve from my forefathers with pure conscience, that *without ceasing I have remembrance of thee in my prayers night and day; greatly desiring to see thee,* being mindful of thy tears, that I may be filled with joy; when I call to remembrance the unfeigned faith that is in thee, which dwelt first in thy grandmother Lois, and thy mother Eunice; and I am persuaded that in thee also. Wherefore I put thee in remembrance that thou stir up the gift of God, which is in thee by the putting on of my hands" (II Tim. 1:1−6).

So Paul chose Timothy to go with him on his second missionary journey, *"and took and circumcised him because of the Jews which were in those quarters."* Many people—even scholars—have asked, "Why did Paul do this?" The Apostle Paul defended the grace of God as few men have defended pure grace; but Paul was a Jew and he emphatically declared that his prayer and heart's desire for Israel was *that they be saved* (Rom. 10:1). He also confessed to *"great heaviness and continual sorrow"* in his heart because his kinsmen according to the flesh were *not* saved. So dearly did he love the Jews that he

would have been willing to be *"accursed from Christ"* if such a sacrifice would lead them into salvation (Rom. 9:1−3). He knew that they had "a zeal of God, but *not according to knowledge"* (Rom. 10:2).

Therefore, in his concern for the Jews, fearful lest he drive them *from* the grace of God, Paul requested the circumcision of Timothy because the Jews in that part of the country all knew that Timothy's father was a Gentile, but Timothy himself, because of his Jewish mother, was reckoned a Jew. There is no doubt that Paul believed he was doing the right thing to avoid opposition and reproaches from the Jews in that area. The question of circumcision as being binding in itself was settled in the church council at Jerusalem (as discussed fully in the preceding chapter); but to neglect it in this instance would invite contention and bitter opposition from the Jews, even from some of the Jewish *believers,* and it would greatly hinder the cause of the Gospel in that locality. It must be remembered that the decree of the church in Jerusalem only related to the exemption of Gentiles from being circumcised. It was a very different thing at this early period of the New Testament Church for a Jew to consent to worship with a Gentile who was uncircumcised and to tolerate the non-observance of the rite by one who was counted a Jew.

I am not attempting to defend what Paul did. I am simply saying that whatever he did was done with a clear conscience and a sincere heart. He testified before Felix, "Herein do I exercise myself, to have always *a conscience void of offence toward God, and toward men"* (Acts 24:16). Before he was converted, Paul stood ready to give his life for the religion of his fathers; and when he met Jesus on the Damascus road and was born again, he was just as zealous for God, determined to do nothing that might drive away even one soul from the Lord Jesus Christ. In I Corinthians 9:19−22 he testified:

"Though I be *free from ALL men,* yet have I made

myself *servant* unto all, that I might gain the more.   And unto the Jews I became as a Jew, *that I might gain the Jews.*   To them that are under the law, as under the law, *that I might gain them that are under the law.*   To them that are without law, as without law, (being not without law to God, but under the law to Christ,) *that I might gain them that are without law.*   To the weak became I as weak, *that I might gain the weak:   I AM MADE ALL THINGS TO ALL MEN, that I might by all means save some!"*

What Paul did in having Timothy circumcised was an act of expediency for the sake of the Gospel, and it was in accord with his uniform and declared principle of Christian conduct.   In connection with this, I believe it will be time well spent and space well used to give you the full text of Paul's inspired "law of love concerning doubtful things," as recorded in Romans chapter 14:

"Him that is weak in the faith receive ye, but not to doubtful disputations.   For one believeth that he may eat all things:   another, who is weak, eateth herbs.   Let not him that eateth despise him that eateth not; and let not him which eateth not judge him that eateth:   for God hath received him.   Who art thou that judgest another man's servant?   to his own master he standeth or falleth.   Yea, he shall be holden up:   for God is able to make him stand.

"One man esteemeth one day above another:   another esteemeth every day alike.   Let every man be fully persuaded in his own mind.   He that regardeth the day, regardeth it unto the Lord; and he that regardeth not the day, to the Lord he doth not regard it.   He that eateth, eateth to the Lord, for he giveth God thanks; and he that eateth not, to the Lord he eateth not, and giveth God thanks.

"For none of us liveth to himself, and no man dieth to himself.   For whether we live, we live unto the Lord; and whether we die, we die unto the Lord:   whether we

live therefore, or die, we are the Lord's. For to this end Christ both died, and rose, and revived, that he might be Lord both of the dead and living.

"But why dost thou judge thy brother? or why dost thou set at nought thy brother? For we shall all stand before the judgment seat of Christ. For it is written, As I live, saith the Lord, every knee shall bow to me, and every tongue shall confess to God. So then every one of us shall give account of himself to God. Let us not therefore judge one another any more: but judge this rather, that no man put a stumblingblock or an occasion to fall in his brother's way.

"I know, and am persuaded by the Lord Jesus, that there is nothing unclean of itself: but to him that esteemeth any thing to be unclean, to him it is unclean. But if thy brother be grieved with thy meat, now walkest thou not charitably. Destroy not him with thy meat, for whom Christ died.

"Let not then your good be evil spoken of: for the kingdom of God is not meat and drink; but righteousness, and peace, and joy in the Holy Ghost. For he that in these things serveth Christ is acceptable to God, and approved of men. Let us therefore follow after the things which make for peace, and things wherewith one may edify another. For meat destroy not the work of God. All things indeed are pure; but it is evil for that man who eateth with offence. It is good neither to eat flesh, nor to drink wine, nor any thing whereby thy brother stumbleth, or is offended, or is made weak. Hast thou faith? Have it to thyself before God. Happy is he that condemneth not himself in that thing which he alloweth. And he that doubteth is damned if he eat, because he eateth not of faith: for whatsoever is not of faith is sin" (Rom. 14:1–23).

Verse 4: *"And as they went through the cities, they delivered them the decrees for to keep, that were ordained of the apostles and elders which were at Jerusalem."*

*"The cities"* mentioned here are the cities of Syria, Cilicia, and other areas where Paul and Barnabas had preached the Gospel and churches had been established. Paul, Silas, Timothy, and others of their party went through those cities, visiting the various churches and *delivering "the decrees"*—the letters that had been written at the council just held in Jerusalem. These decrees were fully discussed in chapter 15, as concerning the ceremonial laws of Moses and the relation of those laws to salvation by faith in the finished work of Jesus.

*"Decree"* usually refers to a law or an edict of a legislature or a king. However in the case of the Church it was not a law. It was simply a decision agreed upon by the members of the council in Jerusalem when the case under discussion was submitted to the elders, the apostles, and other believers in the assembly. The problem was thoroughly considered, under the direction of the Holy Spirit an agreement was reached, and the results of that agreement were written in a letter, a copy of which was dispatched by chosen messenger to all of the churches where there were Gentile believers.

They delivered these decrees *"for to keep"*—that is, regardless of the fact that these "decrees" did not force the Gentile Christians to observe Jewish law, they were nevertheless to be *kept*. They were to be observed to the good of all, that Jewish believers might not be offended. It was made clear that abstaining from meats and other questionable things had nothing to do with salvation, but that such observance was in the interest of unity among brethren, that they might be able to fellowship as the Lord intended His children to fellowship together in His Church.

Verse 5: *"And so were the churches established in the faith, and increased in number daily."*

We think of *"establish"* as meaning to make steadfast, firm, or stable—in other words, to settle on a firm or

permanent basis. This can be applied to the churches here. As Paul and his traveling companions revisited the churches, they not only distributed *the letter from the council in Jerusalem,* but gave personal help where needed, taught the Word, encouraged and strengthened the believers in the various assemblies. As a natural child grows and develops from proper feeding and care, so does the born again child of God grow and develop in Christian character as he feeds on the Word and walks from day to day in the increased light shed on his pathway by his study and knowledge of God's way and will.

Thus as the missionaries traveled from one church to another those churches grew and the believers *"increased in number daily."* That is God's method. Today we see great denominations put on visitation programs, push "membership drives," and use whatever enticement they can design in order to take more members into their congregation and increase attendance records. But you will notice in Acts 2:47 that *"the LORD* added to the Church daily such as should be (were being) *SAVED."*

Certainly there is nothing wrong with visitation. Christians should be interested in soul winning, and in the interest of soul winning we *should* spend time in visiting, meeting new people, inviting them to services, even taking them in our own car if need be; but there is not one name added to the record in heaven except the names of those who are saved by the grace of God, washed in the blood, born again through faith in the finished work of Jesus! Then, and only then, God adds them to His Church.

It is plainly evident that the Apostle Paul was not satisfied to simply lead men into the knowledge of salvation and then leave them to get along the best they could in a world filled with temptations and dangers for the babes in Christ. Paul believed that every child of God should know his spiritual birthright, and that he should be instructed in the ways of righteousness in order

that he *live, speak, and think* to the glory of God.

He begged the Roman believers to present their bodies "a living sacrifice, holy, acceptable unto God," *a reasonable service* (Rom. 12:1). He pleaded with the Ephesian Christians, "Be not drunk with wine . . . but *be filled with the Spirit*" (Eph. 5:18). In Romans 6:12, 13 he urges, "Let not sin therefore reign in your mortal body, that ye should obey it in the lusts thereof. Neither yield ye your members as instruments of unrighteousness unto sin: but yield yourselves unto God, as those that are alive from the dead, and your members as instruments of righteousness unto God!"

Wherever Paul was used of the Lord to establish a church, the believers in that church were his children in the Lord and he loved them. He was concerned about their spiritual welfare, he prayed for them without ceasing, and at every possible opportunity he returned to visit with them and encourage them that they might be established and built up in the faith.

## The Macedonian Vision

Verse 6: *"Now when they had gone throughout Phrygia and the region of Galatia, and were forbidden of the Holy Ghost to preach the Word in Asia."*

Paul and Silas traveled *"throughout Phrygia."* At this time this was the largest Roman province in Asia Minor. It was divided into two parts—Asian Phrygia and Galatian Phrygia—but the line between them was never strictly drawn. We know from Acts 2:10 that Jews from Phrygia were present at Pentecost. Today the population there consists of Turks, Greeks, Armenians, Jews, and other smaller tribes of uncertain ancestry and peculiar customs. Sheep and goat raising are the leading industries. Through this large, mountainous province Paul and Silas passed, and entered *"the region of Galatia,"* a province directly east of Phrygia.

This area was formerly conquered by the Gauls. They settled there and called it after their own name. Galatia as Paul knew it was a Roman province, but there were many Jews in that area and it was due to this that it was so easy for controversy to arise there between Jewish believers and Gentile believers, as evidenced by Paul's letter to the Galatian Christians.

However, Paul and Silas *"were forbidden of the Holy Ghost to preach the Word in Asia."* So we see that the Holy Ghost *forbids* as well as leading. Luke does not explain *how* the Spirit conveyed this message forbidding these missionaries to preach the Gospel in Asia. Personally, I believe the message was given by revelation, and I believe it was given because it was God's intention to extend the Gospel farther into the regions of Greece than would have been done had Paul and Silas remained in Asia Minor. God is omniscient, He knew the end in the beginning, and He knew exactly how to map out the routes His ministers were to travel.

The territory here called *"Asia"* was, according to Bible authorities, called Ionia. It was the region of Proconsular Asia, and Ephesus was its capital. Here, too, were such cities as Smyrna, Thyatira, Philadelphia, and other cities within which were established the seven churches of Revelation chapters 1 through 3. The Gospel was later preached with great success in all of these regions, but at the time of Paul's second missionary journey a more important and much wider field was opened to him, for when the Spirit forbade Paul and Silas to preach the Gospel in Asia, the door into Europe was opened to the Gospel for the first time.

Verses 7 and 8: *"After they were come to Mysia, they assayed to go into Bithynia: but the Spirit suffered them not. And they passing by Mysia came down to Troas."*

Mysia, too, was a province of Asia Minor, with Propontis on the north, Bithynia on the east, Libya on the

south, and the Aegean Sea on the west. When Paul and Silas reached Mysia *"they assayed* (endeavored, desired, or made plans) *to go into Bithynia: but the Spirit SUFFERED THEM NOT."*

Again the Holy Spirit forbade Paul and Silas following their own wishes. I am sure Paul had a good reason for wanting to go into Bithynia, I am sure he felt that there was a need there—*and so there was;* but God would take care of that need in His own good time and according to His eternal plan. Meanwhile, through the Holy Spirit He instructed Paul not to go into Bithynia to preach the Gospel. Paul yielded to the Spirit, knowing that Jesus saved him, called him, and by revelation gave him the message he was to deliver. Therefore, as the Spirit *directed,* he kept traveling. They left Mysia and *"came down to Troas."*

*Troas* is a name of historic interest. It can refer to either the city, or to the district surrounding it. The city of Troas is situated on the coastline of Asia Minor, and along that coastline many historic battles have been fought—bloody battles which are recorded in the annals of history. It was in this province that the ancient city of Troy stood, and the region was celebrated in the early and powerful period of Grecian history. It was here that many of the events recorded in Homer's writings are supposed to have taken place. The city of Troas has long since been completely destroyed, and only the ruins, barely discernable now, testify to the size, importance, and majesty which history declares characterized it in ancient times. *Troas* is mentioned several times in the New Testament, and in Acts 20:6 we will find Paul preaching there. It was also in that city that he raised Eutychus from the dead.

Verse 9: *"And a vision appeared to Paul in the night: There stood a man of Macedonia, and prayed him, saying, Come over into Macedonia, and help us."*

*"A vision appeared to Paul in the night."* When God closes a door to His servants, He always opens another door. The Holy Spirit had forbidden Paul and Silas to preach the Word in Asia and, obedient to the Spirit's leading, they traveled to Troas. There, in a vision, God gave further direction. This was not unusual; God often spoke to His chosen vessels in such a manner. The Old Testament prophets—Isaiah, Ezekiel, Daniel—even faithful Abraham, received messages from God in visions. In Acts 10:3 Cornelius was instructed in a vision to send for Peter. At the same time *Peter* was being instructed in a vision to *answer* the call from Cornelius (Acts 10:3—16). It was in a vision that God commissioned Ananias to call on Saul of Tarsus just after Saul's meeting with Jesus on the Damascus road (Acts 9:10). In Numbers 12:6 the Lord God declared, "If there be a prophet among you, I the Lord will make myself known unto him in a vision, and will speak unto him in a dream."

*"There stood a man of Macedonia."* Macedonia was an extensive Grecian area, bordered on the north by Thrace, on the south by Thessaly, on the west by Epirus, and on the east by the Aegean Sea. It eventually became a Roman province, and it is to this province that the New Testament writings refer when speaking of Macedonia. It has been suggested that the inhabitants of that area were descendants of Kittim, son of Javan (Gen. 10:4); however, the long and varied history of Macedonia would indicate that it was later inhabited by people of many nationalities among whom were Turks, Albanians, Greeks, Bulgarians, and Jews. That kingdom rose to great power under the reign of Philip II and his son, Alexander the Great; and in the New Testament record it was the first region in Europe in which the Gospel of the saving grace of God was preached.

In Paul's vision the man from Macedonia "prayed him, saying, *Come over into Macedonia, and help us.*" Here again we are afforded an intimate look at the

Apostle Paul. He had not intended to travel in Europe at this time, he did not leave Antioch on his second missionary journey with any idea of preaching the Gospel in Europe. But *the Holy Spirit* had that mission field in mind, and Paul was ever obedient to the Spirit. I do not doubt that he wondered *why* he was forbidden to preach in Asia; certainly there was a need for evangelism there and Paul's heart reached out to those fertile fields. But in spite of what may have been a puzzled mind, his obedience to the Spirit drove him on toward Troas, and the unmistakeable direction of God in the vision directed him to Macedonia.

In his conversion from Judaism to Christianity, Paul did not make partial surrender. He was *completely* given over to God's service, a bondslave of Jesus Christ. He testified, *"I KNOW WHOM I have believed"*—not a program, not a ceremony, but *a Person*—"and am persuaded that He is able to keep that which I have committed unto Him against that day" (II Tim. 1:12). Paul had a personal Saviour to whom he was a bondslave. He was no longer his own. He was crucified to the old life and to everything connected with it, and the life he lived was not lived by sight or by might, but by faith (Gal. 2:20). He had a deep sense of responsibility to the One with whom he was crucified and in whom he lived.

Paul's personal testimony was always positive, never negative:

*"I serve"*—"There stood by me this night the angel of God, whose I am, and whom I serve" (Acts 27:23).

*"I can"*—"I can do all things through Christ which strengtheneth me" (Phil. 4:13).

*"I do"*—"This one thing I do, forgetting those things which are behind, and reaching forth unto those things which are before, I press toward the mark for the prize of the high calling of God in Christ Jesus" (Phil. 3:13, 14).

*"I keep"*—"I keep under my body, and bring it into subjection: lest that by any means, when I have preached

to others, I myself should be a castaway (disapproved)"
(I Cor. 9:27).

"*I am*"—"I am debtor both to the Greeks, and to the
Barbarians; both to the wise, and to the unwise. . . . I
am ready to preach the Gospel . . ." (Rom. 1:14,15). "I
am now ready to be offered, and the time of my departure is at hand" (II Tim. 4:6).

"*I have fought*"—"I have fought a good fight . . . ."

"*I have finished*"—"I have finished my course . . . ."

"*I have kept*"—"I have kept the faith" (II Tim. 4:7).

And finally, with a "Hallelujah!" he could say:
*"Henceforth there is laid up for me A CROWN OF
RIGHTEOUSNESS, which the Lord, the Righteous Judge,
shall give me at that day:* and not to me only, but
unto all them also that love His appearing" (II Tim. 4:8).

That the Holy Spirit perfectly directed Paul is proved
and demonstrated by the record of happenings in Philippi,
Thessalonica, Berea, Athens, Corinth, Ephesus—wherever
the Gospel was preached on this missionary journey.
Churches were established, and only eternity will reveal
how many hundreds or thousands of souls were saved.
If Paul had been allowed to preach in Asia he might
have remained there, or if he reached Europe at all he
might have done so at an inopportune time. What then
would have happened to the Philippian jailer, Lydia,
and others among the heathen people in idol-worshipping
localities such as Ephesus and the wicked city of Corinth?
God in His omniscience saw it all, the Holy Spirit directed in all undertakings, Paul was obedient in all that
he did, and thus the will of God was done to His glory
and to the good of mankind.

The Holy Spirit still guides God's preachers today—
not always through flaming visions, not always in words
spoken in order that mankind might hear and understand;
but by circumstances and everyday occurrences—*commonplace things*, sometimes difficult, sometimes dark and
disappointing, but always by His perfect design.    We

may not always understand, we may stand perplexed for awhile, but if we are obedient to His direction we soon discover the truth of Romans 8:28 and realize that all things *do* work together for good to them that love God and are called according to *His* purpose!

If we are completely surrendered to God's service according to His divine will, if we are attuned to the voice of the Holy Spirit as was the Apostle Paul, then difficulties will become definite opportunities of faith and service.    Let us rest in the Lord in times of darkness, trusting until the light breaks through—as indeed it will!  God's shortest route to "Troas" may be in direct opposition to our personal plans, but it is better to go God's route *with Him* than anywhere else on earth *without* Him.

Verse 10:    *"And after he had seen the vision, immediately we endeavoured to go into Macedonia, assuredly gathering that the Lord had called us for to preach the Gospel unto them."*

*"After HE had seen the vision"*—indicating that the Holy Spirit spoke only to Paul, the others in his company did not see the vision—*"IMMEDIATELY we endeavoured to go into Macedonia."*  No excuses were offered here, no questions asked, no time given over to hesitation.   Paul certainly knew by this time that trials, tribulations, dangers, and hardships awaited him in the heathen land whereunto he had been called.   The people there knew nothing of the saving grace of God, they had never heard the message of salvation *by* grace.   But Paul recognized the invitation of the Spirit, he knew the Macedonian call had come from God, and where God led *he was willing to go.*   Therefore he did not consider the hardships, trials, dangers, and likely persecution.   *Immediately* he took his little company of men and started on his way to Macedonia.

We notice something else of importance in this verse:

Luke changes from third person to first person in his narrative. From *"he"* (speaking of Paul) he now says, *"WE endeavoured to go* into Macedonia," indicating that he is now in Paul's company. Probably he joined the missionaries at about this time, since this is the first instance in which he refers to himself as being one of Paul's traveling companions. In Galatians 4:13 Paul spoke of an "infirmity of the flesh," and it is quite likely that God gave him a personal physician to travel with him. How good God is!

We know from the Scriptures that Luke was with Paul on the greater part of his missionary journeys, and in Colossians 4:14 Paul speaks of him as "Luke, the *beloved* physician." Then in his parting message to Timothy, his son in the ministry, Paul wrote, *"Only Luke is with me."*

In the last part of our present verse we note Paul's complete confidence in the direction of the Holy Spirit— *"ASSUREDLY gathering that the Lord had called us for to preach the Gospel"* in Macedonia. Again we see the personal pronoun is in the first person—"the Lord had *called US."* We must not miss the fact that every man in this party of missionaries was called of God. The Apostle Paul had already become the leader and outstanding man in the group, but the Holy Spirit would never have directed as He did had not all of them been called to that work, just as every believer *today* is called of God. Oh, no—not all Christians are called to stand in pulpits, or go to mission fields in foreign lands, or teach a Bible class, or sing, or play an instrument; but from the moment a person is saved, that person is called to the service of God! Whatever your occupational duties, no matter how great or how insignificant, those duties are to be rendered *as unto God.* Paul declares emphatically that *whatsoever* we do—eating, drinking, daily living—is to be done to the glory of God (I Cor. 10:31).

Luke was not an apostle, nor were Silas and Timothy. But these men who traveled with the Apostle Paul, regardless of their place in the background, were *called of God* to go into Macedonia with the message of salvation by the grace of God through faith in the finished work and shed blood of the Lord Jesus Christ. That is Luke's testimony here.

I wonder how many "Macedonians" are calling today —all around us, in the places where we work, living right next door to us, meeting us every day as we go about our daily tasks—and we are not attuned to hear their call? Perhaps we are too busy in our place of business—or even too busy in the program of our church—to be aware of those with whom we come in frequent contact who desperately need our help. The Gospel of the grace of God is still the only message of salvation, and the souls of men and women today are still as important as in the days when the Apostle Paul carried the living Word to the Macedonians.

Verse 11: *"Therefore loosing from Troas, we came with a straight course to Samothracia, and the next day to Neapolis."*

*"Loosing* (setting sail) *from Troas,"* the missionary band went to Samothracia, an island in the Aegean Sea not too far from Thrace. Since the inhabitants of the island were from Samos and from Thrace, it was called by a combination of those two names. It was a small island, about twenty miles in circumference, and was considered to be an asylum for criminals and fugitives. Thus it furnished a rich field in which to sow the seed of the Gospel.

*". . . and the next day to Neapolis."* This was a maritime city of Macedonia, located near the borders of Thrace and about ten miles from Philippi. The fact that it occupied a position on a neck of land between two bays made it an excellent harbor on both sides. It is

said to be here that the fleet of Brutus and Cassius was moored at the time of the battle of Philippi in 42 B. C.

Verse 12: *"And from thence to Philippi, which is the chief city of that part of Macedonia, and a colony: and we were in that city abiding certain days."*

From Neapolis, Paul and his companions traveled to *Philippi, "the chief city of that part of Macedonia."* The former name of this city was *Dathos.* It was rebuilt and beautified by Philip II and was renamed *Philippi* in his honor. During the civil war of the Romans many outstanding battles were fought there. The city of Philippi was famous as the site of the decisive battle between Brutus and Anthony, and it was there that Brutus committed suicide.

Luke also tells us that Philippi was *"a colony."* The entire region had been conquered by the Romans, and it was then divided into four provinces. The rendering of the original language indicates that Philippi was a city or province occupied by Roman citizens, it had the rank and dignity of a Roman colony, and old Roman coins still in existence today declare this as fact.

When Rome's soldiers took possession of an area, they reproduced Rome *in miniature.* Government and habits of life were Roman. Ruled by Rome, such a colony was *continuously in touch* with that great city. Its magistrates were *appointed* by Rome, sent *from* Rome, and they did that which was *pleasing and beneficial* to Rome.

Thus at Philippi Paul found himself closer to the great center of world government. He was a Roman citizen and he looked with longing eyes toward the capital, yearning to reach that city and take it for Jesus through the sword of the Spirit, the Word of God. He declared, *"I must also see Rome!"* (Acts 19:21). It was not his desire to see Rome as *we* might see Rome, Cairo, Paris, or London today—through the eyes of a tourist. Paul would see that great city through the eyes of a missionary

with a passion for souls.

It is noteworthy that in Paul's missionary journeys he invariably settled at strategic centers, places from whence roads led out into surrounding communities, smaller cities, and out-of-the-way places. That was one reason he longed to reach Rome. The slogan in that day was *"All roads* lead to Rome," and *from* Rome great highways led throughout the known world. Paul had a vision of a lost world, and he longed to preach the Gospel to as many souls as he could possibly reach in the time allotted to him in God's eternal plan.

When Paul arrived in Philippi the church had been established in Jerusalem for about twenty years. The world of unregenerate men, ignorant concerning the divine movements of Almighty God as He works out His eternal program, little knew at that time that a man had moved into the city of Philippi and started a movement which would eventually bring about the fall of the great Roman empire! Paul entered the city without fanfare or advance notice, and it is not unreasonable to suppose that he entered into a few hours of rest before opening his campaign of evangelism, preaching the grace of God. Yes, the preaching of the Gospel by Paul and his companions in the area of Philippi was the beginning of the fall of Rome.

*"And we were in that city abiding certain days."* That could mean a week, a month, or longer. We have no way of ascertaining how long Paul remained in Philippi, but if you will read the four short chapters of his epistle to the Philippian Christians you will see how genuine and how great was his love for his converts there.

Verse 13: *"And on the Sabbath we went out of the city by a river side, where prayer was wont to be made; and we sat down, and spake unto the women which resorted thither."*

At that time there were Jews scattered throughout the

world, but from this verse we see their pitiful position in Philippi. There were not even ten Hebrews of eminence there, for if there had been as many as ten they would have established a synagogue. Paul and Silas found only a little group of women at the appointed place of prayer—dedicated women who recognized God and their relationship to Him.

Yet in that city which was the center of idolatry under the rule of Rome, Paul sought and found vantage ground for carrying on his ministry: he learned of a little Bible class that met outside the city *"by a river side,"* and he attended their meeting on the Sabbath—whether by his own choice or by invitation from the women we are not told.

We notice that *"prayer was wont to be made"* in this particular place. It was not just a casual prayermeeting, but the usual place of prayer. It was the common thing for the Jews to erect a definite place of prayer, particularly where there were Jewish families but not enough in number to have a synagogue. The established place of prayer was very important in their worship—in fact, it is necessary for them to have their synagogue or its equivalent in order to worship at all. So important is this custom that even passenger ships today have a small synagogue for the use and convenience of Jews who travel on the ocean liners.

Thanks be unto God, that is not true of Christianity! Christ is the *end of the law* with all of its ceremonies and buildings. Believers are living stones builded together into an habitation of God, and where two or three are gathered together in His name He is in the midst of them to own and to bless. But in the transition period many true believers still met in the Jewish synagogues. It was Paul's custom to go into the synagogues on the Sabbath, as did many other Jewish believers, in order to give out the Gospel message to Israel.

That the Apostle Paul attended this prayermeeting

where only women were present testified to the genuine-
ness of his conversion. He was a Pharisee of the Pharisees, and it was their custom to repeat every day, "O
God, I thank thee that I am neither Gentile, nor slave,
*nor woman!"* These words were repeated daily by the
Pharisees and leaders in the Jewish religion; yet Paul,
after meeting Jesus on the Damascus road, declared,
"There is neither Jew nor Greek, there is neither bond
nor free, *there is neither MALE NOR FEMALE: for
ye are all ONE in Christ Jesus"* (Gal. 3:28). Thus did
he contradict what he had said for many years as a
Pharisee. He abandoned the Jewish religion and therefore abandoned contempt for a woman. He was a new
creation in Christ Jesus, and through his sermon to this
little group of women, Christianity gained a foothold
in Europe.

*"We sat down, and spake unto the women which re-
sorted thither."* Evidently Paul was the spokesman here
(v. 14), and although his sermon is not recorded, there is
no doubt in my mind as to what he took for his subject.
To the Corinthian believers he said, "I determined not
to know any thing among you, save *Jesus Christ, and
Him crucified"* (I Cor. 2:2). That was his message, no
matter where or to whom he preached. It was always
centered on the death, burial, and resurrection of Jesus
(I Cor. 15:1–4).

### The First Convert In Europe

Verse 14: *"And a certain woman named Lydia, a seller of purple, of the city of Thyatira, which worshipped
God, heard us: whose heart the Lord opened, that she
attended unto the things which were spoken of Paul."*

Several facts about Lydia are given in this verse. She
was *"a seller of purple"*—or of "purple-dyed garments."
This alone tells us that she was a woman of rank, a
member of the elite class. Purple was a most valuable

color, obtained in that day from shellfish. It was very expensive, chiefly worn by rich people, and therefore a merchant dealing in purple would of necessity be a person of some financial means in order to be able to deal in a commodity as profitable—and costly—as the wares Lydia handled.

She was *"of the city of Thyatira."* This was one of the cities which Paul was compelled to by-pass on his way to Troas since the Spirit forbade his preaching in that area. It was an outstanding city, a metropolis where much business was carried on. The art of dying materials was early cultivated in Thyatira, and it is possible that Lydia brought her merchandise from there, although she was a resident of Philippi.

This verse also tells us that she *"worshipped God."* She was evidently a Jewish proselyte. Like Cornelius (Acts 10:2), she was religious, she had a deep desire to know God in truth; and when any person truly wants to know the truth God will *make it possible* for that person to *know* the truth. Lydia heard the message preached that Sabbath, the message of salvation through the death, burial, and resurrection of Jesus. Luke tells us that the Lord opened her heart, and *"she attended unto the things which were spoken of Paul."*

It was God who opened Lydia's heart, and the only possible way for Him to open a heart is through the hearing of the Gospel. Lydia heard the Word of God, it opened her heart, she listened attentively to Paul's message. She believed, she was born again, and became the first convert in Europe.

Verse 15: *"And when she was baptized and her household, she besought us, saying, If ye have judged me to be faithful to the Lord, come into my house, and abide there. And she constrained us."*

*"She was baptized and her household."* Lydia here gave testimony to her saving faith, and as in the case of

Cornelius (Acts 10:47, 48) she and her entire household were baptized. I repeat here what I have said many times before—the New Testament teaches *household salvation.*

It seems that in those days it was customary for a saved person to be baptized immediately after believing. This was true at Pentecost (Acts 2:41), it was true of the Ethiopian eunuch (Acts 8:37, 38), it was true of Cornelius and his household (Acts 10:48), and it was true of the Philippian jailer and his household (Acts 16:33).

Then Lydia besought Paul and his companions to stay in her home. She said, *"If ye have judged me to be faithful to the Lord"*—that is, "If you count me as a sister believer, if you believe that I am truly saved, then I invite you to *come into my house, and abide there."* To me, this is another suggestion of Lydia's financial affluence since she had a home large enough to accommodate several abiding guests. It was customary among believers to offer hospitality to other Christians who came into a city or community. In Corinth, Paul stayed with Aquila and Priscilla (Acts 18:1—3).

*"And she constrained us."* The Greek word here translated "constrained" is found only one other time in the New Testament—in Luke 24:29—where it is used with reference to Christ's walking with the two disciples on the way to Emmaus. Therefore we conclude that the word is peculiar to Luke's writings. The two disciples "constrained" Jesus, that He tarry with them; He accepted their invitation, and as He broke bread with them they recognized Him. They then returned to Jerusalem with the good news that "the Lord is risen indeed!" (Read Luke 24:13—34.)

Now in our present Scripture Lydia "constrains" Paul and Silas and their company and offers them the hospitality of her house. In this day of "bigness"—world churches, world programs, great denominations boasting thousands of members—the conversion of *one woman*

*and her household* seems a small thing; but it was through Lydia and her hospitality that the Gospel had a vantage point in the idolatrous city of Philippi, and from that point it spread abroad and victory came to the hearts of thousands. I believe this is evidenced in Paul's letter to the Philippians, for in chapter 1 verses 3 through 5 he said, *"I thank my God upon every remembrance of you,* always in every prayer of mine for you all making request with joy, *for your FELLOWSHIP IN THE GOS-PEL from the first day until now."* I believe "the first day" here refers to that day when Paul preached his first sermon in the ladies' Bible class in Philippi and God opened the first heart in Europe—the heart of Lydia, and opened her home as well.

Yes, only one woman and her household comprised the beginning of the church in Philippi; but Paul looked upon that church with unusual joy, and I am inclined to believe that he considered it the crowning result of his ministry. Sometimes in our Bible study we miss precious things and pass over them as being insignificant; but if it had not been for Lydia the record of the Gospel in Philippi might have told an altogether different story. By comparison, if it were not for the godly women in most churches today the work of spreading the Gospel would be tragically hindered. I look out over the con-gregations before whom I speak, and often wonder, "Where are the *men?"* There are far more women than men in the churches today.

There are many instances in the Bible where God used women in His service. In addition to Lydia we might mention *Deborah,* a prophetess who is also listed among the judges of Israel. God used her as a leader of His people at a time of national distress, and it was largely due to her courage that Barak won the battle against Sisera, captain of the army of Jabin, king of Canaan, "and the hand of the children of Israel prospered." Read the story in Judges 4:4—24. Deborah's song of victory is

recorded in Judges chapter 5.

*Esther,* an orphan girl who became queen, was used of God for a great purpose. Her clear judgment and spirit of self-sacrifice saved the Hebrew nation from extermination at the hands of their enemies. Her story is recorded in the book of the Bible that bears her name.

*Dorcas,* about whom we studied in Acts 9:36—43, was a humble woman, noted chiefly for her good works and almsdeeds among the poor; yet she was the only woman in the New Testament to be called a "disciple." Her life and her testimony brought glory to God.

We could not pass over *Mary Magdalene,* the last person at the cross, the first at the tomb on resurrection morning. In Mark 16:9 we read, "Now when Jesus was risen early the first day of the week, *He appeared FIRST to Mary Magdalene,* out of whom He had cast seven devils." What would be the magnitude or scope of the testimony of such a woman, her untiring devotion to her Lord bringing her to face dangers which caused even the chosen twelve to desert Him?

We could mention so many more—Rahab the harlot, hiding the spies in order that they might carry back to Israel the needed information from the land of Canaan (Joshua chapter 2). Mary and Martha, sisters of Lazarus, are familiar figures in the ministry of Jesus as they offered their home, their hospitality, and their service that He who had no place to lay His head might find rest and comfort.

Solomon, the man of great wisdom, pronounced blessing upon godly women in general when he wrote, "Who can find a virtuous woman? for her price is far above rubies. The heart of her husband doth safely trust in her, so that he shall have no need of spoil. . . . Strength and honour are her clothing; and she shall rejoice in time to come. . . . Her children arise up, and call her blessed; her husband also, and he praiseth her" (Prov. 31:10—28 in part).

Thank God for women whose hearts are open to Jesus and whose homes are open to preachers of the Gospel of the grace of God! Thousands of men have been saved because of the faithfulness of a godly woman who opened her heart to the Gospel message, was saved, and through faithful prayer and consecrated living was used of God to melt the hard heart of an ungodly husband and lead him to Christ.

## A Demon Cast Out—Paul and Silas Imprisoned

Verse 16: *"And it came to pass, as we went to prayer, a certain damsel possessed with a spirit of divination met us, which brought her masters much gain by soothsaying."*

*"As we went to prayer"*—perhaps returning to the same place mentioned in verse 13—"a certain damsel possessed with *a spirit of divination* met us." It is not clear whether this happened on the same day Lydia was saved, or whether it occurred a day or several days later. This "certain damsel" was demon-possessed. The word here translated *"divination"* is *Python* (sometimes spelled Pythios), one of the names given to Apollo, the Grecian god of music, poetry, fine arts, eloquence, and medicine. He was esteemed to have been the third son of Jupiter and Latona. Beautiful temples were erected to him, and people came from far and wide to worship him in the temples. One priestess of Apollo claimed to be inspired and at times gave answers to questions which were regarded as the oracles of God.

The art of divination (fortune telling) was practiced extensively throughout that area, and was the source of much gain. This young woman who met Paul and Silas *"brought her masters much gain by soothsaying."* But regardless of what legend and tradition taught concerning this practice or the inspiration of those who practiced it, Paul regarded the whole thing as a case of

*demon possession.*

Verses 17 and 18: *"The same followed Paul and us, and cried, saying, These men are the servants of the most high God, which shew unto us the way of salvation. And this did she many days. But Paul, being grieved, turned and said to the spirit, I command thee in the name of Jesus Christ to come out of her. And he came out the same hour."*

There is no explanation of *why* this damsel followed the missionaries for "many days," but all the while she cried out, *"These men are the servants of the most high God!"* We know that Satan and his demons know much about God and about the Scriptures. Every time demons met Jesus during His public ministry they immediately confessed Him as the Son of God. When He met the demon-possessed men of Gadara, the demons cried out, "What have we to do with thee, Jesus, thou Son of God? Art thou come hither to torment us before the time?" (Matt. 8:29).

In Capernaum He met a man with an unclean spirit which cried out, "Let us alone; what have we to do with thee, thou Jesus of Nazareth? Art thou come to destroy us? I know thee who thou art, the Holy One of God" (Mark 1:24). In Mark 3:11 we read that when unclean spirits saw Jesus they fell down before Him and cried, "Thou art the Son of God!"

The demon who possessed the girl at Philippi recognized Paul and Silas as men of God, and the girl herself revealed what the demon recognized. It could be that this poor, demented damsel, under the power of the demon, hoped to acquire more popularity and a more prominent reputation as being *inspired* if she prophesied by telling who these men were and what they were doing. Naturally this would impress the multitudes who did not understand that she was under the power and motivation of demons—but she did not fool Paul for one moment.

The devil was using her as a dangerous weapon against the Church.

This girl was declaring the truth about Paul and Silas and their company, but when the devil tells the truth about the Bible, about Jesus, or about believers, a peril is created. It is said that *truth must win,* no matter who utters it; but dear friend, this is the master lie which has cursed the Church of God for almost twenty centuries! The Spirit of the living God within the Apostle Paul revealed to him what the devil was doing through this girl, Paul rejected her testimony, rebuked the demon and cast him out.

All through the ministry of Jesus, while men denied Him and called Him an imposter, the demons cried out, "Thou art the Son of God!" But every time the demons told the truth about Him, Jesus refused their testimony, commanded them to be quiet, and cast them out. Paul possessed the indwelling Spirit, the same Holy Spirit that led him to Philippi. He was in perfect fellowship with Jesus, and he well knew that it was the devil's plan and program to hinder the message of grace and defeat the Gospel in that great city of idolatry and sin.

If the devil is once permitted to cooperate, he will tell the truth. Liberals and modernists tell the truth— that is, *as far as they go.* They preach just enough truth to lead many well-meaning, sincere people away from the true fundamentals of the faith. The girl in Philippi was telling the truth; but Paul stopped her testimony because it was not bringing glory to God, and in the end it would greatly hinder the cause of Christ in that city.

Ministers today should follow Paul's example. Many religious leaders (so-called) invite the cooperation of liberals and modernists who deny the virgin birth, the verbal inspiration of the Scriptures, and the blood atonement even while accepting the *fact* of God and believing many of the cardinal truths of Christianity. Therefore when

these men are admitted into the fellowship of funda
mental, Bible-believing Christians and allowed to lead
in prayer or otherwise take part in the work of the
church, they do great harm to the cause of Christ.  Allow
the devil to enter into the fellowship of the preaching
of the Gospel, and before long he will twist and distor
the truth, add a bit here, take away a bit there, modify
and tone down, until the truth of God is changed into
deadly and damnable heresy!  This has happened *many
times over* in this present day.

Some ministers feel that we can *help* liberals and
modernists by allowing them to come into our fellowship
and work with us, but this is not true.  God's Word
asks, *"Can two walk together, except they be agreed?"*
(Amos 3:3).

We are further commanded, *"Be ye not unequally
yoked together with unbelievers:* for what fellowship
hath righteousness with unrighteousness? and what com
munion hath light with darkness?  And what concord
hath Christ with Belial? or *what part hath he that believeth with an infidel?*  And what agreement hath the
temple of God with idols? for *ye* are the temple of the
living God; as God hath said, I will dwell in them, and
walk in them; and I will be their God, and they shal
be my people.  *WHEREFORE COME OUT FROM A
MONG THEM, AND BE YE SEPARATE, saith the
Lord, AND TOUCH NOT THE UNCLEAN THING*
and I will receive you, and will be a Father unto you
and ye shall be my sons and daughters, saith the Lord
Almighty"* (II Cor. 6:14—18).

Another clear warning and commandment from God's
Word is found in II John 7—11: "Many deceivers are
entered into the world, who confess not that Jesus Chris
is come in the flesh.  This is a deceiver and an anti
christ. . . . Whosoever transgresseth, and abideth not in
the doctrine of Christ, hath not God.  He that abideth
in the doctrine of Christ, he hath both the Father and

the Son. *If there come any unto you, and bring not this doctrine, receive him not into your house, neither bid him God speed: FOR HE THAT BIDDETH HIM GOD SPEED IS PARTAKER OF HIS EVIL DEEDS!"*

The devil's ministers and false apostles look so much like the true ministers of God that many people are deceived by them. Paul warns against this in his second letter to the Corinthian believers. He explains, "Such are false apostles, deceitful workers, transforming themselves into the apostles of Christ. And no marvel; for *Satan himself is transformed into an angel of light! Therefore it is no great thing if his ministers also be transformed as the ministers of righteousness;* whose end shall be according to their works" (II Cor. 11:13—15).

However, there are some ministers — pastors, evangelists, missionaries, and Bible teachers — who are strong in the Lord. They reject the cooperation of friends of the enemy of pure, unadulterated Gospel. Some people say, "I attend a church where a liberal is pastor, but I take the *good* and reject the *bad."* Beloved, this is spiritual ignorance! Even if it were possible to "take the good and reject the bad" it would still be against God's will for a born again believer to attend and support such a church. His command is, *"COME OUT from among them,"* and have no fellowship with them at all. To contribute to the support of a church pastored by a liberal or modernist is to contribute to the enemies of the Lord Jesus Christ.

When the demon-possessed damsel at Philippi had followed Paul and his companions for *"many days,"* Paul turned to her and said to the spirit, *"I command thee in the name of Jesus Christ to come out of her. And he came out the same hour."* Some people contend that there is no such thing as a genuine fortuneteller, they laugh at the idea of spiritualism and witchcraft; but I assure you that this is no laughing matter. There are people who are *sold out to Satan* — mind, body, and

soul. I have just pointed out, by way of God's holy Word, that the devil has ministers who transform themselves (disguise themselves) as ministers of righteousness. They are messengers of hell, they possess Satanic power, and Satan speaks through them. When Paul began to preach the Gospel in Philippi, his greatest danger was not the peril of being arrested and imprisoned—oh, no! His gravest peril was this demented damsel with the spirit of divination following him about and telling the truth about him.

The evil spirit came out of her at Paul's command. *"The same hour"* does not mean that the spirit came out of the girl at some time within the next sixty minutes, but *immediately*. The Spirit of God is more powerful than the spirit of Satan, and the command given by God's man *"in the name of Jesus Christ"* was instantly obeyed. "Ye are of God, little children, and have overcome them: *because greater is He that is in you, than he that is in the world"* (I John 4:4).

Verses 19—21: *"And when her masters saw that the hope of their gains was gone, they caught Paul and Silas, and drew them into the marketplace unto the rulers, and brought them to the magistrates, saying, These men, being Jews, do exceedingly trouble our city, and teach customs, which are not lawful for us to receive, neither to observe, being Romans."*

The devil does not give up easily. Failing in his efforts to hinder the Gospel by proclaiming *the truth* through the soothsayer, he immediately changed his tactics, adopted the method of antagonism, and passed from sight. But even though he was not *seen*, he was still operating in a most effective way—he was now active *behind the men of the world.*

*"When her masters saw that the hope of their gains was gone"* they wasted no time in planning strategy against Paul and Silas. They immediately went into

action. They had been making merchandise of this poor
girl, and in verse 16 we were told that she brought them
*"much gain by soothsaying."* Now, by her deliverance
from the evil spirit, their bank account was affected and
they decided to be rid of these preachers who had cost
them that avenue of income. So *"they caught Paul and
Silas, and drew them into the marketplace unto the
rulers."*

The *marketplace* was a court or forum where crowds
could assemble. Therefore court was often held in or
near the marketplace. The *"rulers"* in this instance
were the civil magistrates, not the religious leaders. Since
Philippi was a Roman colony the magistrates there were
of military status, probably officers in the Roman army
who executed double duty as both civil and military
authorities.

*"These men, being Jews, do exceedingly trouble our
city."* This of course was untrue. Paul and Silas were
not "troubling" the city of Philippi. They had cut off
the financial gain of these unscrupulous men when they
led the young soothsayer to Jesus. Free of demon possession, indwelt by the Spirit of God, she was a new
creation in Christ Jesus and was no longer of gainful use
to her masters. However, they did not come out openly
and publicly announce that the men of God had robbed
them of their questionable source of income and put an
end to their merchandising at the expense of the poor
fortuneteller. Instead of telling the truth about Paul and
Silas they falsely charged them with disturbing the public
peace.

Not satisfied to bring only one accusation against the
missionaries, they went further and declared, "They teach
*customs which are not lawful for us to receive."* Suddenly these greedy men became concerned about their city
and the laws of the land! They had no respect for the
law, they were simply *pretending* concern in order to
rid the city of these preachers of the Gospel who had

*already* interfered with their money-making scheme—
and there was no telling what kind of upheaval might
result from their being allowed to *remain* in Philippi!

This was the attitude the Jews had expressed toward
Jesus after the raising of Lazarus. They said, "If we
let Him thus alone, all men will believe on Him: and
the Romans shall come and take away both our place
and nation" (John 11:48). They were fearful lest the people, converted to Christianity by the miracles and message of Jesus, would turn against them and refuse to
follow their directions, thus causing them to lose both
position and power. The men at Philippi had already
felt the impact of Christianity, it had cost them their
source of income, and they wanted it stopped before it
gained further hold on the people. Their god was money.

The Apostle Paul declared, *"The LOVE of money is
the root of all evil"* (I Tim. 6:10), and the men at Philippi were not the last to oppose God's ministers because
of money. It is unbelievable what men will do to rid
the community of a true minister of the Gospel if his
preaching causes them to lose business and thus restricts
the flow of dollars into their bank accounts! There are
men who claim to be Christians, yet they rent property
to the liquor crowd and other ungodly people who operate night clubs, dance halls, and houses of ill repute
where young women are robbed of their virtue and young
men become habitual drunkards.

The men who own such property may live in a re-
spectable neighborhood—even in a restricted area where
beautiful, well-kept homes are the order of the day. They
may be members of a local church, and from their ill-
gotten gains they may contribute liberally to the *support*
of that church; but when God's minister comes in and
preaches against sin, and under his preaching souls are
saved and the people begin to turn away from sinful
practices, business drops off in the gambling houses and
night clubs. The men who own property in such dis-

tricts, seeing that their income is in jeopardy, will suddenly become concerned about their town and the church. They themselves live quietly, and they maintain that there is nothing wrong with what they are doing. Thus year after year they pursue their wicked ways of getting financial gain, and they despise any form of religion which would cut into their profits. Then when their true character is exposed these same men become suddenly filled with zeal for the betterment of the community, and appear most pious in church affairs in order to forestall any threat to their source of income.

Men who have money as their idol are the most hypocritical people on earth, and even while plying their wicked trade they can appear to have the utmost reverence for the law and for the church. When they determine to rid their city of God's preacher they (like the men in Philippi) do not give their *real reason* for their determination. They accuse the minister of preaching too loudly, or too long, or without proper education. Or perhaps there is something wrong with his wife—she is extravagant, she does not dress with enough style, or she dresses *too* fashionably and thus brings the world into the church! The preacher may not visit enough, or he visits too much and neglects his other duties. He does not have enough ambition and the church is not advancing, or he has *too much* ambition and not enough spirituality. It is the same old scheme in new clothes, the same devil working behind the scenes to hinder the cause of Christ.

So it was with the men in Philippi who had gotten "much gain" from the damsel's fortunetelling. They were so angry with the missionaries that they were determined to create enough excitement and turmoil to cause the civil authorities to take action against them.

*"Customs"* here means religious rites or forms of worship. The enemies of Paul and Silas were actually charging them with introducing a new religion which was not

in accord with Rome and was therefore unauthorized
by Roman law. This was a cunning, undermining accusation. These men were not concerned about defending
their beliefs, they cared nothing for either the religion
of Rome or the religion of the Jews. They were simply
hiding behind the laws of Rome.

Historians tell us that the Romans had a law which
forbade the introducing of a new religion into Roman
territory. *Wetstein* tells us that the Romans allowed
foreigners to worship their own gods if it were done
secretly, so that the worship of those gods would not
interfere with the allowed worship of Rome. Neither
was it lawful among the Romans that a *new* religion be
recommended to the citizens, a religion contrary to that
which was confirmed and established by public authority.
Much care was taken among the Romans and the Athenians that no one introduce a new religion, and it was
on this account that *Socrates* was condemned. It was
also for this reason that the Chaldeans and Jews were
banished from the city of Rome. Cicero said, "No person shall have any separate gods or new gods, nor shall
he privately worship any strange gods unless they be
publicly allowed."

Verse 22: *"And the multitude rose up together against
them: and the magistrates rent off their clothes, and
commanded to beat them."*

I am sure the devil chuckled when these men finished
their complaint against Paul and Silas, because *"the
multitude rose up together against them"* and mob violence became evident. This verse indicates that the
entire episode was done in a popular tumult without
even the *form* of trial by law. Paul later complained
about this as a violation of his privileges as a freeborn
Roman citizen (v. 37). These men who claimed to be
so zealous in upholding the law, so filled with concern
for the honor of Rome, were the first to *disregard* Roman

law; and when the proper time came, Paul reminded them of it.

"*And the magistrates*"—the very men who should have demanded the mob to disperse, the men who should have seen that Paul and Silas had a fair trial—"*rent off their clothes, and commanded to beat them.*" According to Roman law, when prisoners were to be whipped they were stripped down to a loincloth, thus laying bare the back and legs. In the writings of Cicero pertaining to such punishment we read, "He commanded the man to be seized, and to be stripped naked in the midst of the forum, and to be bound, and rods to be brought." The actual beating was done by *lictors*, officers of the Roman army. The punishing of prisoners was one of their duties.

Verses 23 and 24: "*And when they had laid many stripes upon them, they cast them into prison, charging the jailor to keep them safely: who, having received such a charge, thrust them into the inner prison, and made their feet fast in the stocks.*"

"*When they had laid MANY stripes upon them . . . .*" This may have been one of the beatings Paul mentioned in II Corinthians 11:25 when he said, "Thrice was I *beaten with rods.*" The Jews were prohibited by law from laying more than forty stripes on a prisoner, and just to be on the safe side they usually gave *only thirty-nine.* It was to this punishment that Paul had reference when he said, "Of the Jews five times received I forty stripes *save one*" (II Cor. 11:24). But there was no law limiting the number of stripes the *Romans* could administer, and it stands to reason that they gave Paul and Silas a very thorough beating—or, as Paul mentions in II Corinthians 11:23, "stripes *above measure.*"

"*They cast them into prison.*" Undoubtedly the magistrates did this for a twofold reason—as punishment for the charge of troubling the city, and to please the men who had brought the complaint against them. They also

charged the jailer *"to keep them safely."* This meant that if the jailer should allow his prisoners to escape he would pay with his own life, and for this reason he put Paul and Silas *"into the INNER prison."*

These men of God were given the treatment afforded Public Enemy Number One today. They were guilty of no crime against the state, no misdemeanor, yet they were confined under such security measures as would be used against the most dangerous criminals. As an extra precaution against Paul and Silas escaping, the jailer then *"made their feet fast in the stocks."* The Greek reads, "made their feet secure to wood."

Stocks were used both as a form of punishment and as a means of absolute security. They were constructed of wood, with holes through which the prisoners' feet (and sometimes the hands, also) were placed; and when locked into position it was impossible for the hands and feet to be withdrawn until the jailer opened the stocks. Thus, Paul and Silas were not only in severe pain from the beating they had endured, they were also in a position of extreme discomfort.

### A Midnight Prayermeeting—A Jailer Saved

Verse 25: *"And at midnight Paul and Silas prayed, and sang praises unto God: and the prisoners heard them."*

Think of the intense pain these men were suffering! Their backs were a mass of torn and bloody flesh from the beating they had just undergone. They were held almost immovable in the stocks in the cold, damp recesses of a Roman prison, without food and water, without any consideration for their physical comfort or well-being. But did they grumble? Did they ask, "What have we done to deserve this?" No. We read, *"At midnight, Paul and Silas PRAYED."* That is one thing a believer can do no matter where he is, no matter how

severe his pain may be or what may be his posture. God
is always attuned to the sincere prayers of His children.

Paul and Silas not only prayed, they also *"sang praises unto God."* Yes, God *"giveth songs in the night"*
(Job 35:10). The Psalmist wrote, "The Lord will command
His lovingkindness in the *daytime,* and *in the night His
song shall be with me,* and my prayer unto the God of
my life" (Psalm 42:8). In Psalm 149:5 we read, "Let the
saints be joyful in glory: let them *sing aloud upon their
beds!"*

*"And the prisoners heard them."* This was no secret
praise service, no silent prayermeeting, no whispered
hymns of praise. After a season of prayer, Paul and
Silas *sang*—and they sang so loudly that the prison cells
echoed with their voices and the other prisoners heard
them. Can you imagine the amazement of those other
prisoners when they heard the songs of praise coming
from the inner cell where God's men were confined?
They must have known that these two men were in serious trouble, otherwise they would not have been locked
in the inner prison. Perhaps they knew of the beating
that had been administered to the missionaries. But
whatever they might have known of the circumstances
that put Paul and Silas in jail, they certainly knew that
they were in no position to be rejoicing and singing
praises to God—*humanly* speaking, that is. Prisoners
who have been as cruelly and unjustly treated as these
men were would not be singing hymns of praise, especially not at the midnight hour. But notice how God answered their prayer.

Verse 26: *"And suddenly there was a great earthquake,
so that the foundations of the prison were shaken: and
immediately all the doors were opened, and every one's
bands were loosed."*

God's men can be *locked in,* but *God* cannot be locked
out! In the midst of the songs of praise, *God spoke:*

*"Suddenly there was a great earthquake!"* This was one of the things that happened during the transition period which established the Gospel message in the lives of early Christians, and by which God revealed the truth to unbelievers. It was of such testimony that Paul wrote of *"so great salvation,* which at the first began to be spoken *by the Lord,* and was *confirmed unto us* by them that heard Him; *God also bearing them witness, both with SIGNS AND WONDERS, AND WITH DIVERS MIRACLES*, and gifts of the Holy Ghost, according to His own will" (Heb. 2:3,4). The earthquake furnished proof that God was present, and that He defended and cared for His own. The earth rocked and reeled with a mighty convulsion as God answered the prayer of His servants and testified to those who had abused them!

"The foundations of the prison were shaken *and immediately ALL the doors were opened."* There is more in this miracle than simply an earthquake which would set Paul and Silas free. Insofar as the sacred record tells us, they were the only born again believers in the prison; yet the Scripture tells us that every door in the prison was opened *"and every one's bands were loosed."* Miraculous indeed! Normally, the building would have collapsed and many prisoners would have been killed. I have traveled in countries where great earthquakes have struck, and even after many years had passed, the scars of destruction remained—places where the earth broke asunder and left great gorges and valleys. An earthquake that would shake the foundation of a prison, open all the doors within, and strike the chains from every prisoner was certainly no ordinary earthquake. God was speaking to the city of Philippi!

God did not send an earthquake to release *Peter* from prison (Acts 12:5—10). He sent an *angel* who delivered Peter from prison without even disturbing the guards outside the door. But the circumstances then were entirely different. There was no one in that group who

would listen to the Gospel as in the case of Paul and Silas when God knew that the jailer would be converted and his entire household saved. So we see that God did not send the earthquake simply to set His men free; He could have accomplished their freedom just as Peter was set free. The earthquake was sent in order that an entire household might hear the Gospel and be born again. (There is no record that anyone but the jailer and his household was converted, but I sincerely believe that other prisoners were born again as a result of that great earthquake and the testimony of God's servants.)

There are so many practical things that we can learn from the experience of Paul and Silas here. *Jesus Christ is the same "yesterday, and today, and for ever"* (Heb. 13:8). The source of the believer's peace, assurance, and happiness lies within the heart, and external things cannot take it away. External circumstances cannot destroy that which abides in the bosom of every born again believer. The enemies of the Gospel cannot destroy the peace that Jesus gives—*perfect* peace (Isa. 26:3). In John 14:27 Jesus bequeathed peace to His children. He said to His disciples, *"Peace I leave with you, MY peace I give unto you;* not as the world giveth, give I unto you. Let not your heart be troubled, neither let it be afraid."

The devil may take away the comforts of God's ministers and missionaries, he may cause them to be put behind bars; but he cannot take away the peace and rest of the soul! Physical freedom may be denied God's preacher, but no prison can take away the liberty Jesus gives. "If the *Son* therefore shall make you free, *ye shall be free indeed!"* (John 8:36).

Verse 27: *"And the keeper of the prison awaking out of his sleep, and seeing the prison doors open, he drew out his sword, and would have killed himself, supposing that the prisoners had been fled."*

The keeper of the prison was probably enjoying a

good night's rest.    He had thrust Paul and Silas into the inner cell of the prison, fastened their feet securely in the stocks, and there was no chance of their escape even if he discounted the terrible scourging they had endured.    Therefore he felt safe in retiring to his own quarters for the night.    But he had reckoned without the fact of Almighty God!

He was awakened from sleep when the earthquake rocked the foundations of the prison, he saw the prison doors were open, and his first thought was undoubtedly of the price he would have to pay if his prisoners had escaped.    It was the law of the land that if a jailer or guard allowed the escape of a prisoner he forfeited his own life in payment for his carelessness. The jailer knew that if his prisoners had fled he would be put to death by his superiors, so he decided to take his own life, *"SUPPOSING that the prisoners had been fled."*

*Supposition* can be extremely costly.    Let us look at some other instances recorded in the Scriptures where people "supposed" and paid a dear price for their supposition:

In Luke 2:41—46 we read that when Jesus was twelve years old, Mary and Joseph took Him with them to Jerusalem to attend the feast of the Passover.    "And when they had fulfilled the days, as they returned, the child Jesus tarried behind in Jerusalem; and Joseph and His mother knew not of it.    *But they, SUPPOSING Him to have been in the company, went a day's journey;* and they sought Him among their kinsfolk and acquaintance. And when they found Him not, they turned back again to Jerusalem, seeking Him.    And it came to pass, that *after THREE DAYS they found Him* in the temple, sitting in the midst of the doctors, both hearing them, and asking them questions."

Webster's dictionary defines "suppose" as "an opinion entertained without positive knowledge or special thought of error."    It is dangerous to *suppose* concerning eternal

matters.  The Bible is a book of exclamation points, not a book of question marks.  When dealing with spiritual matters we should be sure; we should *know WHOM* we have believed (II Tim. 1:12).  If I should ask you, "Are you an American citizen?" you would immediately answer, "Yes, I am"—or "No, I am not," as the case might be.  But ask the average church member, "Are you born again?  Are you *saved?*" and most of the time the answer will be, "I *suppose* I am," or "I *hope* I am," or "I am doing the best I can."

Peter warns us to *give diligence* to make our calling and election sure (II Pet. 1:10).  We should leave nothing to chance where things eternal are concerned.  *We CAN know* beyond any shadow of doubt whether or not we have been born again, for *"the Spirit Himself beareth witness with OUR spirit, that we are the children of God"* (Rom. 8:16).

By *"supposing"* Jesus to have been with them, Mary and Joseph lost fellowship with Him, but His *relationship* to them remained the same.  It is entirely possible for believers to become so involved in the affairs of this life—even religious activities—that they lose fellowship with Jesus.  Born again?  Yes—but out of fellowship. To every born again believer I say with Peter, "Sanctify the Lord God in your hearts:  and be ready always to give an answer to every man that asketh you a reason of the hope that is in you with meekness and fear" (I Pet. 3:15).

Mark 6:45—52 records another instance where someone "supposed" instead of being sure.  Just after the Lord Jesus fed five thousand people, He sent the disciples by boat to the other side of the Sea of Galilee.  The location of that body of water makes it subject to sudden storms, and such a storm arose while the disciples were yet "in the midst of the sea."  Jesus saw them toiling at the oars, "for the wind was contrary unto them:  and about the fourth watch of the night He cometh unto

them, walking upon the sea, and would have passed by them. But when they saw Him walking upon the sea, *they SUPPOSED it had been a spirit,* and cried out: for they all saw Him, and were troubled. And immediately He talked with them, and saith unto them, Be of good cheer: it is I; be not afraid."

Then Jesus entered into the ship, the wind ceased, and the disciples "were sore amazed in themselves beyond measure, and wondered." Supposition could have been very costly to the disciples that night. If Jesus had not joined their company the little fishing boat might have capsized and they could all have been drowned.

*Joseph and Mary,* "supposing" Jesus to be in their company, lost fellowship with Him, traveled a day's journey without Him, and then spent *three* weary, frightful days retracing their steps.

*The disciples,* "supposing" Jesus to have been a spirit, could have capsized and lost their lives.

*The Philippian jailer,* "supposing" his prisoners had all fled when the prison doors were opened, almost took a short-cut to hell. If he had taken his own life before he heard the message of salvation, that is exactly what would have happened!

I thank God that it is not necessary to "suppose" concerning spiritual matters. Anything we need to know about from the spiritual aspect we can learn from God's Word. When the Bible declares "Thus saith the Lord" we can believe it, stand upon it, live by it, and die by it, for God cannot lie (Heb. 6:18; Tit. 1:2).

Verses 28 and 29:   *"But Paul cried with a loud voice, saying, Do thyself no harm: for we are all here. Then he called for a light, and sprang in, and came trembling, and fell down before Paul and Silas."*

Surely the jailer was astonished beyond measure! Here was further evidence of God's hand at work. Not only

had the building not collapsed in the earthquake, not only had *every* door been open and *every* bond removed, but the prisoners had remained in the jail! They could have fled, they could have disappeared into the night amid the pandemonium that undoubtedly reigned at that moment. Yet Paul assured the jailer that his prisoners were all present. These were things the mind of the jailer could not fathom.

Paul was the spokesman, and the fact that he *"cried with a LOUD voice"* indicates that there was much noise and confusion there.

Then the jailer called for a light—and you will notice he did not just casually walk into the presence of the missionaries. He *"sprang in, and came trembling,* and fell down before Paul and Silas."

It is not necessary to *run to the altar* to be saved, it is not necessary to *tremble* in order to be saved. I have *seen* people come running to the altar, I have seen many weep, I have heard some wail and moan under deep conviction. But I have seen others sit quietly with bowed head, and claim the joy of salvation without outward emotional signs. The *jailer* "sprang in" where Paul and Silas were, and he fell down before them. He meant business. He wanted to be saved.

It is not necessary to fall down on one's knees in order to be saved—Zacchaeus was saved coming down a sycamore tree! You can be saved in an automobile, in a plane, in the field, sitting quietly at home. God does not designate a *place* to be saved, He only designates a *WAY*—the *one way* of salvation.

### Believe — Receive — Trust

Verse 30: *"And brought them out, and said, Sirs, what must I do to be saved?"*

Everything up to this point occurred behind prison walls; but when Paul and Silas assured the jailer that

the prisoners were all present, no one had escaped, he *"brought them out,"* probably into a courtyard. Then he asked them the most important question that can be asked:

*"Sirs, WHAT MUST I DO TO BE SAVED?"* The word here translated "sirs" actually reads "lords"—not Jehovah God, but a title, a form of address, usually used by slaves when addressing their masters. It has been suggested that the jailer was asking what he must do to be saved from the arm of the Roman law, but this is absurd under the recorded circumstances. The answer Paul and Silas gave him *proves* that he was not thinking of his physical safety. It seems plain that this man realized his need of salvation, he knew he was in the presence of the servants of Almighty God, and while it is clear from his question that he did not *understand* the way of salvation, he knew these men of God could *show* him the way, and he desperately longed for the right relationship with his Creator. He knew from what had happened in the jail that these were the most unusual prisoners he had ever locked behind bars. He knew the hand of God had rocked the prison with a mighty earthquake, and he knew that a power greater than the power of man's laws had kept the prisoners from running away. There is no reason to think that the jailer asked the question for any reason except to be saved from sin and eternal damnation.

Someone may ask, "Where did the Philippian jailer *learn* about salvation?" This offers good grounds for speculation. In the first place, it would be unreasonable to suppose that he did not know why Paul and Silas were imprisoned. Certainly he knew they had been severely beaten—perhaps he had *assisted* with their punishment. I doubt that the conversion of the soothsaying damsel had gone undiscussed, and it is entirely possible that word from the happenings at the ladies' prayer-meetings (vv. 13 and 14) had also reached his ears. It

had evidently meant little to him when these prisoners had been turned over to his keeping after their scourging, for the Scripture says nothing to indicate that he felt, at that time, either pity or concern for them as he "thrust them (roughly, no doubt) into the inner prison, and made their feet fast in the stocks."

But the subsequent events convinced him that these men *did* have something to offer. They *did* have a relationship with Almighty God that proved to him the truth they had been preaching. Whether he had heard their messages or had gleaned information as it was passed from one person to another, we cannot know. But God's miracle at the prison convinced him of his need for the salvation these men were preaching.

It is not the usual thing for a jailer to be on his knees before his prisoners; but this man was filled with distress and terror. Happenings so evidently of divine origin had taken place around and before him, and the men who *should* have been trembling with fear were calm with the peace that only Jesus gives! Salvation bestows upon the believer that which nothing *on earth* can give. It brings peace "which passeth all understanding" (Phil. 4:7). It gives calm in times of stress, and confidence in the hour of tragedy and anxiety. The true believer passes through trying hours and dark days with assurance—even joy; but the *sinner* has no anchor for the soul, and in times of tragedy and darkness he lives in dread and anxiety. The Philippian jailer, filled with godly fear, fell on his knees before Paul and Silas and cried out, "What must I do to be saved?"

Verses 31 and 32: *"And they said, Believe on the Lord Jesus Christ, and thou shalt be saved, and thy house. And they spake unto him the Word of the Lord, and to all that were in his house."*

This is the simple, plain, *and only* plan of salvation. Paul and Silas did not instruct the jailer to pray, seek,

or beg.    They simply said, *"Believe on the Lord Jesus Christ."*

What does it mean to *believe?*    James 2:19 declares that the *demons* believe and tremble—but we know the demons are not saved.    Salvation is not of intellectual belief; it is *with the HEART* that man "believeth unto righteousness; and with the mouth confession is made unto salvation" (Rom. 10:10).

People who have been brought up in a Christian home, those who have attended Sunday school regularly and have heard many Gospel sermons, do not find it difficult to believe.    But to many others, *believing* and *faith* are deep mysteries which they cannot grasp.    They cannot understand what it means to have faith unto salvation. Many unsaved people will say, "I have *always* believed the *Bible,* and I have always believed in Jesus as the Son of God—but I know I am not saved."    But when we learn from the Word of God what faith is and how it is obtained, the matter of *believing* is no longer difficult.

The Apostle Paul explained, "If our Gospel be hid, it is hid to them that are lost:  in whom the god of this world hath blinded the minds of them which believe not, lest the light of the glorious Gospel of Christ, who is the image of God, should shine unto them" (II Cor. 4:3, 4). The devil has blinded the minds of unbelievers, and it is difficult for them to understand the way of salvation, simple though it is.  Paul further explained, "The *natural man* receiveth not the things of the Spirit of God:   for they are foolishness unto him:   neither can he know them, because they are spiritually discerned" (I Cor. 2:14).

Since the natural man is unable to receive the things of God, since he is blinded by the god of this age, dead in trespasses and sins, *how can he ever come to the place where he can exercise faith in God unto salvation?* Paul and Silas said to the Philippian jailer, *"Believe on the Lord Jesus Christ,* and thou shalt be saved"—but

note: "and *they spake unto him THE WORD OF THE LORD.*"

*Jesus* said, "He that heareth my WORD, and believeth on Him that sent me, hath everlasting life, and shall not come into condemnation; but is passed from death unto life" (John 5:24).

*Paul* said, "By *grace* are ye saved *THROUGH FAITH* . . .*" (Eph. 2:8); and Romans 10:17 declares, *"Faith cometh by hearing,* and hearing by *the Word of God.*"

From John 1:1, 14 we know that *Jesus was the Word:* "In the beginning was the Word, and the Word was with God, and the Word was God. . . . and *the Word was made flesh,* and dwelt among us, (and we beheld His glory, the glory as of the only begotten of the Father,) full of grace and truth."

Jesus was the Word of God brought down to man. He said, "He that heareth my word . . ."—but *what are His words?* He said, "For God so loved the world, that He gave His only begotten Son, that whosoever believeth in Him should not perish, but have everlasting life. For God sent not His Son into the world to condemn the world; but that the world through Him might be saved. He that believeth on Him is not condemned: but he that believeth not is condemned already, because he hath not believed in the name of the only begotten Son of God" (John 3:16—18).

Ephesians 2:8 tells us that salvation is by grace, through faith—the gift of God. A *gift* is something *received.* John 1:12 tells us, "As many as *received HIM* (Jesus), to them gave He power to become the sons of God, even to them that believe on His name."

Therefore: *to "believe on the Lord Jesus Christ"* is to simply believe what the Bible teaches about God's *love* for sinners and what God *did* for sinners. Believe it, receive it—accept it simply because *God said it.* (Read Hebrews 6:18 and Titus 1:2.) "Faith cometh by hearing, and hearing by the Word of God" (Rom. 10:17). You are

reading the Word of God in this message. If you are not saved, *receive* what the Word of God says. *Believe* that Jesus died for you, *repent of your sins,* accept the Word of God and ask Him to save you for Jesus' sake. Just bow your head and talk to Jesus about it just as you would talk to your doctor or a very dear friend. He has promised to save you if you will *accept* the salvation He bought and paid for on Calvary's cross—and He cannot, He *will not,* break His promise!

When the Philippian jailer asked, "What must I do to be saved?" Paul and Silas replied, "Believe on the Lord Jesus Christ"—but they did not stop there. They "spake unto Him the Word of the Lord—*and to all that were in his house.*" In other words, Paul and Silas taught the Scriptures—and that included God's love for sinners and His gift of the Lord Jesus. The jailer, hearing the message of salvation, believed it, received it, and it bore fruit immediately.

Verse 33:  *"And he took them the same hour of the night, and washed their stripes; and was baptized, he and all his, straightway."*

What a change salvation wrought in the life of this man! A short while before, he had consented to, if not actually participating in, the cruel scourging of these men of God. His treatment of them when they were assigned to his care after the beating evidenced no concern on his part except for their safety. He had offered them neither care, consolation, nor comfort. But when *salvation* came to his heart "he took them *the same hour of the night*" and ministered to their physical needs. He began by washing their stripes—caring for the wounds inflicted by the rods as the beating was administered, making them as comfortable as he possibly could. I imagine this was a new experience for the jailer. He was no doubt used to such punishment being administered to prisoners and had grown hardened to it. This is

evident in his treatment of Paul and Silas when, immediately following their scourging, he thrust them into the inner prison and locked them in the stocks. More than likely he did not even bother to give them food and water.

*". . . and was baptized, he and all his, straightway."* They did not even wait until daylight. I am not advocating that a person needs to be baptized immediately upon believing, but certainly every born again Christian should follow Christ in baptism—not to *be* saved, not to be *better* saved, but *because he IS saved.* Baptism signifies the death, burial, and resurrection of Jesus. It is an outward testimony that one has been buried with Christ and raised to walk in newness of life with Him. The true believer is dead to the world, buried with Christ; but baptism does not make us any more fully redeemed. It simply testifies to an unbelieving world that we *are* redeemed.

The jailer was baptized, *"he and all his."* The jailer did not believe *FOR* his household, he was not *baptized* for his household; but *each and every member* of his household heard, believed, and was baptized. The salvation Jesus purchased through His sufferings on Calvary is for each and every member of a household.

Verse 34: *"And when he had brought them into his house, he set meat before them, and rejoiced, believing in God with all his house."*

Here is further testimony that the jailer was genuinely saved. He brought Paul and Silas into his home and *"set meat* (or food) *before them."* We are not told when these missionaries had had their last meal, but considering what they had been through it seems reasonable to assume that they were hungry. They probably had quite a feast that night. It was a happy time for all concerned.

The jailer *"rejoiced, believing in God with all his*

*house."* Rejoicing is the effect of believing. *Salvation produces joy,* but there is no singular rule for rejoicing, no specific definition of the kind of joy salvation brings to each individual heart. Peter says Christians rejoice "with joy unspeakable and full of glory" (I Pet. 1:8), but as I have stated previously, there is no set rule for exhibiting that joy. Perhaps the jailer *laughed.* He might have *cried,* as some people do when they are exceedingly happy. He might have simply rejoiced by rendering joyful service to these men of God who had given him the plan of salvation. By whatever outward demonstration he might have shown his rejoicing, we know that he was filled with the joy of sins forgiven. He was a new man, a new creation in Christ Jesus, and he had much to rejoice *about*—not only for himself, but for his entire family, all who were in his house.

Verses 35 and 36: *"And when it was day, the magistrates sent the serjeants, saying, Let those men go. And the keeper of the prison told this saying to Paul, The magistrates have sent to let you go: now therefore depart, and go in peace."*

From verses 22 through 24 it is evident that the magistrates did not intend to release Paul and Silas the next morning. The Scripture does not tell us what brought about this change of mind on the part of the magistrates, but it stands to reason that the earthquake, the conversion of the jailer, and other events that occurred after midnight had a strong bearing on their desire for these men to leave the city as soon as possible. The Romans in that day regarded an earthquake as an omen of the anger of their gods. So whether the magistrates regarded *Jehovah God* or heathen gods, they knew that a power beyond the power of man had produced the earthquake and they were justifiably alarmed.

*"The magistrates sent the serjeants, saying, Let those men go."* The "serjeants" here refers to the lictors—or

"those having rods." These were no doubt the same men who had scourged Paul and Silas the day before, and now they were being sent to tell them they were free, "and the keeper of the prison told this saying to Paul."

It is not clear whether this "keeper" was the jailer who had been converted the night before, or whether he was someone in a higher executive position. But whoever he was, he was concerned for the outcome of this imprisonment and wanted these men out of town for what he considered to be the good of all concerned. So he insisted that they immediately put themselves out of harm's reach. He said to them, *"Therefore depart, and go in peace."*

Verse 37: *"But Paul said unto them, They have beaten us openly uncondemned, being Romans, and have cast us into prison; and now do they thrust us out privily? Nay verily; but let them come themselves and fetch us out."*

If Paul had wanted to leave Philippi secretly he could have done so when the prison doors were opened and his feet were loosed from the stocks. Now the magistrates send word that he is free to go, and they request that he leave the city without further ado. But Paul refused to leave. Instead, he stood his ground and made *three just complaints* against the magistrates:

First of all, the magistrates had ordered Paul and Silas to be beaten *contrary to Roman law* since they were Roman citizens.

Secondly, the beating had been administered *publicly,* thus humiliating them before the masses of the people.

In the third place, they had been scourged and imprisoned *without a trial.*

Although Paul was a Jew, he was also a Roman freeborn. An educated man, he knew Roman law and was well aware of his privileges under that law. Therefore, at

the proper time and in the interest of justice he did not hesitate to declare his knowledge of Roman law and demand that its requirements be met. Thus would he present a testimony against the enemies of the Gospel and vindicate the cause of Christ. It was not personal pride that caused Paul to make his demands upon the magistrates, but his concern for the faith he represented.

*"They have beaten us OPENLY, being uncondemned . . . now do they cast us out PRIVILY?"* Humiliated publicly, Paul demanded a public apology. Let these enemies of the Gospel admit publicly that they had been in the wrong. He knew he had broken no law, therefore the magistrates had no legal right to arrest him. Since he was a Roman they had *even less right* to scourge him. In the writings of Cicero we read, "The body of every Roman citizen is inviolable. The Porcain Law has removed the rod from the body of every Roman citizen." Since he had been condemned unjustly, publicly beaten and then imprisoned without a trial, Paul refused to leave the city quietly, without public acknowledgement of the injustice that had been meted out to him.

*"Let them come themselves and fetch us out!"* Paul was concerned for his testimony as a preacher of the Gospel. He had been accused of stirring up the people and teaching customs not in accord with the law of Rome. He knew that he and Silas were not lawbreakers, they had been falsely accused, and the men who had demanded his arrest and carried out his punishment were in the wrong. This they must publicly admit, for the outcome of this affair would have a direct bearing on Lydia and the other converts, as well as upon those who would be converted in the future.

Paul here gave a beautiful example of dignity and humility. Christian principles were involved. Paul instructed young Timothy that Christians should "lead a *quiet and peaceable life* in all godliness and honesty" (I Tim. 2:2). In Romans 12:18 he said, *"If it be possible,*

as much as lieth in you, live peaceably with all men."
But there comes a time in the life of every child of God
when a definite stand must be taken if we are to give
testimony to the cause of Christ and the saving grace
of God. The believer who refuses to take such a stand
is detrimental to the Church and to the community in
which he lives. Such would have been the case in Philippi if Paul and Silas had not demanded justice. They
had been falsely accused, unjustly arrested and scourged,
imprisoned without a trial, and now for the sake of their
Christian testimony they demanded public exoneration.
It was in the interest of justice that they used their
Roman citizenship.

Verse 38: *"And the serjeants told these words unto
the magistrates: and they feared, when they heard that
they were Romans."*

It was not true repentance toward God that caused
these magistrates to fear. When the men delivered Paul's
message to them and they learned that they had ordered
the scourging of a Roman citizen, they feared the punishment they knew could be dealt out to them for having
violated the laws of the Roman empire. To unjustly
punish a citizen of Rome was to offend the majesty of
the Roman people, and the one who inflicted or ordered
the unjust punishment was himself severely punished under the law. Historians tell us that frequently the punishment in such cases was death, with the Roman government confiscating the guilty person's property. Small
wonder, then, that these magistrates feared the heavy
hand of Roman law when they learned that they had
mistreated Roman citizens.

Verse 39: *"And they came and besought them, and
brought them out, and desired them to depart out of the
city."*

How things had changed! At the time of their arrest

Paul and Silas had not even been given a chance to offer a defense or explain what had really happened. They were given no opportunity to declare their innocence and prove that the charges against them were false. *But now*—the magistrates *"came and BESOUGHT them . . . and desired them to depart out of the city."* These men knew that if Paul and Silas reported their unjust actions to higher Roman authorities, they might have to pay with their lives. So they begged the men of God to leave the city without pressing the matter further. Perhaps they told them that what they had done was done in ignorance, since they did not know Paul and Silas were Roman citizens. Perhaps they told Paul he should have *made it known* that he was a citizen of Rome. (Of course, Paul could have replied that they did not ask!) At any rate, the magistrates lost no time in going to the prison, bringing Paul and Silas out, and asking them to leave the city.

The missionaries granted the request of the magistrates. They did not pursue the matter further. They could have brought charges, but to stir up further trouble could bring reproach upon the name of Jesus. They had accomplished the main purpose of their visit to Philippi— they had preached the Gospel of the grace of God and laid the foundation for a New Testament Church. They had now received public acknowledgement of the injustice of their imprisonment and the illegality of their scourging. The Gospel would not be furthered by additional demands upon the magistrates.

Verse 40:  *"And they went out of the prison, and entered into the house of Lydia:  and when they had seen the brethren, they comforted them, and departed."*

Ever mindful of his testimony before the world and of the example he set before other believers, Paul did not hasten from Philippi.  He took time to visit the home of Lydia and to converse with other converts,

thereby showing that he was neither frightened nor discouraged by what had happened to him. He was not leaving the city under duress, but in his own good time when he had finished God's business there and the Holy Spirit directed him elsewhere.

That Paul and Silas *"comforted them"* undoubtedly refers to a season of exhortation and instruction, perhaps using the immediately past events as proof of the power of prayer, the faithfulness of God in caring for His own, and the need for stedfastness in the Christian life. These were new converts, the church had just been established in the city of Philippi, and there would be trying times ahead for these believers. Then, having taken leave of Lydia and the brethren, Paul and Silas departed.

In Philippians 2:19−24 Paul wrote of Timothy's service in the church at Philippi: "I trust in the Lord Jesus to send Timotheus shortly unto you . . . who will naturally care for your state. . . . Ye know the proof of him, that, as a son with the father, he hath served with me in the Gospel. Him therefore I hope to send presently, so soon as I shall see how it will go with me. But I trust in the Lord that I also myself shall come shortly."

Paul and Silas traveled to Thessalonica, and we will follow their ministry there in the next chapter. It might be well to take a comparative look at the three conversions recorded in the chapter we have just studied. They are not recorded here by accident, but by the direction and inspiration of the Holy Spirit; and in each of them we see the grace of God in action.

There is the quiet conversion of Lydia—a godly woman insofar as she understood the Scriptures. We find nothing spectacular about the conversion of this lady of the elite. She listened attentively to Paul's message, and she was saved. How? By grace through faith, just as *every* believer is saved.

I am thankful for the record of Lydia's conversion. Today we read of movie stars, gangsters, and others who

have great testimonies to give and great experiences to relate in telling of their conversion. But may I remind you that in the true sense of the word, the only kind of experience God *gives* is great! The greatest miracle this side of the Virgin Birth of Jesus is the conversion of a soul, whether it be the emotionally mild experience of someone like Lydia, or a shouting, "hallelujah!" experience that may be heard echoing from one end of town to the other.

The second conversion in our chapter was that of a young soothsayer who was in bondage to wicked men, making money for them with her fortunetelling. She knew nothing of God, but as she followed Paul and Silas she kept crying out, "These men are the servants of the most high God, which shew unto us the way of salvation!" Paul recognized the evil spirit within this damsel, and after several days of such testimony he turned to her and commanded the evil spirit to come out of her. "And he came out the same hour!"

This was a far more spectacular conversion than Lydia's, though certainly no greater. If this had happened in some great city-wide evangelistic campaign such as is often held today, this young lady would undoubtedly be invited to various places to give her testimony. Someone would write a book giving the details of this girl's conversion. But I repeat—in spite of the spectacular way in which the fortuneteller was brought into salvation, her conversion was no greater than Lydia's. It was simply evidenced in a different manner.

It was the conversion of the fortuneteller that led to the conversion of the Philippian jailer; for the masters of the young soothsayer had the missionaries arrested, brought before the magistrates under false accusations, and, after having them soundly beaten, the magistrates consigned them to prison. There, under very discouraging conditions, Paul and Silas prayed and sang at midnight. God answered with an earthquake that shook

the foundations of the prison, opened all the doors, and broke open the bonds of every prisoner. In terror, the jailer was ready to take his own life; but being assured by Paul that the prisoners were all present, he fell down before the two men of God and asked what he must do to be saved. They instructed him in the Word of God, and he and his household were saved. He then rendered Christian service to them by taking them to his home, caring for their needs, and placing food before them — and he rejoiced with all his house.

These three conversions teach us clearly that we should not try to lead others to have the same kind of emotional experience we had when we were converted. *Lydia,* sitting quietly and receiving Jesus with no emotional display; *the soothsayer,* noisy, demon-possessed, spectacularly delivered of the demon and brought into the knowledge of saving grace; and *the jailer*—frightened, at the point of suicide, falling on his knees and crying out, "What must I do to be saved?" Yet of these three people with their varying display of emotion, one was no more fully saved than the other.

There is but *one way* of salvation: Jesus said, *"I am the Way,* the Truth, and the Life. No man cometh unto the Father but by me!" (John 14:6). It is not the emotional display that indicates salvation, but faith in the heart, faith exercised in the finished work of the Lamb of God.

Beloved, *have YOU believed on Jesus?* Are you born again? Do not try to have the same kind of emotional experience someone else had. Do not try to weep as they wept, or laugh as they laughed, or do whatever they did in responding emotionally to salvation. Just simply trust in Jesus, believe on His name, receive Him by faith — and you will be just as gloriously saved as anyone who has been saved since the dawn of creation!

# CHAPTER XVII

1. Now when they had passed through Amphipolis and Apollonia, they came to Thessalonica, where was a synagogue of the Jews:

2. And Paul, as his manner was, went in unto them, and three sabbath days reasoned with them out of the scriptures,

3. Opening and alleging, that Christ must needs have suffered, and risen again from the dead; and that this Jesus, whom I preach unto you, is Christ.

4. And some of them believed, and consorted with Paul and Silas; and of the devout Greeks a great multitude, and of the chief women not a few.

5. But the Jews which believed not, moved with envy, took unto them certain lewd fellows of the baser sort, and gathered a company, and set all the city on an uproar, and assaulted the house of Jason, and sought to bring them out to the people.

6. And when they found them not, they drew Jason and certain brethren unto the rulers of the city, crying, These that have turned the world upside down are come hither also;

7. Whom Jason hath received: and these all do contrary to the decrees of Caesar, saying that there is another king, one Jesus.

8. And they troubled the people and the rulers of the city, when they heard these things.

9. And when they had taken security of Jason, and of the other, they let them go.

10. And the brethren immediately sent away Paul and Silas by night unto Berea: who coming thither went into the synagogue of the Jews.

11. These were more noble than those in Thessalonica, in that they received the word with all readiness of mind, and searched the scriptures daily, whether those things were so.

12. Therefore many of them believed; also of honourable women which were Greeks, and of men, not a few.

13. But when the Jews of Thessalonica had knowledge that the word of God was preached of Paul at Berea, they came thither also, and stirred up the people.

14. And then immediately the brethren sent away Paul to go as

it were to the sea: but Silas and Timotheus abode there still.

15. And they that conducted Paul brought him unto Athens: and receiving a commandment unto Silas and Timotheus for to com to him with all speed, they departed.

16. Now while Paul waited for them at Athens, his spirit wa stirred in him, when he saw the city wholly given to idolatry.

17. Therefore disputed he in the synagogue with the Jews, and with the devout persons, and in the market daily with them tha met with him.

18. Then certain philosophers of the Epicureans, and of the Sto icks, encountered him. And some said, What will this babble say? other some, He seemeth to be a setter forth of strange gods because he preached unto them Jesus, and the resurrection.

19. And they took him, and brought him unto Areopagus, saying May we know what this new doctrine, whereof thou speakest, is?

20. For thou bringest certain strange things to our ears: w would know therefore what these things mean.

21. (For all the Athenians and strangers which were there spen their time in nothing else, but either to tell, or to hear some new thing.)

22. Then Paul stood in the midst of Mars' hill, and said, Y men of Athens, I perceive that in all things ye are too super stitious.

23. For as I passed by, and beheld your devotions, I found a altar with this inscription, TO THE UNKNOWN GOD. Whor therefore ye ignorantly worship, him declare I unto you.

24. God that made the world and all things therein, seeing tha he is Lord of heaven and earth, dwelleth not in temples mad with hands;

25. Neither is worshipped with men's hands, as though he need ed any thing, seeing he giveth to all life, and breath, and a things;

26. And hath made of one blood all nations of men for to dwe on all the face of the earth, and hath determined the times befor appointed, and the bounds of their habitation;

27. That they should seek the Lord, if haply they might feel a ter him, and find him, though he be not far from every one of u.

28. For in him we live, and move, and have our being; as ce tain also of your own poets have said, For we are also his of spring.

29. Forasmuch then as we are the offspring of God, we ough not to think that the Godhead is like unto gold or silver, or ston graven by art and man's device.

30. And the times of this ignorance God winked at; but no

commandeth all men every where to repent:

31. Because he hath appointed a day, in the which he will judge the world in righteousness by that man whom he hath ordained; whereof he hath given assurance unto all men, in that he hath raised him from the dead.

32. And when they heard of the resurrection of the dead, some mocked: and others said, We will hear thee again of this matter.

33. So Paul departed from among them.

34. Howbeit certain men clave unto him, and believed: among the which was Dionysius the Areopagite, and a woman named Damaris, and others with them.

The movement of Christianity in Europe began at Philippi with the conversion of Lydia, the soothsayer, and the jailer. In this chapter that movement extends *further* into Europe. Because of persecution and tribulation it became imperative for Paul to leave Philippi. Many times God permits adversity to move His children from one place to another to spread the Gospel to other peoples. I do not say that this was true of Paul and Silas at Philippi, but certainly God allowed that which happened to them in that city.

From Philippi Paul and Silas traveled to Thessalonica, passing through other cities on the way—but there is no record that they preached in those cities. Apparently they traveled directly from Philippi to Thessalonica where a church was founded—the church to which Paul later addressed two of his epistles.

In this chapter we will also find Paul and Silas ministering at Berea, and at Athens where Paul preached his noted sermon from Mars' hill. Wherever Paul preached the Gospel, the story is the same—victory and travail.

### Founding of the Church at Thessalonica

Verse 1: *"Now when they had passed through Amphipolis and Apollonia, they came to Thessalonica, where was a synagogue of the Jews."*

*Amphipolis* was the capital of the eastern district of

Macedonia. It was originally a colony of the Athenians, but at the time of Paul's visit there, it was under Roman rule. It was near Thrace and was not far from the mouth of the river Strymon, which made it a strategic commercial center. The ancient name of Amphipolis was *"Nine Ways,"* so called because of the number of Thracian and Macedonian roads which met at this point.

*Apollonia* was approximately thirty miles from Amphipolis. It was situated on the Via Egnatia, the great Roman road which was one of the main military and commercial highways of Macedonia. It is believed to have been founded about 432 B. C. Since Amphipolis was about thirty-three miles from Philippi, and Apollonia was a bit less distance from Amphipolis, it seems reasonable to suppose that Paul and Silas took three days for their journey from Philippi to Thessalonica, since the distance between each of these cities could have been made in one day, and there is no indication that the missionaries spent more time in either Amphipolis or Apollonia than was necessary for a night's lodging.

Thus *"they came to Thessalonica."* This was one of the chief cities of Macedonia, and even in this present day it is a thriving metropolis known as Saloniki. The earlier name of Thessalonica was Therma, but in 315 B. C. the Macedonian king Cassander enlarged the city and strengthened it, and then renamed it after his wife *Thessalonica,* who was the daughter of Philip II and stepsister of Alexander the Great. The city soon became populous and wealthy, the headquarters of the Macedonian navy, seat of the governor, and extremely important as a harbor with a large import and export trade. Today it is still a city of vast commercial activity. It is inhabited by Greeks, Romans, and Jews, and it is said that there are as many as thirty-six Jewish synagogues there. Some Bible scholars suggest that our present verse in the Greek declares that Paul and Silas came to Thessalonica "where was THE synagogue of the Jews," suggesting that there

was no synagogue in the other two cities through which they passed.

Verses 2 and 3: *"And Paul, as his manner was, went in unto them, and three sabbath days reasoned with them out of the Scriptures, opening and alleging, that Christ must needs have suffered, and risen again from the dead; and that this Jesus, whom I preach unto you, is Christ."*

*"Paul, as his manner was,"* went into the synagogue. Wherever Paul went it was his custom to attend worship services in the Jewish synagogues. He *spoke* in the synagogues, but he preached the Gospel of the grace of God in hopes of leading his brethren in the flesh into the knowledge of Jesus as Saviour and Lord. We have noticed throughout our study that when Paul entered a city he went first to the synagogue if there was one. He preached the Gospel "to the Jew first," as in Acts 9:20 and 13:5.

So in Thessalonica, as was his custom, he went to the synagogue *"and three sabbath days reasoned with them out of the Scriptures."* I like the wording here. Paul "reasoned" with the Jews, and his reasoning concerned the words of their prophets as related to the Messiah whom they had crucified. In the Greek, the word here translated *"opening"* is used many times in connection with the eye—i. e., to open the eye when it is closed. Therefore Paul opened unto the Jews the Scriptures from the Old Testament prophets, showing them that Jesus of Nazareth was the One of whom the prophets wrote. He explained that according to their prophets, *"Christ must needs have suffered, and risen again from the dead."* This was plainly and unmistakeably foretold by the prophets. The Jews were expecting Messiah—they were not expecting the suffering Christ. They looked for a majestic, powerful, royal leader who as their king would deliver them from the oppression of Rome, and they

could not see that the crown of thorns must precede the crown of glory. Therefore Paul opened the Scriptures to them, alleging that Jesus is Christ, the Messiah for whom they waited, "that Prophet" of whom Moses wrote.

I think it would be well worth our time to read some of those prophecies and then see when and how they were fulfilled:

The Messiah was to be the Seed of the woman, not the seed of man. In Genesis 3:15 God promised a Redeemer. He said to Satan, "I will put enmity between thee and the *woman,* and between thy seed and *HER seed;* it shall bruise thy head, and thou shalt bruise His heel." *This was fulfilled.* In Luke 1:26—33 we read, "In the sixth month the angel Gabriel was sent from God unto a city of Galilee, named Nazareth, to *a virgin* espoused to a man whose name was Joseph, of the house of David; and the virgin's name was Mary. And the angel came in unto her, and said, Hail, thou that art highly favoured, the Lord is with thee: blessed art thou among women.

"And when she saw him, she was troubled at his saying, and cast in her mind what manner of salutation this should be. And the angel said unto her, Fear not, Mary: for thou hast found favour with God. And, behold, thou shalt conceive in thy womb, and bring forth a Son, and shalt call His name JESUS. He shall be great, and shall be called the Son of the Highest: and the Lord God shall give unto Him the throne of His father David: and He shall reign over the house of Jacob for ever; and of His kingdom there shall be no end."

The Apostle Paul also declared this fulfillment. In Galatians 4:4, 5 he said, "When the fulness of the time was come, God sent forth His Son, *made of a woman,* made under the law, to redeem them that were under the law, that we might receive the adoption of sons."

Micah clearly prophesied that Messiah would be born

in Bethlehem: "But thou, *Bethlehem Ephratah,* though thou be little among the thousands of Judah, yet *out of thee shall He come forth unto me that is to be Ruler in Israel;* whose goings forth have been from of old, from everlasting" (Mic. 5:2).

We read the fulfillment of this prophecy in Matthew 2:1, 2: "Now when Jesus was born in Bethlehem of Judaea in the days of Herod the king, behold, there came wise men from the east to Jerusalem, saying, Where is He that is born King of the Jews? for we have seen His star in the east, and are come to worship Him."

In Genesis 49:10 it was prophesied that the coming of Messiah would be through the lineage of the tribe of Judah and that He would be born a king—King of the Jews: *"The sceptre shall not depart from Judah,* nor a lawgiver from between his feet, until *Shiloh* come; and unto Him shall the gathering of the people be."

The seed through which Messiah came was of the lineage of Abraham, Isaac, and Jacob. In Galatians 3:16 the Apostle Paul declared, "Now to Abraham and his seed were the promises made. He saith not, And to *seeds,* as of many; but as of One, And *to thy SEED,* which is Christ."

We know that Jesus was born through the lineage of the tribe of Judah as promised, for in II Samuel 2:4 we read, "The men of Judah came, and there they anointed *David* king over the house of *Judah."* Jesus came through Jesse and the royal line of David. In Isaiah 11:1 we read, "There shall come forth a rod out of the stem of Jesse, and a Branch shall grow out of his roots." From the human side, Jesus is the Son of David, through the seed of David; but from the divine side He is the Son of God. Mary gave Jesus His flesh, but God Almighty gave Him His blood. In Luke 1:35 Gabriel said to Mary, "The Holy Ghost shall come upon thee, and *the power of the Highest shall overshadow thee:* therefore also that holy thing which shall be born of thee shall be called *the Son*

*of God."* Then in Acts 20:28 Paul said to the Ephesian elders, "Take heed therefore unto yourselves, and to all the flock over the which the Holy Ghost hath made you overseers, to feed *the Church of God, which He hath purchased with HIS OWN BLOOD."* Since the Church was purchased through the shed blood of Jesus, we know that the blood that flowed in His veins was the blood of God.

It was also revealed to *David* that Messiah would be of his family, through his seed. In Psalm 132:11 he wrote, "The Lord hath sworn in truth unto David; He will not turn from it: *Of the fruit of thy body will I set upon thy throne."*

Malachi prophesied that Messiah would be preceded by a forerunner who would declare His coming: "Behold, I will send my messenger, and he shall prepare the way before me: and the Lord, whom ye seek, shall suddenly come to His temple, even the messenger of the covenant, whom ye delight in: behold, He shall come, saith the Lord of hosts" (Mal. 3:1).

We see this fulfilled in Matthew 3:1—3: "In those days came John the Baptist, preaching in the wilderness of Judaea, and saying, Repent ye: for the kingdom of heaven is at hand. For this is he that was spoken of by the prophet Esaias, saying, The voice of one crying in the wilderness, Prepare ye the way of the Lord, make His paths straight."

To Daniel God revealed that Messiah would appear at a specific time and that He would be cut off in death at the end of the sixty-ninth week of the seventy weeks of years shown to Daniel: "Know therefore and understand, that from the going forth of the commandment to restore and to build Jerusalem unto the Messiah the Prince shall be seven weeks, and threescore and two weeks . . . and after threescore and two weeks shall Messiah be cut off, but not for Himself . . ." (Dan. 9:25, 26). If you will study the prophecies in the Bible, run the

references and add up the years, you will see that Jesus came at the exact time prophesied by Daniel, and He was *crucified* exactly as Daniel prophesied He would be.

To Zechariah God revealed that Messiah would be betrayed and sold for thirty pieces of silver: "And the Lord said unto me, Cast it unto the potter: a goodly price that I was prised at of them. And I took the *thirty pieces of silver,* and cast them to the potter in the house of the Lord" (Zech. 11:13).

This was fulfilled in Matthew 26:14—16 when Judas sold the Lord for the price of a common slave: "Then one of the twelve, called Judas Iscariot, went unto the chief priests, and said unto them, What will ye give me, and I will deliver Him unto you? *And they covenanted with him for THIRTY PIECES OF SILVER.* And from that time he sought opportunity to betray Him."

To Isaiah God revealed that the Lord Jesus Christ would die for the sins of the people, that He would be numbered with the transgressors, that He would pray for His executioners, that He would make His grave with the rich: "He was taken from prison and from judgment: and who shall declare His generation? For He was cut off out of the land of the living: for the transgression of my people was He stricken. And He made His grave with the wicked, and with the rich in His death; because He had done no violence, neither was any deceit in His mouth. Yet it pleased the Lord to bruise Him; He hath put Him to grief: when thou shalt make His soul an offering for sin, He shall see His seed, He shall prolong His days, and the pleasure of the Lord shall prosper in His hand. He shall see of the travail of His soul, and shall be satisfied: by His knowledge shall my righteous servant justify many; for He shall bear their iniquities.

"Therefore will I divide Him a portion with the great, and He shall divide the spoil with the strong; because He hath poured out His soul unto death: and He was numbered with the transgressors; and He bare the sin

of many, and made intercession for the transgressors"
(Isa. 53:8–12).

To the Psalmist God revealed that Jesus would die
by crucifixion: "I am poured out like water, and all my
bones are out of joint: my heart is like wax; it is melted
in the midst of my bowels. My strength is dried up like
a potsherd; and my tongue cleaveth to my jaws; and thou
hast brought me into the dust of death. For dogs have
compassed me: the assembly of the wicked have in-
closed me: they pierced my hands and my feet. I may
tell all my bones: they look and stare upon me. They
part my garments among them, and cast lots upon my
vesture" (Psalm 22:14–18).

If you will make a thorough study of the Gospels you
will find that every detail of these prophecies from Isaiah
and David was fulfilled. The quotation just given from
Psalm 22 is a graphic description of the scene at Calvary
when the Lord Jesus Christ died for the sins of the world.

Not only did Jesus Himself declare that He would
rise from the grave on the third day, but centuries before
the Incarnation God revealed to David that Messiah
would rise from the dead: "For thou wilt not leave my
soul in hell; neither wilt thou suffer thine Holy One to
see corruption. Thou wilt shew me the path of life: in
thy presence is fulness of joy; at thy right hand there
are pleasures for evermore" (Psalm 16:10, 11).

The Old Testament Scriptures given here should have
been familiar to every Jew, and it was from such passages that Paul spoke to the Jews in Thessalonica, reasoning with them, opening up the Scriptures, proving that
the crucified, risen, and ascended Christ was none other
than their expected Messiah.

Verse 4: *"And some of them believed, and consorted
with Paul and Silas; and of the devout Greeks a great
multitude, and of the chief women not a few."*

*"SOME of them believed."* From Isaiah chapter 53 it

should be possible to prove to any Jew that Christ must needs have suffered and died in order to save lost sinners; but the majority of these Jews had closed minds, they refused to believe that Jesus of Nazareth was their Messiah. Their minds were made up that He was an impostor and they would not hear Paul even though he reasoned with them from their own Scriptures which clearly declared Messiah's coming, His suffering, His death, and His resurrection.

Yet we need not be critically surprised by the attitude of the Jews in not believing the prophecies concerning the first advent of Jesus as related to their Messiah. There are hundreds of thousands of people—yes, *church members*—who have heard the Gospel message and the prophecies of our Lord's *second* coming, but they do not believe it. The Scriptures plainly and emphatically teach that Jesus is coming back to this earth—literally and bodily; but just as the Jews expected a powerful leader who would at that time restore the glories of Israel, so the majority of church people today expect to convert the world and bring in a reign of righteousness on earth!

Beloved, the Bible does not teach that there will be a world-wide revival. It does not teach that the Church will convert the world and bring in the kingdom. On the contrary, it teaches that this earth will become a place of gross sin even as it was in the days of Noah and in the days of Lot. In II Timothy 3:13 we are told that "evil men and seducers shall wax worse and worse."

Jesus Himself asked, "When the Son of man cometh *shall He find FAITH on the earth?*" (Luke 18:8). Only eight souls were saved in Noah's day. I wonder if the ratio would not be about the same, from the spiritual aspect, if we compared the population of Noah's day with the billions of earth's inhabitants today? How many truly born again, God-fearing believers do you know in *your* community? The majority of people today are fulfilling Paul's words to young Timothy—they will not

*"endure sound doctrine,"* they have heaped to themselves teachers, *"having itching ears,"* they have turned away their ears from the truth and have turned *"unto fables"* (II Tim. 4:3, 4).

God promises, "My Word . . . shall not return unto me void, but it shall accomplish that which I please, and it shall prosper in the thing whereto I sent it" (Isa. 55:11). Therefore, whether it be preached by the Apostle Paul or by ministers called and ordained of God today, when the Word is faithfully preached *SOME will be saved,* even though *not all* will believe.

In Thessalonica some who heard Paul's message *believed,* they were saved, "and consorted with Paul and Silas." In other words, they united with the missionaries and became their disciples, students of the Word. They believed on Jesus, they were saved, but they longed to know more about their new way of life. Therefore they became learners and continued under the teaching of Paul and Silas.

*"Of the devout Greeks a great multitude"* believed. These Greeks were "religious"—that is, they worshipped God to the best of their ability with what understanding they possessed. They knew nothing of salvation by grace through faith, but being proselytes they knew the God of the Jews through Judaism and they had not the prejudices which clung so closely to the Jews. Now through hearing the Gospel preached by the Apostle Paul they believed on Jesus, they were saved, and they became members of the New Testament Church, charter members of the local church in Thessalonica to which Paul's Thessalonian letters were penned.

Not only were some Jews and a multitude of Greeks converted, but *"of the chief women not a few."* In other words, a number of the outstanding women of Thessalonica also believed and were saved. We note this in contrast with the "honorable women" of Antioch in Pisidia who joined with the "chief men" there in

stirring up opposition against Paul and Barnabas.

## Jewish Opposition in Thessalonica

Verse 5:   *"But the Jews which believed not, moved with envy, took unto them certain lewd fellows of the baser sort, and gathered a company, and set all the city on an uproar, and assaulted the house of Jason, and sought to bring them out to the people."*

Jealousy and envy are extremely ugly qualities, regardless of the object toward which they are directed— whether it be jealousy of another's education, wealth, personality, or social standing; but the ugliest and most subtle of all jealousy and envy is found in the field of religion.   These unconverted Jews envied Paul and Silas because so many people were coming out to hear them, many of those who heard were being converted, and that meant that they were turning away from Judaism.

There is entirely too much of this same attitude in religious circles today.   If a minister is doing what God called him to do, if he is giving of his best to the ministry God has given into his care, then why should he be envious of *another's* ministry?   The Word of God teaches that a believer should not be jealous of another believer's success.   Paul declares of the New Testament Church "that there should be no schism in the body; but that the members should have the same care one for another.   And whether one member suffer, all the members suffer with it; or one member be honored, all the members rejoice with it" (I Cor. 12:25, 26).

Beloved, if God calls you to be a janitor, then vow by His grace to be the best janitor Jesus has.   If He calls you to pastor a church, whether that church have fifty members or five thousand, vow by God's grace to be the most dedicated pastor He has in the field!   When we are where God wants us, doing what He has given us to do, we have no reason on earth to envy anyone

or to be jealous of our brethren in Christ. We are all members of the same body; so may God help us to be *one*, as Jesus prayed for believers in John 17:21—"That they all may be one; as thou, Father, art in me, and I in thee, that they also may be one in us: that the world may believe that thou hast sent me."

These Jews "which believed not" and who were "moved with envy" gathered together "certain lewd (or vile) men of the baser sort." The Greek is more nearly represented in modern English by "vile fellows of the rabble"—or, to use an English colloquialism—"*loafer.*" Bible authorities tell us that these were men who gathered about the forum or the marketplace where it was customary for the unemployed to assemble and wait for someone to hire them for a day's work. This is borne out in Matthew 20:2, 3 where Jesus gave the parable of the man who went to the marketplace to hire laborers for his vineyard. That the men in our present verse were "of the baser sort" indicates that they were suited for the mob violence to which the Jews planned to incite them. With the assistance of these "lewd fellows" they "*set all the city on an uproar and assaulted the house of Jason*" where Paul and Silas were staying.

Not much is known of Jason, but from Romans 16:21 some Bible scholars believe that he was a relative of Paul.

Verses 6 and 7: "*And when they found them not, they drew Jason and certain brethren unto the rulers of the city, crying, These that have turned the world upside down are come hither also; whom Jason hath received: and these all do contrary to the decrees of Caesar, saying that there is another king, one Jesus.*"

The Scriptures do not tell us where Paul and Silas were at that moment, but the mob did not find them in the home of Jason. Evidently the Holy Spirit had prompted them to move to safer quarters, for had they not been protected, the angry, unreasoning crowd would have

torn them to bits.

Not finding Paul and Silas, *"they drew Jason and certain brethren unto the rulers of the city."* This would be civil rulers, not the religious leaders. The charge brought against the missionaries was that they "turned the world upside down." I deeply appreciate this statement, especially considering those from whom it came. Would to God that ministers today had such spiritual power in their lives that the same thing would be said of them when they go into a city or community to preach the Gospel.

There have been times in the history of the New Testament Church when God called men on the scene—men so fully surrendered and so completely dedicated that the world dreaded to see them come into a community to hold services. Those men preached the Gospel with such power that the wicked men of the area knew their businesses would suffer because revival in the hearts of the people would stop the flow of income into the coffers of the worldly and ungodly business men.

This is but the realization of what Jesus expressed in John 15:18, 19 when He said to His disciples, "If the world hate you, ye know that it hated me before it hated you. If ye were of the world, the world would love his own: but because ye are not of the world, but I have chosen you out of the world, therefore the world hateth you." He also promised those who follow Him, *"In the world ye shall have tribulation:* but be of good cheer; I have overcome the world" (John 16:33).

Failing to find Paul and Silas in the house of Jason, the mob presented their accusation against them anyway, and then charged Jason with having received the missionaries into his house and given them hospitality. Their accusation against Jason and "certain brethren"—that is, other believers—was, *"These all do contrary to the decrees of Caesar, saying that there is another king, one Jesus."* Not only were they accusing the Christians of

introducing a new religion contrary to the laws of Rome, but also with sedition and rebellion against the Roman emperor. The title of "king" was not to be used in any of the vanquished provinces except by special permission from the emperor. Certainly Paul knew that Jesus was not to be King on earth at that time, he thoroughly understood the Church Age and all that lay between the days of his preaching and the Millennium. Therefore those who brought accusation against Paul and Silas and the other believers in Thessalonica perverted their teaching, for if they did declare that Jesus was King of the Jews they did it in the light of prophecy and not from the standpoint of overthrowing the Roman government.

The same accusation was brought against Jesus in His trial before Pilate. The Jews said to Pilate, "We found this fellow perverting the nation, and forbidding to give tribute to Caesar, saying that He Himself is Christ a King" (Luke 23:2). In John 18:33—36 we read that when Pilate asked Jesus, "Art thou King of the Jews?" the Lord replied, "My kingdom is not of this world: if my kingdom were of this world, then would my servants fight, that I should not be delivered to the Jews: but now is my kingdom not from hence."

Verses 8 and 9: *"And they troubled the people and the rulers of the city, when they heard these things. And when they had taken security of Jason, and of the other, they let them go."*

The rulers feared mob violence. If the crowds became excited enough, things could get out of hand. They also feared the reaction of Rome if the emperor heard the charge that there were rebels in Thessalonica. There is no indication here that Paul and Silas were found, or that they were seen again by any save the brethren. And when the rulers "had *taken security*" of Jason and of the other believers, they were released and allowed to return to their homes.

The *"security"* here mentioned means that Jason and the others gave satisfaction to the rulers and magistrates, assuring them that Paul and Silas were *not* seditionists and were not attempting to overthrow the Roman government. Probably Jason and the other Christians promised to be responsible for the two visitors. Whatever the "security" might have included, Jason convinced the rulers that they were doing nothing that was not in accord with Roman law, and gave sufficient security for the good conduct of Paul and Silas.

Verse 10 tells us that the brethren *"immediately"* sent Paul and Silas to Berea. Undoubtedly the Christians knew where to find the missionaries, and they were taking no chances on exposing them again to the threatening mob. Therefore, under cover of night, they sent them on to Berea, about fifty miles away.

Paul spent approximately one month in the city of Thessalonica, but it was probably one of the richest months of his entire ministry; for when Paul and Silas left that city the Gospel had taken deep root in the hearts of many of the people there, the Thessalonian church was established, and that church spread its influence abroad. It maintained a testimony which brought joy to the heart of the Apostle Paul, as revealed in his epistles to that church.

It is believed that Paul's first epistle to the Thessalonians was the earliest of all his writings. It was written from Corinth about 54 A. D., shortly after he left Thessalonica, and in the opening verses of that letter he expressed his regard for the believers in that city. He wrote, "We give thanks to God always for you all, making mention of you in our prayers; remembering without ceasing your work of faith, and labour of love, and patience of hope in our Lord Jesus Christ, in the sight of God and our Father; knowing, brethren beloved, your election of God" (I Thess. 1:2—4).

In II Thessalonians 1:3, 4 he said, "We are bound to

thank God always for you, brethren, as it is meet, because that your faith groweth exceedingly, and the charity of every one of you all toward each other aboundeth; so that we ourselves glory in you in the churches of God for your patience and faith in all your persecutions and tribulations that ye endure."

During his ministry in Thessalonica Paul taught all of the cardinal truths and fundamental doctrines of Christianity. He preached the Word of God in all of its fulness and power. It would be well to consider some of these truths in passing, for Paul's preaching is as applicable today as it was when he penned the inspired words of his epistles.

First of all, he preached Bible election—not hyper-Calvinism, not that some were elected to be saved while others were elected to be damned. He believed in and preached scriptural election; but he also believed in the free will of man. In I Thessalonians 1:4 he said, "Knowing, brethren beloved, your election of God." Jesus came to be a propitiation for the sins of the whole world and the invitation is to all—to "whosoever will."

Paul preached the doctrine of the Holy Spirit. He declared to the believers in Thessalonica, "Our Gospel came not unto you in word only, but also in power, and in the Holy Ghost, and in much assurance; as ye know what manner of men we were among you for your sake. And ye became followers of us, and of the Lord, having received the Word in much affliction, with joy of the Holy Ghost: So that ye were ensamples to all that believe in Macedonia and Achaia" (I Thess. 1:5—7).

Paul also preached Bible *assurance.* In the passage just quoted he spoke of the Gospel which came not in word only, but in power, in the Holy Ghost, *"and in MUCH ASSURANCE."*

He preached one God manifested in three Persons—Father, Son, and Holy Ghost (I Thess. 1:1, 5).

Paul believed in and preached *the second coming of*

*Christ.* In his writings collectively he mentions the Lord's second coming thirteen times as often as he mentions baptism. In I Thessalonians 1:10 he speaks of the believers in Thessalonica waiting for God's Son from heaven, "whom He raised from the dead, even Jesus, which delivered us from the wrath to come."

In I Thessalonians 2:19 he asks, "What is our hope, or joy, or crown of rejoicing? Are not even ye in the presence of our Lord Jesus Christ at His coming?"

He said, "The Lord make you to increase and abound in love one toward another, and toward all men, even as we do toward you: to the end He may stablish your hearts unblameable in holiness before God, even our Father, at the coming of our Lord Jesus Christ with all His saints" (I Thess. 3:12, 13).

In I Thessalonians 4:13—18 Paul explained in detail the second coming of Christ in the Rapture—encouraging the believers concerning their loved ones who had died in the Lord. He said, "I would not have you to be ignorant, brethren, concerning them which are asleep, that ye sorrow not, even as others which have no hope. For if we believe that Jesus died and rose again, even so them also which sleep in Jesus will God bring with Him. For this we say unto you by the Word of the Lord, that we which are alive and remain unto the coming of the Lord shall not prevent them which are asleep.

"For the Lord Himself shall descend from heaven with a shout, with the voice of the archangel, and with the trump of God: and the dead in Christ shall rise first: Then we which are alive and remain shall be caught up together with them in the clouds, to meet the Lord in the air: and so shall we ever be with the Lord. Wherefore comfort one another with these words!"

Yes, the Apostle Paul was a pre-millennialist—he taught the Rapture of the Church, as these verses point out; but he also taught that there would come a day of judgment, the time when this earth will be judged and sudden

destruction will come upon the wicked. In I Thessalonians 5:1–3 we read, "But of the times and the seasons, brethren, ye have no need that I write unto you. For yourselves know perfectly that the day of the Lord so cometh as a thief in the night. For when they shall say, Peace and safety; then sudden destruction cometh upon them, as travail upon a woman with child; and they shall not escape."

Paul taught the Thessalonian believers how they should live—he instructed them in the Christian walk. He exhorted them to "walk worthy of God, who hath called you unto His kingdom and glory" (I Thess. 2:12). Then in chapter 4, verses 1 and 2, he declared, "Furthermore then we beseech you, brethren, and exhort you by the Lord Jesus, that as ye have received of us how ye ought to walk and to please God, so ye would abound more and more. For ye know what commandments we gave you by the Lord Jesus."

Certainly Paul taught the resurrection of believers, for in the same passage where he declared the second coming of Christ he also said, "The dead in Christ shall rise *first*" (I Thess. 4:16); but he did not mention the resurrection of unbelievers as declared by John in Revelation 20:5, 6.

Paul believed and taught that man is a trinity. In I Thessalonians 5:23 he said, "The very God of peace sanctify you wholly; and I pray God your whole *spirit* and *soul* and *body* be preserved blameless unto the coming of our Lord Jesus Christ."

Paul was forced to leave Thessalonica for the preservation of his life and for the sake of Jason and the other Christians there; but in the short time he preached in that city God gave him such a blessed ministry that he could later write to the believers in the Thessalonian church and say, "Ye are our glory and joy!" (I Thess. 2:20).

Verse 10:    *"And the brethren immediately sent away*

*Paul and Silas by night unto Berea: who coming thither went into the synagogue of the Jews."*

Wherever we find Paul we also find a sharp contrast of opinion about him. The Jews and enemies of the Gospel hated him with burning hatred, while his converts *loved* him as deeply as the Jews hated him! Here in Thessalonica the believers contrived to get him safely out of the city *by night,* just as in Damascus the believers had lowered the apostle over the wall by means of a rope and a basket (Acts 9:25), just as they had helped him escape from Jerusalem when the Jews set about to slay him (Acts 9:30).

*Berea* (sometimes spelled *Beroea*) is a city of southwestern Macedonia. Located on the eastern slope of the old Olympian range of mountains and commanding an extensive and beautiful view of a vast plain watered by the Haliacmon river, it has many natural advantages. Historians describe it as having had many beautiful gardens due to the abundance of water there.

Arriving in Berea, Paul followed his usual custom of going *"into the synagogue of the Jews,"* carrying the Gospel to his own brethren in the flesh, preaching the same message he had preached since the day he was converted on the Damascus road.

Verse 11: *"These were more noble than those in Thessalonica, in that they received the Word with all readiness of mind, and searched the Scriptures daily, whether those things were so."*

*"These were more noble."* These people were more noble by birth than the people in Thessalonica, they had descended from more illustrious ancestors; but that is not the primary meaning of this statement. The Greek word here translated *"noble"* expresses a quality of mind and heart. It means that the Bereans were more disposed to hear, inquire, and study concerning the message Paul and Silas preached. They were more disposed to study

the doctrines and compare the preaching of these two men with the Old Testament Scriptures and prophecies.

*"They received the Word with all readiness of mind."* Whereas in Thessalonica a vast majority of the people had resisted the teaching of Paul and Silas even when Paul reasoned with them out of the Scriptures and pointed out that Jesus of Nazareth was the Christ, the Messiah, the Bereans were willing to listen with open minds. They heard the message and then *"searched the Scriptures"* to see whether or not Paul had spoken the truth.

The person who hears and recognizes the truth of the Scriptures—but *rejects* that truth—is inviting the judgment of God. The Jews have paid a tremendous price for resisting the truth. Their minds have been blinded for two thousand years, and the vast majority of them are still willingly ignorant concerning the fulfillment of the prophecies of their Old Testament Scriptures. But the Bereans were of a different moral and mental character. They did not resist the Word. On the contrary they heard Paul's message, they allowed him to bear testimony which was directly against everything they had been taught, and then they searched the Scripture to prove whether or not the roots of that message were founded in the truth of God.

Notice one thing here: This verse does not tell us that the Bereans simply *read* the Scriptures. *They SEARCHED*—and they *searched DAILY*. It is one thing to read the Bible, it is altogether another thing to *search* the Scriptures, to *dig deep* into the Word of God and pray for the Holy Spirit to give light and understanding. *Reading* may bring knowledge, but to know God's will and way we must search, and our searching must be of such quality as the Bible recommends. Hear the words of Solomon in Proverbs 2:1–5:

"My son, if thou wilt receive my words, and hide my commandments with thee; so that thou incline thine ear unto wisdom, and apply thine heart to understanding;

yea, if thou criest after knowledge, and liftest up thy voice for understanding; if thou seekest her as silver, and searchest for her as for hid treasures; *then shalt thou understand the fear of the Lord, and find the knowledge of God!"*

The Bereans searched the Scriptures — not for the sake of material for argument, but *to learn "whether those things were so."* Were Paul and Silas preaching the truth? Was their teaching in accord with the Old Testament prophecies? If so, they would receive it. If not, they would reject it. This is the wise thing for believers to do today. We should compare the preaching we hear from the pulpit with what God's Word has to say. Doctrine should be examined in the light of the Scripture, and "if there come any unto you, and bring not this doctrine, receive him not into your house, neither bid him God speed: for he that biddeth him God speed is partaker of his evil deeds" (II John 7—11 in part). Believers should not give comfort or aid to the enemies of the Gospel; and those who do so will lose their reward at the end of life's journey — yes, even if they have been born again. You will note I said they will lose their *reward* — not their salvation.

Verse 12: *"Therefore many of them believed; also of honourable women which were Greeks, and of men, not a few."*

*"THEREFORE many of them believed."* It is just as true today as in the days of Paul that those who diligently *search the Scriptures for truth* will eventually believe, because the Word of God will convince any sincere seeker of truth. The Word of God is the living Word. It is *light,* and the entrance of light brings life. Faith to be saved comes by hearing, and hearing comes by the Word of God.

Jesus declared, "Verily, verily, I say unto you, He that heareth my Word, and believeth on Him that sent me,

hath everlasting life, and shall not come into condemnation; but is passed from death unto life" (John 5:24).

Jesus also said, "It is the Spirit that quickeneth; the flesh profiteth nothing: *the WORDS that I speak unto you, they are spirit, and they are LIFE"* (John 6:63).

The Word of God is the incorruptible seed that brings the new birth (I Pet. 1:23). The Bereans searched the Word daily, and as a result of their sincere searching many of them believed.

We do not know *how many* believed, but we are told that among them were *"honourable women* which were Greeks, and *of men, not a few."*

Verse 13: *"But when the Jews of Thessalonica had knowledge that the Word of God was preached of Paul at Berea, they came thither also, and stirred up the people."*

As I have said before, the devil does not give up easily. This was not the first time Paul's enemies followed him from one place to another to stir up persecution against him. From Antioch in Pisidia and from Iconium they followed him to Lystra where they influenced the enemies of the Gospel to stone Paul (Acts 14:19). And now, those who had incited mob violence against him in Thessalonica heard that the Word of God was being preached fruitfully at Berea, and *"they came thither also, and stirred up the people."*

The Greek word here translated *"stirred"* denotes agitation or excitement. It can be illustrated by the waves of the sea as they are activated by the wind and caused to roll and tumble. There are several passages in the Old Testament where the corresponding Hebrew expression is used to denote agitation and tumult which resembles the troubled sea when the waves and billows are tossed by contrary winds. For example, in Isaiah 17:12, 13 we read, "Woe to the multitude of many people, *which make a noise like the noise of the seas;* and to

the rushing of nations, *that make a rushing like the rushing of mighty waters!* The nations shall rush *like the rushing of many waters:* but God shall rebuke them, and they shall flee far off, and shall be chased as the chaff of the mountains before the wind, and like a rolling thing before the whirlwind."

Jeremiah speaks of *Egypt* as rising up *like a flood:* "Who is this that cometh up as a flood, whose waters are moved as the rivers? Egypt riseth up like a flood, and his waters are moved like the rivers; and he saith, I will go up, and will cover the earth; I will destroy the city and the inhabitants thereof" (Jer. 46:7, 8).

Verse 14: *"And then immediately the brethren sent away Paul to go as it were to the sea: but Silas and Timotheus abode there still."*

Again Paul's converts sent him away for his own safety, as they had done several times before. They sent him away *"to go as it were to the sea."* The route Paul took was uncertain. *"As it were"* could indicate that they took him *as if* to send him by sea, thus assuring that the Jews would not follow him. It could mean that they actually *sent him by sea,* since he could have reached Athens by water. The latter seems to be the meaning, for it is difficult to understand that Paul would have gone by land through all the intervening districts and not have sought to preach the Word anywhere along the way until he reached Athens. Also, due to the condition of his health, the trip by sea would have been much easier for him than traveling overland.

*"But Silas and Timotheus abode there still."* Apparently only Paul was in great danger. Probably since he was the *principal speaker* and therefore the primary offender of the Jews, it was *his* life that was in jeopardy, with no threats made against Silas and Timothy. Therefore the believers sent Paul away while Silas and Timothy remained in Berea for a short time to continue the

work there.

## Paul At Athens

Verse 15: *"And they that conducted Paul brought him unto Athens: and receiving a commandment unto Silas and Timotheus for to come to him with all speed, they departed."*

*"They that conducted Paul"* evidently refers to those who spirited him out of Berea and away from the Jews. They brought him safely to Athens and then carried word back to Silas and Timothy that they were to join Paul *"with all speed."* Perhaps he anticipated greater success in Athens than actually came to him there. There is no doubt of the challenge that presented itself to him. This was Paul's first recorded visit to that city—it could have been the first visit of any born again believer, or at least of anyone who preached the Gospel of grace to the idolatrous people who lived there.

Verse 16: *"Now while Paul waited for them at Athens, his spirit was stirred in him, when he saw the city wholly given to idolatry."*

*"While Paul waited . . . ."* How did this godly minister conduct himself in a pagan city while he waited for his co-workers to join him? We must assume that Paul knew the history of this center of world paganism, for of the three "university cities" of that day (Athens, Tarsus, and Alexandria) Athens was the most outstanding. Since Paul's home was in Tarsus, and in view of his own education and background, it is most reasonable that he was acquainted with the art, literature, philosophy, and learning which distinguished the Greek city to which he now brought his message of the saving grace of God.

As the capital of Greece, Athens was also known for its military men. It boasted many statesmen, and its warriors have been written up in history, poetry, and

legend. The city was founded by Cecrops, an Egyptian, in 1556 B. C., and for a time was an Egyptian colony. It was named Athens in honor of *Athena,* the Greek goddess of wisdom (corresponding to the Roman goddess Minerva).

Some of the walls of the ancient city still stand, although it was often subjected to terrible wars. It was burned twice by the Persians, destroyed by Philip II of Macedon, destroyed again by Sylla, plundered by Tiberius, ravished by the Goths in the reign of Claudius, and ruined by Alaric. From the reign of Justinian to the thirteenth century, Athens remained in obscurity but continued to be at the head of a very small state. The Turks and the Greeks fought there on many occasions, but in spite of its history of mighty wars, Athens today is again a flourishing city and its artistic, architectural, and literary fame has stood through the centuries.

So you see, there was much in the city of Athens that might have interested the ordinary traveler—or "tourist," as we would call such people today—and some Bible scholars have criticized Paul because of the fact that not once, by recorded word or epistle, did he seem to have taken any interest in the things which would have attracted other men, even scholars. We must remember, however, that the Apostle Paul did not visit Athens as either tourist or student of the arts and sciences. He was not inspired by things that inspired other men. As he looked out over Athens in all of its magnificence *even then, under Roman rule*—the universal seat of Grecian Art, Science, and Philosophy—he was not concerned with the splendor of its temporal things. I do not say that Paul did not love beauty, but where others saw majesty, grandeur, and beauty beyond description, he saw the slavery, the agony of heartache expressed in the degenerate philosophies which were being taught daily to the tens of thousands of that city's inhabitants.

I believe Paul had a normal and appreciative curiosity,

but he was not in Athens to satisfy his artistic tastes or his love for things classic. Perhaps as he entered the city he saw the "winged victory" of the mighty gateway. Perhaps in passing down the narrow, crooked streets he observed the passages filled with masterpieces of art. Perhaps as he lifted his eyes heavenward he saw the Parthenon which adorned the rugged Acropolis with its many marble statues and shields of victory. But over and above the materialistic beauty Paul saw the degradation of humanity, with nothing to satisfy the longing of the human heart, a longing which only God can satisfy.

This man who counted all things loss for Christ's sake, he who carried such a crushing burden for the lost, *felt his spirit "stirred in him, when he saw the city wholly given to idolatry."* The city of Athens was filled with idols—statues in every public place, on every street corner, before every door, in the vestibule of every home. It has been said that there were so many statues in Athens that it was easier to find *a god* than to find *a man* in that city. Greek mythology was written in all the graciousness and beauty of the sculptor's chisel—but Paul saw only that the statues represented false gods and false religions. They were dedicated to the limitless gratification of an indescribable sensualism and perversion of human nature. Therefore, as Paul realized the spiritual blindness of the people, bound with the fetters of sin and held captive by the devil, as he saw the misery and hopelessness of idolatry, his spirit was stirred within him. (The Greek word here rendered *"stirred"* actually means "provoked" or irritated. Paul rebelled against the evidence of idol-worship all around him.)

What Paul saw in Athens can be seen around the world today—not necessarily in stone gods, but the world today is a world of idolatry and there are tens of thousands of idol-worshippers. To some men, *business* is their idol. To others, *wealth*. To others, *self-gratification*. The great goddess of our cities is *Amusement*—and

untold millions worship at her shrine!    Paul declared
that one of the outstanding signs of the end of this age
is that men will be "lovers of pleasures more than lovers
of God; having a form of godliness, but denying the
power thereof" (II Tim. 3:4, 5).

In his epistle to the Corinthian church the Apostle
Paul urged believers to flee from idolatry (I Cor. 10:14)
and made it clear that there can be no agreement between
idols and believers (who are the temple of God).    Read
II Corinthians 6:14−18.

John the Beloved cried out against idolatry.    To the
believer he said, "Little children, keep yourselves from
idols" (I John 5:21), and in Revelation 21:8 he tells us
that idolaters "shall have their part in the lake which
burneth with fire and brimstone, which is the second
death!"

Small wonder, then that Paul's spirit was stirred as
he looked upon the magnificent city of Athens *"wholly
given to idolatry."*

Verse 17:    *"Therefore disputed he in the synagogue
with the Jews, and with the devout persons, and in the
market daily with them that met with him."*

*"Disputed"* in this instance does not mean that Paul
*argued* with these people, but rather that he *reasoned*
with them.    He engaged them in *discussion,* but not in
angry debate.    You will also notice that his first discussion was *"in the synagogue with the Jews."*    The
people of Athens were constantly searching, ever seeking
more knowledge, continually looking for something new,
and even Judaism was perverted by this practice.

It was Paul's custom to reason with the Jews out of
their own Scriptures, and we have no reason to think
that his reasoning here was otherwise.    And in other
places we read, "Some believed . . . some received his
message"—but not so in Athens.    There is no suggestion
that even one Jew believed.

The *"devout persons"* mentioned here were those who worshipped God after the manner of the Jews—Jewish proselytes who had renounced idolatry but had not been fully admitted into the privileges of the Jewish religion. Paul reasoned with these people in an effort to win them and thus have an open door to persuade the idol worshippers that their stone gods could not help them.

Paul also spoke *"in the market, daily."* This was the place where the people gathered to buy and sell various commodities and also to hear speakers. The Greek philosophers were frequently found in public discussion, for Athens was a city of such learning that it boasted an abundance of men who surpassed all others in the fields of science, literature, art, and other subjects. Thus someone spoke daily in the marketplace. Finding the people assembled there, Paul took advantage of the opportunity to declare the marvelous grace of God.

Verse 18: *"Then certain philosophers of the Epicureans, and of the Stoicks, encountered him. And some said, What will this babbler say? Other some, He seemeth to be a setter forth of strange gods: because he preached unto them Jesus, and the resurrection."*

Athens was distinguished for great numbers of refined—but subtle—philosophers who boasted of being the wisest of men. But Paul did not approach the people from the standpoint of philosophy. He changed neither his method nor his message. He preached Jesus—crucified, risen, ascended, and coming again!

The *"Epicureans"* were a group of philosophers named in honor of Epicurus who in 341 B. C. established his school of philosophy in Athens. The Epicureans denied that the universe was created by God—in fact, they denied that the gods exercised any care or providence over humanity in any way. They also denied the immortality of the soul of man. They declared *pleasure* as the chief good, and virtue was to be practiced only as it contrib-

uted to pleasure. Epicurus did not mean *sensual* pleasure or degrading appetites and vices, but *rational* pleasure properly regulated and governed—in other words, "the achievement of happiness by serene detachment."

However, by the time the Apostle Paul arrived on the scene in Athens, the followers of Epicurus did not adhere to his doctrine. They had perverted his teaching and they practiced pleasure in its vilest form, devoting themselves to a life of gaiety and sensuality, seeking happiness in the lowest of illicit sexual practices. They were confident that there was no God, therefore they had no fear of Divine intervention in life or punishment after death. They completely gave themselves over to every imaginable passion, and practiced no control over their degenerate appetites. Thus when Paul preached against such doctrine and expounded the truth of the Gospel (including the resurrection) they found his preaching unacceptable.

The *"Stoicks"* (or Stoics) took their name from the Greek *stoa*—meaning a porch or portico—because Zeno, founder of this sect of philosophers, held his classes in a porch in the city of Athens. Although born on the island of Cyprus, Zeno came to Athens at an early age and the greater part of his life was spent there. He taught publicly for forty-eight years, and died in 264 B. C. at the age of ninety-six.

The Stoics accepted the *fact* of God, but maintained that all things were fixed by fate and that even God Himself was under the dominion of fatal necessity. They taught that the "fates" were to be submitted to, passions and affections were to be suppressed and restrained, and happiness consisted in the soul's insensibility to pain, that man should gain absolute mastery over all the passions and affections of his nature. They were stern in their views of virtue and like the Pharisees they took great pride in their own self-righteousness. They reasoned that matter was eternal, that God was the animating

principle (or soul) of the world, and that all things were a part of God. Not all of them agreed on the future state of man—some of the Stoic philosophers believed that the soul would exist until the destruction of the universe and then all souls would be destroyed *with the universe*, and others believed that the soul would finally be absorbed into the divine essence of Almighty God and thus all men would eventually become part of God.

Like the Pharisees and Sadducees, these two groups of philosophers differed in doctrine concerning God, the universe, the soul of man; but when they decided to find out what kind of "babbler" Paul was, they laid aside their disagreement, got together, and *"encountered him."*

The Greek word here translated *"babbler"* means "base fellow" and it does not occur anywhere else in the New Testament. It literally means "one who collects seeds" and it was applied by the Greeks to the very poor persons who collected the grains of wheat, barley, and oats in the fields after the harvest (the gleaners), and to the poor people who gathered the scraps of food around the marketplaces and in the streets. The term was also applied to birds that picked up grain from the fields and around the marketplaces. Sometimes it was used in speaking of tellers of tales—men who gathered scraps of information and who sometimes entertained people by telling tales of what they had seen, or where they had been, or adventures they had had. Thus the term denoted the poor, needy, and vile—the refuse of society, as well as the birds which, while acting as scavengers, were troublesome with their continual noise-making, chirping and chattering as they fluttered about picking up grains and crumbs.

The word is used metaphorically here with reference to Paul, indicating that he was a gatherer of scraps of information to be dispensed secondhand. It was an expression of contempt for this foreigner who had come into the city attempting to teach these learned men.

Thus they accused Paul of being a merchant of scraps. Perhaps it was this experience to which the apostle referred in his letter to the Corinthians when he said:

"I think that God hath set forth us the apostles last, as it were appointed to death: for we are made a spectacle unto the world, and to angels, and to men. We are fools for Christ's sake, but ye are wise in Christ; we are weak, but ye are strong; ye are honourable, but we are despised. Even unto this present hour we both hunger, and thirst, and are naked, and are buffeted, and have no certain dwellingplace; and labour, working with our own hands: being reviled, we bless; being persecuted, we suffer it: being defamed, we intreat: *we are made as the filth of the world, and are the offscouring of all things unto this day*" (I Cor. 4:9—13).

Verses 19 and 20: *"And they took him, and brought him unto Areopagus, saying, May we know what this new doctrine, whereof thou speakest, is? For thou bringest certain strange things to our ears: we would know therefore what these things mean."*

The philosophers brought Paul *"unto Areopagus."* This was Mars' hill, the place where the court met. Here the celebrated supreme judges of Athens assembled for hearings and court procedures. Located almost in the very center of the city, Mars' hill rose to a height which commanded a view of the marketplace, thus affording Paul a full view of the statues which studded the streets of Athens. The hill was steep, its sides were jagged, and ascent to its summit was gained by means of steps which led up one side. Even today traces of those stone steps remain, and the flat summit of the hill still bears traces of the smoothing of the stone for seats. It was my privilege to visit there on one occasion, and I walked to the place where it is said Paul stood when he gave the address we will study in these next verses.

The confidence of the masses was placed in the court which met on Mars' hill. The judges heard cases concerning murder, immorality, and all kinds of vice. The virtuous were rewarded, and severe judgment was meted out to those who committed murder or immorality, or who insisted on being idle. The court was peculiarly attentive to blasphemies against their gods and the performance of sacred mysteries having to do with their religion. At the time Paul arrived in Athens, that city was almost one hundred percent idolatrous, and they naturally wanted to hear more regarding the doctrine the apostle was teaching and the "strange gods" of which he spoke.

*"May we know"* suggests that Paul was not brought into court for trial, but simply that they might inquire of him concerning this *"new doctrine."* They had idols to every known god (even an idol to an *unknown* god) and if Paul knew a god they did not know they wanted to set up an idol to him, too. The spirit of the Athenians was to *hear* a person before they condemned him and to *examine* him before they approved him. Therefore they brought Paul to the Areopagus—not as a criminal, not to bring accusations against him, but to hear what he had to say. He was not to be either condemned or approved until they knew more about him and about the doctrine he taught.

*"Thou bringest certain strange things to our ears."* The Greek language here suggests things unusual or remarkable, things pertaining to a foreign country or people of another land. Paul certainly taught something different from what the Greek philosophers taught, something vastly different from what the people were accustomed to hearing. Therefore they wanted to know *"what these things mean."*

Verse 21: *"(For all the Athenians and strangers which were there spent their time in nothing else, but either to tell, or to hear some new thing.)"*

I have already pointed out the general character of the Athenians. They were constantly learning, ever eager to hear something new, searching for new revelations. The *"strangers"* mentioned here were people who visited Athens in the interest of learning. Since that city stood at the head of the literary world as well as being the center of the arts and sciences of that day, people came there from other cities and countries to study and to hear the Athenian philosophers and teachers. Thus the people of Athens were willing to examine anything that was new and which might add to their knowledge in any phase of learning.

*"Some new thing"* literally translated simply means something newer than the *latest* new thing the Athenians had heard. Historians tell us that these were the most curious of peoples. They not only inquired into things which were of interest to them at that particular time, they also inquired respecting those things which did not interest them. Whatever the subject, they were curious about it. One historian tells us that there were more than three hundred places in Athens where the people met for discussion on many and varied subjects.

The Athenians deified the mind, making a god of the intellect. I wonder if we are not repeating that same sin today? We probe the heavens, we delve into the secrets of outer space. We have made gods of Science, Astronomy, and various other great themes of learning. *Demeter*, Greek goddess of agriculture and fruits of the harvest, glorified the physical. Are we not doing that today? *Zeus*, the Greek god who supposedly ruled all other gods, was always portrayed in great strength and power—usually with a thunderbolt in his hand. In other words, he was the god of *force*. Certainly this is in evidence today. Around the world great nations are depending upon their mighty planes, ships, submarines, bombs, guided missiles, and hydrogen warheads. Is this not the day when men literally bow at the altar of force

and might? When I think on these things I ask myself, "Where is Paul? Where are Timothy, Silas, and Luke?" God give us men today who will stand behind the sacred desk in churches throughout America and declare that Jehovah is God and *beside Him there IS no God!*

### Paul's Sermon On Mars' Hill; Theme: God Will Judge the World By Jesus Christ

Verse 22: *"Then Paul stood in the midst of Mars' hill, and said, Ye men of Athens, I perceive that in all things ye are too superstitious."*

In this and the remaining verses of this chapter we see the final scene of Paul's ministry in the city of Athens insofar as the New Testament records. In verse 15 Paul sent word to Silas and Timothy that they should join him immediately in Athens; but there is no record of their missionary work there, no church was established, and Scripture does not refer to Paul's ever having returned to that city. The philosophers and scholars *heard* the message of the Gospel of grace, they gave Paul opportunity to expound the "new doctrine" he brought to them, but they rejected his message and only a meager few believed unto salvation.

*"Paul stood in the midst of Mars' hill."* We have already discussed the importance and prominence of Mars' hill. It was from this place that Socrates had faced his accusers in trial for his life more than four hundred years before. Athens offered no place of greater honor from which Paul could have addressed his listeners.

*"I perceive that in all things ye are too superstitious."* The Greek adjective which the apostle here uses has two shades of meaning—*"superstitious"* as used here and, more accurately, *"religious."* As Paul looked out over this gathering of the men of Athens he recognized the fact that they were inclined to worship. They were religious—as well as superstitious. He knew they were

religious because below Mars' hill lay the marketplace with idols on every hand. He knew they were superstitious because after having built an altar to every god they knew, they then built an altar to an "unknown" god, just in case they had omitted one! But their religion was empty and vain. However, Paul did not address them in harshness. He spoke first of all in a manner which would let them know that he was not unobservant of their city or their habits, and continued by describing what he had seen.

Verse 23: *"For as I passed by, and beheld your devotions, I found an altar with this inscription, TO THE UNKNOWN GOD. Whom therefore ye ignorantly worship, Him declare I unto you."*

It is said that in Athens there were altars to Philosophy, Beneficence, Rumor, and Shame. The Athenians not only deified *men,* but also made gods of ideas, capacities, and philanthropy. The very fact that there were so many idols in Athens proved that the people desired knowledge of a higher Being, someone who could satisfy the longing of their hearts. The presence of so many idols, so many altars, together with the beautiful temples in the city, told Paul that in spite of the great knowledge and wisdom of these people they were still seeking for the satisfaction and peace which their learning and wisdom could not give. Therefore he used one of their altars as an open door through which to speak to them.

He said, *"I found an altar . . . to the UNKNOWN God."* They had accused Paul of setting forth "strange gods," and he was here to tell them that he was in their midst to declare the God to whom they had already erected an altar. But since they worshipped Him in ignorance, their worship was to no avail.

*"Him declare I unto you."* Paul spoke in Christian courtesy and in the spirit of kindness. I am not suggesting that he compromised—indeed not! But he wanted to

win these men for Christ, he wanted to capture their complete attention, and then denounce their idolatry and
present his message of the grace of God. His message
was positive and he spoke with authority, letting these
Greeks know that he knew and proclaimed the God who
was "unknown" to them.

Verses 24 and 25: *"God that made the world and all
things therein, seeing that He is Lord of heaven and
earth, dwelleth not in temples made with hands; neither
is worshipped with men's hands, as though He needed
any thing, seeing He giveth to all life, and breath, and
all things."*

Now what did Paul preach to the Athenians? First
of all, he declared that the one true God is the sovereign
Creator of all things, Lord of heaven and earth. To us
who have been brought up in the Christian atmosphere
of America these truths seem commonplace, but they
were new to the Grecians. The Stoics did not acknowledge God as a personality. They believed that God is
everything and everything is God. The view of the Epicureans was the view of atheism. But Paul stood before
them and declared that God was Creator and Sustainer
of the universe. Such teaching denied the whole theol-
ogy of the men who had invited him to speak.

As Lord of heaven and earth God cannot be expressed
in the sum total of *"things"*—things visible, things of
which men are conscious and with which they come in
contact. God is far greater than things. He is greater
than the universe with all of its beauty and power and
mystery. He is great beyond the realm of man's imagination, and He upholdeth *all things* "by the word of
His power" (Heb. 1:3).

But God *"dwelleth not in temples made with hands."*
In Isaiah 66:1, 2 we read, *"Thus saith the Lord: The
heaven is my throne, and the earth is my footstool:
Where is the house that ye build unto me? and where*

is the place of my rest? *For all those things hath mine hand made . . . ."* Athens boasted beautiful temples, temples that held idols intricately carved of ivory and wood, or chiseled in stone, or cast in gold and silver. But God did not dwell in those temples. He dwells in the hearts of believers (I Cor. 3:16).

*"Neither is worshipped with men's hands."* From one end of Athens to the other Paul saw evidence of the work of men's hands. They worshipped *many* gods, these learned Athenians, and the magnificent temples and beautiful idols and statues were the work of their hands, executed in honor of their gods. The one true God is not worshipped in this way. Jesus declared, "God is a Spirit: and they that worship Him must worship Him in spirit and in truth" (John 4:24).

*"As though He needed any thing."* God needs nothing, for He is the Creator of *all* things. He speaks—and whatsoever He calls forth *immediately IS.* He spoke the world into being. He said, "Let there be *light"*—and there was light. He said, "Let there be a firmament in the midst of the waters . . . and it was so." At His Word the earth *produced*—grass, herbs, fruit. At His Word the sun, moon, and stars shone forth from the heavens. He spoke the animal world into being—all living things. And finally He said, "Let us make man in our image, after our likeness"—and into man, made from the dust of the earth, God breathed the breath of life! How puny would have been the offerings of these Greek philosophers, even if those offerings had been made to the true God instead of to idols, *"seeing He giveth to all life, and breath, and ALL THINGS."*

Verses 26 and 27: *"And hath made of one blood all nations of men for to dwell on all the face of the earth, and hath determined the times before appointed, and the bounds of their habitation; that they should seek the Lord, if haply they might feel after Him, and find Him,*

*though He be not far from every one of us."*

God is not only the Creator of all things material, He is the One who orders the cycles and the centuries. He fashions the ages and determines the bounds of man's habitation. He created man and placed him on this earth. He gave men their habitation among the wonderful works of His hands in order that they might *see* His wonderful works and realize His power and wisdom and thus come to a knowledge of God's existence and His character. There is actually no excuse for ignorance toward God. In Psalm 19:1—3 David tells us, *"The heavens* declare the glory of God, and the firmament sheweth His handywork. Day unto day uttereth speech, and night unto night sheweth knowledge. *There is NO SPEECH NOR LANGUAGE where their voice is not heard."*

Job said, "Ask now the beasts, *and they shall teach thee;* and the fowls of the air, *and they shall tell thee:* or speak to the earth, *and it shall teach thee:* and *the fishes of the sea* shall declare unto thee. Who knoweth not in all these that the hand of the Lord hath wrought this? In whose hand is the soul of every living thing, and the breath of all mankind" (Job 12:7—10).

In Romans 1:20 the Apostle Paul explains, "The invisible things of Him from the creation of the world are clearly seen, being understood by the things that are made, even His eternal power and Godhead; so that they are without excuse." Then in Romans 2:1 he thunders out, *"THEREFORE thou art inexcusable, O man!"*

It was evident that the Athenians thus far had not discovered the true God nor learned of His character. Therefore instead of being wise they were ignorant and wicked. Paul was pointing out the folly and foolishness of idolatry, showing that God had given each nation—including Greece—the opportunity to know Him; and if man had not discovered God through *God's* works, how could he (who is himself God's creation) discover his

Creator through the works of *his own* hands? How empty, foolish, and vain is idolatry!

*"If haply they might feel after Him."* The Greek word
here translated *"feel"* means "to touch or handle." The
same word is used in Luke 24:39 and in Hebrews 12:18.
It suggests searching diligently, untiringly, and accurately for the true God, to learn that He does exist and to
know His character. Paul expresses this in Hebrews 11:6:
"Without faith it is impossible to please Him: for he
that cometh to God must believe that *He is*, and that
He is a rewarder of them that *diligently seek Him.*"

In the last part of our verse Paul sets forth the glorious truth that those who diligently search for God, who
truly desire to *know* Him, can find Him for *"He be not
far from every one of us."* The Word of God clearly
teaches that God's presence fills all things—in heaven and
in earth. The Psalmist exclaimed, "Whither shall I go
from thy Spirit? or whither shall I flee from thy presence? If I ascend up into heaven, thou art there: if I
make my bed in hell, behold, thou art there. If I take
the wings of the morning, and dwell in the uttermost
parts of the sea; even there shall thy hand lead me, and
thy right hand shall hold me" (Psalm 139:7—10).

In Jeremiah 23:23, 24 we read, "Am I a God at hand,
saith the Lord, and not a God afar off? Can any hide
himself in secret places that I shall not see him? saith
the Lord. Do not I fill heaven and earth? saith the
Lord."

In Solomon's prayer of dedication for the magnificent
temple God had authorized him to build, he asked, "Will
God indeed dwell on the earth? *Behold, the heaven and
heaven of heavens cannot contain thee;* how much less
this house that I have builded?" (I Kings 8:27).

Where did the heathen come from? *Adam and Eve*
knew God. They were personally acquainted with Him
in the Garden of Eden, and even after they sinned they
knew Him through a blood sacrifice. They taught their

children about God, as evidenced by their sons bringing an offering to Him. Abel brought of the firstling of his flock—a blood offering. Cain brought of the fruit of the ground. Abel's offering was accepted, Cain's offering was rejected. In the process of time, as men multiplied on the earth, wickedness increased until God sent judgment. He sent the flood and destroyed all living things— except Noah and his family. *THEY knew God*—and since the flood all men have come through the seed of that family who knew God personally. So why were the Athenians pagan? Why are there millions of heathen people on earth today? The answer is found in the Word of God, in Romans 1:21—32:

Men who knew God did not glorify Him *AS God.* They were unthankful, they professed to be *wise,* but refusing to glorify God caused them to become fools. They changed the glory of God into "an image made like to corruptible man, and to birds, and fourfooted beasts, and creeping things." Because of this, *God "gave them up to uncleanness* through the lusts of their own hearts."

They changed the truth of God into a lie and worshipped creatures instead of worshipping God the Creator. Therefore *"God gave them up to vile affections."* Man was created to love God and to love righteousness; but when he changed God's truth into a lie and loved wickedness, *God gave him up* to love things vile.

Men did not like to think about God, they did not want to retain God in their knowledge. Therefore *"God gave them over to A REPROBATE MIND,* to do those things which are not convenient; being filled with all unrighteousness, fornication, wickedness, covetousness, maliciousness; full of envy, murder, debate, deceit, malignity; whisperers, backbiters, haters of God, despiteful, proud, boasters, inventors of evil things, disobedient to parents, without understanding, covenantbreakers, without natural affection, implacable, unmerciful."

When God gives up the heart, soul, and mind of man, man then becomes heathen.  Therefore heathen peoples today are reaping what their forefathers sowed.

Verses 28 and 29:  *"For in Him we live, and move, and have our being; as certain also of your own poets have said, For we are also His offspring.  Forasmuch then as we are the offspring of God, we ought not to think that the Godhead is like unto gold or silver, or stone, graven by art and man's device."*

*"In Him we live, and move, and have our being."* Paul's doctrine concerning the true God is discovered in his insistence that God is transcendent—*above* all and *beyond* all.  This statement presented a startling challenge to the Greeks.  *In effect* Paul said to them, "You are the offspring of God; so why try to express Him in these dumb idols which at best are feeble and foolish *imitations of yourselves?"*  The artistic beauty of their idols, the gold and silver with which they were so richly inlaid, was nothing when compared to the worth of the soul of one Athenian.  Jesus asked, "What is a man profited, if he shall gain the whole world, and lose his own soul? or what shall a man give in exchange for his soul?" (Matt. 16:26).

Peter expressed the same truth in his first epistle: "Forasmuch as ye know that *ye were not redeemed with corruptible things, as silver and gold,* from your vain conversation received by tradition from your fathers; *but with the precious blood of Christ,* as of a lamb without blemish and without spot" (I Pet. 1:18, 19).

*"As certain also of your own poets have said."*  Here Paul revealed his knowledge of Greek culture and his familiarity with Greek literature.  The quotation he gave is found in the writings of Aratus and Cleanthes:  *"For we are also His offspring."*  Both of these philosophers preceded Paul by more than three hundred years, and by quoting from their writings which he knew the Athenians

would recognize, he let them know that he did not discount their claim to artistic and literary fame insofar as education was concerned, at the same time declaring the emptiness and vanity of worshipping idols, since their own poets had declared that man is the offspring of God.   Why, then, should man think *"that the Godhead is like unto gold or silver, or stone, graven by art and man's device"*?   God is far above any of these.

Verse 30:    *"And the times of this ignorance God winked at; but now commandeth all men every where to repent."*

There was a time when God *"winked"* at such ignorance—i. e., He overlooked it.  Paul did not mean that God overlooked *sin*.   The thought is best expressed in Acts 14:16 where Paul explained that God "in times past suffered all nations *to walk in their own ways."*   The meaning here is that God passed over those times without immediate and direct punishment being inflicted upon the wrongdoers.  This He did for a purpose:  He allowed men to walk in ignorance, that man might experiment and show himself that apart from God he can do nothing but fail.

However, the time when God winked at ignorance is past forever.  Jesus commissioned His disciples to evangelize the whole world.  "Repentance and remission of sins" was to be preached in His name "among all nations, beginning at Jerusalem" (Luke 24:47).  Therefore *ALL men* are commanded to repent—not just the Jews who were God's favored nation.   Jesus removed that middle wall of partition and now the call to repentance is to all men throughout the earth. Thus to the Athenians Paul pointed out that God had seen their foolish idols, their vain altars, their magnificent temples, and He had overlooked them in pity and compassion.  But a new day has dawned, a day in which God commands that all men repent—Jew, Gentile, rich, poor, bond or free.

Verse 31:   *"Because He hath appointed a day, in the which He will judge the world in righteousness by that Man whom He hath ordained; whereof He hath given assurance unto all men, in that He hath raised Him from the dead."*

Here Paul declares the whole fact of Christianity. God does not *suggest* or *recommend* that men repent. *He COMMANDS* that men repent—*all* men, *everywhere.* And why do men need to repent? Because the true God *"hath appointed a day in which He will judge the world in righteousness."*   How are we to know that this is true?   We know it is true because God has *"given assurance* unto all men" in that He raised Jesus from the dead.

God not only *willed* that the world should be *governed* upon principles of true righteousness; He also ordained *"that Man"*—the Man Christ Jesus—who is to be King of the earth.   Thus Paul made known to the Athenians the fact that the righteous government of this world will not be brought about by idols, nor by altars built to an "unknown god," but by a MAN—and God gave assurance of this fact by raising that Man from the dead.

To deny the bodily resurrection of Jesus is to destroy the message of God's grace.   *Salvation* depends upon His bodily resurrection, *the Millennium* depends upon His bodily resurrection, and *the deliverance of this earth from the curse* depends upon the bodily resurrection of the Lord Jesus Christ.   This is made very clear in I Corinthians 15:13−26:

"If there be no resurrection of the dead, then is Christ not risen:   and if Christ be not risen, then is our preaching vain, and your faith is also vain.   Yea, and we are found false witnesses of God; because we have testified of God that He raised up Christ:   whom He raised not up, if so be that the dead rise not.   For if the dead rise not, then is not Christ raised:   and if Christ be not raised, your faith is vain; ye are yet in your sins.   Then

they also which are fallen asleep in Christ are perished. If in this life only we have hope in Christ, we are of all men most miserable.

"*But now is Christ risen from the dead,* and become the firstfruits of them that slept. For since by man came death, by man came also the resurrection of the dead. For as in Adam all die, even so in Christ shall all be made alive. But every man in his own order: Christ the firstfruits; afterward they that are Christ's at His coming.

"Then cometh the end, when He shall have delivered up the kingdom to God, even the Father; when He shall have put down all rule and all authority and power. For He must reign, till He hath put all enemies under His feet. The last enemy that shall be destroyed is death."

Yes, Jesus is the Righteous Judge. God will judge the secrets of men *by Jesus Christ and according to the Gospel* (Rom. 2:16). He will judge in righteousness and everyone who stands before Him will receive justice. In Romans 14:11, 12 we read, "For it is written, As I live, saith the Lord, every knee shall bow to me, and every tongue shall confess to God. So then every one of us shall give account of himself to God."

In II Corinthians 5:10 Paul declares, "We must all appear before the judgment seat of Christ; that every one may receive the things done in his body, according to that he hath done, whether it be good or bad." Then in II Timothy 4:1 Paul speaks of "the Lord Jesus Christ, who shall judge the quick (the living) and the dead at His appearing and His kingdom."

Verse 32: *"And when they heard of the resurrection of the dead, some mocked: and others said, We will hear thee again of this matter."*

"*Some mocked.*" This bears out the truth of I Corinthians 1:18 where Paul declares, "The preaching of the

cross is *to them that perish* foolishness; but unto us which are saved it is the power of God." The doctrine of the resurrection was not accepted by the Greeks—to them it was incredible, so absurd that no Greek would believe it.

Down through the ages, so-called "learned men" have mocked and jeered at the simple doctrine of Christianity. Oh, yes—I know there are some well educated men in every field who do believe the written Word of God, who have accepted His only begotten Son as Saviour; but the majority of the masses today reject the pure and unadulterated truth as Paul preached it. Many times, not having an excuse to reject the Word, they find an intellectual excuse; and when the Gospel declares something beyond their ability to reason out through mental process, they flatly reject it as unreasonable and absurd, therefore untrue.

But God is not found through reason. He is found through simple faith, and without faith it is impossible to know Him. Many intellectuals and religionists will listen attentively to the minister until he says, "But now *repent!*" And when that cry is heard they begin to mock and sneer. Like the Athenians, they decide to put it off and hear of it another day.

"Others said, *We will hear thee again of this matter.*" The "others" were probably the Stoics. The Epicureans would mock in no hesitation because they denied any future state of man. The doctrine of the resurrection would be unacceptable to them because according to their philosophy there was nothing beyond the grave. On the other hand, the Stoics did not deny the future existence of man and to them it was not entirely unbelievable that Jesus could have been raised from the dead. Therefore, they might have considered the matter worth looking into a bit further—but not at that moment. They would hear more of it at some future time.

Beloved, that is still the devil's program! Pharaoh

said, "Tomorrow!" but for him that tomorrow never came, spiritually speaking. When Paul testified before Felix, "he reasoned of righteousnes, temperance, and judgment to come. Felix trembled, and answered, Go thy way for this time; when I have a convenient season, I will call for thee" (Acts 24:25). But if that "convenient season" ever came for Felix, the sacred record does not mention it. Solomon warned, "Boast not thyself of to morrow; for thou knowest not what a day may bring forth" (Prov. 27:1). Paul himself said, *"NOW is the accepted time . . . NOW is the day of salvation"* (II Cor. 6:2). If the Athenians ever heard Paul again, it is not recorded—and somehow I believe that if they had heard him again, the Holy Spirit would have told us. We do know that no church was founded in Athens and there is no account of any further contact with Paul by these philosophers or any of the Athenians.

Verse 33:  *"So Paul departed from among them."*

Paul left Athens immediately and went to Corinth. In Matthew 7:6 Jesus said, "Give not that which is holy unto the dogs, neither cast ye your pearls before swine, lest they trample them under their feet, and turn again and rend you." Dogs cannot appreciate that which is holy, and pigs have no consideration for precious gems except to trample them under foot. Paul did not argue with the philosophers on Mars' hill. He stated Gospel facts—not in an argumentative manner, but in kindness and simplicity. It is to be noted that when men *persecuted* Paul he returned to the place of persecution to preach the same Gospel and encourage the babes in Christ; but for these intellectuals in Athens, these "wise" men who had become fools and were filled with moral dishonesty, the apostle had no further word. He simply left their presence.

The Gospel is not to be argued before those who mock and sneer at the truth of God. I have never debated an

atheist, and I never will. I believe in preaching the Word and declaring the truth, I believe in being kind and considerate and Christian; but I also believe that when a man goes behind the sacred desk he should not do so for the purpose of debate or argument. It is not pleasing to God for His minister to be cowardly and "soft pedal" the absolute truths laid down in the Word. Neither should God's man hide behind the pulpit to lambast and villify the people in the pew. He should declare the truth, the whole truth, nothing but the truth— and let the chips fall where they may. The Word of God is not to be argued with ungodly men. Therefore when Paul presented his message in clear, understandable language and the people of Athens rejected the truth, he wasted no more time on them. He walked away from them and prepared to take up his ministry in Corinth.

Verse 34: *"Howbeit certain men clave unto him, and believed: among the which was Dionysius the Areopagite, and a woman named Damaris, and others with them."*

These *"certain men"* heard Paul attentively and with open minds, they believed what he taught and they embraced the Christian doctrine. *"Among the which was Dionysius the Areopagite."* We find no other statement about this man, but from the fact that he was an Areopagite we know that he was connected in some way with the high court of Athens. He could even have been one of the supreme judges. His conversion would have made a deep impression on many of the Athenians, perhaps leading to others' being saved at a later date. This would have made Paul's labor in Athens worth everything he had put into it.

*"And a woman named Damaris."* It would be interesting to know more about this woman, but the Scripture gives no further information about her. Was she another "Lydia"? Was she prominent in the social life

of Athens so that her conversion, like that of Dionysius, would have widespread effect on those with whom she came in contact? We do not know. Whatever fruit her life brought forth is not recorded for us to read in this life, but God keeps the record and we know she will be justly rewarded.

"*. . . and others with them.*" We are not told *how many* "others," nor do we have any further record of their activity.

Some scholars have suggested that since Paul did not give *details* here concerning the resurrection, he was undoubtedly interrupted at that point. He gave details proving the resurrection in I Corinthians chapter 15, and his first epistle to the church in Thessalonica gave detailed explanation concerning the Lord's return and the resurrection of the saints (I Thess. 4:13—18); but his discourse from Mars' hill contained neither of these explanations. The doctrine of the resurrection of the body was so radically foreign to many of the Athenians that they could have rudely mocked and jeered Paul at the point of his introduction of that truth. It could be that he was forced to stop speaking, and if that were true it would certainly account for his sudden departure from among them.

I have often wondered if Paul felt that he had failed in Athens. It would appear that he was disappointed, to say the least, by the seemingly meager results of his ministry there. Certainly he felt that he had gone as far as he should in presenting the doctrine of the grace of God in the face of the skepticism and unbelief which he encountered. He moved on to Corinth where he was to have his major campaign and launch his major assault on the Greek world.

# CHAPTER XVIII

1. After these things Paul departed from Athens, and came to Corinth;

2. And found a certain Jew named Aquila, born in Pontus, lately come from Italy, with his wife Priscilla; (because that Claudius had commanded all Jews to depart from Rome:) and came unto them.

3. And because he was of the same craft, he abode with them, and wrought: for by their occupation they were tentmakers.

4. And he reasoned in the synagogue every sabbath, and persuaded the Jews and the Greeks.

5. And when Silas and Timotheus were come from Macedonia, Paul was pressed in the spirit, and testified to the Jews that Jesus was Christ.

6. And when they opposed themselves, and blasphemed, he shook his raiment, and said unto them, Your blood be upon your own heads; I am clean: from henceforth I will go unto the Gentiles.

7. And he departed thence, and entered into a certain man's house, named Justus, one that worshipped God, whose house joined hard to the synagogue.

8. And Crispus, the chief ruler of the synagogue, believed on the Lord with all his house; and many of the Corinthians hearing believed, and were baptized.

9. Then spake the Lord to Paul in the night by a vision, Be not afraid, but speak, and hold not thy peace:

10. For I am with thee, and no man shall set on thee to hurt thee: for I have much people in this city.

11. And he continued there a year and six months, teaching the word of God among them.

12. And when Gallio was the deputy of Achaia, the Jews made insurrection with one accord against Paul, and brought him to the judgment seat,

13. Saying, This fellow persuadeth men to worship God contrary to the law.

14. And when Paul was now about to open his mouth, Gallio said unto the Jews, If it were a matter of wrong or wicked lewd-

ness, O ye Jews, reason would that I should bear with you:

15. But if it be a question of words and names, and of your law, look ye to it; for I will be no judge of such matters.

16. And he drave them from the judgment seat.

17. Then all the Greeks took Sosthenes, the chief ruler of the synagogue, and beat him before the judgment seat. And Gallio cared for none of those things.

18. And Paul after this tarried there yet a good while, and then took his leave of the brethren, and sailed thence into Syria, and with him Priscilla and Aquila; having shorn his head in Cenchrea: for he had a vow.

19. And he came to Ephesus, and left them there: but he himself entered into the synagogue, and reasoned with the Jews.

20. When they desired him to tarry longer time with them, he consented not;

21. But bade them farewell, saying, I must by all means keep this feast that cometh in Jerusalem: but I will return again unto you, if God will. And he sailed from Ephesus.

22. And when he had landed at Caesarea, and gone up, and saluted the church, he went down to Antioch.

23. And after he had spent some time there, he departed, and went over all the country of Galatia and Phrygia in order, strengthening all the disciples.

24. And a certain Jew named Apollos, born at Alexandria, an eloquent man, and mighty in the scriptures, came to Ephesus.

25. This man was instructed in the way of the Lord; and being fervent in the spirit, he spake and taught diligently the things of the Lord, knowing only the baptism of John.

26. And he began to speak boldly in the synagogue: whom when Aquila and Priscilla had heard, they took him unto them, and expounded unto him the way of God more perfectly.

27. And when he was disposed to pass into Achaia, the brethren wrote, exhorting the disciples to receive him: who, when he was come, helped them much which had believed through grace:

28. For he mightily convinced the Jews, and that publickly, shewing by the scriptures that Jesus was Christ.

The city of Corinth was the capital of Roman Greece. Destroyed by the Romans in 146 B. C. it was rebuilt by Julius Caesar and was re-located on a narrow isthmus making it convenient to the sea. It became a great commercial center, crowded by merchants and agents of trade and commerce, and visited by thousands of travelers from all over the known world at that time.

It is therefore understandable that Corinth was cursed with all the vices which have been found in big cities and seaports for centuries. *Poseidon* was the pagan deity who presided over the city. He was the Greek god of the sea (corresponding to the Roman god Neptune). Games were held in his honor, and it is of these games that Paul wrote in chapter 9 of his first letter to the Corinthian church, comparing believers to the runners in a race. Poseidon was believed to protect the people in the days when Greeks fought against Greeks before the Romans came to fight and conquer them. The fleets of Corinth had sailed against the ships of Athens, and the merchantmen of Corinth had fought with the Phoenicians for the trade of the islands of the seas.

High above the city towered the two thousand foot bulk of the Acrocorinthus where the shrine of Aphrodite stood. This goddess was served by a host of priestesses and courtesans whose influence contributed greatly to the degraded immoral conditions which existed in Corinth at the time of Paul's arrival there. Lewd shows, vulgar and obscene displays of immorality and wickedness mingled with all kinds of corrupt and indecent practices.

In order to appreciate even a little of what Paul actually saw and experienced when he arrived in Corinth, one must study his later epistles to the Corinthian church. We need to see the church founded there, and study the way in which Satan attacked that church in his attempt to hinder the spread of the Gospel in that city. We also need to see how Paul dealt with the situations that arose in the church there—but we need to see more than that. We need to see *the city itself,* for the things that happened to some of the believers in the Corinthian church were but reflections of the real status of their surroundings and the corruption that existed there.

Corinth held a strange mixture of humanity, a strange mixture of poverty and wealth. As one of the great commercial centers of that time, the merchants dealt in

Arabian balsam, Egyptian papyrus, Phoenician dates, Lybian ivory, Babylonian carpets of all kinds, goats' hair from Cilicia, and wool from Lycaonia—but they also dealt in human slaves from Phrygia. The *rich* led lives of luxury, frivolity, lust, and sin. The lives of the *poor* were no less sinful and debauched. The corruption of the city had permeated even the lives of the slaves. In fact, the city of Corinth was so notorious for its immorality and debauchery that the phrase "to play the Corinthian" found a prominent place in the Greek language as an expression of the lowest level of moral living. Even in our modern English, "a Corinthian" at one time meant a polished rake.

This background of the Corinthian people makes it understandable that when Paul's preaching touched upon spiritual matters and moral conduct these people could not accept his preaching—and some who did accept the saving grace of God and were born again did not completely sever relations with the carnal things in Corinth, so deeply were the masses in that city affected by the corrupt manner of life there.

Into this center of immorality, a city steeped in sin, came the Apostle Paul with the bold declaration, *"I am determined not to know any thing among you, save Jesus Christ, and Him crucified!"* He entered the city of Corinth *preaching* "Jesus Christ and Him crucified," lifting up the bloodstained banner, going forth conquering and to conquer in the name of the greatest Conqueror of all— He who conquered death, hell, and the grave. Paul was confident that the preaching of the cross would prove a force which would eventually convince the Corinthians of the wisdom and power of God unto salvation. The prince of apostles believed in the power of the Gospel— and his faith was not in vain, for the church of God in Corinth—with all of its weaknesses, defects, and failures—became one of the greatest evangelistic centers of Paul's day. His success in that city was as great as

had been his seeming failure in Athens.

## Paul At Corinth

Verses 1 and 2: *"After these things Paul departed from Athens, and came to Corinth; and found a certain Jew named Aquila, born in Pontus, lately come from Italy, with his wife Priscilla; (because that Claudius had commanded all Jews to depart from Rome:) and came unto them."*

After Paul's sad experience in Athens where his message of the cross and the resurrection was rejected and flatly refused, he came to one of the happiest experiences of his entire ministry. There is no doubt that the founding of the church in Corinth was one of his mountain-top achievements. Athens was the center of clouded light. The Athenians professed to be both learned and wise, yet their minds were so clouded by sin and idolatry that the Gospel penetrated into the hearts of only a few of them.

Athens had been filled with idolatry, Corinth was filled with sensuality. Therefore Paul's work in Corinth was not easy, but it was joyful because people were born again and the church, soon established, grew rapidly.

In Corinth Paul "found *a certain Jew named Aquila . . . with his wife Priscilla."* Paul had left Athens with a heavy spirit, and this no doubt contributed to his physical problems. He was subject to periodic illnesses, though of exactly what nature we do not know. To the Thessalonian believers he wrote, "We were comforted over you *in all our affliction and distress* by your faith" (I Thess. 3:7). In II Corinthians 12:7, 8 he speaks of *"a thorn in the flesh,"* and although Paul's particular "thorn" is not defined, we know from Scripture that he prayed thrice for the Lord to remove it, and each time God replied, *"My grace is sufficient for thee,* for *my strength* is made perfect in weakness!"

Whatever Paul's illness, it is reasonable to assume that when he arrived in Corinth he was not in the best of health and his appearance at that time may not have been attractive and inviting to the Corinthians—especially to the Greeks who were aesthetically minded and to whom beauty was a god. According to I Corinthians 2:3 Paul appeared in Corinth weak and trembling. He said, "I was with you in weakness, and in fear, and in much trembling." This undoubtedly had to do with the physical weakness of the apostle. His bodily presence was not that of an athlete or soldier, although he used both of those terms in apt comparison to the Christian life. Paul himself describes his physical weakness in II Corinthians 10:9, 10 where it was said of him that his *letters* were weighty and powerful, *"but his bodily presence is weak, and his speech contemptible."*

However, God takes care of His own. In Corinth Paul found friends. God opened up the home of Aquila and Priscilla and they took him to live with them. Aquila was a Jew by birth, but it is evident that he had been converted to the Christian faith, and later references to him give us to understand that he became a bosom friend of the Apostle Paul. In Romans 16:3, 4 Paul speaks of Aquila and Priscilla as *"my helpers in Christ Jesus, who have for my life laid down their own necks:* unto whom not only I give thanks, but also all the churches of the Gentiles." In I Corinthians 16:19 he said, "Aquila and Priscilla salute you much in the Lord, *with the church that is in their house."* In his last letter to young Timothy, Paul sends salutations to Aquila and Priscilla. So undoubtedly the friendship formed upon his entrance into Corinth ripened into a lifelong attachment and became one of the apostle's treasured associations.

Claudius the Roman emperor had commanded all the Jews to leave Rome, and it was his decree that caused Aquila and Priscilla to leave their home in Italy and settle in Corinth. I do not doubt, however, that God's

hand and God's design entered into it—unrecognized, of course, by the emperor—for in His omniscience God foresaw the part they would carry out in the life and ministry of the Apostle Paul.

Verse 3: *"And because he was of the same craft, he abode with them, and wrought: for by their occupation they were tentmakers."*

It was the custom in Jewish families for every Jewish boy to be taught a trade. Even though they might receive a higher education, as Paul did, they were trained in some practical form of employment lest in adult years they be dependent upon the charity of their fellowman. If our government today would take some lessons from the Jewish fathers we would find a solution to the poverty problem in this day when the hard-working people of this nation pay millions upon millions of dollars in taxes to be given out to those who do not desire to work! In Paul's day, the person who did not *work* did not *eat* (II Thess. 3:10).

Paul was not too proud to labor with his hands in order to earn his livelihood. He carried the Gospel into virgin territory where no churches had been established, in some instances there was no small nucleus of believers,. and he worked to support himself in order to preach the Gospel. He worked for his livelihood in Ephesus and in Thessalonica, and no doubt in other places where the Scriptures do not record his labors. To the Ephesian elders he said, "I have coveted no man's silver, or gold, or apparel. Yea, ye yourselves know, that *these hands have ministered unto my necessities, and to them that were with me"* (Acts 20:33, 34).

To the Thessalonians Paul wrote, "Yourselves know how ye ought to follow us: for we behaved not ourselves disorderly among you; *neither did we eat any man's bread for nought; but wrought with labour and travail night and day, that we might not be chargeable to any of you"*

(II Thess. 3:7, 8).

Since Paul was *"of the same craft"* (or trade) as Aquila and Priscilla he worked with them in Corinth, *"for by their occupation they were tentmakers."* This was not an easy trade to follow. It involved a great deal of hard work. Tents as we know them today are made of heavy canvas material; but in Paul's day they were made of skins or of strips of goats'-hair sewn together by hand. The finished product was heavy and substantial, furnishing lodging for the nomadic peoples who traveled from place to place. There were many shepherds in that country, and tentmaking was a profitable business. It was also a very logical trade for *Paul* to follow, for he was a native of Tarsus in Cilicia, a province noted for goats'-hair cloth which was exported to other countries to be used in making tents.

## The Founding of the Corinthian Church

Verse 4: *"And he reasoned in the synagogue every sabbath, and persuaded the Jews and the Greeks."*

Again we are reminded of Paul's deep love for his own people. Wherever he went he visited the synagogue first and reasoned with the Jews, using their own Old Testament Scriptures to present the Gospel truth—the fact that Jesus of Nazareth was their long-awaited Messiah.

*"He reasoned in the synagogue every sabbath."* We are not told here what subject Paul announced or what text he read, but as we look into his first epistle to the church at Corinth we see that he preached the Gospel of the grace of God in words easily understood. He preached without fear, favor or compromise. In the short time he stayed in that city he preached every fundamental doctrine of Christianity and also emphasized the coming of the Lord Jesus Christ.

*"And persuaded the Jews and the Greeks."* In I Corinthians 1:18—24 Paul said, "The preaching of the cross

is to them that perish foolishness; but unto us which
are saved it is the power of God. For it is written, I
will destroy the wisdom of the wise, and will bring to
nothing the understanding of the prudent. Where is the
wise? Where is the scribe? Where is the disputer of
this world? Hath not God made foolish the wisdom of
this world? For after that in the wisdom of God the
world by wisdom knew not God, it pleased God by the
foolishness of preaching to save them that believe. *For
the JEWS require a SIGN, and the GREEKS seek after
WISDOM: but WE PREACH CHRIST CRUCIFIED,*
unto the Jews a stumblingblock, and unto the Greeks
foolishness; but *unto them which are called, BOTH
JEWS AND GREEKS, Christ the power of God, and
the wisdom of God."*

In the second chapter of I Corinthians, verses 1 through
5, Paul declared, "And I, brethren, when I came to you,
came not with excellency of speech or of wisdom, declaring unto you the testimony of God. For I determined
not to know any thing among you, save Jesus Christ,
and Him crucified. . . . And my speech and my preaching
was not with enticing words of man's wisdom, but in
demonstration of the Spirit and of power: that your
faith should not stand in the wisdom of men, but in
the power of God."

Therefore we know that in "reasoning" with the Jews
and "persuading" both Jews and Greeks, Paul presented
the Lord Jesus Christ, the Lamb of God whom God set
forth to be a propitiation for sin through faith in His
shed blood. He preached the power of God, that their
faith might stand in Christ and not in philosophy or in
excellent speech.

Verse 5: *"And when Silas and Timotheus were come
from Macedonia, Paul was pressed in the spirit, and testified to the Jews that Jesus was Christ."*

The Greek word here translated *"pressed"* means con-

strained or convicted. By the time Silas and Timothy arrived in Corinth Paul was *"pressed in the spirit,"* so constrained by the Word and so burdened for the lost people around him, that his burdened spirit was almost more than he could bear. So great was Paul's devotion to the Lord Jesus Christ and so strong was his conviction of the truth of the Gospel of grace, that he out-paced, out-prayed, and out-passioned all other ministers of all time. The Apostle Paul put more into a life surrendered to Christ than any other man history has revealed.

Paul truly counted everything loss for Jesus' sake. To the Philippians he testified, "What things were gain to me, those I counted loss for Christ. Yea doubtless, and *I count all things but loss for the excellency of the knowledge of Christ Jesus my Lord: for whom I have suffered the loss of all things, and do count them but dung, that I may win Christ!"* (Phil. 3:7, 8).

To the Corinthians he wrote, "Though I be *free from all men,* yet have I made myself *servant* unto all, that I might gain the more. And unto the Jews I became as a Jew, that I might gain the Jews; to them that are under the law, as under the law, that I might gain them that are under the law; to them that are without law, as without law, (being not without law to God, but under the law to Christ,) that I might gain them that are without law. To the weak became I as weak, that I might gain the weak: *I am made ALL THINGS TO ALL MEN, that I might by all means save some"* (I Cor. 9:19—22).

So *in Corinth also* Paul *"testified to the Jews that Jesus was Christ."* He had left Timothy and Silas at Berea when he went to Athens. He sent word back for them to join him there, but the book of Acts does not clearly indicate that they did so. They now join him in Corinth with news from the church in Thessalonica— *good* news. We know this from I Thessalonians 3:1—8 where Paul speaks of sending Timothy back to Thessa-

lonica to work with the church there. Whether he sent
word to Timothy at Berea telling him that he should return to Thessalonica instead of coming on to Athens as
he had first been instructed, or whether Timothy came to
Athens and was immediately sent back to Thessalonica
we do not know. But in some way Paul directed him to
return to that city and strengthen the believers there, con-
tinuing to teach them in the Word. Perhaps since Athens
proved to be unproductive ground the apostle felt there
was more need for Timothy in the Thessalonian church
than on the mission field in Athens. At any rate, when
Silas and Timothy finally joined Paul at Corinth, they
brought glorious news of the work being carried on in
Thessalonica, and Paul penned these touching words
addressed to that church:

"Now when Timotheus came from you unto us, and
brought us *good tidings of your faith and charity*, and
that ye have good remembrance of us always, desiring
greatly to see us, as we also to see you: Therefore, brethren, *we were comforted over you in all our affliction and
distress by your faith: FOR NOW WE LIVE, IF YE
STAND FAST IN THE LORD*" (I Thess. 3:6—8).

Athens, a city which had so much to offer and which
so desperately needed to know the grace of God, had
withheld understanding of (and sympathy with) Paul's
preaching of the Gospel. Such an experience would be
disheartening to any minister, and certainly to one of
Paul's dedication and zeal it would have been extremely
so. But when Timothy and Silas came to him in Corinth
with news of the flourishing church in Thessalonica, he
was refreshed, the Word took a still mightier grasp upon
him, and he was stirred to preach with even more intensity and power than he had ever preached before. His
message, however, remained the same: "Jesus is the
Christ!"

Verse 6:   *"And when they opposed themselves, and
blasphemed, he shook his raiment, and said unto them,*

*Your blood be upon your own heads; I am clean: from henceforth I will go unto the Gentiles.''*

"*They opposed themselves, and blasphemed.''*     The Jews opposed Paul, they opposed his message—and they spoke contemptuously of Jesus, which was *blasphemy.* At this, Paul "*shook his raiment,''* which signifies the act of shaking off the guilt of their condemnation.  He had delivered his soul.  He had warned them of their wicked ways and they had rejected his message.  So, having done all that he could to lead them into the light of salvation, he shook his raiment.   This is the same principle laid down by the Lord Himself when He instructed His disciples, "*Whosoever shall not receive you, nor hear your words, when ye depart out of that house or city, SHAKE OFF THE DUST OF YOUR FEET. Verily I say unto you, It shall be more tolerable for the land of Sodom and Gomorrha in the day of judgment, than for that city!''* (Matt. 10:14, 15).

There is no point in trying to force salvation upon anyone.   Salvation is for all who will accept the Lord Jesus Christ by faith and trust in His shed blood, but God is love and love does not force.   Therefore when Paul delivered the message of the Gospel of grace and the people blasphemed and spoke contemptuously against the Lord Jesus Christ, he shook his raiment by way of signifying that he had nothing more to say to them.   In effect, Paul was saying to them what God said about Ephraim.  In Hosea 4:17 we read, "*Ephraim is joined to idols: LET HIM ALONE!''*

"*Your blood be upon your own heads; I am clean.''* In other words, "The guilt for your destruction is *yours,* not mine.''   When Pilate asked the Jews, "What shall I do then with Jesus which is called Christ?'' they shouted, "Let Him be crucified!''   Pilate then took water, and washed his hands before the multitude and said, "I am innocent of the blood of this just Person:  see ye to it.'' The Jews then cried out, "*His blood be on US, and on*

*our children!"* (Matt. 27:22—25).

In Luke 13:34, 35, as Jesus wept over the city of Jerusalem, He said: "O Jerusalem, Jerusalem, which killest the prophets, and stonest them that are sent unto thee; *how often would I have gathered thy children together, as a hen doth gather her brood under her wings, and ye would not! Behold, YOUR HOUSE IS LEFT UNTO YOU DESOLATE:* and verily I say unto you, Ye shall not see me, until the time come when ye shall say, Blessed is He that cometh in the name of the Lord."

It has been said, "As long as there is *life,* there is *hope"*—but that is not true. In Genesis 6:3 God clearly warned, *"My Spirit shall not always strive with man . . . ."* There comes a time when God says, "Let him alone." One cannot *hear* the Gospel, *reject the message* of the Gospel, and remain the same. Once exposed to the Gospel of grace one either *receives* Jesus or *rejects* Him—there is no neutral ground; and to reject the Lord Jesus Christ is to go further and further into wickedness and sin.

Paul made it clear to these Jews that he was not to be blamed for the judgment that was sure to come upon them. He had preached the Gospel in all its purity and truth. They had heard his message and had deliberately rejected it. Therefore the Apostle Paul declared, *"I will go unto the Gentiles"*—and he did!

Verse 7: *"And he departed thence, and entered into a certain man's house, named Justus, one that worshipped God, whose house joined hard to the synagogue."*

*"Justus"* is a Latin name often used by Jews and Jewish proselytes, sometimes combined with a Jewish name. The man in this verse is *Titus Justus,* undoubtedly a Gentile and possibly one of Paul's first converts in Corinth. Little is known of him beyond what we read here. His house was near the synagogue, and when Paul left off reasoning with the Jews he moved into the home

of Justus.  From there he carried on his ministry to the Gentiles.

Verse 8:   *"And Crispus, the chief ruler of the syna-gogue, believed on the Lord with all his house; and many of the Corinthians hearing believed, and were baptized."*

*"Crispus"* is also a Latin name, but the fact that this man was *"chief ruler of the synagogue"* marks him as a Corinthian Jew.  As we have said so often before, not all who hear the Gospel will be saved, but there is al-ways *some fruit* when the incorruptible seed, the Word of God, is faithfully given out.   This was no ordinary man.  He was an outstanding person and his conversion unquestionably carried more weight because of the fact that he was chief ruler of the synagogue.  It would be interesting to know how the other Jews reacted to the conversion of Crispus, but the Holy Spirit did not see fit to give us a detailed account of that event.

Crispus *"believed on the Lord with all his house."* Here is another instance of household salvation, and it is also to be noted that Crispus was one of the believers whom Paul baptized in the Corinthian church.  In I Co-rinthians 1:14, after dissension arose in the church there, Paul said, "I thank God that I baptized none of you, but Crispus and Gaius."

*"And many of the Corinthians hearing believed."* Romans 10:17 should be familiar to every soul winner: "Faith cometh by *hearing,* and hearing by *the Word of God."* The Corinthians heard Paul's message, the Word opened their hearts, and they believed unto salvation.

I Corinthians 15:3, 4 gives a brief outline of the points of Paul's preaching in Corinth.  He said, "I delivered unto you first of all that which I also received, how that *Christ died for our sins* according to the Scriptures; and that *He was buried,* and that *He rose again the third day* according to the Scriptures."

Paul preached to the Corinthians *that which he had*

*received of God* (I Cor. 11:23). In Galatians 1:11, 12 he said, "The Gospel which was preached of me *is not after MAN*, for I neither *received* it of man, neither was I *taught* it, *but BY THE REVELATION OF JESUS CHRIST.*" Paul preached the pure, unadulterated Word of God as he received it from the Lord Jesus Christ. The points of his sermon were three:

*1. Christ died for our sins*—to make atonement for sin "according to the Scriptures." Prophecy pointed to the manner of His death. Psalm 22 describes the scene of the crucifixion, Isaiah 53 plainly portrays His sacrificial death, and Jesus Himself declared, "As Moses lifted up the serpent in the wilderness, *even so MUST THE SON OF MAN BE LIFTED UP*" (John 3:14).

*2. He was buried*—and this, too, was "according to the Scriptures." Isaiah 53:9 declared that He was "with *the rich* in His death." He was buried in the tomb of Joseph of Arimathaea, a rich and influential member of the Sanhedrin who, with the assistance of Nicodemus, took the body of Jesus from the cross, wrapped it in linen burial clothes, and laid it in Joseph's new tomb "wherein was never man yet laid" (John 19:38–42).

*3. He rose again the third day*—"according to the Scriptures." In Psalm 16:10, 11 David foresaw and declared the resurrection. Jesus said to the Pharisees, "As Jonas was three days and three nights in the whale's belly, *so shall the Son of man be three days and three nights in the heart of the earth*" (Matt. 12:40).

Therefore Paul preached to the Corinthians the message he had received "by the revelation of Jesus Christ"— he preached Christ crucified, buried, risen—yes, and ascended and coming again! Many of the Corinthians heard Paul's message, they believed and received the Word, they were saved—and here we have the beginning of the Corinthian church, in the house of a Gentile and in the very shadow of the Jewish synagogue!

What a blessing the Jews missed. There are people

today who say that our first ministry should be to the Jews and that the firstfruits of our missionary offering should go to the Jews.    Do not misunderstand me.    I pray for the Jews, I believe in evangelizing the Jews, and this ministry has contributed thousands of dollars in money and equipment to Jewish missions; *but the Jews had the Gospel first,* they rejected it, and today the message of God's grace is to "whosoever will."    There are no firstfruits from the standpoint of nationality.

It is true that Jesus instructed His disciples to preach to the Jew first, they were not to go into the way of the Gentiles (Matt. 10:5, 6), and *Paul* obeyed that commission. But when the Jews rejected the Gospel he turned to the Gentiles.    In Acts 1:8 Jesus told His disciples that they would be witnesses for Him in Jerusalem and in all Judaea, then in Samaria, and finally *"unto the uttermost part of the earth."*    In Luke 24:47 Jesus declared "that repentance and remission of sins should be preached in His name *among all nations, BEGINNING at Jerusalem."* He knew the Jews, as a nation, would reject the Gospel and the message would then be to the Gentiles.    Paul and Barnabas said to the Jews in Antioch in Pisidia, "It was *necessary* that the Word of God should *first* have been spoken *to YOU:*    but seeing ye put it from you, and judge yourselves unworthy of everlasting life, lo, *we turn to the Gentiles"* (Acts 13:46).

Although the Apostle Paul never completely gave up his attempt to win his brethren to Christ and whenever opportunity presented itself he *preached* to the Jews, he was quick to acknowledge that his call and ordination was as *minister to the Gentiles.*    In Romans 11:13 he said, "I speak to you Gentiles, inasmuch as *I am the apostle of the Gentiles,* I magnify mine office."

In Galatians 2:7, 8 he acknowledges that as Peter was primarily the apostle to the *Jews,* Paul himself was committed to the Gentiles.    Then in Ephesians 3:1−9 he wrote:

"For this cause I Paul, *the prisoner of Jesus Christ for you Gentiles,* if ye have heard of the dispensation of the grace of God which is given me to you-ward: How that *by revelation* He made known unto me the mystery; (as I wrote afore in few words, whereby, when ye read, ye may understand my knowledge in the mystery of Christ) which in other ages was not made known unto the sons of men, as it is now revealed unto His holy apostles and prophets by the Spirit; *that the Gentiles should be fellowheirs, and of the same body, and partakers of His promise in Christ by the Gospel: Whereof I was made a minister,* according to the gift of the grace of God given unto me by the effectual working of His power. Unto me, who am less than the least of all saints, is this grace given, *that I should preach among the Gentiles the unsearchable riches of Christ;* and to make all men see what is the fellowship of the mystery, which from the beginning of the world hath been hid in God, who created all things by Jesus Christ."

The prophets declared that the Jews would reject the Gospel and that it would then be given to the Gentiles. In Deuteronomy 32:21 God declared through Moses, "They have moved me to jealousy with that which is not God; they have provoked me to anger with their vanities: and I will move them to jealousy *with those which are not a people;* I will provoke them to anger with a foolish nation."

In Matthew 21:43 Jesus said to the unbelieving Jews, "The kingdom of God shall be taken from you, and given to a nation bringing forth the fruits thereof."

However, Paul makes it very clear that God has not *cast away* His people, but rather that *blindness* is come to Israel for a season. "Have they stumbled that they should fall? God forbid: but rather *through their fall salvation is come unto the Gentiles,* for to provoke them to jealousy. Now if the fall of them be the riches of the world, and the diminishing of them the riches of the

Gentiles, how much MORE their FULNESS?" (Please read Romans 11:1—12.) The time will come when Israel as a nation will be saved (Isa. 66:8; Zech. 13:6). In this Day of Grace, since Jesus has broken down that middle wall of partition, Jew and Gentile alike are saved by the grace of God through faith in the finished work of the Lord Jesus Christ, and all are baptized by the Spirit into the New Testament Church, the body of Christ.

When Paul turned from the synagogue in Corinth and set up his headquarters in the house of Justus, many Corinthians believed, they were saved, *"and were baptized."* Christians are commanded to be baptized—not in order *to be saved,* but because we *are* saved. Jesus commanded His disciples, "Go ye therefore, and teach all nations, baptizing them in the name of the Father, and of the Son, and of the Holy Ghost" (Matt. 28:19).

In Acts 2:41 when Peter preached at Pentecost, *"they that gladly received his word were baptized:* and the same day there were added unto them about three thousand souls."

The Samaritans were baptized when Philip held revival there. "When they believed Philip preaching the things concerning the kingdom of God, and the name of Jesus Christ, they were baptized, both men and women" (Acts 8:12). When the Ethiopian eunuch asked for baptism, Philip said, "If thou believest with all thine heart, thou mayest." The eunuch replied, "I believe that Jesus Christ is the Son of God." Philip then baptized him and he went on his way rejoicing (Acts 8:36—39).

The Apostle Paul was baptized immediately after Ananias came to speak with him. "Immediately there fell from his eyes as it had been scales: and he received sight forthwith, and arose, and was baptized" (Acts 9:18).

The Gentiles in the house of Cornelius believed and were baptized. Peter asked, "Can any man forbid water, that these should not be baptized, which have received the Holy Ghost as well as we? And he commanded them

to be baptized in the name of the Lord . . ." (Acts 10:47, 48).

Lydia and her entire household were baptized at Philippi, as were the Philippian jailer and his household (Acts 16:15, 33). In Acts 19:5 we will find that Paul baptized the disciples of John the Baptist. They had been baptized "unto John's baptism," but Paul baptized them "in the name of the Lord Jesus."

The Gospel order in this Dispensation of Grace is *hear* the Word, *believe* the Word, *receive* the Word, follow the Lord Jesus in *baptism,* and receive the bread and the fruit of the vine thereby showing forth His death, burial, and resurrection until He comes again for His Church. Jesus Himself instituted that ordinance just before His crucifixion (Matt. 26:26−29; Mark 14:22−25; Luke 22:19, 20) and Paul taught that doctrine in the Corinthian church (I Cor. 11:23−34).

Verses 9 and 10: *"Then spake the Lord to Paul in the night by a vision, Be not afraid, but speak, and hold not thy peace: For I am with thee, and no man shall set on thee to hurt thee: for I have much people in this city."*

*"Then spake the Lord to Paul . . . by a vision."* It is not to be supposed that God will speak to us in visions today. In this Dispensation of Grace God manifests Himself to us according to His promises laid down in His completed Word. The "perfect law of liberty" is ours, all Scripture is God-breathed and is profitable to us for instruction and correction, for reproof and for doctrine, "that the man of God may be perfect, throughly furnished unto all good works" (II Tim. 3:16, 17).

When Jesus was asked "Lord, how is it that thou wilt manifest thyself unto us, and not unto the world?" the answer He gave was very enlightening. He said, "If a man love me, He will keep my words: and my Father will love him, *and WE WILL COME UNTO HIM AND*

*MAKE OUR ABODE WITH HIM"* (John 14:22, 23). We have God's completed Word, and the third Person of the Trinity, the Holy Spirit, makes His abode in the heart of every believer. Therefore since we are indwelt by the Spirit (Rom. 8:9), led by the Spirit (Rom. 8:14), taught by the Spirit (John 16:13; I John 2:20, 27), it is not necessary for God to speak to us in visions. Paul did not have the completed Word of God as we have it today, the New Testament had not yet been written, and then too, God gave Paul special revelation for the special ministry unto which He had called him.

*"Be not afraid . . . I am with thee."* I do not believe this indicates that the apostle was showing cowardice, or that he was fearful for his physical safety. Such would be contrary to his character. He had boldly retraced his steps on other missionary journeys, going back into towns where he had been forbidden to preach, even into Lystra where he had been stoned. But we must consider that Paul at this particular time was not strong physically, he had had a very discouraging ministry in Athens, and now things were going quite well in Corinth. It just might have occurred to him to wonder if his success in Corinth would bring down upon him the wrath of the Jews and cause them to drive him from the city, as they had done on several previous occasions. If Paul was fearful, I am sure he was fearful for the Gospel, not for his own safety. But God let him know that He was with him, and that he should speak boldly, and no man should set upon him to hurt him.

*"For I have much people in this city."* As Paul looked out over the city of Corinth with its wickedness and immorality, did he wonder if there *could be* revival, if it were *possible* for a church to be established in such a city? If such thoughts came to his mind, they did not remain there long, for Paul believed God. When God said, "Be not afraid . . . no man shall set on thee to hurt thee . . . I have much people in this city," Paul was

assured of victory there. He could not *see* the "much people" of whom God spoke, any more than *Elijah* could see the seven thousand men in Israel who had not bowed to Baal (I Kings 19:18). The Lord mercifully by this vision gave His servant assurance that his preaching would be greatly blessed, and rising up comforted he was ready to speak boldly in the Lord, and he could leave the results with God.

There is no doubt that Paul's success in the city of Corinth was a most amazing achievement. A church in such deplorable surroundings is definitely a monument to the omnipotence of God's marvelous saving grace. When we look at the list of some of those who constituted the foreseen "much people" we cannot but stand in reverence and awe. Paul himself tells us that before their conversion these people were fornicators, idolaters, adulterers, effeminate, abusers of themselves with mankind, thieves, covetous, drunkards, revilers, extortioners. To the Corinthians Paul declared that those who were guilty of such ungodly practices would not "inherit the kingdom of God," and then added, *"and such were SOME OF YOU!"* (I Cor. 6:9—11).

It is interesting to note the material from which the church at Corinth was made. Among the members we find Titus Justus in whose home Paul preached and where the Corinthian church was founded (v. 7); Aquila and Priscilla in whose home Paul stayed (v. 2); Crispus, chief ruler in the synagogue (v. 8); Gaius and the household of Stephanas (I Cor. 1:14, 16); Quartus, and Erastus the chamberlain (or treasurer) of the city (Rom. 16:23); and Sosthenes (I Cor. 1:1). Outside of these, "not many wise men after the flesh, not many mighty, not many noble" were called (I Cor. 1:26). The rest of the Corinthian church was composed of members who had been among the most vicious, vile, and sinful people on earth—and from Paul's epistles to that church we know that some of them had difficulty in breaking away from former

habits, even after they were saved.

The miracle of the Gospel in the founding of the church in Corinth bears out the truth of Isaiah 1:18— ". . . though your sins be as scarlet, they shall be as white as snow; though they be red like crimson, they shall be as wool." The blood of Jesus Christ can wash away every sin. Any sinner on earth can be justified, regenerated, and made a son of God through the miracle of God's saving grace—but that miracle can happen to an individual *only by faith in the finished work of God's only begotten Son.*

Verse 11: *"And he continued there a year and six months, teaching the Word of God among them."*

You will note that during his year and six months in Corinth Paul was *"teaching the Word of God."* He did not teach reformation, although he certainly had opportunity to do so because he saw the need for reformation on every hand. For example, atop the Acrocorinthus stood the temple of Venus, beautiful beyond description and served by more than one thousand courtesans and priestesses who were devoted to unrestrained lust. The doors of this exquisite temple were flung wide to all, and every passerby who sought to satisfy lascivious and sensual desires could enter—officially and without money. If Paul had wanted to preach reformation he could certainly have cried long and loud for these people to "turn over a new leaf" and reform; but he knew that reformation was not the answer. They needed redemption through the blood of Jesus. Therefore Paul did not preach reformation. He preached Christ—crucified, buried, risen, ascended, and coming again.

The government in Corinth was as rotten with official corruption as the city itself was steeped in sensuality, vice, and shame—but Paul did not preach civic righteousness. He did not go down to the slums and preach morality in order to get the drunks, harlots, and whore-

mongers to leave the vileness of their sins and begin a new life. Instead, he preached the Gospel of the grace of God and relied on the Holy Spirit to bear the Word of God home to hearts, that the power of God might convict, convince, regenerate, and redeem.

Then, after the Corinthians heard and received the Gospel and were born again, Paul sought to teach them how they should live as true believers, that they might be good examples to others and bear fruit to the glory of God. So for eighteen months he preached the Gospel of God's saving grace and taught the Scriptures to the people of Corinth.

One of the sad needs in the church today is the teaching of the Word of God. There is a vast difference between *preaching* and *teaching the Word.* It is in the program of God that men preach the Gospel, exhort, cry aloud and spare not; but believers grow in grace and in the knowledge of the Lord and Saviour Jesus Christ as they are *taught.* Jesus commissioned His disciples to go "into all the world, and *preach the Gospel* to every creature" (Mark 16:15), but He also commissioned them to *TEACH all nations,* "baptizing them in the name of the Father, and of the Son, and of the Holy Ghost: *TEACHING them to observe ALL THINGS whatsoever I have commanded you . . ."* (Matt. 28:19, 20).

The church today needs to be taught. Christians need to know the doctrines of the Word of God and how to *rightly divide* the Word. Paul declared himself "a *preacher,* and an *apostle,* and a *teacher* of the Gentiles" by appointment of God, and urged Timothy to "hold fast the form of *sound words*" (II Tim. 1:10−13). In writing to Titus, Paul listed the qualifications of a bishop and one of those qualifications was "holding fast *the faithful Word* as he hath been taught, that he may be able *by sound doctrine* both to exhort and convince the gainsayers" (Tit. 1:9).

Paul also instructed Timothy, *"PREACH THE WORD.*

Be instant in season, out of season; reprove, rebuke, exhort with all longsuffering and *doctrine."* And then he warned, *"For the time will come when they will not endure sound doctrine;* but after their own lusts shall they heap to themselves teachers, having itching ears; and they shall turn away their ears from the truth, and shall be turned unto fables"* (II Tim. 4:2—4).

It is a sad tragedy that the local church today is attempting to meet the need of the people through social and recreational programs, fellowship suppers, and in many other ways.   Some of these things are fine, but even so, nothing will take the place of the preaching of the pure Gospel of God's saving grace. And after people are saved they need to be taught sound doctrine that they may be built up in the faith.

## The Man Who Cared For None of These Things

Verses 12 and 13: *"And when Gallio was the deputy of Achaia, the Jews made insurrection with one accord against Paul, and brought him to the judgment seat, saying, This fellow persuadeth men to worship God contrary to the law."*

When the Romans conquered Greece they divided it into two provinces—Macedonia and Achaia—and each of these provinces was governed by a proconsul.  Gallio was made proconsul of Achaia in 53 A. D. and is mentioned by ancient historians as having been a mild and lovable man.   He was brother to the celebrated philosopher Seneca who described him as being a man of extraordinary, most unusual lovely temper.   He said, "No mortal was ever so mild to anyone as he was to all, and in him there was such a natural power of goodness that there was no semblance of art or dissimulation."   Some writers have called him the very flower of pagan courtesy and pagan culture.

It was before this man that the Jews brought Paul

after they had *"made insurrection with one accord"* against him. Their charge? That he *"persuadeth men to worship God contrary to the law."* Since they did not specify *Roman* law or the laws of *Israel* they evidently meant that his teaching was contrary to *all* laws, whether Roman or Jewish. The Jews in Greece were permitted to worship God according to their own belief, but they could easily have pretended that Paul was teaching a form of worship which did not agree with their laws for worshipping God, and certainly it would not have been difficult for them to suggest that his teaching was contrary to *Roman* law and religion. It appears that they were trying to convince Gallio that Paul was teaching men to worship God contrary to *any* laws in the entire Roman empire. Their chief aim was to be rid of him and it mattered not how false their accusation might be.

Verses 14 and 15: *"And when Paul was now about to open his mouth, Gallio said unto the Jews, If it were a matter of wrong or wicked lewdness, O ye Jews, reason would that I should bear with you: but if it be a question of words and names, and of your law, look ye to it; for I will be no judge of such matters."*

*"When Paul was now about to open his mouth"* to testify in his own defense, Gallio interrupted him and addressed the Jews, thus closing the door of salvation in his own face. Paul was ready at all times to give an answer for what he believed and for what he preached. If he had been allowed to speak in defense of his conduct he would have given testimony to the saving grace of God. He would undoubtedly have reasoned with Gallio in much the same manner as he had reasoned with Felix and Agrippa "concerning the faith in Christ." He would have reasoned "of righteousness, temperance, and judgment to come" (Acts 24:24, 25). But Gallio gave Paul no opportunity to speak, and thereby he shut out a

message from the living God.

*"If it were a matter of wrong or wicked lewdness . . . I should bear with you."* The original text here denotes an act committed by one who is skilled in iniquity, a veteran offender. In other words, if Paul had committed a crime against the city, Gallio would hear the case.

*"But if it be a question of words and names . . . ."* The Jews disputed much about words, and probably Gallio had heard something of the nature of the controversy and understood that they were disputing over whether Jesus were Messiah, King of the Jews, or an impostor, a false prophet. To him this would be a matter pertaining entirely to the Jewish religion and would have nothing to do with civil affairs of the city.

*"Look ye to it, for I will be no judge of such matters."* We are reminded here of the attitude of *Pilate* toward the Jews when they brought Jesus before him as a malefactor. He said to them, *"Take ye Him, and judge Him according to your law."* But since by the law the Jews could not condemn anyone to death they insisted that the Roman governor should try the case. Therefore when they continuously cried out, "Crucify Him! Crucify Him!" he said to them, *"Take ye Him, and crucify Him: for I find no fault in Him"* (John 18:31; 19:6).

Gallio had much the same attitude toward the charges brought against Paul. Since those charges did not pertain to civil affairs he declared that they did not come under his jurisdiction and he did not feel called upon to settle the matter.

Verse 16:   *"And he drave them from the judgment seat."*

The Greek here offers no suggestion of violence. Gallio simply refused to hear the case against Paul and invited the Jews to leave his office.

Verse 17:   *"Then all the Greeks took Sosthenes, the chief ruler of the synagogue, and beat him before the*

*judgment seat. And Gallio cared for none of those things."*

*"The Greeks"* spoken of here had witnessed the Jews' persecution of Paul and the tumult that resulted from their false accusations when they brought him before Gallio and accused him of breaking the law. Since Sosthenes was the chief ruler of the synagogue, the Greeks no doubt considered him to be the ringleader in opposition against Paul and therefore they held him responsible for the unpleasantness that had just occurred. They were indignant because of the bigotry of the Jews, because of their contentious spirit, and they set upon Sosthenes *"and beat him."* Since the Greek word here translated "beat" is not the word used to denote judicial scourging, it seems evident that Sosthenes was actually given a beating with fists or with whatever the Greeks had in their hands.

All of this happened *"before the judgment seat."* Apparently the Greeks fell upon Sosthenes before he left the courtroom. We are not told how severely he was beaten, and nothing further is said of him here; but later, when Paul wrote back to the Corinthians at the close of his missionary work in Ephesus, he sent greetings from himself *"and Sosthenes our brother"* (I Cor. 1:1), and from this we know that this man was eventually converted and became a minister of the Gospel of the grace of God.

*"And Gallio cared for none of those things."* The attitude of this man provides an interesting study. When the Jews brought Paul before him, he told them that if their charges against the apostle pertained to civil affairs he would hear their complaint; but if they were charging Paul with breaking some religious custom, "a question of words and names," then it was no affair of his. Then the Greeks seized Sosthenes, ruler of the Jewish synagogue, and administered a beating to him before the judgment seat—and Gallio cared not at all! He was

unwilling to make either case a matter of legal discussion or even of investigation. He refused to try Paul, and he refused to interfere in the beating of Sosthenes. He had nothing to do with the question concerning proselytes, either to or from Judaism. Perhaps he felt that Sosthenes, instrumental in provoking persecution against Paul, should feel the effects of that persecution in the excited passions of the mob against himself. He did what was only common practice among the Romans, for they regarded the Jews with contempt and cared little how much they were exposed to persecution and hatred. In spite of the fact that he had the wrong spirit, it was a matter of total indifference to him that a Jew had been severely beaten.

He was equally indifferent toward Paul. He was not interested in the apostle's ministry, he had no concern for life hereafter, and he could not have cared less about the true God whom Paul preached. Gallio, like many of the Romans in his day, lived only for the pleasures of this life, and for the gratification of those pleasures. Yet this man was strangely modern—for there are millions of people today who care nothing for things eternal. They spend all of their time and a great deal of their wealth *thinking* of pleasure, *planning* for pleasure, never taking time to prepare to meet God!

We might note here that Sosthenes probably took his position as chief ruler of the synagogue after Crispus was converted (v. 8). Crispus would naturally have resigned his position immediately after his conversion, and if he had not resigned he would have been excommunicated at once.

## Paul Takes A Jewish Vow

Verse 18: *"And Paul after this tarried there yet a good while, and then took his leave of the brethren, and sailed thence into Syria, and with him Priscilla and Aquila; having shorn his head in Cenchrea: for he had a vow."*

Paul left Corinth with a firm determination to reach Jerusalem in time for the festival which was soon to take place there. (See verse 21.) Taking leave of the believers in Corinth he set sail for Syria, *"and with him Priscilla and Aquila."* These two believers he left at Ephesus when he arrived there, as we will soon learn.

Cenchrea was a town about ten miles from Corinth. A church had been established there, possibly through Paul's ministry in Corinth, and it was to that church that Phoebe belonged and in which she served (Rom. 16:1, 2). It would be interesting to know just what happened at Cenchrea when Paul shaved his head; but Luke penned down only what the Holy Spirit gave to him and the Spirit did not see fit to tell us what happened at Cenchrea. Verses 18 through 23 in this chapter form a strangely compact narrative. Under inspiration Luke penned them down, seeming anxious to hurry on to the next part of his writing and describe the evangelistic work in Ephesus.

*". . . having shorn his head . . . for he had a vow."* Some have suggested that it was Aquila whose head was shorn, but properly interpreted there can be no question that it was Paul, and he did this to seal a Jewish vow he had taken.

There has been much discussion as to why Paul made this vow, and on what occasion it was made. Some Bible scholars have been critical of the apostle, declaring that there was no reasonable excuse for his doing such a thing. I personally believe Paul took this vow in an effort to convince his own people that he did not oppose the laws of Moses or the religion of their fathers and was simply teaching that *Christ was the fulfillment* of all sacrifices and rituals, the *end of the law* for righteousness to all who believe.

In chapter 15 of our present study we discussed in detail how Paul stood in the council in Jerusalem and declared that Gentiles should not be taught that circum-

cision was necessary to salvation. He always took a clear and uncompromising stand for the Gospel of the grace of God and Christianity, but in spite of this he was also ready at all times to do anything or go anywhere in order to win the Jews, his own people, to Christ.

Paul was a staunch defender of the grace of God and he declared that anyone who preached any other gospel should be accursed (Gal. 1:8, 9). It is therefore reasonable to believe that he took this Jewish vow primarily to convince the Jews that he did not despise their law and that he was not an enemy of the teachings of Moses. In taking such a vow Paul observed a custom of the Israelite people. He complied with a law which in itself was not wrong. He knew he was saved by grace, pure grace, only grace; but he was trying to convince his brethren in the flesh that the grace of God *did* save, and the vow he took did not frustrate the grace of God in his own heart and life. He did not take the vow to become more fully redeemed, but simply to convince the Jews that he was not against Moses, Abraham, and the fathers, and that he was preaching the fulfillment of the prophecies given by their own prophets.

We find vows observed throughout the Old Testament. Since a vow is a solemn promise made to Almighty God respecting one of many things, when a man made a vow he was under divine obligation to keep it:

"When thou shalt vow a vow unto the Lord thy God, thou shalt not slack to pay it: for the Lord thy God will surely require it of thee; and it would be sin in thee. . . . That which is gone out of thy lips thou shalt keep and perform; even a freewill-offering, according as thou hast vowed unto the Lord thy God, which thou hast promised with thy mouth" (Deut. 23:21, 23).

An example of such a vow is found in Genesis 28:20-22, when Jacob at Bethel vowed one-tenth of his estate to the honor and glory of God:

"And Jacob vowed a vow, saying, If God will be with me, and will keep me in this way that I go, and will give me bread to eat, and raiment to put on, so that I come again to my father's house in peace; then shall the Lord be my God: and this stone, which I have set for a pillar, shall be God's house: *and of all that thou shalt give me I WILL SURELY GIVE THE TENTH UNTO THEE!"*

The most remarkable vow in the Old Testament economy was the vow of the Nazarite. Under this vow a man made a solemn promise to God to abstain from wine or any other intoxicating drink. He also did not cut his hair for the duration of his vow, nor did he enter into a house polluted by having a dead body within. He attended no funerals. The Nazarite vow was for a definite period fixed by the person who made the vow. It might be for eight days, or for thirty days—or, in some instances, for a lifetime. At the end of the time allotted for the vow, specified offerings were made by the priest, *the head of the Nazarite was shaved* and the hair was burned on the fire of the altar in the tabernacle. (The entire ritual of the Nazarite vow is given in Numbers chapter 6. Time and space will not permit us to give the entire text here.)

Sometimes a man took the vow of a Nazarite while he was away from Jerusalem and could not reach the temple when the vow was ended. Therefore he simply observed the abstenance required by the vow, and his head was shaved wherever he happened to be at the time the vow ended. This was probably true of Paul. His hair was shaved at Cenchrea; and later, when he reached Jerusalem, he went through the proper ceremonies of the vow he had taken. (Read Acts 21:23, 24.)

Verse 19: *"And he came to Ephesus, and left them there: but he himself entered into the synagogue, and reasoned with the Jews."*

The historian Josephus tells us that there were many Jews in Ephesus at that time, some of whom had even obtained citizenship there. Paul's stay in that city was very brief on this occasion, since it was merely a stopover on his way to Jerusalem. We note, however, that he took advantage of that time to go into the synagogue and *reason with the Jews.*

Taking the first part of this verse last, we also note that Aquila and Priscilla remained in Ephesus when Paul set sail for Jerusalem, and in verse 26 we see them *expounding "the way of God"* as they awaited Paul's return.

Verses 20 and 21: *"When they desired him to tarry longer time with them, he consented not; but bade them farewell, saying, I must by all means keep this feast that cometh in Jerusalem: but I will return again unto you, if God will. And he sailed from Ephesus."*

*"When they desired him to tarry longer"* seems to indicate that some of those present in the synagogue heard Paul's message with open minds and willing hearts and were anxious to learn more about the truth he preached. We might also conclude that since he tarried there such a short time no opposition was stirred up among the Jews such as was customary in other cities where Paul preached successfully. We will see in our next chapter that the apostle did run into some difficulty in Ephesus when his preaching affected the business of those who were engaged in promoting the worship of the goddess Diana.

Paul *"consented not"* to stay longer in Ephesus at that time. He said, *"I must by all means keep this feast that cometh in Jerusalem."* This was probably the feast of the Passover. The Holy Spirit did not see fit to reveal Paul's specific reason for hastening on to the Holy City to keep this particular feast, but his determination could have been prompted by a twofold reason: He needed to go to Jerusalem to complete his vow, and

because of the unusually large crowds assembled at the time of the Passover celebration he would have unlimited opportunity to preach the Gospel—especially to the Jews. He would have another chance to convince the Jewish leaders in Jerusalem that he was not against them, but was simply trying to lead them into the truth concerning the Messiah of whom Moses wrote.

Therefore his stay in Ephesus was very brief, but he left the Ephesians with the promise, *"I will return again unto you, if God will."* And he did return to that city for a fruitful and extended ministry, as we will see in our next chapter. According to Acts 20:31, Paul's ministry in Ephesus continued "by the space of three years."

Verses 22 and 23: *"And when he had landed at Caesarea, and gone up, and saluted the church, he went down to Antioch. And after he had spent some time there, he departed, and went over all the country of Galatia and Phrygia in order, strengthening all the disciples."*

*"When he had landed at Caesarea, and gone UP . . . ."* Jerusalem was referred to as "up" from surrounding areas. It was the center of Jewish worship, the temple was there, and people spoke of "going up" to that city. (Please note Luke 2:42; John 2:13; 7:8, 10; Acts 15:2 for examples.) That Paul *"saluted the church"* means that he expressed his love and regard for the believers in Jerusalem, but no more is said about his visit there at this particular time. It has been suggested that Paul met with a cold and ungracious reception, and that the position he assumed toward the law in his preaching to Gentile converts raised up adversaries among the Christians in Jerusalem who were zealous for the law.

It is strange that the name of the city is not mentioned, nor are we told a word about the fulfilment of the vow Paul had taken. Evidently he left almost immediately and *"went down to Antioch,"* where he tarried for a time—we are not told for how long a time.

Leaving Antioch he *"went over all the country of Galatia and Phrygia . . . strengthening all the disciples."* Paul had preached the Gospel in Galatia and Phrygia when he and Silas had traveled through that area on his second missionary journey (Acts 16:6). He now made another visit to the churches there to strengthen and encourage believers in those areas.

The Apostle Paul preached the Gospel with a fervor and clarity that reached men for Christ. He was an ardent and faithful soul winner. But he was possessed of *more* than a burning desire to see men *saved*. He longed to see them grow in grace and reach upward toward maturity in their spiritual life. He constantly encouraged his converts to walk as believers *should* walk. For example:

In Romans 6:4 he declares that Christians should "walk *in newness of life."*

In Romans 8:1 he says, "There is therefore now no condemnation to them which are in Christ Jesus, *who walk NOT after the flesh, but after the SPIRIT."*

He said to the Ephesians, "We are His workmanship, created in Christ Jesus unto *good works, which God hath before ordained that we should WALK IN THEM"* (Eph. 2:10).

In Ephesians 4:1−3 he said, "I . . . beseech you that ye *walk WORTHY of the vocation wherewith ye are called,* with all lowliness and meekness, with longsuffering, forbearing one another in love; endeavouring to keep the unity of the Spirit in the bond of peace."

In Ephesians 5:2 he urged the believers at Ephesus to *"walk IN LOVE,* as Christ also hath loved us, and hath given Himself for us . . . ."

In Ephesians 5:8 he urged believers to *"walk as CHILDREN OF LIGHT."*

To the Colossians he wrote that they should *"walk WORTHY of the Lord* unto all pleasing, being fruitful in every good work, and *increasing in the knowledge of*

*God"* (Col. 1:10).

In Colossians 2:6, 7 he said, "As ye have therefore received Christ Jesus the Lord, *so walk ye IN HIM:* rooted and built up in Him, and stablished in the faith, as ye have been taught, abounding therein with thanksgiving."

According to Colossians 4:5, Christians are also to *"walk IN WISDOM" toward them that are outside the Church.*

Paul constantly *taught* his converts, returning to the various fields of his ministry whenever he had opportunity. He carried a great responsibility for other believers, especially those who had been saved under his ministry. He wanted to present them *"holy and unblameable and unreproveable"* in the sight of God (Col. 1:22).

To the Thessalonian believers he wrote, "The Lord make you to *increase and abound* in love one toward another, and toward all men, even as we do toward you: *to the end He may stablish your hearts unblameable in holiness before God,* even our Father, at the coming of our Lord Jesus Christ with all His saints" (I Thess. 3:12, 13).

### Apollos At Ephesus

Verses 24 and 25: *"And a certain Jew named Apollos, born at Alexandria, an eloquent man, and mighty in the Scriptures, came to Ephesus. This man was instructed in the way of the Lord; and being fervent in the Spirit, he spake and taught diligently the things of the Lord, knowing only the baptism of John."*

The glowing description of Apollos as given here is certainly understandable when we consider his background as an Alexandrian Jew. The city of Alexandria (founded by Alexander the Great and named for him) was the home of many Greeks, Jews, and native Egyptians, thus holding a strange mixture of cultures. It was a

brilliant seat of learning. It was also the *banking center* of Egypt, which made it a city of wealth and distinction. Since Apollos was *"an eloquent man"* it seems reasonable that to a natural gift of eloquence he had added the learning and culture of his background. He was an outstanding orator, and through his oratory was manifested the fact of his culture and refinement.

We know very little about Apollos beyond what is given in this passage. In I Corinthians 1:12 and 3:5, 6 Paul mentions him in connection with the ministry in Corinth, and from Titus 3:13 we know that he later became an outstanding and distinguished minister of the Gospel.

That he was *"mighty in the Scriptures"* tells us that Apollos was endowed with a special and singular gift. Although he had not yet learned the full truth concerning the coming of the Holy Spirit, the new birth, the infilling of the Spirit and other facts pertaining to the Dispensation of Grace, he possessed a distinct ability and power to master the Scriptures and to see the inter-relationship set forth in them. He was familiar with the prophecies of the Old Testament concerning the coming Messiah, and evidently he knew much about the ministry of Jesus and the miracles wrought by Him. He was also gifted with the ability to impart to his fellowman his intricate knowledge of things scriptural.

Apollos was *"instructed in the way of the Lord."* This does not mean that he knew of Pentecost, nor is it suggested that he knew of the coming of the Holy Spirit or the birth of the New Testament Church.

*"Being fervent in the Spirit, he spake and taught diligently the things of the Lord."* That is, as far as he *understood* the things of the Lord. He enthusiastically proclaimed such truth as he knew, but his knowledge was imperfect concerning the Dispensation of Grace. He had been instructed in Messianic prophecy, he understood the purpose of Messiah's coming, and he *"taught diligently"* everything that had been revealed to him up to that

time.

Apollos knew *"only the baptism of John."* This of course refers to John the Baptist. What was "the baptism of John"? In Matthew 3:1—3, 11 we read, "In those days came John the Baptist, preaching in the wilderness of Judaea, and saying, Repent ye: for the kingdom of heaven is at hand. For this is he that was spoken of by the prophet Esaias, saying, The voice of one crying in the wilderness, Prepare ye the way of the Lord, make His paths straight. . . . I indeed baptize you with water unto repentance: but He that cometh after me is mightier than I, whose shoes I am not worthy to bear: He shall baptize you with the Holy Ghost, and with fire."

As a disciple of John the Baptist, Apollos was baptized unto repentance and he was looking for the coming of Messiah; but he knew nothing of the meaning of the cross, the fact of the resurrection, or the coming of the Spirit at Pentecost. He preached the views of John the Baptist, forerunner of the King. He had been baptized unto John's baptism, but it is clear that he had not heard that the Lord Jesus Christ was the Messiah for whom he waited.

Verse 26: *"And began to speak boldly in the synagogue: whom when Aquila and Priscilla had heard, they took him unto them, and expounded unto him the way of God more perfectly."*

Apollos *"began to speak boldly in the synagogue."* This man was no hypocrite. He was entirely sincere, he preached the *truth* insofar as he had *heard* the truth, and he preached with conviction—*"boldly."*

*"Whom when Aquila and Priscilla had heard . . . ."* These godly people knew the full message of salvation by grace through faith. Undoubtedly they recognized Apollos as a learned, sincere, and devout man, but one whose knowledge of the saving grace of God was incomplete. Therefore *"they took him unto them"* (to their

home or to some place aside where they could speak
with him privately) *"and expounded unto him the way
of God more perfectly."*

The Scripture does not record in detail what Aquila
and Priscilla taught Apollos, but we can be assured that
they instructed him concerning the virgin-born Messiah—
Son of God, very God in flesh—crucified, buried, risen,
and ascended "according to the Scriptures." These two
believers were co-workers with the Apostle Paul, and Paul
was a preacher of the cross—the message of saving grace.
So we know that Aquila and Priscilla taught Apollos
concerning salvation by grace through faith *plus nothing;*
and since he had accepted and believed the preaching of
John the Baptist, he received this further instruction with
ready heart and mind—and from verse 28 we know that
he immediately preached the truth that Jesus was Messiah.

Verse 27:    *"And when he was disposed to pass into
Achaia, the brethren wrote, exhorting the disciples to receive him:  who, when he was come, helped them much
which had believed through grace."*

Apollos left Ephesus to go into Achaia, and he carried
with him a written message from *"the brethren"* at Ephesus—a message urging the believers in Achaia to receive
Apollos as a brother in Christ and a teacher of the Gospel of grace.

*"Who, when he was come, helped them much which
had believed through grace."* I am sure that Apollos not
only helped the *believers* in Achaia, but through his gift
of oratory and his more perfect knowledge of salvation by
grace through faith in the finished work of Jesus he undoubtedly led others to believe.

The *Corinthian* church classified Apollos with Peter
and Paul, being greatly impressed by his eloquence and
his knowledge of the Scriptures. In I Corinthians 1:12
Paul wrote to the Corinthians, "Now this I say, that
every one of you saith, I am of *Paul;* and I of *Apollos;*

and I of *Cephas;* and I of Christ." We read the same thing in I Corinthians 3:4—6: "For while one saith, I am of *Paul;* and another, I am of *Apollos;* are ye not carnal? Who then is *Paul,* and who is *Apollos,* but ministers by whom ye believed, even as the Lord gave to every man? *I have planted, Apollos watered;* but God gave the increase."

The statement *"which had believed through grace"* could refer to the believers in Achaia, or it could refer to Apollos himself. If it speaks of Apollos it means that he was *enabled by grace* to strengthen the brethren in Achaia, those who had believed through the preaching of the Apostle Paul. If it refers to the believers in Achaia it means that they had been saved through believing *Paul's preaching of the Gospel of grace.*

Verse 28: *"For he mightily convinced the Jews, and that publickly, shewing by the Scriptures that Jesus was Christ."*

That Apollos *"MIGHTILY convinced the Jews"* manifests the fact of his eloquence as well as his knowledge of the Scriptures. That he convinced them *"publickly"* would indicate that he spoke in the synagogue—and very likely in any other place where he could assemble an audience.

*"Shewing BY THE SCRIPTURES that Jesus was Christ."* This would be the Old Testament Scriptures, the prophecies of Isaiah and others, which plainly foretold the coming and the character of Messiah.

Beloved, this is still the effective method of soul winning! People care not what you or I may *"think"* about Jesus and salvation—and some of them will even argue with the Word of God. But most sinners do respect the Word, and when we give them "thus saith the Lord" then *the Word*—"quick, and powerful, and sharper than any twoedged sword" (Heb. 4:12)—reaches the heart; and through the power of the Holy Spirit sinners are brought

to Christ.   It was the power of the Word, the Scriptures in which Apollos was so thoroughly versed, that convinced the Jews of Christ's messiahship and showed them that Jesus of Nazareth corresponded perfectly with the Old Testament prophecies concerning Messiah.

# CHAPTER XIX

1. And it came to pass, that, while Apollos was at Corinth, Paul having passed through the upper coasts came to Ephesus: and finding certain disciples,

2. He said unto them, Have ye received the Holy Ghost since ye believed? And they said unto him, We have not so much as heard whether there be any Holy Ghost.

3. And he said unto them, Unto what then were ye baptized? And they said, Unto John's baptism.

4. Then said Paul, John verily baptized with the baptism of repentance, saying unto the people, that they should believe on him which should come after him, that is, on Christ Jesus.

5. When they heard this, they were baptized in the name of the Lord Jesus.

6. And when Paul had laid his hands upon them, the Holy Ghost came on them; and they spake with tongues, and prophesied.

7. And all the men were about twelve.

8. And he went into the synagogue, and spake boldly for the space of three months, disputing and persuading the things concerning the kingdom of God.

9. But when divers were hardened, and believed not, but spake evil of that way before the multitude, he departed from them, and separated the disciples, disputing daily in the school of one Tyrannus.

10. And this continued by the space of two years; so that all they which dwelt in Asia heard the word of the Lord Jesus, both Jews and Greeks.

11. And God wrought special miracles by the hands of Paul:

12. So that from his body were brought unto the sick handkerchiefs or aprons, and the diseases departed from them, and the evil spirits went out of them.

13. Then certain of the vagabond Jews, exorcists, took upon them to call over them which had evil spirits the name of the Lord Jesus, saying, We adjure you by Jesus whom Paul preacheth.

14. And there were seven sons of one Sceva, a Jew, and chief of the priests, which did so.

15. And the evil spirit answered and said, Jesus I know, and Paul I know; but who are ye?

16. And the man in whom the evil spirit was leaped on them, and overcame them, and prevailed against them, so that they fled out of that house naked and wounded.

17. And this was known to all the Jews and Greeks also dwelling at Ephesus; and fear fell on them all, and the name of the Lord Jesus was magnified.

18. And many that believed came, and confessed, and shewed their deeds.

19. Many of them also which used curious arts brought their books together, and burned them before all men: and they counted the price of them, and found it fifty thousand pieces of silver.

20. So mightily grew the word of God and prevailed.

21. After these things were ended, Paul purposed in the spirit, when he had passed through Macedonia and Achaia, to go to Jerusalem, saying, After I have been there, I must also see Rome.

22. So he sent into Macedonia two of them that ministered unto him, Timotheus and Erastus; but he himself stayed in Asia for a season.

23. And the same time there arose no small stir about that way.

24. For a certain man named Demetrius, a silversmith, which made silver shrines for Diana, brought no small gain unto the craftsmen;

25. Whom he called together with the workmen of like occupation, and said, Sirs, ye know that by this craft we have our wealth.

26. Moreover ye see and hear, that not alone at Ephesus, but almost throughout all Asia, this Paul hath persuaded and turned away much people, saying that they be no gods, which are made with hands:

27. So that not only this our craft is in danger to be set at nought; but also that the temple of the great goddess Diana should be despised, and her magnificence should be destroyed, whom all Asia and the world worshippeth.

28. And when they heard these sayings, they were full of wrath, and cried out, saying, Great is Diana of the Ephesians.

29. And the whole city was filled with confusion: and having caught Gaius and Aristarchus, men of Macedonia, Paul's companions in travel, they rushed with one accord into the theatre.

30. And when Paul would have entered in unto the people, the disciples suffered him not.

31. And certain of the chief of Asia, which were his friends, sent unto him, desiring him that he would not adventure himself into the theatre.

32. Some therefore cried one thing, and some another: for the assembly was confused; and the more part knew not wherefore they were come together.

33. And they drew Alexander out of the multitude, the Jews putting him forward. And Alexander beckoned with the hand, and would have made his defence unto the people.

34. But when they knew that he was a Jew, all with one voice about the space of two hours cried out, Great is Diana of the Ephesians.

35. And when the townclerk had appeased the people, he said, Ye men of Ephesus, what man is there that knoweth not how that the city of the Ephesians is a worshipper of the great goddess Diana, and of the image which fell down from Jupiter?

36. Seeing then that these things cannot be spoken against, ye ought to be quiet, and to do nothing rashly.

37. For ye have brought hither these men, which are neither robbers of churches, nor yet blasphemers of your goddess.

38. Wherefore if Demetrius, and the craftsmen which are with him, have a matter against any man, the law is open, and there are deputies: let them implead one another.

39. But if ye enquire any thing concerning other matters, it shall be determined in a lawful assembly.

40. For we are in danger to be called in question for this day's uproar, there being no cause whereby we may give an account of this concourse.

41. And when he had thus spoken, he dismissed the assembly.

In this chapter we take up the study of Paul's work and ministry in Ephesus. It was a great day in Christianity when the church in Ephesus was born. This is the outstanding and representative church in the New Testament. It is the church to which two epistles are addressed—one, the book of Ephesians—written by Paul under inspiration of the Holy Spirit; and one given by the Spirit to John the Beloved on the Isle of Patmos (Rev. 2:1—7).

Paul's letter to the church in Ephesus soars higher in spiritual truths than any of his other epistles. It was to the church in Ephesus that he was able to write concerning those profound matters having to do with the vocation of the Church of the living God in this Dispensation of Grace. For example, to the church in *Corinth*

Paul wrote:

*"I, brethren, could not speak unto you as unto SPIR-ITUAL, but as unto CARNAL,* even as unto babes in Christ.   I have fed you with *milk,* and not with *meat:* for hitherto ye were not able to bear it, neither yet now are ye able.   *For ye are yet carnal:*  for whereas there is among you envying, and strife, and divisions, *are ye not carnal, and walk as men?*   For while one saith, I am of Paul; and another, I am of Apollos; are ye not carnal?" (I Cor. 3:1—4).

But to the church at Ephesus he wrote, "Paul, an apostle of Jesus Christ by the will of God, to the saints which are at Ephesus, and *TO THE FAITHFUL in Christ Jesus:*  Grace be to you, and peace, from God our Father, and from the Lord Jesus Christ.   Blessed be the God and Father of our Lord Jesus Christ, *who hath blessed us with ALL SPIRITUAL BLESSINGS IN HEAV-ENLY PLACES in Christ:*  according as He hath chosen us in Him before the foundation of the world, *that we should be HOLY AND WITHOUT BLAME BEFORE HIM IN LOVE:*  having predestinated us unto the adoption of children by Jesus Christ to Himself, according to the good pleasure of His will, to the praise of the glory of His grace, *wherein He hath made us ACCEPTED IN THE BELOVED"* (Eph. 1:1—6).

The sacred record of the coming of the Apostle Paul to Ephesus and the founding of the church there is of special interest. The church at Ephesus occupies a singular place in the New Testament revelations to the Church of the living God—revelations concerning doctrine and the position and walk of the individual believer.   Also, Paul's ministry in Ephesus was the last of his ministry in liberty.   He ministered after that, but he ministered in chains and as a prisoner of the Roman empire.   I do not mean to imply that he saw no freedom after his imprisonment in Rome.   He could have been set at liberty and possibly re-visited these churches; but insofar

as this record is concerned, we see here the last of Paul's free ministry.

## Paul At Ephesus

Verses 1 and 2: *"And it came to pass, that, while Apollos was at Corinth, Paul having passed through the upper coasts came to Ephesus: and finding certain disciples, he said unto them, Have ye received the Holy Ghost since ye believed? And they said unto him, We have not so much as heard whether there be any Holy Ghost."*

*"While Apollos was at Corinth . . . ."* In the last five verses of chapter 18 we saw Apollos at Ephesus preaching the doctrine of John the Baptist until Aquila and Priscilla took him under their personal care and instructed him more fully in things concerning the death, burial, and resurrection of Jesus. He then went on to Achaia to preach the truth of the Gospel and to prove by the Scriptures "that Jesus was Christ." Therefore when Paul began his three-year ministry in Ephesus, Apollos had already moved on to other fields.

The Apostle Paul had already been to Ephesus, as we noted in verses 18—21 in chapter 18; but his stay there was very brief at that time, since he was on his way to Jerusalem. However, he left Aquila and Priscilla at Ephesus, and his return visit recorded in our present verse was about a year later. The Holy Spirit did not see fit to reveal through the pen of Luke any detailed account of Paul's activities and labors during that year. Only such incidents as have to do with spiritual lessons are recorded for us.

Ephesus was a celebrated city in Asia Minor and was of strategic importance as a commercial, political, and religious center. It was also the center of worship of the goddess Diana (corresponding to the Greek *Artemis*). The temple of Diana was one of the wonders of the world. A

massive structure 425 feet long and 220 feet wide, it over-shadowed the city (and everyone in it). To this temple came vast numbers of visitors and pilgrims, and much wealth was brought into it. Thus when Paul arrived in Ephesus to begin his extended ministry he found the city largely given over to witchcraft, sorcery, and magic.

However, Paul did not preach against the worship of Diana as such. Under the power of the Holy Ghost he preached the Gospel and lifted up Jesus. God used Paul in Ephesus in a very singular way. His ministry was accompanied by special miracles and outstanding signs and wonders, and his message broke down the stronghold of idolatry and great revival swept the city. He labored there for a period of three years—the longest ministry in one place recorded for his entire missionary work.

*"Finding certain disciples, he said unto them, Have ye received the Holy Ghost since ye believed?"* This is one of the very familiar sections in the book of Acts. It is also one of the most often misinterpreted passages in all of the Word of God. Many people use the first seven verses of this chapter in an attempt to prove that the baptism of the Holy Spirit does not occur at conversion but at a later time—sometimes soon after conversion, sometimes much later, even *years* after a person has been saved. But let us see Paul's investigation of the parties concerned here, and the instruction he gave them.

It is not by accident that this portion of our present chapter comes *immediately* after the passage describing the ministry of Apollos in Ephesus. Apollos was preaching as much truth as he knew, but he did not know the full truth until Aquila and Priscilla explained it to him. Therefore he preached "the baptism of John"—that is, he preached the same message John the Baptist had preached. Finding these disciples, Paul asked them, *"Did ye receive the Holy Ghost when ye believed?"*

I am sure some folk will suggest that I have misquoted the Scripture—but not so. Any Greek scholar will assure

you that this phrase in verse 2 reads, "Have ye received the Holy Ghost since ye believed?" and (in parentheses following) *"Did* ye receive the Holy Ghost *when ye believed?"* Both verbs—"receive" and "believe"—are in the past tense; therefore, with no damage to the Scriptures this can be read, "Received ye the Holy Ghost when ye believed?"

Thus we see that Paul did not actually ask these men if they had received the Holy Ghost *SINCE they believed.* He did not believe or teach that we believe unto salvation, and then at some later time receive the baptism of the Holy Ghost; nor did he at any time suggest that a believer should *seek* the baptism of the Spirit. It was Paul who declared, "If any man *have NOT* the Spirit of Christ, *he is none of His. . . .* For as many as are *led* by the Spirit of God, they are the sons of God. . . . The Spirit Himself *beareth witness with our spirit,* that we are the children of God" (Rom. 8:9, 14, 16).

"And they said unto him, *We have not so much as heard whether there BE any Holy Ghost."* Now I ask, How *could* these men have received the baptism of the Holy Ghost when they had not even *heard* of the Holy Ghost? Remember, they knew only the preaching of Apollos, the doctrine of John the Baptist. They had not heard of Pentecost, they did not know of the coming of the Spirit, nor of the beginning of the New Testament Church.

Verse 3: *"And he said unto them, Unto what then were ye baptized? And they said, Unto John's baptism."*

John made it clear that he was not *"that Light,"* he was not *"that Prophet"* of whom Moses wrote (John 1:8, 21). He was a voice crying, *"Prepare ye the way!"* (Matt. 3:3). John declared that his ministry was unto repentance and baptism, but he also declared that there was a fuller baptism to come—not through his ministry, but through the ministry of the One whom he announced.

He said, "I indeed baptize you with water unto repentance: but He that cometh after me is mightier than I, whose shoes I am not worthy to bear: *He shall baptize you with the HOLY GHOST*, and with fire" (Matt. 3:11). Thus did John *foretell* the coming of the Holy Ghost. Therefore these disciples at Ephesus implied by their answer to Paul's question—not that the "Holy Ghost" was strange, but that they were not *acquainted* with the ministry of the Holy Ghost for they had not heard that the Holy Spirit was *given*.

It may be asked, "Why did Paul question these men in the first place? Why did he ask them if they were possessors of the Holy Spirit?" The only reasonable answer is that as he observed them and listened to their testimony he recognized the fact that they had not been fully instructed in the way of salvation by grace through faith. They knew nothing of the miracle of the new birth and the indwelling of the Holy Spirit. A man who was as fully surrendered to God's direction as *Paul* was surrendered would surely know that something was lacking in the experience of these men.

Verses 4 and 5: *"Then said Paul, John verily baptized with the baptism of repentance, saying unto the people, that they should believe on Him which should come after him, that is, on Christ Jesus. When they heard this, they were baptized in the name of the Lord Jesus."*

Paul did not minimize John's preaching or John's baptism. He simply told them that John's baptism was preparatory to the coming of Jesus—His death, burial, resurrection, glorification, and then the coming of the Holy Spirit on the Day of Pentecost.

In Romans 10:14 Paul asked, "How then shall they call on Him in whom they have not *believed?* and how shall they believe in Him of whom they have not *heard?* and how shall they *hear* without a preacher?" These disciples of John had not heard, therefore they could not

believe.

"*When they heard this . . . .*" When they heard *what?* When they heard that they should believe on Jesus, the One for whom John the Baptist prepared the way. Even though the details of Paul's instructions are not recorded here it would stand to reason that he gave them the same message he had given wherever he had preached: the message of the death, burial, and resurrection of the Lord Jesus Christ, the Lamb of God. And hearing that message, "*they were baptized in the name of the Lord Jesus.*"

Verses 6 and 7: "*And when Paul had laid his hands upon them, the Holy Ghost came on them; and they spake with tongues, and prophesied. And all the men were about twelve.*"

Jesus came that we might have life and have it abundantly. Since God saved me I have *desired* that life in its fullest. I have searched diligently concerning the baptism of the Holy Spirit, and to me the Scriptures make it clear that this is the last time a group of believers were baptized in the Holy Ghost, with that baptism evidenced by speaking in tongues and prophesying as these men did. After this account there is no scriptural record where any servant of God laid hands on anyone that they might receive the Holy Ghost; nor is there any record where any apostle, minister, evangelist, or missionary invited an individual to *seek* the baptism of the Holy Ghost.

The Scripture tells of four groups of believers who received the baptism of the Holy Ghost:

1. The one hundred and twenty believers at Pentecost, all Jews, all waiting with one accord in the upper room. They were baptized with the Holy Spirit and they spoke with "other tongues" so that every man present heard the Gospel message in his own language (Acts 2:1—11).

2. The second group were Samaritans who had believed under Philip's preaching, and when Peter and John had prayed for them and laid their hands on them they received the Holy Ghost—but there is no suggestion that they spoke in tongues (Acts 8:14—17).

3. The third group was composed entirely of Gentiles in the house of Cornelius when Peter preached the Gospel to them. There was no laying on of hands, no praying for the baptism of the Spirit. But while Peter was still speaking the Holy Spirit fell on all who believed, and they spoke with other tongues (Acts 10:44—48).

4. The fourth group were the twelve men of whom we read in our present verses. They received the Holy Spirit when Paul laid his hands on them, they spoke with other tongues, and they prophesied.

These four groups were all baptized into one body—the body of Christ—where there is neither Jew nor Greek, there is neither bond nor free, there is neither male nor female: but believers are all ONE in Christ Jesus (Gal. 3:28).

We see in these groups a wide difference of experiences. Therefore when anyone outlines an experience that believers must follow in order to have the baptism of the Holy Ghost, that person is wrongly dividing the Word of Truth and needs to study to show himself approved unto God (II Tim. 2:15).

Since the day Paul laid his hands on these men in Ephesus and they received the baptism of the Holy Spirit evidenced by their speaking in tongues and prophesying, every person who has heard and believed the Gospel, believing unto salvation, has immediately received the baptism of the Holy Spirit—as clearly spelled out in I Corinthians 12:12—27:

"For as the body is one, and hath many members, and all the members of that one body, being many, are one body: so also is Christ. For by one Spirit are we all baptized into one body, whether we be Jews or Gen-

tiles, whether we be bond or free; and have been all made to drink into one Spirit. For the body is not one member, but many.

"If the foot shall say, Because I am not the hand, I am not of the body; is it therefore not of the body? And if the ear shall say, Because I am not the eye, I am not of the body; is it therefore not of the body? If the whole body were an eye, where were the hearing? If the whole were hearing, where were the smelling? But now hath God set the members every one of them in the body, as it hath pleased Him. And if they were all one member, where were the body? But now are they many members, yet but one body. And the eye cannot say unto the hand, I have no need of thee: nor again the head to the feet, I have no need of you.

"Nay, much more those members of the body, which seem to be more feeble, are necessary: and those members of the body, which we think to be less honourable, upon these we bestow more abundant honour; and our uncomely parts have more abundant comeliness. For our comely parts have no need: but God hath tempered the body together, having given more abundant honour to that part which lacked: that there should be no schism in the body; but that the members should have the same care one for another. And whether one member suffer, all the members suffer with it; or one member be honoured, all the members rejoice with it. *NOW YE ARE THE BODY OF CHRIST, and members in particular.*"

In his letter to the Ephesians the Apostle Paul wrote: "The husband is the head of the wife, *even as Christ is the head of the Church: and He is the Saviour of the body.* Therefore as the Church is subject unto Christ, so let the wives be to their own husbands in every thing.

"Husbands, love your wives, *even as Christ also LOVED THE CHURCH, AND GAVE HIMSELF FOR IT;* that He might sanctify and cleanse it with the wash-

ing of water by the Word, that He might present it to Himself a glorious Church, not having spot, or wrinkle, or any such thing; but that it should be holy and without blemish.

"So ought men to love their wives as their own bodies. He that loveth his wife loveth himself. For no man ever yet hated his own flesh; but nourisheth and cherisheth it, *even as the Lord the Church: FOR WE ARE MEMBERS OF HIS BODY, OF HIS FLESH, AND OF HIS BONES.* For this cause shall a man leave his father and mother, and shall be joined unto his wife, and they two shall be one flesh.

*"This is a great mystery: but I speak concerning Christ and the Church"* (Eph. 5:23—32).

We become members of the body of Christ through the miracle of the spiritual birth—the baptism and work of the Holy Spirit; and this occurs when we are born again. It is impossible to be saved *apart from* the baptism of the Spirit. That is the only way to become a member of the New Testament Church.

In Acts 2:47 the Lord added to the Church daily such as were being saved. They were added to the Church, the body of Christ, the moment they believed on Jesus and trusted Him as personal Saviour. Beloved, if the baptism of the Holy Ghost is an experience that *follows* the new birth, why did Paul not instruct the jailer at Philippi *concerning that baptism?* The Apostle Paul preached *all* of the Gospel—always and under all circumstances. When the Philippian jailer asked, "What must I do to be saved?" the apostle replied, *"Believe on the Lord Jesus Christ, and thou shalt be saved . . . and they spake unto him THE WORD OF THE LORD"* (Acts 16:31, 32). The jailer believed, his entire household believed, they were all baptized—but the account says not one word about anyone speaking with other tongues, prophesying, or giving any outward sign of their inward experience. The Scripture simply tells us that the jailer

sat at meat with Paul and Silas *"and rejoiced, believing in God with all his house"* (Acts 16:34).

Every believer, every person who has sincerely trusted in the shed blood and finished work of the Lord Jesus Christ, has been united to the body of Christ through the baptism of the Holy Ghost, and it is utterly impossible to be a Christian *apart* from the Holy Ghost. Jesus Himself said to Nicodemus, "Except a man be *born again,* he cannot see the kingdom of God. . . . Except a man be *born of water AND OF THE SPIRIT,* he cannot enter into the kingdom of God" (John 3:3, 5).

In Romans 8:9 Paul declared, ". . . Now if any man *have NOT the Spirit of Christ,* he is none of His!" And in Ephesians 4:30 Paul tells us that we should "grieve not *the Holy Spirit of God, whereby ye are SEALED* unto the day of redemption."

## Paul In the Synagogue At Ephesus

Verse 8: *"And he went into the synagogue, and spake boldly for the space of three months, disputing and persuading the things concerning the kingdom of God."*

*"He went into the synagogue."* As we have noticed so often before, this was always Paul's custom when he entered a new field. He went first to the synagogue and taught the Jews from the Old Testament Scriptures showing that Jesus was Messiah.

In the synagogue at Ephesus he *"spake boldly for the space of three months"*—and I do not doubt that he spoke *daily,* perhaps several times a day—*"disputing and persuading the things concerning the kingdom of God."* This means that he preached the death, burial, and resurrection of Jesus "according to the Scriptures," reminding the Jews that their own prophets had declared that Messiah would suffer and die but would rise again.

Paul *disputed* (or reasoned) and then *persuaded.* No doubt he answered questions asked by some of the Jewish

leaders. They probably declared that the Old Testament Scriptures meant one thing, and Paul clearly pointed out that the Scriptures meant exactly what they said. He *reasoned* with them and then used *persuasive* words to show them how their prophets had minutely described the suffering Saviour, the Messiah, and that those descriptions also applied to Jesus of Nazareth whom the Jews had crucified.

Verse 9: *"But when divers were hardened, and believed not, but spake evil of that way before the multitude, he departed from them, and separated the disciples, disputing daily in the school of one Tyrannus."*

*"When divers were hardened, and believed not . . . ."* The Gospel either *softens* hearts, or *hardens* hearts. When God's Word is heard and *received*, the heart is softened; but when it is heard and *rejected*, the heart is hardened. Most of the Jews rejected Paul's message, therefore they were hardened. When they refused to believe the truth, the next step was automatic—that is, they *heard* the truth, they *rejected* the truth, *and they were hardened.*

Next, they *"spake evil of that way before the multitude."* The *"WAY"* here refers to the way of salvation, the way that leads to heaven, the manner in which God redeems men. We find the same expression in Acts 9:2 when Saul of Tarsus obtained warrants for the arrest of Christians in Damascus—"that if he found *any of this WAY*, whether they were men or women, he might bring them bound unto Jerusalem." In Acts 22:4 Paul testified, "I persecuted *this WAY* unto the death, binding and delivering into prisons both men and women."

This of course refers to *the JESUS way.* To Thomas Jesus said, *"I am the WAY . . .* no man cometh unto the Father, but by ME" (John 14:6). In Philippi the girl who was possessed of demons followed Paul and Silas and continually cried out, "These men are the servants of the most high God, which shew unto us *the WAY of*

*salvation"* (Acts 16:17).

In His Sermon on the Mount, Jesus said, ". . . Strait is the gate, and *narrow is the WAY, which leadeth unto life,* and few there be that find it" (Matt. 7:14).

When the Jews *spoke evil of "that way"* Paul did not try to *force* his message upon them. He knew that salvation must be received willingly, *by FAITH.* Therefore he *"departed from them, and separated the disciples."* In other words, Paul and the other believers left the synagogue and moved their activities to *"the school of one Tyrannus."*

*"Disputing daily"* does not mean that the Christians were angry, argumentative, or contentious. They simply met with the people daily and continued reasoning and teaching concerning the way of salvation—i. e., Jesus Christ—crucified, buried, risen, ascended, seated at the right hand of the Majesty. Paul preached the Gospel—not according to tradition as it was handed down by the Jewish fathers, nor even as given to him by the other apostles; but *as he received it from the Lord BY REVELATION.* In the school of Tyrannus he continued to teach publicly and to reason with the people, showing them how Christ died for their sins and was raised for their justification.

We are not told who *Tyrannus* was. He was probably a Jew, and from the context we conclude that he was in charge of the place where Paul now held his meetings. The Greek word here translated *"school"* generally refers to a place where groups met for lectures and discussions. Thus Paul and his co-workers were permitted to assemble there to discuss the Scriptures and preach the Gospel without such annoyances as they had encountered in the synagogue.

Verse 10: *"And this continued by the space of two years; so that all they which dwelt in Asia heard the Word of the Lord Jesus, both Jews and Greeks."*

*"This continued by the space of two years."* Here

we learn the secret of the great and powerful church established in the city of Ephesus. Today most churches have *week-end* revivals. A scattered few have as much as a *week* of meetings with services nightly, and occasionally services are held both morning and evening for a week. But in Ephesus Paul held what we might call a Bible Conference that lasted for twenty-four months, with services being held daily.

If Christians are to grow strong in the Lord and become good soldiers for Christ, if we are to be effective soul-winners, we must be instructed in the Word of God. In the spiritual life, as well as in the physical, *milk* precedes *meat*. Babes in Christ must be fed with the milk of the Word if they are to become mature Christians where they can be fed with the *meat* of the Word. I Peter 2:2 tells us that we should, "as newborn babes, desire the sincere milk of the Word," *that we may grow thereby.* So for two years Paul taught daily those who came to hear him in the city of Ephesus. This is the longest period of time spent by the apostle *in one place* during his entire ministry.

And *"ALL they* (that is, great multitudes) *which dwelt in Asia heard the Word of the Lord Jesus."* We have previously noted the importance of the city of Ephesus in the province of Asia Minor, and because of that city's being a center of commerce and idol-worship a constant stream of humanity flowed through it. Thousands of people visited there—some for commercial reasons, some because of religion (which, of course, was idolatry). Thus Paul had the privilege of preaching the Gospel to great multitudes during the two years he spent in Ephesus, and as those crowds returned home they in turn carried the message of salvation until *"all who dwelt in Asia"* heard that message.

To *"both Jews and Greeks"* Paul preached *"the Word of the Lord Jesus."* Paul had no other message to deliver. He had neither the desire nor the time to discuss

current events or political issues. He simply *preached the Word* concerning the Lord Jesus Christ.

Paul was greatly challenged by what he found in the city of Ephesus. From there he wrote to the church in Corinth explaining, "I will tarry at Ephesus until Pentecost. For *a great door and effectual is opened unto me, and there are MANY adversaries*" (I Cor. 16:8, 9). Paul had stayed for a long period at Corinth. He did not tarry long in Athens for there were no "adversaries" there —the Athenians were not even concerned enough to persecute him for his preaching! The devil so completely controlled that city that the people did not raise opposition to the Gospel and there was little opportunity for Paul to preach the grace of God effectively. But of Ephesus he could say, "A great and effectual *door* is opened . . . there are *many adversaries.*" The difficulties he encountered in Ephesus were blessings in disguise. The adversaries who would destroy him actually contributed to the mighty victory he won there, as we will see later in our study.

Verses 11 and 12: *"And God wrought special miracles by the hands of Paul: so that from his body were brought unto the sick handkerchiefs or aprons, and the diseases departed from them, and the evil spirits went out of them."*

*"God wrought SPECIAL miracles by the hands of Paul."* Most remarkable and extraordinary miracles were brought to pass through Paul—a manifestation of *the power of God* which was needed to bring to nought the evil powers of darkness, demons, wicked spirits, and magic so active in the city of Ephesus.

In Hebrews 2:1—4 Paul wrote, "Therefore we ought to give the more earnest heed to the things which we have heard, lest at any time we should let them slip. For if the Word spoken by angels was stedfast, and every transgression and disobedience received a just recompence

of reward, how shall we escape, if we neglect so great salvation; which at the first *began to be spoken by the Lord, and was CONFIRMED unto us by them that heard Him; GOD ALSO BEARING THEM WITNESS both with signs and wonders, and with DIVERS MIRACLES*, and gifts of the Holy Ghost, according to His own will?"

So God wrought special miracles by the hands of Paul in order to bear witness to the message Paul preached, thus manifesting extraordinary power in this city where *Satan* had manifested such great power. Jewish instruments of Satan in the person of men like the seven sons of Sceva (v. 14) were powerful in Ephesus, and God sent special power upon Paul and used him to show the truth of I John 4:4: "Ye are of God, little children, and have overcome them: because *greater is He that is in YOU, than he that is in the world!"*

We are not to assume, however, that this power was upon Paul (or within him) to remain forever. Such manifestations of power did not continue with him even until the climax of his ministry. God did this for a special reason in Ephesus.

There is much superstition and fanaticism in religion today, and those who claim to be miracle-workers base their authority on portions of Scripture such as the statement in our present verse. They say, "If God wrought miracles by the hands of Paul, *He can do the same today."* They do not accept the fact that the signs and wonders of the transition period were direct testimony that the Gospel preached by the apostles was truly God's Word. We need no such testimony today because we have the complete written Word, and *all that we need to know* about time, eternity, God, Satan, salvation, sin, or anything else having to do with things eternal *can be found IN HIS WORD.* If we refuse to believe the Word God has given us, we would not believe if we saw mighty miracles! We must remember that even when God *did* work miracles by the hands of His servants

many of the people who *witnessed* those miracles *still refused to believe.*

Such special miracles were wrought through Paul *"that from his body were brought unto the sick handkerchiefs or aprons."* Bible scholars tell us that the Greek word here translated *"handkerchief"* is of Latin origin and denotes a piece of cloth, particularly linen, with which a person removed sweat from his face. It also referred to a piece of cloth used for tying up something, such as bread or grain. The same word is used in John 11:44 with reference to the *napkin* which was bound about the face of Lazarus when Jesus called him forth from the tomb. It is used again in John 20:7, speaking of the *napkin* which had been about the head of Jesus, "not lying with the linen clothes, but wrapped together in a place by itself."

The Greek word here rendered *"apron"* comes from a Latin word meaning "half-girdle," a piece of linen or cloth girded about the waist to prevent soiling the clothes of those who were engaged in certain types of work which would otherwise be detrimental to the clothing.

The modernists and liberals have attempted to explain away the miracles wrought through Paul by means of these handkerchiefs and aprons, saying that they were only superstitions—but not so! The miracles were genuine. Paul touched the handkerchiefs and aprons brought to him by the sick or by those who had sick loved ones, *"and the disease departed from them, and the evil spirits went out of them."*

A similar instance is recorded in Matthew 9:20—22 when the woman who had had "an issue of blood twelve years" pressed into the crowd and touched the hem of Jesus' garment. She said, "If I may but touch His garment, I shall be whole." But notice: It was not touching the hem of the Lord's garment that healed the woman; *it was FAITH.* Jesus said to her, "Daughter . . . *thy FAITH hath made thee whole."*

By like token, there was no efficacy or healing power in the handkerchiefs and aprons brought to Paul and then returned to those who were sick of various diseases or possessed of demons. It was not Paul's touching these pieces of cloth that gave the power to heal. The people were healed *because they had FAITH IN THE GOSPEL Paul was preaching.*

Verses 13 and 14: *"Then certain of the vagabond Jews, exorcists, took upon them to call over them which had evil spirits the name of the Lord Jesus, saying, We adjure you by Jesus whom Paul preacheth. And there were seven sons of one Sceva, a Jew, and chief of the priests, which did so."*

*"Vagabond Jews"* in the Greek reads "Jews going about," and of course that description is aptly used. A vagabond is a person who wanders from one place to another without settling down. These Jews were itinerants, having no fixed abode, but not necessarily wandering beggars or idlers.

These "vagabond Jews" were *exorcists*—men who claimed to cast out evil spirits by religious or magical ceremonies, incantations, and adjurations. There were many such people in that day, magicians who pretended to cast out evil spirits and demons and to cure diseases by means of charms and amulets.

These particular Jews *"took upon them to call over them which had evil spirits the name of the Lord Jesus."* It was the practice of exorcists to use the name of some god, or some other "magical" name, when they adjured the evil spirits to come out of the one in whom they had taken up their abode. You will recall that in Matthew 12:22−30 when Jesus healed a man who was blind, mute, and possessed of a demon, the Pharisees accused Him of casting out demons by *Beelzebub*, prince of demons. Jesus, knowing their thoughts, said to them, "If Satan cast out Satan, he is divided against himself; how

hall then his kingdom stand?    And if I by Beelzebub ast out devils, *by whom do your children cast them ut?"*

In this instance the vagabond Jews used *the name of esus* because it was through His name that Paul wrought pecial miracles, and they probably knew that Jesus had ast out many evil spirits during His own public min- stry.    Therefore they supposed that name to hold some harm which would dispel evil spirits, and they said, *"We adjure you by Jesus whom Paul preacheth."*

To *"adjure"* means "to bind by an oath," or to lay under the obligation of an oath.    A similar word is used n I Thessalonians 5:27 when Paul closed his letter with hese words:    *"I CHARGE YOU by the Lord* that this pistle be read unto all the holy brethren."    To *adjure* vas a form of putting one under oath.    We find an ex- mple of this in I Kings when Solomon put Shimei under n oath and said to him, "Did I not make thee to swear y the Lord . . . ?    Why then hast thou not *kept* the oath f the Lord, and the commandment that I have charged hee with?" (I Kings 2:42, 43).    Study also Genesis 24:37, I Kings 11:4, and Nehemiah 13:25.

There were many of these vagabond Jews in the days f Paul, and the art of commanding evil spirits to come ut of people *under oath* was practiced extensively.    This as been proved by the writings of historians—by Jo- ephus and many other trustworthy writers of that time; nd from Bible history we learn that the name most ften used was the name of Jehovah.

*"There were seven sons of one Sceva, a Jew, and hief of the priests, which did so."* Although Sceva was Jew he bore a Greek name, and all that we know of im is recorded in this verse.    We are told that he was *chief of the priests."* The Greek reads, "a chief priest." Ve do not know why the title was given to him, but is most likely that the name was applied to the twenty- ur courses of the Levitical priesthood, who are called

in the Old Testament "heads of fathers' houses." We know that Sceva was a Jewish chief priest and held the office of a ruler, but he was not God's high priest.

We might note that this is the fourth time in the book of Acts where we have read of Satanic instruments:

*Simon Magus* who claimed to be converted—and then proved his claim false by attempting to *buy* the power of the Holy Spirit (Acts 8:9—20).

*Elymas the sorcerer* opposed the message of the Gospel going forth to the Gentiles (Acts 13:6—12). This man was a type of the Jewish nation's blind opposition to the Messiah.

*The young soothsayer* at Philippi who, controlled by the spirit of witchcraft and divination, followed Paul and Silas until finally Paul turned to her, rebuked the demon and cast him out. The soothsayer was converted but Paul and Silas were arrested, beaten, and thrown in jail at the demand of the men who had been making merchandise of the poor fortuneteller and her peculiar powers.

*The seven sons of Sceva* in our present verse formed the fourth example of Satan's use of human instruments to hinder the Gospel. They were professional exorcists, they traveled from place to place declaring that they had the power to cast out evil spirits, and they tried to imitate the power of God which had been manifested through the Apostle Paul.

Verse 15: *"And the evil spirit answered and said Jesus I know, and Paul I know; but who are ye?"*

The name of Jesus used by the sons of Sceva did not accomplish what had been accomplished through the miracles of Paul! Even while Jesus was on earth He said, *"Not every one that saith unto me, Lord, Lord, shall enter into the kingdom of heaven; but he that doeth the will of my Father which is in heaven. Many will say to me in that day, Lord, Lord, have we not proph-*

esied in thy name? *and in thy name have cast out devils?* and in thy name done many wonderful works? And then will I profess unto them, I never knew you: depart from me, ye that work iniquity" (Matt. 7:21—23).

To these vagabond Jews the evil spirit replied, *"JESUS I KNOW, and Paul I know; but who are YE?"* The demons always recognized the Lord Jesus Christ. They knew His power was superior to their own and when they came in contact with Him as He tabernacled among men they acknowledged Him and confessed that He was the Son of God. When Jesus met the man of Gadara, a man possessed of a *legion* of demons, the demons cried out, *"What have we to do with THEE, JESUS, THOU SON OF GOD?* Art thou come hither to torment us before the time?"* (Matt. 8:29).

Yes, the demons knew Jesus, they knew Paul and his power to cast them out; but they did not know the seven sons of Sceva. They demanded, *"Who are YE?"* In other words, "By *what right* do YOU command us to come out of this body in which we dwell?" When demons came in contact with Jesus they recognized His power, and they recognized the power of God in the Apostle Paul; but they also knew that these Jews did not possess that power. Therefore they could not cast out demons *in the name of Jesus.*

Verse 16: *"And the man in whom the evil spirit was leaped on them, and overcame them, and prevailed against them, so that they fled out of that house naked and wounded."*

Although these Jews had used the *name* of Jesus in commanding the evil spirit to come out of the man, *they had not acknowledged the DEITY of Jesus.* The demon who possessed this poor man recognized their lack of power, and energized by superhuman strength he *"leaped on them and overcame them."* He tore the clothes from them and put them to flight—*"naked and wounded."*

Beloved, one day all who have used the name of Jesus wrongly, all who have made merchandise of the souls of men and of sick people, will meet with a worse fate than did the sons of Sceva!

Verses 17 and 18: *"And this was known to all the Jews and Greeks also dwelling at Ephesus; and fear fell on them all, and the name of the Lord Jesus was magnified. And many that believed came, and confessed, and shewed their deeds."*

*"This was known to all."* News of the fate of the seven sons of Sceva spread rapidly through the city of Ephesus. Jews and Gentiles alike heard of it and *"fear fell on them all."* They now knew that the miracles wrought by the Apostle Paul were genuine, wrought in the name of Jesus by the power of God. They saw clearly that there was a real, vital, and *divine difference* between Paul and the impostors who had attempted to cast out demons in the name of Jesus.

Faith comes by hearing, and hearing by the Word of God. Many people who had heard Paul's message recognized the truth of that message, were deeply convicted of their sins, and they believed the Word. Thus *"the name of the Lord Jesus was magnified."*

*"And many that believed came, and confessed."* You may rest assured that when one believes unto salvation he will *confess* that belief. To the believers in Rome Paul wrote, "With the heart man believeth unto righteousness; and with the mouth confession is made unto salvation" (Rom. 10:10).

The next step the Ephesians took proved that their confession was sincere. They came, they confessed, *and "SHEWED THEIR DEEDS."* We are not saved by works—*"by grace* are ye saved through *faith;* and that not of yourselves: *it is the gift of God: NOT OF WORKS,* lest any man should boast" (Eph. 2:8, 9). Salvation is totally *apart from works,* but all who are saved *produce*

works—not all bring forth a hundredfold, some produce thirty, some sixty—but there is no such thing as saving faith *entirely apart* from fruit-bearing.

God's grace saves us, and God's grace becomes ours *through FAITH*. Faith comes through hearing the Word of God, therefore salvation is the gift of God and is entirely apart from works. BUT—*"We are HIS WORK-MANSHIP, created in Christ Jesus UNTO good works, which God hath before ORDAINED THAT WE SHOULD WALK IN THEM"* (Eph. 2:10).

*Faith alone saves us* and justifies us in the sight of God, but *works* justify us in the sight of men. James said, "Wilt thou know, O vain man, that *FAITH WITH-OUT WORKS is dead?* Was not Abraham our father *justified by works, when he had offered Isaac his son upon the altar?* Seest thou how faith wrought with his works, and by works was faith made perfect? And the Scripture was fulfilled which saith, *Abraham believed God, and it was imputed unto him for righteousness:* and he was called the Friend of God.

"Ye see then how that by works a man is justified, and not by faith only. Likewise also *was not Rahab the harlot justified by works, when she had received the messengers, and had sent them out another way? FOR AS THE BODY WITHOUT THE SPIRIT IS DEAD, SO FAITH WITHOUT WORKS IS DEAD ALSO"* (James 2:20—26).

Jesus explained it in these words: "Let your light so shine before men, *that they may SEE YOUR GOOD WORKS, and glorify your Father which is in heaven"* (Matt. 5:16). So you see, while works have nothing to do with redemption, *works prove that we ARE redeemed.* The many who believed in Ephesus confessed their faith in Jesus and then *proved* their salvation by their actions.

Verse 19:    *"Many of them also which used curious arts brought their books together, and burned them before*

*all men: and they counted the price of them, and found it fifty thousand pieces of silver.''*

"*Curious arts*" speaks of the practice of magic or spiritualism. The men who believed under Paul's preaching were secretly attached to these curious arts, but under the power of Paul's message from the Word of God they were deeply convicted that these things were sinful—tools of the devil. So they confessed their sins and separated themselves from former sinful practices.

Please note that these people did not forsake the practice of these "curious arts" in a half-hearted manner. They "*brought their books together, and BURNED them before all men.*" These books contained magic formulas, incantations, and adjurations, some of which had been handed down from generation to generation. It is a matter of historical record that such "curious arts" were practiced extensively at Ephesus. It was believed that combinations of letters or words pronounced with a certain intonation of voice were powerful and effective in casting out demons and healing diseases. People who engaged in or patronized such arts also believed that those same letters or words inscribed on parchment and worn on the body had power to ward off evil spirits and all kinds of diseases. In fact, these arts were so accepted that rulers claimed to have won battles by the use of such incantations and amulets.

The people of Ephesus were not the last to believe in "magic" and spiritualism. There are people today who deal in familiar spirits and claim to be able to communicate with the dead. These things are of the devil. They are as deadly as the magic of Ephesus, and God's Word warns us to be alert and on guard against such doctrine.

"Now the Spirit speaketh expressly, that in the latter times some shall depart from the faith, giving heed to seducing spirits, and doctrines of devils; speaking lies in hypocrisy; having their conscience seared with a hot iron" (I Tim. 4:1, 2).

John the Beloved warns, "Beloved, believe not every spirit, but try the spirits whether they are of God: because many false prophets are gone out into the world" (I John 4:1).

The people who believed Paul's message and put their faith and trust in the crucified, buried, risen Lord *"brought their books together . . . ."* We see *unity* among these believers—i. e., they brought their books of magic together in a unified effort to destroy evil and put away evil practices. This points out the fact that the Holy Spirit was in command, and the Holy Spirit is not the author of division among God's people.

Notice too that the Ephesian believers brought their books of magic into a public place *"and burned them BEFORE ALL MEN."* Today, liberals and modernists would suggest that those who are determined to burn their books of superstition should do it at home in secret lest they *offend* someone else who prefers to continue the use of such literature! But the believers in Ephesus brought all their books together, piled them in one great heap, and had a public bonfire—thus giving testimony that they were finished with such sinful practices.

Beloved, this was a real testimony! These people had *practiced* their arts publicly, now they publicly *renounced* them, turning from "books" to THE ONE BOOK—the Word of God; and there was to be no turning back. These men who had misled and deceived many of the Ephesians wanted those whom they had deceived to know that they were no longer indulging in "curious arts"—and dearly beloved, the only way to do business with the devil is to go all out and completely destroy that which would destroy others. Whatever things a person must get rid of when he is born again, those things should be *destroyed*, not given to someone else!

*"And they counted the price of them, and found it fifty thousand pieces of silver."* Bible scholars tell us that it is impossible to definitely ascertain the coin in-

dicated by the Greek word used here denoting silver. If the coin refers to the Jewish shekel (which was worth about fifty cents of our American money) the value of the books would have been approximately $25,000. In Greek or Roman coin the value would have been much less. Some Bible scholars suggest that the total cost of the books could have been anywhere from $8,500 to $25,000, but the important thing is that these Ephesian Christians burned their evil books when they found the Lord Jesus Christ as personal Saviour. Whatever the exact value of the books, fifty thousand pieces of silver represented a lot of money—and even this sum does not represent the entire sacrifice made in the burning of the books, for the hopes of further financial gain from the *use* of the books by those who dealt in curious arts was also part of their sacrifice. The record is here to show us that Christianity had—and still has—the power to change the lives of men and women, and those changes will be evidenced by their deeds and daily lives.

Dear reader, as you and I read this passage in God's Word, does the Holy Spirit remind us that *we* should put away certain things from *our* lives? Are we as obedient as these believers were? It is true that the church in Ephesus finally drifted away from its first love (Rev. 2:4); but in its early days the believers there had a deep love for Jesus, and they willingly separated themselves from all things that pertained to the powers of darkness.

Christians today need to hear—and heed—the words Paul later wrote to the believers in Ephesus, words penned under the inspiration of the Holy Spirit. Read these words. Let them sink deep into your heart. Let them search your soul:

*Ephesians 2:19—22:* "Now therefore ye are no more strangers and foreigners, but fellowcitizens with the saints, and of the household of God; and are built upon the foundation of the apostles and prophets, Jesus Christ Himself being the chief corner stone; in whom all the

building fitly framed together groweth unto an holy temple in the Lord: in whom ye also are builded together for an habitation of God through the Spirit.''

*Ephesians 4:30—32:* "And grieve not the Holy Spirit of God, whereby ye are sealed unto the day of redemption. Let all bitterness, and wrath, and anger, and clamour, and evil speaking, be put away from you, with all malice: and be ye kind one to another, tenderhearted, forgiving one another, even as God for Christ's sake hath forgiven you.''

*Ephesians 5:1—21:* "Be ye therefore followers of God, as dear children; and walk in love, as Christ also hath loved us, and hath given Himself for us an offering and a sacrifice to God for a sweetsmelling savour.

"But fornication, and all uncleanness, or covetousness, let it not be once named among you, as becometh saints; neither filthiness, nor foolish talking, nor jesting, which are not convenient: but rather giving of thanks. For this ye know, that no whoremonger, nor unclean person, nor covetous man, who is an idolater, hath any inheritance in the kingdom of Christ and of God.

"Let no man deceive you with vain words: for because of these things cometh the wrath of God upon the children of disobedience. Be not ye therefore partakers with them. For ye were sometimes darkness, but now are ye light in the Lord: walk as children of light: (For the fruit of the Spirit is in all goodness and righteousness and truth;) PROVING WHAT IS ACCEPTABLE UNTO THE LORD. AND HAVE NO FELLOWSHIP WITH THE UNFRUITFUL WORKS OF DARKNESS, BUT RATHER REPROVE THEM. For it is a shame even to speak of those things which are done of them in secret. But all things that are reproved are made manifest by the light: for whatsoever doth make manifest is light. Wherefore he saith, Awake thou that sleepest, and arise from the dead, and Christ shall give thee light.

"See then that ye walk circumspectly, not as fools,

but as wise, redeeming the time, because the days are evil. Wherefore be ye not unwise, but understanding what the will of the Lord is. And be not drunk with wine, wherein is excess; but BE FILLED WITH THE SPIRIT; speaking to yourselves in psalms and hymns and spiritual songs, singing and making melody in your heart to the Lord; giving thanks always for all things unto God and the Father in the name of our Lord Jesus Christ; submitting yourselves one to another in the fear of God."

Verse 20:    *"So mightily grew the Word of God and prevailed."*

The city of Ephesus was indeed a city of darkness; but when Paul came—God's minister with God's message—light came into the city. Paul preached the Word of God, and the entrance of the Word gives light (Psalm 119:130). God's Word is like a fire—warming the heart, burning out the dross of sin, kindling the fires of God's love within the bosom; and like a hammer it breaks stony hearts and crushes stubborn wills. (Read Jeremiah 23:29.)

Hebrews 4:12 declares, "The Word of God is *quick, and powerful, and sharper than any twoedged sword,* piercing even to the dividing asunder of soul and spirit, and of the joints and marrow, and is a discerner of the thoughts and intents of the heart."

In Romans 1:16 Paul declared that the Gospel of Christ —the Word of God—"is *the POWER of God unto salvation* to every one that believeth." The WORD which Paul ministered—and which we minister today—is the POWER—the explosive and disruptive power—of God. The Greek word used here for "power" is a word filled with strength. It is the same word scientists have adopted for (in our terms) *"dynamo,"* *"dynamite,"* and *"dynamic."* Yes, the Word of God is indeed powerful, and in the city of Ephesus it grew mightily and *prevailed,* causing men to forsake their evil ways to follow in the

footsteps of Jesus. So we who are saved by God's grace today should follow the example set by the men of Ephesus when Paul preached the Gospel there.

Suppose a man who operates a liquor store hears the Gospel and is born again. Should he sell his liquor store to some other man who will continue to operate it? Indeed he should not! He should destroy every bottle of booze in the store and then see that the building is converted to some useful purpose. If a distributor of pornographic literature is converted he should unload all of his filthy books in the back lot, saturate them with kerosene or gasoline, and set fire to them. Suppose the owner of a huge distillery should be converted. Would it be right for him to destroy the hundreds of thousands of dollars worth of distilled liquors on hand? The answer is clear: Indeed it *would* be right—unless the alcohol could be converted into a product to be used for beneficial commercial purposes such as disinfectants for hospital use. If the man who owns the biggest distillery on earth should be converted, he should do what the Ephesians did with their evil books—he should destroy his ungodly property or convert it into that which would be beneficial to mankind.

Beloved, every defensive argument ever used by the money-loving owners of distilleries could have been used by the men of Ephesus in defense of their curious arts! If the excuses of the liquor crowd are valid, then the conduct of the Ephesians was vain and foolish.

Salvation is the gift of God—apart from works, apart from any human effort; but being saved is only *the beginning* of the Christian life. Jesus came into the world to save us and give us life—*abundant life;* but He cannot give us the abundance of grace which is our spiritual birthright unless we are willing to surrender soul, spirit, and body to Him. Jesus is not calling upon us to *die* for Him. He wants us to be *living sacrifices.*

Paul pleaded with the believers at Rome, "I beseech

you therefore, brethren, by the mercies of God, that ye *present your bodies a living sacrifice, holy, acceptable unto God, which is your REASONABLE service.* And be not conformed to this world: but be ye transformed by the renewing of your mind, that ye may prove what is that good, and acceptable, and *perfect, will of God*" (Rom. 12:1, 2).

The Apostle Paul was much concerned that his converts walk in the faith as children of God *should* walk. In Romans 6:11−23 he wrote, "Likewise reckon ye also yourselves to be *DEAD INDEED UNTO SIN, but A-LIVE UNTO GOD through Jesus Christ our Lord.* Let not sin therefore reign in your mortal body, that ye should obey it in the lusts thereof. *Neither yield ye your members as instruments of unrighteousness unto sin: but yield yourselves unto God, as those that are alive from the dead, and your members as instruments of righteousness unto God.*

"For sin shall not have dominion over you: for ye are not under the law, but under grace. What then? Shall we sin, because we are not under the law, but under grace? God forbid! Know ye not, that to whom ye yield yourselves servants to obey, his servants ye are to whom ye obey; whether of sin unto death, or of obedience unto righteousness?

"But God be thanked, that ye were the servants of sin, but ye have obeyed from the heart that form of doctrine which was delivered you. *Being then made free from sin, ye became the servants of righteousness.*

"I speak after the manner of men because of the infirmity of your flesh: for as ye have yielded your members servants to uncleanness and to iniquity unto iniquity; even so now yield your members servants to righteousness unto holiness. For when ye were the servants of sin, ye were free from righteousness. What fruit had ye then in those things whereof ye are now ashamed? For the end of those things is death. But now being

made free from sin, and become servants to God, ye have your fruit unto holiness, and the end everlasting life. For the wages of sin is death; but the gift of God is eternal life through Jesus Christ our Lord!"

When we become children of God, the world and weaker Christians watch every move we make. We do not live to ourselves, we are not our own. "So then every one of us shall give account of himself to God. Let us not therefore judge one another any more: but judge this rather, that no man put a stumbling block or an occasion to fall in his brother's way. . . . It is good neither to eat flesh, nor to drink wine, nor any thing whereby thy brother stumbleth, or is offended, or is made weak. Hast thou faith? Have it to thyself before God. Happy is he that condemneth not himself in that thing which he alloweth. And he that doubteth is damned if he eat, because he eateth not of faith: *for WHATSOEVER IS NOT OF FAITH IS SIN*" (Rom. 14:12, 13, 21—23).

To the church in Corinth Paul wrote: "Whether therefore ye eat, or drink, *or WHATSOEVER ye do, do all to the glory of God.* Give none offence, neither to the Jews, nor to the Gentiles, nor to the Church of God: Even as I please all men in all things, not seeking mine own profit, but the profit of many, that they may be saved" (I Cor. 10:31—33).

It was when the Ephesian Christians reached the point of complete surrender that the Word of God grew mightily *"and PREVAILED"*—over man and over demons! I cannot but wonder as I study this account and find the secrets here revealed, if we as Christians today would like to see the Word of God grow and prevail in our own home town? Do we *really want* revival? If we do, then we must yield ourselves unreservedly to the Spirit of God, serving the Lord Jesus in humility and lowliness of mind, bringing sincerity of heart and the sacrificial earnestness so evident in the life of the Apostle Paul. God's Word

is the same today as it was in Paul's day (Psalm 119:89). Jesus Christ is the same *"yesterday, and TO DAY, and for ever"* (Heb. 13:8).

## The Apostle Paul Looks Upon Fields White Unto Harvest

Verse 21: *"After these things were ended, Paul purposed in the spirit, when he had passed through Macedonia and Achaia, to go to Jerusalem, saying, After I have been there, I must also see Rome."*

The Gospel now being firmly established in the city of Ephesus, Paul felt that he could leave the converts there for a season, and even the great victory he had won in that city did not satisfy his heart. He looked out over fields white unto harvest, and he saw no laborers. Therefore he *"purposed in the spirit* (in his mind) ... *to go to Jerusalem,"* and on the way to the Holy City he would pass *"through Macedonia and Achaia."* In both of these places Paul had ministered earlier and churches had been established there (chapters 16—18). He would revisit those churches—and from chapter 15 of his letter to the Romans we might conclude that at least part of his purpose in going through Macedonia and Achaia was to take up a collection and receive gifts for the poorer saints in Jerusalem. He speaks of this in Romans 15:25, 26:

"But now I go unto Jerusalem to minister unto the saints. For it hath pleased them of Macedonia and Achaia to make a certain contribution for the poor saints which are at Jerusalem."

*"After I have been there, I must also see Rome."* Paul was not speaking here as a tourist. His interest in seeing Rome was not in that city's ancient buildings, its historical streets and its celebrated monuments. His "must" was the MUST of God's missionary. Rome was the strategic center of the known world, and from the

heart of that great city highways led out over a vast territory. "All roads lead to Rome" was a popular and trustworthy saying in that day. Along the Roman highways traveled not only the Roman military legions, but merchants, scholars, and sightseers as well. Therefore if that great city could be won for Jesus, those highways would become the *highways of the Lord,* and God's messengers would carry the message of salvation which would bring peace to the soul and happiness to the heart, with every need supplied. Therefore the cry of Paul's heart was "I MUST see ROME!"

Verse 22:    *"So he sent into Macedonia two of them that ministered unto him, Timotheus and Erastus; but he himself stayed in Asia for a season."*

Although Paul "purposed in the spirit" to visit Jerusalem and then go on to Rome, he did not immediately begin his journey toward those cities. Instead, he sent Timothy and Erastus on ahead of him while he remained in Asia "for a season"—for how *long* a "season" we are not told. I believe one reason for his tarrying at Ephesus is found in I Corinthians 16:8, 9 where he said, "I will tarry at Ephesus until Pentecost. *For a great door and effectual is opened unto me, and there are MANY ADVERSARIES."* We will learn more about these "adversaries" in the next few verses.

Certainly *Timothy* was an efficient person to send to visit the churches because he was with Paul when those churches were established (Acts 16:3; 17:14). *Erastus* is not mentioned often, but from Romans 16:23 we know that he was "chamberlain" of the city of Corinth—a position which would correspond to our office of *treasurer.* Thus he, too, was well qualified to receive a collection for the poor. Later Paul himself took the offering to Jerusalem.

### The Uproar of the Silversmiths

Verses 23—25:    *"And the same time there arose no*

*small stir about that way. For a certain man named Demetrius, a silversmith, which made silver shrines for Diana, brought no small gain unto the craftsmen; whom he called together with the workmen of like occupation, and said, Sirs, ye know that by this craft we have our wealth."*

At *"the same time"* Timothy and Erastus left Ephesus for Macedonia and Achaia, *"there arose no small stir about that WAY."* The "Way" here refers to the Jesus Way, the plan of salvation according to the preaching of the Gospel of the grace of God. The *results* of Paul's preaching were plainly evident, and the "stir" (or great excitement) that arose was occasioned by the realization of the silversmiths that their income was adversely affected when so many of the Ephesians accepted Jesus and turned from idol worship.

The silversmiths carried on a flourishing business in the city of Ephesus. Their main source of income was from the designing and manufacturing of little silver shrines to be used in the worship of the goddess Diana, and there was great demand for these little articles of idolatry. Diana (corresponding to the Roman goddess Artemis) was one of the greatly celebrated goddesses of the pagan religion. She was one of the twelve superior deities. She was sometimes represented as having a great number of breasts, denoting that she was the fountain of great and plentiful blessings. Sometimes she was represented as goddess of the hunt, dressed in hunting clothes and carrying a bow in her hand.

The little silver shrines fashioned by the silversmiths were of varied design. Sometimes they showed Diana set into a tiny recess with her lions in attendance. Sometimes they were souvenir models of the famous temple of Diana which at that time was regarded as one of the seven wonders of the world. These shrines or silver amulets were purchased even by people who did not worship Diana, for travelers who came to visit the city

of Ephesus would naturally want to own a miniature temple, a tiny replica of the celebrated temple of Diana.

It has always been a pagan custom to carry small images of pagan gods. Such fashion of worship is still practiced today in the jungles and in heathen lands where the Gospel of God's grace has not yet penetrated. When I traveled in Ecuador, Colombia, Brazil, and to various places in Africa, I brought back several such miniature idols which I purchased as souvenirs in those countries. The Romans in Paul's day had images (which they called *penates* or "household gods") in their homes— nor is such practice a thing of the past. There are millions of people all over the world today who have little images in their homes, in their places of business, even on the dashboard of their automobile or hung on a chain around their necks! Evidently the business of manufacturing images and shrines is still flourishing!

It was during the month of May when the silver-smiths in Ephesus rose up against Paul. This was a special time of devotion to the goddess Diana, and since she was worshipped in Egypt, Cilicia, Athens, and other heathen places there was a great gathering of people from all over proconsular Asia. In May they came from all directions to gather in Ephesus to do homage to their favorite goddess, and the largest temple ever built in her honor was located there.

*"A certain man named Demetrius"* called the silver-smiths together to remind them that by their craft of designing and making the shrines honoring Diana, they earned their living. Evidently Demetrius was a leader among such craftsmen. We might refer to him today as president of the silversmiths' labor union. So he called together all who were "of like occupation" and warned them that their livelihood was being endangered by Paul's preaching of the Gospel, and it did not seem reasonable to him that *they* should stand idle while Paul declared a God and a Gospel which would put them

out of business!

Verse 26: *"Moreover ye see and hear, that not alone at Ephesus, but almost throughout all Asia, this Paul hath persuaded and turned away much people, saying that they be no gods, which are made with hands."*

Here is recorded a most noble testimony given by a heathen man, a testimony confirming the zeal of the Apostle Paul's preaching and his success in turning idolaters to the true God.

*"Not alone at Ephesus, but almost throughout all Asia"* Paul had indeed preached that *there is ONE GOD*, and "saying that *they be no gods, which are made with hands!"* To the Corinthians Paul declared, ". . . we know that *an idol is nothing* in the world, and that *there is none other God but one"* (I Cor. 8:4); and in I Corinthians 12:2 he said, "Ye know that ye were Gentiles, carried away *unto these DUMB IDOLS*, even as ye were led." To the Thessalonians he also spoke of their having *"turned to God from idols to serve the LIVING AND TRUE GOD"* (I Thess. 1:9). So wherever Paul preached, idolatry suffered as the Gospel touched the hearts of men and turned them to Jesus.

Verse 27: *"So that not only this our craft is in danger to be set at nought; but also that the temple of the great goddess Diana should be despised, and her magnificence should be destroyed, whom all Asia and the world worshippeth."*

*"This our craft is in danger to be set at nought."* This was the first complaint Demetrius made against Paul's preaching—and that is the first thought that comes to the mind of any unbeliever whose business is threatened by revival! Blinded by the god of this age, the unbeliever cannot realize the truth of Matthew 16:26 when Jesus asked the all-important question, *"What is a man profited, if he shall gain the whole world, and lose his*

*own soul? or what shall a man give in exchange for his soul?"* The unbeliever takes no notice of the wages of sin and thinks only of the material. Therefore when his means of income is threatened he becomes greatly disturbed.

*"Also . . . the temple of the great goddess Diana should be despised, and her magnificence should be destroyed."* This was the second charge Demetrius made against Paul. He feared that the worship of Diana would cease if Paul and his companions were allowed to continue preaching the Gospel of the God whom Paul declared to be the one true God. If what Paul preached was true, and if the people accepted his message, the end result would be refutation of the contention that people needed the little shrines which the craftsmen prepared and sold for use in the worship of Diana. Those same little amulets would then become objects of contempt and ridicule, and Demetrius and his co-workers would be out of business.

In this contention Demetrius was telling the truth, because the message of salvation by grace through faith in the finished work of the Lord Jesus Christ renders all other religious articles, programs, shrines and trinkets useless and empty. When Jesus cried out on Calvary, "It is finished!" He meant exactly that. He accomplished the work which He came to accomplish and there is not one thing that can be added to His finished work. When Christianity prevails, it puts men out of business if they are engaged in traffic of vice and vanity—that which tends to satisfy the lust of the flesh. I thank God that I am an American; but if this great country of ours were truly *"Christian* America" as it is nominally considered to be, hundreds of thousands of business men would be *out* of business within a matter of hours! The liquor traffic would cease because there would be no drinkers. The drug traffic—and many other occupations which it is not necessary to name here—would die on their feet

because there would be no customers. Truly born again people do not participate in gambling, drinking, and such pastimes of the world.

There are some folk who will say, "If this is true, then it would not be economically healthy for our nation to become *a truly Christian nation.*" I disagree. If every individual now engaged in the manufacture and distribution of that which is evil should be converted and come to know the Lord Jesus Christ as personal Saviour, the billions now being spent for strong drink and other vices would be channeled into avenues which would advance good and fill up the way of life for all peoples. It would not then be necessary for men to pay billions of dollars in taxes and welfare, not to mention the billions expended on penitentiaries and prisons.

There will come a time when the knowledge of the Lord will cover the earth as the waters now cover the sea, when men will beat their swords into plowshares and their spears into pruning hooks. There will be peace on earth and good will among men. But that time will not come until Jesus returns to set up His kingdom on earth and sit on the throne of David to reign.

*"The temple of the great goddess Diana"* is said by historians to have been two hundred and twenty years in the building and the expense was shared by all of Asia Minor. The temple was four hundred and twenty-five feet long, two hundred and twenty feet wide, and was supported by one hundred and twenty-seven marble pillars sixty feet in height and weighing one hundred and fifty tons each. These pillars were of solid marble, some of them intricately carved, others polished to brilliant perfection. The doors of the temple were paneled in cypress wood, the roof was made of cedar, the interior was lavishly decorated in gold and hung with the finest paintings by ancient artists. Such magnificence challenges the imagination—but the beautiful temple of Diana was burned by the Goths in 260 A. D. and today archeol-

ogists tell us that it is impossible to pinpoint the exact location where it stood! Thus it is when men build for time and not for eternity, when they think only of the flesh and not of the spirit. The glory of this world will pass away, but they who do the will of God shall abide forever in that celestial city that will never pass away.

*"Asia and the world"* refers of course to the known world at that time—and it is true that the worship of Diana extended far and wide. It was this widespread worship of that goddess that brought the multitudes to Ephesus during the month of May, and Demetrius realized that the overflowing crowds would give Paul and his fellow Christians a great opportunity to advance the cause of Christianity. If that should happen, certainly the trade of the silversmiths would be hampered and the magnificent temple of Diana could fall into disrepute. This Demetrius intended to prevent, if at all possible.

Verse 28: *"And when they heard these sayings, they were full of wrath, and cried out, saying, Great is Diana of the Ephesians."*

*"When they heard these sayings . . . ."* Demetrius had begun his discourse by calling the craftsmen together (v. 25) and reminding them that they earned their livelihood by the manufacture of silver shrines or trinkets in honor of Diana. These shrines were purchased by worshippers and visitors—especially at that particular time of year when multitudes poured into Ephesus for the festival to be held in honor of the goddess.

Demetrius then declared that wherever Paul had preached, his message had "turned away much people" from idolatry, and if that happened in Ephesus the silversmiths would be in danger of losing their income. In addition to the effect this new way of life would have on *their* profession, the goddess Diana would be held in contempt and her temple would be despised. Thus did *"these sayings"* of Demetrius fill the craftsmen with

wrath, and they cried out, *"Great is Diana of the Ephesians!"*

Verse 29:    *"And the whole city was filled with confusion:    and having caught Gaius and Aristarchus, men of Macedonia, Paul's companions in travel, they rushed with one accord into the theatre."*

Historians tell us that this *"theatre"* was the scene of all the great games and exhibitions of the city and had a seating capacity of thirty thousand people!  The city was filled with worshippers at that time, and the silversmiths were doing a booming business with sales of the silver shrines to be used in worship.   Thus when the people assembled in such a large building, it seems reasonable to suppose that the crowd was large enough to require that much space.   And now *"the whole city was filled with confusion."*   Considering the multiplied hundreds present, such confusion would be nothing short of mob violence, with thousands crying out, "Great is Diana of the Ephesians"—not thinking, but simply following the spirit of the crowd.

They *"caught Gaius and Aristarchus,"* two Macedonian companions of Paul who were laboring with him in Ephesus.   "Gaius" was a very common name in those days, and Bible scholars find it difficult to establish the exact relationship of this man to others of the same name. We can assume, however, that this is the same Gaius mentioned by Paul as being his host in Corinth (Rom. 16:23) and also as being one of the believers whom Paul baptized at Corinth (I Cor. 1:14).

*"Aristarchus"* is introduced to us here, but we read of him again in Acts 20:4 as Paul's traveling companion after leaving Ephesus, and in Acts 27:2 he is mentioned as being on the ship with Paul on the way to Rome. Then in Colossians 4:10 Paul wrote of him as a fellow-prisoner with him in Rome.

So we know enough about these two men to know

that they were devout and diligent servants of the living
God, and they had probably been outstanding in the
ministry of Paul at Ephesus.  Therefore they were well
known to all, and when Demetrius stirred up the people
to the point of mob hysteria these two Christians were
immediately seized upon and *"rushed with one accord
into the theatre."*   Bear in mind that there was very
likely a crowd of people already assembled in the theatre.
Since it had a seating capacity of thirty thousand, it
seems reasonable to suppose that it held a multitude of
worshippers when Gaius and Aristarchus were brought in.

Verse 30:    *"And when Paul would have entered in
unto the people, the disciples suffered him not."*

*"Paul would have entered . . . ."*  It was Paul's custom
to give testimony before his accusers, testimony of the
saving grace of God.  It must also be considered that
Paul was devoted to those who labored with him in the
Gospel.   Perhaps he felt that he could say or do something that would be to the benefit of his co-workers, and
in utter disregard for his own personal safety he sought
to enter the theatre where Gaius and Aristarchus were
being held.   But *"the disciples suffered him not."*  We
are not told how the believers restrained Paul, whether
by force or by persuasion.   At any rate, they did not
allow him to put himself in the precarious position of
appearing before the already enraged mob which had
seized his companions.

Verse 31:    *"And certain of the chief of Asia, which
were his friends, sent unto him, desiring him that he
would not adventure himself into the theatre."*

*"The chief of Asia"* refers to men who presided over
the public games and religious festivals in the arena.
They were elected yearly and their election had to be
confirmed at Rome before it was valid in Ephesus, since
these men were held responsible for suitable honor being

rendered to the emperor of Rome.

"*. . . which were his* (Paul's) *friends . . . .*" We have no reason to believe that these men were Christians, but being friendly toward Paul they were well aware that he was not a rabble rouser and trouble maker. At any rate, Paul had won their confidence and friendship even though they might not have realized that he was preaching the only true religion, the Gospel of grace and salvation through faith in the finished work of the Lord Jesus Christ. It is certainly probable that these chief men of Asia had seen uproars like this before, and they were experienced enough in handling such uprisings to know that Paul's presence in the theatre would only add fuel to the flame which already threatened to go beyond all bounds of control. No doubt they also feared for his life. So they added their words of caution to the efforts of the disciples, desiring Paul not to enter the theatre—which had now become a courtroom, so to speak.

Verse 32: "*Some therefore cried one thing, and some another: for the assembly was confused; and the more part knew not wherefore they were come together.*"

"*Some . . . cried one thing, and some another.*" Here is a fitting description of a mob. These people had assembled for a purpose—to worship the goddess Diana— and only a few of them actually knew what was taking place. Therefore "some cried one thing, and some another." Hopeless confusion! and the greater part of the people "*knew not wherefore they were come together.*"

Verses 33 and 34: "*And they drew Alexander out of the multitude, the Jews putting him forward. And Alexander beckoned with the hand, and would have made his defence unto the people. But when they knew that he was a Jew, all with one voice about the space of two hours cried out, Great is Diana of the Ephesians!*"

The exact identity of this "*Alexander*" is not given

here. It is supposed by most Bible scholars that he was "Alexander the coppersmith" against whom Paul warned young Timothy in II Timothy 4:14. If that be true, then this man was Paul's enemy and perhaps welcomed the opportunity to speak against him. Be that as it may, the Jews selected him as their spokesman and drew him out of the crowd to stand before the mob and *make "his defence unto the people."*

This was not Alexander's personal defense, he was not defending *himself* before the multitude; but since most civil disturbances under Roman rule were blamed on the Jews, it was Alexander's design to explain to the crowd that the Jews were in no way connected with the Christian endeavor that had so stirred the city. So standing before the people, Alexander *"beckoned with the hand"*—in other words, he raised his hand to silence the tumult in order to be heard above the roar of the crowd.

*"But when they knew that he was a Jew . . . ."* The appearance of Alexander had the opposite of the intended effect. The people recognized him as a Jew, and his presence before them was all that was needed to throw them completely out of control. Lifting their voices in unison they drowned out anything he might have said, shouting, *"Great is Diana of the Ephesians!"*

*Paul* was a Jew, *many* of the Christians were Jews, and the Ephesians who were *not* Jews were prejudiced against them. Unacquainted as they were with the new Christian movement, they considered Paul and his group as simply another sect of the Jews. Therefore they raised the cry in honor of Diana and refused to listen to Alexander, thinking, no doubt, that he was standing before them to defend Paul.

The largest mob starts with but a handful of dissatisfied people. The most devastating riot begins with one brick thrown or one fire ignited. Then it spreads as others join in—not all of them knowing *what* they are doing, or *why*. And as the crowd gathers in number, the riot

gathers in force and momentum until its frenzy lays
waste whatever it reaches. So it was with the uproar
in Ephesus. It started with one man—Demetrius the
silversmith. He succeeded in arousing the other craftsmen
of that trade, and they joined him in his campaign
against the Apostle Paul and his co-workers. The cry
then spread to the multitudes gathered in the theatre;
and the uproar, gaining momentum as it gained voices,
finally climaxed in shouting that lasted for two hours
as thousands of voices cried out in unison, *"Great is
Diana of the Ephesians!"* (And after this display of devotion to Diana, I am sure many who had joined in with
the crowd in a disinterested manner were convinced that
they, too, were deeply devoted to the heathen goddess.)

Verse 35: *"And when the townclerk had appeased
the people, he said, Ye men of Ephesus, what man is
there that knoweth not how that the city of the Ephesians
is a worshipper of the great goddess Diana, and of the
image which fell down from Jupiter?"*

The Greek word here translated *"townclerk"* is used
in many other places (see Matt. 2:4; Mark 8:31; I Cor.
1:20) but is always rendered "scribe." This is the only
place in the Bible where the word is applied to a heathen
magistrate. He was a keeper of public records and presided at various meetings of the townspeople. He was
an important person, for through him all public com-
munications were made to the city and in his name
replies were given. Evidently the townclerk in our present verse was also a man of influence and popularity, for
he "appeased" the noisy mob and quieted them to a
degree where they would hear what he had to say.

*"Ye men of Ephesus . . . ."* In spite of the disorder
and unruliness of the crowd, the townclerk addressed
them in a dignified and respectful manner.

*"What man is there that knoweth NOT"* (in other
words, it was universally known) *"that the city of the*

*Ephesians is a worshipper of the great goddess Diana
. . . ?"* Here is confidence on the part of the townclerk.
His question was put to the people in such a way as to
indicate that there was no danger of anyone destroying
the religion whereby Diana was so ardently worshipped.
There was sarcasm in his words, too, for indirectly he
was saying that everybody on earth except Paul and a
little handful of fanatics knew that the Ephesians worshipped Diana and would continue to do so. Certainly
such worship would not be destroyed by a few Jews like
Paul and his co-workers. Thus did the magistrate reprove
the howling mob for their unreasonable shouting and their
uncalled-for fears. Little did he know that in days and
years to come, the message Paul preached would not
only destroy the worship of Diana, but would shake the
foundations of the mighty Roman Empire as well!

*". . . and of the image which fell down from Jupiter."*
It was claimed by those who worshipped the goddess
Diana that the first image of her fell from the sky—or
from heaven. Therefore the people of Ephesus felt that
that city was the most honored spot on earth because the
temple of Diana was there, and a great image of her
stood within the temple. Thus they believed Ephesus to
be the custodian of the great goddess.

Verse 36:  *"Seeing then that these things cannot be
spoken against, ye ought to be quiet, and to do nothing
rashly."*

The townclerk simply assumed the attitude that no
one on earth could call into question the zeal of the
Ephesians toward their goddess Diana, or doubt the
endurance of their worship of her. How foolish to think
that such firmly established worship could be destroyed
by the feeble efforts of a small group of Jews, no matter
how zealous, who were endeavoring to bring in a God
whom they claimed to be the one true God, thereby dis-
placing Diana's rightful place among the Ephesians!

*"Ye ought to be quiet."* That is a nice way of saying, "Since we know that our worship cannot be destroyed, since we are not afraid of these upstart Jews who preach a God named Jesus, you should be quiet and continue with your worship. Diana *is* great and the whole world knows it. So there is absolutely no need for all of this shouting and turmoil. *And do nothing rashly."*

Verse 37:    *"For ye have brought hither these men, which are neither robbers of churches, nor yet blasphemers of your goddess."*

There is more here than meets the eye.   This man was a diplomat—a *politician,* if you please.   He agreed with the idolaters, he confirmed the superstitions of the people.   He reassured their belief that the image of Diana had fallen from Jupiter.   But he also defended Paul and the other believers—though whether because of admiration for them or fairness in his administration of the affairs of the city it would be impossible to say.   Whatever his reasons for speaking on behalf of the Christians, his approach to and handling of the matter quieted the people and brought them back to reason.

Underlying his ability as a politician was this man's spirit of patriotism.   He loved Ephesus—that fact is evident.   It was his official duty to keep peace in the city and he spoke *in the interest* of peace and civic quietness. But he also knew that this screaming mob composed of thousands of frenzied people could wreck the entire city if they were not calmed down.   He wanted to save his city from the destruction that would easily come if the crowd in the theatre should spread out into the town in search of Paul and other converts to the Christian faith.

Therefore he assured the people that "these men"— possibly Gaius and Aristarchus, possibly the group of believers—*"are neither robbers of churches . . . ."*—or, better rendered, "robbers of temples."   The temple at

Ephesus had great treasure chambers and all that was placed under the guardianship of the goddess Diana would be for the time the property of the temple. Thus to steal from those treasures would be sacrilege. Paul and his companions were not guilty of committing sacrilege against the temple of Diana, they had stolen nothing from it nor had they destroyed anything belonging to it. They had preached against idols and against idol worship, but they had done no violence to the temple. Their work had been carried on peaceably and in the open for all to see.

*". . . nor yet blasphemers of your goddess."* Paul had not used harsh or reproachful words in reference to the goddess Diana—in fact, he had not preached *against* Diana as such. He had simply preached the truth and pointed people to the one *true* God. The best way to remove darkness is to turn on the light, and that is exactly what Paul did. He opposed idolatry, yes—but he preached a positive Gospel as well as negative. To the *believers* he said, "Have no fellowship with the unfruitful works of darkness." But to the *unbeliever* he preached the pure Word of God and the grace of God, knowing that when one turns to the living God that one automatically turns from idolatry. The most powerful force on earth—the Gospel of God, the power of God unto salvation—is at the disposal of God's minister. But we must preach the Gospel in its simplicity, in love, with a burning desire to see souls saved. That was Paul's approach. He was willing to become anything or do anything honorable and righteous in order to win men to Christ. No sacrifice was too great, no labor too hard. Whatever he did was done to the glory of God, and his work in Ephesus was accomplished not by attacks against the goddess Diana, but by holding forth the crucified, risen, ascended and coming again Son of God, the Lord Jesus Christ.

Verse 38:  *"Wherefore if Demetrius, and the craftsmen*

*which are with him, have a matter against any man, the
law is open, and there are deputies: let them implead
one another.*"

If Demetrius and his craftsmen had a trade dispute, it
should be taken to the courts. If it were a town matter,
a municipal dispute, it should be taken to the assembly
of men which had authority in matters pertaining to the
town.   If injustice had been done to Demetrius and his
men, there were laws to correct that injustice and days
when the courts were open for complaints, days appointed
for judicial trials where such matters could be determined
in proper manner by proper authorities.

*"There are deputies:   let them implead* (accuse) *one
another."*   The deputies were Roman authorities known
as *proconsuls.*   If the silversmiths had just complaint
against Paul and his group of believers they could plead
that case before the proconsul and be assured that they
would receive justice.   But of course Demetrius knew—
and probably most of the other craftsmen knew—that
they had no real charge that they could bring against
the Christians.   Therefore they could not bring a *formal*
charge against them, accuse them in the proper court
where the laws were for all, where equal, impartial justice would be handed down by the Roman authorities.

Verse 39:   *"But if ye inquire any thing concerning
other matters, it shall be determined in a lawful assembly."*

*"Other matters"* would pertain to whatever had to do
with public affairs.   If there were charges of that nature
to be brought up, then an *assembly* must convene—not
a mob or a riot, but an assembly that met in conformity
with the law of Rome.   If there were any public griev-
ances against Paul and the other Christians, those griev-
ances must be presented before a properly-convened assembly under the leadership of government authorities.
Actually, the meaning of "assembly" is a called-out

people, assembled in a legal manner. (The Church in the New Testament is an assembly of "called-out ones," an assembly made up of people who have been delivered from the world through faith in the finished work of the Lord Jesus Christ.) The "assembly" spoken of in our present verse was an assembly called together to take care of legal matters such as any charge that might be brought legally against Paul and the Christians in Ephesus, and that assembly would determine whether or not they had done anything contrary to law or detrimental to the city.

Verse 40: *"For we are in danger to be called in question for this day's uproar, there being no cause whereby we may give an account of this concourse."*

The Roman law read, "He who raises a mob, let him be punished with death!" This is recorded in Roman history. Ephesus was a free city but it stood in danger of losing its freedom if the uproar raised by the silversmiths should be reported to Rome. There were magistrates in the city of Ephesus who could express their displeasure with such an uprising, thereby bringing reprisals from the Roman government if the people could not show just cause for it—and the townclerk knew there was no just cause. The city of Ephesus was in great danger of judgment from Rome, and the townclerk's words and actions were prompted by his concern for the city rather than by his understanding of Christianity.

Beloved, I would like to point out here that the moment the believers in Ephesus came under the protection of the townclerk, *the church* was in greater danger than when Demetrius and his mob were howling in protest against Paul and his fellow Christians! It has been previously mentioned that John the Beloved recorded the condition of that church even before the end of the first century of Christianity. In Revelation 2:1—5 we read:

"Unto the angel of *the church of Ephesus* write: These things saith He that holdeth the seven stars in His right hand, who walketh in the midst of the seven golden candlesticks; I know thy works, and thy labour, and thy patience, and how thou canst not bear them which are evil: and thou hast tried them which say they are apostles, and are not, and hast found them liars: and hast borne, and hast patience, and for my name's sake hast laboured, and hast not fainted. *Nevertheless I have somewhat against thee, BECAUSE THOU HAST LEFT THY FIRST LOVE. Remember therefore from whence thou art fallen, and repent, and do the first works; or else I will come unto thee quickly, and will remove thy candlestick out of his place, EXCEPT THOU REPENT.*"

In the history of the Church down through the centuries we find that when Christians came under the protection of civil authorities, when they were defended by their enemies, there was a tendency for the Church to be "at ease in Zion." On the other hand, history reveals that the Church has flourished and made great advances when under *severe persecution* by the enemies of the Gospel. The "candlestick" has been removed from the church in Ephesus for centuries, and what was once a great, flourishing city is now a Mohammedan village and there remains no trace of the magnificent temple of Diana. The harbor which once bustled with commercial activity is nothing more than a pool filled with reeds. In the stagnant waters around the area where Ephesus once stood there is malaria and pestilence, and oblivion reigns supreme. I repeat: When a local assembly comes under the protective wing of civil authorities, backsliding inevitably results.

*But the Church of the living God marches on!* God's Word is forever settled in heaven, and Jesus promised, "*. . . I will build my Church—AND THE GATES OF HELL SHALL NOT PREVAIL AGAINST IT!*" (Matt. 16:18). "*. . . He hath said, I WILL NEVER LEAVE*

*THEE, NOR FORSAKE THEE.* So that we may boldly
say, The Lord is my helper, and I will not fear what
man shall do unto me" (Heb. 13:5, 6).

Verse 41: *"And when he had thus spoken, he dismissed the assembly."*

The townclerk used his authority well.  He had defended the religion of the idolaters by assuring them
that their worship of the goddess Diana was so well
established and so widely known that nothing could
destroy it.  He had appealed to their reason by reminding them that they should either present their charges
against Christianity through regular legal channels or
stand in danger of being punished by Rome for their
illegal promotion of a riotous assembly.  Having "thus
spoken, *he dismissed the assembly."*  Evidently the
crowd dispersed quietly and went their several ways.

Soon after this incident Paul left Ephesus and started
on his planned trip through Macedonia and Achaia on
his way to Jerusalem.

# CHAPTER XX

1. And after the uproar was ceased, Paul called unto him the disciples, and embraced them, and departed for to go into Macedonia.

2. And when he had gone over those parts, and had given them much exhortation, he came into Greece,

3. And there abode three months.  And when the Jews laid wait for him, as he was about to sail into Syria, he purposed to return through Macedonia.

4. And there accompanied him into Asia Sopater of Berea; and of the Thessalonians, Aristarchus and Secundus; and Gaius of Derbe, and Timotheus; and of Asia, Tychicus and Trophimus.

5. These going before tarried for us at Troas.

6. And we sailed away from Philippi after the days of unleavened bread, and came unto them to Troas in five days; where we abode seven days.

7. And upon the first day of the week, when the disciples came together to break bread, Paul preached unto them, ready to depart on the morrow; and continued his speech until midnight.

8. And there were many lights in the upper chamber, where they were gathered together.

9. And there sat in a window a certain young man named Eutychus, being fallen into a deep sleep: and as Paul was long preaching, he sunk down with sleep, and fell down from the third loft, and was taken up dead.

10. And Paul went down, and fell on him, and embracing him said, Trouble not yourselves; for his life is in him.

11. When he therefore was come up again, and had broken bread, and eaten, and talked a long while, even till break of day, so he departed.

12. And they brought the young man alive, and were not a little comforted.

13. And we went before to ship, and sailed unto Assos, there intending to take in Paul: for so had he appointed, minding himself to go afoot.

14. And when he met with us at Assos, we took him in, and came to Mitylene.

15. And we sailed thence, and came the next day over against Chios; and the next day we arrived at Samos, and tarried at Trogyllium; and the next day we came to Miletus.

16. For Paul had determined to sail by Ephesus, because he would not spend the time in Asia: for he hasted, if it were possible for him, to be at Jerusalem the day of Pentecost.

17. And from Miletus he sent to Ephesus, and called the elders of the church.

18. And when they were come to him, he said unto them, Ye know, from the first day that I came into Asia, after what manner I have been with you at all seasons,

19. Serving the Lord with all humility of mind, and with many tears, and temptations, which befell me by the lying in wait of the Jews:

20. And how I kept back nothing that was profitable unto you, but have shewed you, and have taught you publickly, and from house to house,

21. Testifying both to the Jews, and also to the Greeks, repentance toward God, and faith toward our Lord Jesus Christ.

22. And now, behold, I go bound in the spirit unto Jerusalem, not knowing the things that shall befall me there:

23. Save that the Holy Ghost witnesseth in every city, saying that bonds and afflictions abide me.

24. But none of these things move me, neither count I my life dear unto myself, so that I might finish my course with joy, and the ministry, which I have received of the Lord Jesus, to testify the gospel of the grace of God.

25. And now, behold, I know that ye all, among whom I have gone preaching the kingdom of God, shall see my face no more.

26. Wherefore I take you to record this day, that I am pure from the blood of all men.

27. For I have not shunned to declare unto you all the counsel of God.

28. Take heed therefore unto yourselves, and to all the flock, over the which the Holy Ghost hath made you overseers, to feed the church of God, which he hath purchased with his own blood.

29. For I know this, that after my departing shall grievous wolves enter in among you, not sparing the flock.

30. Also of your own selves shall men arise, speaking perverse things, to draw away disciples after them.

31. Therefore watch, and remember, that by the space of three years I ceased not to warn every one night and day with tears.

32. And now, brethren, I commend you to God, and to the word of his grace, which is able to build you up, and to give you

an inheritance among all them which are sanctified.

33. I have coveted no man's silver, or gold, or apparel.

34. Yea, ye yourselves know, that these hands have ministered unto my necessities, and to them that were with me.

35. I have shewed you all things, how that so labouring ye ought to support the weak, and to remember the words of the Lord Jesus, how he said, It is more blessed to give than to receive.

36. And when he had thus spoken, he kneeled down, and prayed with them all.

37. And they all wept sore, and fell on Paul's neck, and kissed him,

38. Sorrowing most of all for the words which he spake, that they should see his face no more. And they accompanied him unto the ship.

The keynote to this chapter is found in chapter 19, verse 21: "After these things were ended, Paul purposed in the spirit, when he had passed through Macedonia and Achaia, to go to Jerusalem, saying, After I have been there, I must also see Rome."

Chapter 20 records a condensed account of Paul's final trip through this particular region. Penned by Luke as the Holy Spirit gave it to him, the divine record is a specially arranged extract from the Apostle Paul's ministry—a ministry which was full and complete, *extraordinary* in every respect. If *all* that Paul said and did had been written down we would be lost among the many details of it; but the Holy Spirit gave the *heart* of his ministry as our guide to a proper estimate of the entirety of the richness of that ministry. Thus we have the divine truths that this history furnishes—what Paul did, the things he said, the miracles he wrought as the Holy Ghost empowered and led him.

In this chapter we find the story of Paul's strange, contradictory, and changing journey before he left this particular region. We will be dealing with two principal events—the meeting of the apostle with the disciples at Troas, and the remarkable gathering of the Ephesian elders when Paul sent for them and called them together

at Miletus and delivered to them his final charge concerning their duties and ministry in the New Testament Church.

### Paul's Last Visit to Jerusalem; He Goes to Macedonia and Greece

Verse 1:  *"And after the uproar was ceased, Paul called unto him the disciples, and embraced them, and departed for to go into Macedonia."*

*"After the uproar was ceased . . . ,"* speaking of course of the disturbance caused by Demetrius and the silversmiths, as recorded in the preceding chapter. We are not told *how long* after this incident Paul remained in Ephesus, but from the general wording of the verse we conclude that he tarried only until the air had cleared and the people returned to their normal routine. Then Paul called the disciples together, *"embraced them,"* and departed on his journey through Macedonia and Achaia.

The *embrace* here was a token of affectionate farewell, just as a kiss was a token of welcome or farewell. In those days it was the custom in that country for acquaintances and friends to greet each other with a kiss, but this applied to members of the same sex and was free from anything inconsistent with their calling as saints. For example, Jesus rebuked Simon the Pharisee by saying, "Thou gavest me no kiss . . ." (Luke 7:45).

We find this custom throughout the epistles, especially where the Apostle Paul was concerned. In Romans 16:16 he wrote, "Salute one another with an holy kiss." In I Corinthians 16:20 he gave the same exhortation, and again in II Corinthians 13:12 and I Thessalonians 5:26. *Peter* closed his first epistle with the exhortation, "Greet ye one another with a kiss of charity (love) . . ." (I Pet. 5:14). Paul was particularly devoted to his converts, and the believers in Ephesus were no exception. So he called

them together, embraced them, and then left Ephesus.

Verses 2 and 3: *"And when he had gone over those parts, and had given them much exhortation, he came into Greece, and there abode three months. And when the Jews laid wait for him, as he was about to sail into Syria, he purposed to return through Macedonia."*

*"Those parts"* undoubtedly refers to the churches already established in the areas where Paul had formerly traveled and preached the grace of God. His journey would have taken him by way of Philippi, Corinth, Berea, and some of the places where on his other visits he had been persecuted and cruelly mistreated. It was between this second visit to Macedonia and his previous visit there that he wrote his two epistles to the church in Thessalonica.

When Paul had given *"much exhortation"* in these places *"he came into Greece."* The *exhortation* here is suggestive of advocacy and comfort. Thus in these cities through which he traveled Paul defended the cause of Christ and comforted the believers who, in all probability, were suffering persecution because of their faith. He, too, had been threatened and persecuted on his former visit; he would have been killed had not God taken care of him, and it was noble of him to risk his life in returning to those churches to bring exhortation and encouragement to the believers there. Then he moved on into Greece. This was the second part of his plan as expressed in verse 21 of chapter 19.

*"And there abode three months."* Again Paul was on the battleground where he had faithfully fought the devil on previous occasions, but his ministry on this trip was primarily that of encouraging believers and building up the saints in the faith. Some Bible scholars believe that it was during his stay in Greece at this time that Paul was divinely inspired to write his epistle to the believers in Rome. This conviction is based on

the words in Romans 15:25—27, where the apostle speaks of going to Jerusalem "to minister unto the saints," taking with him the gifts and offerings from Macedonia and Achaia to be distributed among the needy believers in the church in Jerusalem.

*"The Jews laid wait for him."* How familiar with such plottings Paul must have become by now! No information is given this time as to what *kind* of plot was designed against the apostle's life—whether he was to be attacked before he reached the ship by which he planned to sail to Syria, or just how the Jews planned to deal with him. But as on previous such occasions Paul somehow learned of their plan, and instead of sailing to Syria *"he purposed to return through Macedonia"* returning by the same route he had used in coming into Greece, traveling overland.

Verses 4 and 5: *"And there accompanied him into Asia Sopater of Berea; and of the Thessalonians, Aristarchus and Secundus; and Gaius of Derbe, and Timotheus; and of Asia, Tychicus and Trophimus. These going before tarried for us at Troas."*

Some scholars consider *"Sopater of Berea"* mentioned here to be the same man called *Sosipater* in Romans 16:21. If this be true, then he was sufficiently well known in the work of the Church to send greetings with Paul to the church at Rome. However, we know nothing more of Sopater than what we find in this Scripture.

*"Aristarchus"* we met in the previous chapter of our study, when with Gaius he was seized by the mob under influence of the silversmiths, and dragged into the theatre where a great crowd had gathered.

No further information is given concerning *"Secundus."* We know him simply as a man of Thessalonica who accompanied Paul on his journey to Jerusalem with collections from the other churches.

*"Gaius of Derbe"* may be assumed to be the same

Gaius who, with Aristarchus, was victim of the silver-smiths (Acts 19:29), although "Gaius" was a common name in those days and it is difficult to determine the specific person referred to here.

With *"Timotheus,"* of course, we are well acquainted, and we will hear more of him as we continue our studies. Paul considered him as his son in the ministry, and the epistles of I and II Timothy are filled with expressions of the apostle's concern for this young man.

*"Tychicus"* was one of Paul's most faithful coworkers. He delivered Paul's letter to the church in Colosse, and in that letter Paul speaks of Tychicus as "a beloved brother, and a faithful minister and fellowservant in the Lord" (Col. 4:7). The same terms are used with reference to this man in Ephesians 6:21, 22, indicating that Tychicus also delivered the Ephesian epistle. In Titus 3:12 we learn that Paul also sent Tychicus to assist Titus, and II Timothy 4:12 also makes reference to him. It is evident that during Paul's long imprisonment in Rome, Tychicus was of great help to him.

*"Trophimus"* was a Greek, his home was in Ephesus. He is mentioned in Acts 21:27−29 as having been seen in Jerusalem with Paul, and the Jews assumed that he was one of the Greeks whom Paul brought into the temple, thus polluting their place of worship. Any Gentile who passed beyond "the Court of the Gentiles" and entered the temple proper was subject to the death penalty. The false declaration by the Jews that Paul had brought Trophimus into the temple caused a riot that would have cost Paul his life had not the Roman soldiers rescued him! Trophimus is also mentioned in II Timothy 4:20 where Paul wrote, ". . . Trophimus have I left at Miletum sick."

These faithful believers preceded Paul to Troas where they waited for him. In Acts 16:12 Paul had left Luke at Philippi; but here in verse 5 Luke writes, *"These . . . tarried for US,"* indicating that he had again joined Paul

as his missionary companion.

Verse 6:   *"And we sailed away from Philippi after the days of unleavened bread, and came unto them to Troas in five days; where we abode seven days."*

*"We sailed away from Philippi."*   It was undoubtedly at this time that Luke rejoined Paul, since he consistently uses the personal pronoun *"we."*

*". . . after the days of unleavened bread"*—that is, after the seven days of the Passover.   During the Passover no leaven was used in the bread.   God commanded, "Seven days shall ye eat unleavened bread; even the first day ye shall *put away leaven out of your houses* . . . Seven days shall there be no leaven found in your houses . . . Ye shall eat nothing leavened; in all your habitations shall ye eat unleavened bread" (Ex. 12:15—20 in part). If you will study the entire chapter of Exodus 12, it will acquaint you with God's order for the Passover.

*". . . and came to Troas in five days."*   Paul had formerly made that same trip in *two* days (Acts 16:11, 12). However, the Aegean Sea was subject to uncertain behavior, and since the stormy season was beginning when Paul and Luke made this crossing, contrary winds could have accounted for the five-day trip as compared with Paul's earlier journey.   Luke then tells us that they stayed in Troas *"seven days,"* which would have kept them there through one Sabbath day.

Verse 7:   *"And upon the first day of the week, when the disciples came together to break bread, Paul preached unto them, ready to depart on the morrow; and continued his speech until midnight."*

*"Upon the first day of the week . . . the disciples came together to break bread."*   This clearly reveals that the disciples observed the first day of the week as a day of worship, rather than the old Jewish Sabbath.   Paul and his traveling companions had been in Troas through a

Sabbath, and yet on the day *following* that Sabbath they came together *to break bread*—i. e., to observe the Lord's Supper.

This is not the only reference to the early Christians' observing the first day of the week. Paul instructed the Corinthians, "Now concerning the collection for the saints, as I have given order to the churches of Galatia, even so do ye. *UPON THE FIRST DAY OF THE WEEK let every one of you lay by him in store, as God hath prospered him,* that there be no gatherings when I come" (I Cor. 16:1, 2). Also, in Revelation 1:10 John the Beloved penned these words: *"I was in the Spirit ON THE LORD'S DAY,* and heard behind me a great voice, as of a trumpet." This was the beginning of John's remarkable vision on the Isle of Patmos.

It is very probable that the disciples celebrated the Lord's Supper with the breaking of bread each Lord's Day. Some churches still observe that ordinance every Sunday. Others observe it once a month, and still others partake of it only every three months—quarterly. The important thing is not *how often* we celebrate the Lord's Supper, but the *spirit* in which we observe it. These first Christians were in the transition period, the time when the old economy was giving way to the new; and it was extremely important that the Lord's Supper be observed each Lord's Day, thus reminding the believers of the death, burial, resurrection, and coming again of the Lord Jesus Christ. Today we have the completed Word of God, the perfect law of liberty is ours to read and feed upon, and it is not necessary to observe the Lord's Supper each Lord's Day. But each time we *do* partake of the bread and the fruit of the vine we show forth the Lord's death until He comes again.

*"Paul preached unto them . . . and continued his speech until midnight."* I would imagine that even though Paul was the principal speaker, others of the believers might have given testimony from time to time,

and no doubt there were many questions to be answered as they were asked by those in attendance. This would be the Apostle Paul's last visit to this area, and many of the converts were still babes in Christ. Therefore the meeting continued *until midnight.*

This meeting attended by the first believers certainly gives scriptural grounds for all-night worship and praise services. Although most ministers today speak only thirty minutes or less, I can remember when we had all-night services in our town. Different ministers spoke at different hours and the Bible was read continuously for one hour. Testimonies were given, special singers sang the old songs of Zion. Such a night was looked forward to with great anticipation and remembered long afterward by all who attended. I know of no church where such services are held today. Admittedly, conducting an all-night service simply for the sake of *having* an all-night assembly would bring no glory to God nor would it profit believers; but it is certainly scripturally proper for Christians to spend long periods of time in worship, prayer, and praise to God when such meetings are conducted because the saints love God and love to hear His Word preached while His people testify to His saving grace!

Verses 8 and 9: *"And there were many lights in the upper chamber, where they were gathered together. And there sat in a window a certain young man named Eutychus, being fallen into a deep sleep: and as Paul was long preaching, he sunk down with sleep, and fell down from the third loft, and was taken up dead."*

*"There were many lights . . . ."* So the "upper chamber," the meeting place of these Christians, was brightly lighted, in contrast to heathen temples and places where in semi-darkness all kinds of abominable things took place. This upper room was not a place of darkness and abomination, but a place of light and truth. There

was no secret about Christianity and its aim. As Paul testified before King Agrippa he said, "The king knoweth of these things, before whom also I speak freely: for I am persuaded that *none of these things are hidden from him; for THIS THING WAS NOT DONE IN A COR-NER"* (Acts 26:26).

*"There sat in a window a certain young man named Eutychus."* Windows in that day were not *glass* windows such as we have today. Wooden shutters opened to let in light and air, and could be closed at night to keep out the cold. The walls of the houses were thick, and an open window would provide ample room for a person to sit. Evidently the upper chamber was crowded, and Eutychus found a comfortable place on the window ledge. The hours passed. Perhaps this young man was weary from the labors and events of the day, the many lights in the room increased the heat and contributed to his drowsiness. At any rate, he fell sound asleep and *"fell down from the third loft, and was taken up dead."*

From the window of the third story of the building to the ground beneath the window was a long way to fall—and Eutychus would have landed on either the pavement of the street or the pavement of the courtyard, depending on which way the window faced. Certainly it is not surprising that he *"was taken up DEAD."* Such a fall could easily have broken his neck or fractured his skull.

There are critics who will suggest that this young man was not actually *dead*, but simply stunned from the fall—in which case he would soon have revived and been able to rejoin the worshippers. I believe the Word of God is to be taken *literally* here. I believe this young man was *dead*, killed by his fall from the third story window of the building where Paul was preaching; and I also believe that he was miraculously *and literally* brought back to life!

Verse 10: *"And Paul went down, and fell on him, and embracing him said, Trouble not yourselves; for his life is in him."*

The meeting came to a halt, at least temporarily, as the Apostle Paul went down to where Eutychus had fallen, *"fell on him,"* and embraced him. This was an act of tenderness and compassion, but it also reminds us of *Elisha's* restoration of life to the son of the Shunammite, as recorded in II Kings 4:32—35:

"And when Elisha was come into the house, behold, the child was dead, and laid upon his bed. He went in therefore, and shut the door upon them twain, and prayed unto the Lord. And he went up, *and lay upon the child, and put his mouth upon his mouth, and his eyes upon his eyes, and his hands upon his hands: and he stretched himself upon the child; and the flesh of the child waxed warm.* Then he returned, and walked in the house to and fro; and went up, and stretched himself upon him: and the child sneezed seven times, and the child opened his eyes."

Paul said to the people around Eutychus, *"Trouble not yourselves."* In other words, "Let there be no weeping and wailing such as unbelievers would do. Have faith. Trust in God and be not troubled about this seeming tragedy."

*"For his life is in him."* Or, "His life is now restored." From the moment of Paul's embrace the young man's life was restored. I believe what God's Word says. After all, this account was penned under the inspiration of the Holy Spirit, and Luke the beloved physician was the scribe! Certainly a physician would be in a position to know whether this young man was dead or whether he was only momentarily unconscious. We are told that he was *dead*, and I believe it. I also believe that his life was restored when Paul fell upon him and embraced him—simply another of the *"special miracles"* which God wrought by the hands of Paul (Acts

19:11).

Verses 11 and 12: *"When he therefore was come up again, and had broken bread, and eaten, and talked a long while, even till break of day, so he departed. And they brought the young man alive, and were not a little comforted."*

Apparently Eutychus and others of the believers returned to the upper room where the meeting had been in progress. The *breaking of bread and eating* here indicates an ordinary meal rather than observance of the Lord's Supper. They *"talked a long while, even till break of day."* We are not told what these believers talked *about*, but it would be difficult to imagine that their conversation concerned anything that would not have been to the glory of God. This would have been a time of blessed fellowship, a time of praise to God for the miracle He had wrought through the Apostle Paul, and the believers *"were not a little comforted"* by the fact of this miracle, and they were strengthened in the faith. Paul then departed and continued on his journey toward Jerusalem.

### From Troas to Miletus

Verse 13: *"And we went before to ship, and sailed unto Assos, there intending to take in Paul: for so had he appointed, minding himself to go afoot."*

*"We went before to ship"* means that Luke and the others who were traveling with Paul preceded him on the next lap of their journey, and again waited for him at a given destination. They *"sailed to Assos, there intending to take in Paul."*

Assos was an outstanding seaport of Asia Minor. It lay just north of the Island of Lesbos. It was an *ancient* city, dating back to more than five centuries before the birth of Christ. It was at one time the home of the

Greek philosopher Aristotle. There are many interesting historical facts available concerning this city, but time and space will not permit us to enlarge on them in this study. Today the city is under Turkish rule, it has lost most of its importance, and it is now called *Bekhram.* The harbor from which Paul sailed in the next step of his journey has been filled up and is now covered with gardens, but a new, modern harbor is nearby.

By land, Assos was only about twenty miles from Troas. By water, sailing around Cape Lectum, the distance was about *forty* miles. Luke and the other disciples went by sea, *"for so had he* (Paul) *appointed, minding himself to go afoot."* We are not told *why* the apostle sent his companions by ship while he traveled overland, but more than likely he needed solitude, a time to be alone with God and commune with Him. Certainly Paul was not a poor sailor, and the accounts recorded in Acts chapter 27 show him to be fearless even in the face of a *storm* at sea. From verses that follow in our present chapter—especially verses 22 through 25—we know that Paul was aware of the uncertainties ahead of him, and he fully realized that he would not pass this way again. So it stands to reason that he needed some time alone with God in preparation for whatever awaited him at the end of this journey when he should reach Jerusalem.

Verse 14: *"And when he met with us at Assos, we took him in, and came to Mitylene."*

Paul joined his companions at Assos and continued the journey with them, coming to anchor at *Mitylene.* This was the capital city of the beautiful island of Lesbos, one of the *larger* islands in the Aegean Sea. Although the island was Greek, it was highly favored by the Romans as a holiday resort. It boasted two excellent harbors and strong fortresses, and its location made it a natural overnight stop for Paul and his companions on

their journey southward toward Jerusalem.

Verse 15: *"And we sailed thence, and came the next day over against Chios; and the next day we arrived at Samos, and tarried at Trogyllium; and the next day we came to Miletus."*

Spending only the night at Mitylene, the travelers set sail next morning and came *"over against Chios"* (now called *Scio*), another beautiful island in the Aegean Sea just off the coast of Asia Minor. Though small, this island was of strategic location, natural beauty, and of great monetary importance because of its export trade. It was the scene of many battles and much turmoil dating back to more than five centuries B. C. Finally, in 1821 A. D. the Turks overran the island and laid it waste. They massacred 23,000 Chians and sold 47,000 into slavery; but in Paul's day Chios was a flourishing seaport of importance. However, Paul and his companions apparently did not stop there, and the next day *"arrived at Samos"*—an island just off the coast of Lydia—*"and tarried"* (spent the night) *"at Trogyllium; and the next day we came to Miletus."*

*Miletus* (also called *Miletum*) was a seaport city as well as being the ancient capital of Ionia. Even in the sixth, seventh, and eighth centuries B. C. this was a flourishing commercial center, and during its years of great prosperity it was the home of such Greek philosophers as Thales, Anaximander, and Anaximenes. However, at the time of Paul's visit there the city had passed the zenith of its glory, it was already on a commercial decline, and had become part of the Roman province of Asia.

Verse 16: *"For Paul had determined to sail by Ephesus, because he would not spend the time in Asia: for he hasted, if it were possible for him, to be at Jerusalem the day of Pentecost."*

The statement that Paul *"determined to sail by Eph-*

*esus"* is a bit misleading as we speak of going "by" a place today. *Our* meaning is that we will stop over in a certain place as we travel to another destination, but Paul meant that he would *sail past Ephesus* without stopping to enter the city. *"He hasted"*—that is, he hurried on—*"if it were possible . . . to be at Jerusalem the day of Pentecost."* Paul wanted to keep the feast of Pentecost at Jerusalem as well as delivering the collections from the other churches to the saints in the church at Jerusalem; and he knew that if he entered the city of Ephesus and delayed his journey he would not reach the Holy City in time for the feast.

## Paul Sends For the Ephesian Elders

Verse 17: *"And from Miletus he sent to Ephesus, and called the elders of the church."*

Ephesus was not more than thirty miles from Miletus, and Paul undoubtedly thought that less time would be lost in summoning the elders of the Ephesian church to come to *him* than in his attempting to stop in Ephesus, possibly encountering more delay than he could make allowance for on his journey to Jerusalem if he were to reach there by Pentecost.

Verses 18 and 19: *"And when they were come to him, he said unto them, Ye know, from the first day that I came into Asia, after what manner I have been with you at all seasons, serving the Lord with all humility of mind, and with many tears, and temptations, which befell me by the lying in wait of the Jews."*

Paul's message to the Ephesian elders, as recorded here, is one of the tenderest, most affectionate, and eloquent addresses to be found anywhere in history—sacred or secular. It is strikingly descriptive of the apostle's manner of life while he was with them in Ephesus, and it also reveals Paul's deep concern for the welfare

of the believers in the Ephesian church. Here is expressed the firm purpose of his soul and spirit, the determination to live to the glory of God even in the face of grave danger—perhaps death. He indicated plainly that he *expected* to meet with persecution and hardship in the days that lay just ahead of him—and I do not doubt for one moment that Paul knew he would one day seal his testimony with his life's blood. The message recorded in the following verses of this chapter expresses the apostle's affectionate and sorrowful farewell to the elders of the church in Ephesus, and surely no one can read that message without realizing that it was delivered by a man whose heart was filled with love, compassion, and kindness as he set forth his one great aim and object—i. e., the promotion of the glory of God through the preaching of God's grace.

*"Ye KNOW . . ."*—that is, "From your own observation during the three years I spent with you, you know the life I lived, the Gospel I preached, and how with all of my being I sought to bring glory to God through the preaching of His grace." This challenging statement by the Apostle Paul declares the purity and holiness of his life. These men of Ephesus had abundant opportunity to know him. He had lived among them, they had heard him speak—both publicly and privately—and they knew him well enough to know that he lived what he preached. Had Paul not had full consciousness of his own integrity he could not have made such a statement.

*"From the first day that I came into Asia . . . at all seasons"* was his way of reminding them that from the moment he came into their city until the moment he stood before them to deliver this message, he had lived a consistent and exemplary Christian life. In fact, in verse 31 of this chapter he said, "Remember, that by the space of three years *I ceased not to warn every one NIGHT AND DAY with tears!"*

*"Serving the Lord"* speaks of the discharge of the

appropriate duties of apostolic office as well as Paul's private life.    Salvation is the gift of God, not of works (Eph. 2:8, 9).    We are saved entirely by grace through faith—*nothing added*.    But apostleship is different.    It *costs* to be an apostle, a faithful servant of the Lord, and Paul was willing to pay the price.

He served the Lord *"with all humility,"* not in pride and arrogance.    He was not a religious dictator, but a bondslave of Jesus Christ, a fully-surrendered and humble servant.    His office of apostleship gave him no feeling of superiority or exaltation, but rather pressed upon him the burden of the realization of his responsibility to his calling, a responsibility to the God who had called him, and a responsibility to the Church, the mystery of which was revealed to him.

From the religious standpoint there has never been a man who had *more to boast of*, either before or after his conversion, than the Apostle Paul had.    Before his conversion he was a dedicated religionist, a Pharisee of the Pharisees, an Hebrew of the Hebrews, of the tribe of Benjamin.    He was also a Roman citizen freeborn. He was one of the best educated men of his day, a student of Gamaliel, a member of the governing body of the Sanhedrin.    Yes, he had much of which to boast. Then he met Jesus on the Damascus road, he was born again and became Paul the prince of apostles.    Called with a special calling, endowed with unusual power, blessed as few men have ever been blessed of God, he *still* had much to boast about—but no more humble servant of God is named in the sacred record of God's Word!

Paul not only served the Lord in humility, but also *"with many tears."*    These were not tears shed from apprehension of danger to his person.    Paul feared no man, and on many occasions he endangered his life in order to preach the Gospel; but he carried a heavy burden of anxiety and concern for his converts and the churches he had established, and his burden for the Jews caused

him to declare, *"I have great heaviness and continual
sorrow in my heart, for I could wish that myself were
ACCURSED FROM CHRIST for my brethren, my kinsmen according to the flesh"* (Rom. 9:2, 3).

A born-again, God-called, Holy Spirit-anointed minister or layman will feel a deep compassion for the unsaved and will shed tears over the pathetic condition of
the unbeliever.   Sinners are blinded by the god of this
age, they cannot see their lost condition, and the dedicated Christian will carry a burden to see men saved.
The Psalmist declared, *"They that sow in tears* shall
reap in *joy.*   He that goeth forth and *weepeth,* bearing
precious seed, shall doubtless *come again with rejoicing,
bringing his sheaves with him"* (Psalm 126:5, 6).

The Apostle Paul was an ardent soul-winner.  He was
called as a special minister to the Gentiles, and to him
God revealed the mystery of the New Testament Church;
but his heart also yearned after his own countrymen,
and at every opportunity he spoke to the Jews concerning
the Lord Jesus Christ and His identification as their
Messiah.   It is little wonder, then, that he served the
Lord "with many tears."

*". . . and temptations, which befell me by the lying
in wait of the Jews."*   The word here rendered "temptations" would be better translated *"trials."*   We are accustomed to speaking of temptation as a Satanic induce-
ment to lead us into sin; but in Scripture it denotes
not only that which leads into sin, but also trials and
tribulations of many kinds.   The "temptations" which
befell Paul are pointed out as coming upon him because
of the opposition of the Jews—their *"lying in wait"* with
a diversity of snares, plots, and pitfalls designed to destroy the apostle, discredit his message, and put a stop
to the rapid spread of Christianity under his preaching.

In his letter to the Corinthian church, Paul speaks
in detail of some of the hardships and dangers he endured in order to preach the Gospel, but we see no hint

of weakness or self-pity there. In II Corinthians 11:23—28 Paul declared that he had been "in labours more abundant, in stripes above measure, in prisons more frequent, in deaths oft. *Of the JEWS five times received I forty stripes save one.* Thrice was I beaten with rods, once was I stoned, thrice I suffered shipwreck, a night and a day I have been in the deep; in journeyings often, in perils of waters, in perils of robbers, *in perils BY MINE OWN COUNTRYMEN,* in perils by the heathen, in perils in the city, in perils in the wilderness, in perils in the sea, in perils among false brethren; in weariness and painfulness, in watchings often, in hunger and thirst, in fastings often, in cold and nakedness. *Beside those things that are without, that which cometh upon me daily, THE CARE OF ALL THE CHURCHES!"* Small wonder, then, that the Apostle Paul labored in tears, as he now reminds the Ephesian elders.

Verses 20 and 21: *"And how I kept back nothing that was profitable unto you, but have shewed you, and have taught you publickly, and from house to house, testifying both to the Jews, and also to the Greeks, repentance toward God, and faith toward our Lord Jesus Christ."*

*"I kept back nothing"* refers to the message Paul had preached in Ephesus during his three-year ministry there. He had preached pure doctrine, everything that was necessary for salvation and for growth in grace. He had preached the death, burial, and resurrection of the Lord Jesus Christ "according to the Scriptures," and he had preached for the purpose of their edification, without timidity or fear of consequences. He had kept back no doctrine or admonition which was to their benefit.

This should be the aim of true ministers today. As the Spirit leads, the minister should preach the Gospel in all of its purity and power. He need not shape his messages to gratify the desires of his congregation nor to flatter their pride, and certainly he should not preach

for the sake of popularity among men. A true minister of the Gospel seeks first to glorify God and to edify his hearers, pointing them to the Lord Jesus Christ.

If God's minister is true to God's Word, he will not always please those who listen. His message will not always be acceptable to all who hear it. There are times when a preacher must reprove and admonish as well as instruct and edify. He may not enjoy delivering such a message, but Paul's instructions to young Timothy were given in these words:

*"Preach the WORD; be instant in season, out of season. REPROVE, REBUKE, EXHORT WITH ALL LONG-SUFFERING AND DOCTRINE.* For the time will come when they will not endure sound doctrine; but after their own lusts shall they heap to themselves teachers, having itching ears; and they shall turn away their ears from the truth, and shall be turned unto fables. But *watch thou in ALL THINGS, endure afflictions, do the work of an evangelist, MAKE FULL PROOF OF THY MINISTRY"* (II Tim. 4:2—5).

Writing to the believers in Thessalonica Paul gave what I call "the sure cure for backsliding"—a message which Christians today may not enjoy but need to hear. He said: "See that none render evil for evil unto any man; but ever *follow that which is good,* both among yourselves, and to all men. *Rejoice evermore. Pray without ceasing. In everything give thanks:* for this is the will of God in Christ Jesus concerning you. *Quench not the Spirit. Despise not prophesyings. Prove all things; hold fast that which is good. Abstain from all appearance of evil.* And the very God of peace sanctify you wholly; and I pray God your whole spirit and soul and body be preserved blameless unto the coming of our Lord Jesus Christ. Faithful is He that calleth you, who also will do it" (I Thess. 5:15—24).

Paul delivered profitable doctrine, admonition, and instruction *"publickly and from house to house."* Here

is expressed the wide range of Paul's ministry. He preached in public assemblies—in the synagogue, in the marketplace, on the street—wherever people gathered. But he also taught in homes, in small groups where he could give personal instruction to those who hungered and thirsted after the deeper things of God. All truly born again people love the Word of God, but there is a small percentage of believers who cherish the Word with a peculiar and singular devotion, seeking a closer and more intimate walk with Him.

Certainly there is a great need for public preaching; but there is also a need for detailed and personal instruction for those who seek after righteousness in its fulness and to its depths. There were instances in the ministry of Jesus when He taught in homes, and on other occasions He taught when only *one person* was present. According to the sacred record, He enjoyed visiting in the home of Mary, Martha, and Lazarus, and Luke 10:38—42 records the fact of His teaching in that home as Mary sat at His feet "and heard His Word." He called *Zacchaeus* from the sycamore tree as He passed by, went home with him, and salvation came to the home of Zacchaeus that day (Luke 19:1—10). He spoke at length with the woman of Samaria, and through her testimony of God's saving grace many of her townsmen were saved (John 4:6—42).

The local church has its place and there is certainly great need for public preaching; but there is no doubt that many people are won to Jesus by personal contact, individual to individual—or, as Paul expressed it, "from house to house."

*"Testifying both to the Jews, and also to the Greeks."* In his epistle to the believers in Rome, the Apostle Paul declared, *"I AM DEBTOR both to the Greeks, and to the Barbarians;* both to the wise, and to the unwise. . . . I am not ashamed of the Gospel of Christ: for it is the power of God unto salvation to every one that believeth;

*to the JEW FIRST, and also to the GREEK"* (Rom. 1:14, 16).

From the day he was saved on the Damascus road, Paul felt himself to be debtor to all who needed Christ. His love for his own people was expressed in Romans 9:1–3 by his declaration that he would be willing to spend eternity in hell if by so doing he could bring salvation to Israel. In Romans 11:13 he acknowledged his call to minister to the Gentiles.

In I Corinthians 9:19–22 he said, "Though I be *free from ALL men,* yet have I made myself *servant unto all,* that I might gain the more. And *unto the JEWS I became as a Jew,* that I might gain the Jews; to them that are *under the LAW,* as under the law, that I might *gain* them that are under the law; to them that are *WITH-OUT law,* as without law, (being not without law to God, but under the law to Christ,) that I might *gain* them that are without law. *To the WEAK* became I as weak, that I might *gain* the weak. *I am made ALL things to ALL MEN, that I might by all means save some!"*

Paul's message to Jew and Greek alike was *"repentance toward God, and faith toward our Lord Jesus Christ."* Paul bore witness to the divine necessity of repentance toward God. He preached the same message Jesus preached. In Luke 13:3, 5 we read these words that fell from the lips of the Son of God: "I tell you, Nay: but, *except ye REPENT,* ye shall all likewise perish. . . . Except ye repent, *ye shall all likewise PERISH!"*

Conveying the same message from Mars' Hill, the Apostle Paul declared, "The times of this ignorance God winked at; but NOW commandeth ALL MEN every where to repent: because He hath appointed a day, in the which He will judge the world in righteousness by that Man whom He hath ordained; whereof He hath given assurance unto all men, in that He hath raised Him from the dead" (Acts 17:30, 31).

Romans 3:23 tells us, *"ALL HAVE SINNED, and come short of the glory of God."* All sin is *against* God. Therefore there must be *repentance TOWARD God* before anyone can—or will—exercise sincere saving faith in the finished work of the Lamb of God. Faith comes by hearing, and hearing by the Word of God (Rom. 10:17). Paul preached the Word, he faithfully preached *repentance toward God* and proclaimed the necessity for *faith in God* unto salvation, wholly apart from works:

*"For by GRACE are ye saved THROUGH FAITH; and that not of yourselves: it is the gift of God: NOT OF WORKS, lest any man should boast"* (Eph. 2:8, 9).

To the Romans Paul wrote, *"Abraham believed God, and it was counted unto him for righteousness"* (Rom. 4:3).

Jesus is the Way, the Truth, and the Life (John 14:6). There is no other way to heaven. The person who denies that Jesus is Christ cannot be saved, but all who come to God in Christ's name, believing in His finished work, God saves for Jesus' sake (Eph. 4:32). These are the spiritual truths Paul preached at Ephesus, to Jew and Greek alike, and he now reminds the Ephesian elders of his manner of preaching.

Verses 22 and 23: *"And now, behold, I go bound in the spirit unto Jerusalem, not knowing the things that shall befall me there: save that the Holy Ghost witnesseth in every city, saying that bonds and afflictions abide me."*

*"Behold, I go BOUND in the spirit unto Jerusalem."* The Greek word used here for "bound" is also used in Matthew 13:30 where Jesus spoke of binding the tares which grew among the wheat until harvest. It is used in Matthew 14:3 where it speaks of Herod's binding of John the Baptist when he put him into prison. Paul uses the same term in Romans 7:2 applying it to a wife being bound (by the law) to her husband for as long as the

husband lived. The word denotes a strong obligation. Thus Paul, *bound in the spirit,* felt an overwhelming, compelling need to go to Jerusalem.

The *"spirit"* in this instance speaks of *Paul's* spirit, not the Holy Spirit. In other words, Paul was compelled by his convictions to go to Jerusalem. He was taking with him the gifts which had been made up in other churches to be presented to the church in Jerusalem, and of course he carried with him the burden to preach the Gospel to the Jews.

*". . . not knowing the things that shall befall me there."* In spite of being compelled in the spirit to go to Jerusalem, there was a feeling of apprehension—not bodily fear, but the foreboding uncertainty of what lay in store for him in the Holy City—and in the next chapter of our study we will see that Paul's premonition of danger was not unfounded.

Paul did not know what kind of trials and tribulations he would face in Jerusalem. On many occasions he had faced death for the cause of Christ, and God had *delivered* him on every occasion; but he did not know whether or not his life would be spared this time. He only knew that persecution would be his lot as it had been so often before.

*"The Holy Ghost witnesseth . . . ."* Paul's premonition of coming events was undoubtedly through the witness of the Holy Spirit. In chapter 21, verse 11 we are told that through "a certain prophet named Agabus" Paul was warned that the Jews at Jerusalem would deliver him into the hands of the Gentiles. But this was the apostle's all-out attempt to bring together the two factions of the New Testament Church and bind Jew and Gentile together in the bonds of Christian love. So he pressed on toward Jerusalem in spite of his forewarning that *"bonds and afflictions"* awaited him there, as *"in every city."*

Paul preached under the direction of the Holy Spirit,

he was *led* of the Spirit; but in spite of the Spirit's leading he encountered persecution, affliction, stoning, imprisonment, and scourgings. Even when Paul was converted the Lord declared, "I will shew him *how great things he must suffer for my name's sake"* (Acts 9:16).

Verse 24: *"But none of these things move me, neither count I my life dear unto myself, so that I might finish my course with joy, and the ministry, which I have received of the Lord Jesus, to testify the Gospel of the grace of God."*

*"None of these things move me."* Paul's knowledge that bonds and afflictions awaited him in Jerusalem did not cause him to change his plans. Persecutions were not worthy of his consideration when compared with the great purpose to which his life was dedicated— the lifting up of the blood-stained banner of the Lord Jesus Christ. To the Corinthians he testified, "I determined not to know any thing among you, save *Jesus Christ, and Him crucified"* (I Cor. 2:2).

To the Philippians he wrote, *"What things were gain to me, those I counted loss for Christ. Yea doubtless, and I COUNT ALL THINGS BUT LOSS FOR THE EXCELLENCY OF THE KNOWLEDGE OF CHRIST JESUS MY LORD: for whom I have suffered the loss of all things, and do count them but dung, that I may win Christ, and be found IN HIM,* not having mine own righteousness, which is of the law, but that which is through the faith of Christ, the righteousness which is of God by faith: *THAT I MAY KNOW HIM,* and the power of His resurrection, *and the fellowship of His SUFFERINGS,* being made conformable unto His death; if by any means I might attain unto the resurrection of the dead. Not as though I had already attained, either were already perfect: but I follow after, if that I may apprehend that for which also I am apprehended of Christ Jesus.

"Brethren, I count not myself to have apprehended: *but this one thing I do, forgetting those things which are behind, and reaching forth unto those things which are before, I PRESS TOWARD THE MARK FOR THE PRIZE OF THE HIGH CALLING OF GOD IN CHRIST JESUS"* (Phil. 3:7—14).

Paul had no fear of man. As long as he was in the will of God, fulfilling the ministry to which God had called him, nothing else mattered. He declared, "I have learned, in whatsoever state I am, therewith to be content. I know both how to be *abased,* and I know how to *abound.* Every where and in all things I am instructed both to be *full* and to be *hungry,* both to *abound* and to *suffer need. I can do ALL THINGS through CHRIST which strengtheneth me!"* (Phil. 4:11—13).

*"Neither count I my life dear unto myself."* Paul had been given a ministry to fulfill, and his vision reached beyond death into the joys that waited for him on the other side. He declared, ". . . *Christ shall be magnified in my body, whether it be BY LIFE, or BY DEATH. For to me to live is Christ, and TO DIE IS GAIN. . . . I am in a strait betwixt two, having a desire to DEPART, AND TO BE WITH CHRIST; which is far better:* nevertheless to abide in the flesh is more needful for you" (Phil. 1:20—24).

Paul knew that with physical death would come release from the infirmities and afflictions of the flesh. He knew that "a crown of righteousness" awaited him. If II Corinthians 12:2—4 speaks of Paul's own experience (and outstanding Bible scholars believe it does) then he had already had a glimpse of Paradise. No wonder he had a desire to depart this life and be with Christ! But his abiding in the flesh was to the benefit of his converts and to the glory of God in the winning of souls. Therefore he would fulfill his ministry, he would *"finish his course with JOY."*

In the epistles, life is represented as a "course," a

"race" to be run.    Paul makes this comparison in his second epistle to young Timothy, just before he was executed under Nero's orders. In II Timothy 4:7 he wrote, "I have fought a good fight, *I have finished my COURSE,* I have kept the faith."

In his first letter to the church at Corinth, Paul compared the Christian life to a race to be run, with a reward to be won:    "Know ye not that they which *run in a race* run all, but *one receiveth the prize?*  So run, that ye may obtain.    And every man that striveth for the mastery is temperate in all things.    Now they do it to obtain a *corruptible* crown; *but we an incorruptible"* (I Cor. 9:24, 25).

To the Hebrew Christians, the Apostle Paul also compared the Christian life to a race.    He said, "Wherefore seeing we also are compassed about with so great a cloud of witnesses, let us lay aside every weight, and the sin which doth so easily beset us, and let us RUN with patience the RACE that is set before us, looking unto Jesus the author and finisher of our faith; who for the joy that was set before Him endured the cross, despising the shame, and is set down at the right hand of the throne of God" (Heb. 12:1, 2).

In Acts 13:25 when Paul preached in the synagogue at Antioch in Pisidia he spoke of John the Baptist as having *"fulfilled his course"* in declaring the coming of the Lord Jesus Christ.

What a wonderful experience for believers to finish their course and come to the end of this life *"with joy"!* There can be perfect peace, the peace of God, in one's heart at the end of life's journey.    It is possible to look back over the Christian experience with no regret, knowing that we have given our best, knowing that we have been good soldiers, faithful runners, successful laborers in God's great vineyard—*for "we are MORE than conquerors THROUGH HIM THAT LOVED US!"* (Rom. 8:37).

"*. . . and the ministry, which I have received of the Lord Jesus.*" Speaking here of the apostolic office given him when he was saved and called to preach the Gospel, Paul consistently made plain the fact that he had been placed in the ministry by the Lord Jesus Christ, not by man, not handed down by apostolic authority.

In the first part of his letter to the Galatian church, Paul gave this testimony: "Do I now persuade men, or God? Or do I seek to please men? For if I yet pleased men, I should not be the servant of Christ. *But I certify you, brethren, that the Gospel which was preached of me is NOT AFTER MAN. For I neither received it of man, neither was I taught it, but by the REVELATION OF JESUS CHRIST.* . . . When it pleased God, who separated me from my mother's womb, and called me by His grace, to reveal His Son in me, that I might preach Him among the heathen; *immediately I CONFERRED NOT WITH FLESH AND BLOOD: neither went I up to Jerusalem to them which were apostles before me;* but I went into Arabia, and returned again unto Damascus. Then after three years I went up to Jerusalem to see Peter, and abode with him fifteen days. But other of the apostles saw I none, save James the Lord's brother" (Gal. 1:10–19 in part).

Paul was a chosen vessel, set apart to preach the good news of salvation by grace through faith plus nothing. The Greek word translated "servant" in the passage just given from Galatians actually means "bond servant," or "bond slave," and a bond slave has only one person to please—*his lord and master.* His one aim is to do the *will* of his master. Paul, as a bond slave of the Lord Jesus Christ, did not seek to please men nor to do the will of men. He sought always to do and say that which would bring glory to the One who had put him into the ministry. This fact he always made clear, just as he made it plain that he was not a minister by his own choice but "through THE WILL OF GOD" (I Cor.

1:1; II Cor. 1:1). He makes the same statement in Ephesians 1:1 and in Colossians 1:1. In I Timothy 1:1 he declares himself to be "an apostle of Jesus Christ *by the COMMANDMENT of God our Saviour, and Lord Jesus Christ . . . .*"

In II Timothy 1:1 Paul again declares his apostleship "by the will of God," and Galatians 1:1 declares that his apostolic appointment was *"not of men, neither by man, but BY JESUS CHRIST, AND GOD THE FATHER,* who raised Him from the dead." In I Corinthians 9:16 he testified, "For though I preach the Gospel, *I have nothing to glory of: for NECESSITY is laid upon me; yea, WOE IS UNTO ME, if I preach not the Gospel!*"

In I Timothy 1:11, 12 Paul speaks of *"the glorious Gospel of the blessed God, which was COMMITTED TO MY TRUST. And I thank Christ Jesus our Lord, who hath enabled me, for that He counted me faithful, PUTTING ME INTO THE MINISTRY."*

Saul of Tarsus met Jesus on the Damascus road. He became Paul the preacher, and having been put into the ministry by the will of God and the Lord Jesus Christ, he faithfully preached *"the Gospel of the grace of God"* until his lips were sealed in martyrdom.

Verse 25:    *"And now, behold, I know that ye all, among whom I have gone preaching the kingdom of God, shall see my face no more."*

That Paul preached *"the Kingdom of God"* tells us that he preached the second coming of the Lord Jesus Christ and the millennial reign of Christ on earth. Although the Jews rejected and crucified their King, the Kingdom of God *will be set up,* Jesus will sit on the throne of David and reign in righteousness, and the earth will be filled with the knowledge of God as the waters now cover the sea. So Paul not only preached the second coming at the time of the Rapture, but also the return of Christ in glory to set up His kingdom.

*"Ye all . . . shall see my face no more."* Parting from his parishioners is always a sad time for a true minister of God. Those who have been edified by his preaching and who have worked in unison with him to the glory of God find a close bond established with a faithful pastor or evangelist. Ties of Christian love bind brothers and sisters in Christ as earthly ties often do not, and the parting in such instances brings sorrow to the hearts of minister and congregation alike. For Paul, this was especially true. He loved his converts with a peculiar devotion and concern for their welfare. He was jealous of the Gospel and he longed to see the believers "come in the unity of the faith, and of the knowledge of the Son of God, unto a perfect man, unto the measure of the stature of the fulness of Christ" (Eph. 4:13). Paul had spent more time in Ephesus than in any other place where he carried the Gospel, and his devotion to the Ephesian believers is certainly understandable.

Also, there is always a close tie between the believer and the person who led him to Christ. When Paul came into the city of Ephesus it was given over to idolatry, the Gospel had no following there, and the people were "dead in trespasses and sins," walking "according to the course of this world, according to the prince of the power of the air, the spirit that now worketh in the children of disobedience." They were living for the lusts of the flesh, "fulfilling the desires of the flesh and of the mind, and were by nature the children of wrath" (Eph. 2:1—3). Then Paul came, with his message of the death, burial, and resurrection of the Lord Jesus Christ. Light came into the city, and Paul's preaching opened up to them that "new and living way"—salvation through faith in the finished work of the Lord Jesus Christ. These people who had once been "without Christ . . . aliens from the commonwealth of Israel . . . strangers from the covenants of promise, having no hope, and without God in the world" were now "no more strangers and foreign-

ers, but fellowcitizens with the saints, and of the household of God" (Eph. 2:12—19 in part). Paul had brought the glorious Gospel to them, the Gospel which had enlightened the eyes of their understanding, and they were saddened by his announcement that he would see them no more (verses 37 and 38 of this chapter).

Paul did not know what would befall him in Jerusalem, but if he was delivered from the trials and persecutions he would certainly face there, he intended taking his ministry to other countries and would not be returning to Ephesus.   In Acts 19:21 he expressed his desire to visit Rome, and in Romans 15:24 he revealed his hope of a journey into Spain on his way to Rome. So he was passing through the cities in Greece and Macedonia for the last time.

Verses 26 and 27:  *"Wherefore I take you to record this day, that I am pure from the blood of all men.  For I have not shunned to declare unto you all the counsel of God."*

*"WHEREFORE . . ."* (that is, because of Paul's past ministry and his labors among them) *"I take you to record"* (he calls them as witnesses) *"that I am PURE from the BLOOD of all men."* Paul had not complicated the simplicity of the plan of salvation. He had preached the grace of God in so simple and plain a way as to make it understandable even to a child. Therefore those who heard his message and then rejected it could not blame him if they died without salvation and were lost forever.

This principle is set forth in Ezekiel 3:18,19 where God instructed Ezekiel to warn the children of Israel: "When I say unto the wicked, Thou shalt surely die; and thou givest him not warning, nor speakest to warn the wicked from his wicked way, to save his life; the same wicked man shall die in his iniquity; but *his BLOOD will I require at thine hand.*  Yet if thou warn

the wicked and he turn not from his wickedness, nor from his wicked way, he shall die in his iniquity; *but thou hast delivered thy soul.*"

The same thing is repeated in Ezekiel 33:8, 9: "When I say unto the wicked, O wicked man, thou shalt surely die; if thou dost not speak to warn the wicked from his way, that wicked man shall die in his iniquity; but *his BLOOD will I require at thine hand!* Nevertheless, if thou warn the wicked of his way to turn from it; if he do not turn from his way, he shall die in his iniquity; but thou hast delivered thy soul."

Paul spoke of this to the Jews in Corinth when they blasphemed in the face of his preaching that Jesus was the Christ. "And when they opposed themselves, and blasphemed, he shook his raiment, and said unto them: *YOUR BLOOD BE UPON YOUR OWN HEADS! I am clean. From henceforth I will go unto the Gentiles*" (Acts 18:6).

Wherever Paul preached he faithfully warned that the wages of sin is death. He had faithfully presented the gift of God—eternal life through the finished work of Jesus. He preached pure Bible doctrine, and he had preached Gospel truth to *"ALL men"*—Jews, Gentiles, rich, poor, bond or free, learned or unlearned. He had not only presented the plan of salvation to the unsaved; he had also fed the babes in Christ with the milk of the Word, and those who were growing in grace he fed with the strong *meat* of the Word. Therefore he could stand before them and declare, "I have delivered my soul, and your blood is not on my hands!"

*"For I have not shunned to declare . . . all the counsel of God."* Here is set forth the reason for what Paul has said in the previous verses. He was innocent of the blood of those to whom he had preached, even if they should be lost. He had not shunned to preach the whole truth of God—that is, he had kept back nothing that would be profitable to their spiritual welfare. He had

not been hindered by fear of man, nor had he held back any detail of truth in order to gain popularity with men. He sought no praise of man, and he preached the pure doctrine of the Word of God in spite of the fact that such preaching was not acceptable to all of his hearers.

The Greek word here translated *"shunned"* also means *to disguise.* Paul did not disguise any important or vital doctrine of Bible truth. He had brought the truth out in the open and declared it in words easily understood.

*"The whole counsel of God"* means the entire purpose (or will) of God as revealed in regard to the salvation of sinners. It was to Paul that God revealed the mystery of the New Testament Church, *a mystery "which in other ages was not made known unto the sons of men,* as it is now revealed unto His holy apostles and prophets by the Spirit; that the *Gentiles* should be *fellowheirs, and of the same body,* and partakers of His promise in Christ by the Gospel" (Eph. 3:2—6 in part).

Paul preached the miracle of salvation by grace through faith (Eph. 2:8). To the Judaists he declared that by the deeds of the law no man ever had been, nor ever would be, justified in the sight of God. "For what the law *could not* do, in that it was weak through the flesh, God sending His own Son *in the likeness* of sinful flesh, and for sin, *condemned sin in the flesh"* (Rom. 8:3). He explained that the sinless Son of God was made to be sin *for US,* "that we might be made *the righteousness of God IN HIM"* (II Cor. 5:21).

Not only did Paul himself declare the whole counsel of God, he also instructed young Timothy and Titus concerning their ministry that they should do as he had done. To Timothy he wrote, *"Preach the WORD!"* (II Tim. 4:2). He admonished Titus, "Speak thou the things which become *sound doctrine"* (Tit. 2:1).

## The Purchase Price of the Church

Verse 28: *"Take heed therefore unto yourselves, and*

to all the flock, over the which the Holy Ghost hath
made you overseers, to feed the Church of God, which
He hath purchased with His own blood."

"Take heed therefore unto yourselves"—i. e., "Be constantly on guard against the dangers that are sure to
beset you, and be careful how you live and how you
conduct yourselves." The first duty of a minister is to
live what he preaches. He should be an example to
the flock. As Paul expressed it in Colossians 4:17, ministers should "take heed to the ministry" which they
have received of the Lord, that they fulfil that ministry.
He admonished Timothy, "Neglect not the gift that is
in thee, which was given thee by prophecy, with the
laying on of the hands of the presbytery" (I Tim. 4:14).

Paul applied these precautions to his own life. He
testified, "I keep under my body, and bring it into subjection: lest that by any means, when I have preached
to others, I myself should be a castaway" (I Cor. 9:27).
He did not fear that he might fail in salvation, but that
he might lose his crown, his reward for faithful service.
Therefore he was determined to keep his body under
control, lest passion or lust overcome him. He practiced
rigid self-denial in order to keep himself spiritually fit
for the Christian work God had called him to do. The
devil places peculiar dangers and unusual temptations
before God's ministers, and it is important that they be
on guard at all times. Therefore Paul warned the elders
to watch over their conduct that they might be good
examples to others.

". . . and to all the flock"—that is, the local assembly
of born again people over whom the Lord had appointed
the elders as His undershepherds. Jesus Himself referred
to Christians in that same manner. John 10:1—16 records
His discourse on the Good Shepherd who "giveth His
life for the sheep." In John 21:15—17 He commissioned
Peter, "Feed my lambs . . . Feed my sheep." There is
to be no partiality. The undershepherd of God is to love

the lambs and the sheep, he is to teach them, guide them, guard them from their enemies, direct them around the pitfalls of the devil. He is also to *feed* the flock—the "sincere milk of the Word" for those who are not yet ready for meat, and the bread and meat of the Word for those who can assimilate it.

"... *over the which the Holy Ghost hath made you overseers.*" Notice—*the Holy Ghost* appointed these overseers, the undershepherds of "the Church of the living God." While these elders were no doubt selected by members of the assembly, the Holy Ghost prompted and led in the selection. I am afraid that in too many churches today the Holy Spirit is not given a chance to have any part in the annual elections held in most churches. On the contrary, committees are appointed, personalities are selected and voted on, and the winner is put into office. They are not always selected for their spirituality and dedication to God and to the church, but for their own political, social, or financial standing. It is evident for all to see that politics has invaded the local assembly today, and all too often it is run by politicians in the field of religion. One need not go to Rome to find a pope, for there are popes, bishops, priests, and religious dictators in all of the big denominations. In the early days of the Church, the Holy Ghost had pre-eminence in all things. He selected the first deacons, He selected the elders at Ephesus, and He selected the leaders of the New Testament Church in its infancy.

The overseers of the assembly were to *"feed the Church of God."* We have already touched on this as one of the duties of God's undershepherds. I Peter 2:2 instructs, "As newborn babes, desire *the sincere MILK of the Word,* that ye may *grow* thereby." To the believers in Corinth Paul said, "I have fed you with *milk,* and *not with MEAT:* for hitherto ye were not able to bear it, neither yet now are ye able. For ye are yet *carnal* . . ." (I Cor. 3:2, 3).

". . . the Church of God, *which He hath purchased WITH HIS OWN BLOOD.*" I do not profess to understand this final statement in our present verse. Each time I read it I feel that I should remove the shoes from my feet because I stand on holy ground! The New Testament Church is *God's* Church—His own purchased possession—and the price paid is *God's own blood.* We know Jesus died and shed His blood for the Church. Therefore *the blood which flowed in the veins of the Lamb of God was the blood of God.*

I repeat: I do not understand this, it is too glorious for my comprehension; *but I BELIEVE it.* I accept it by faith because it is the Word of the living God. Many people today say that men do not need to be born again, that there is no need for sinners to be washed in the blood. They claim that all men have a spark of divinity, and all will eventually be saved. Beloved, if that be true, then there was no reason for Calvary!

Calvary is God's ultimate and final treatment of sin— S-I-N, singular, the sin that damns the soul. John the Baptist said of Jesus, *"Behold the Lamb of God, which taketh away the SIN of the world"* (John 1:29). John 3:18 declares, "He that believeth on Him is not condemned: but *he that believeth NOT is condemned AL-READY*, because he hath not believed in the name of the only begotten Son of God."

*Apart from SIN* the cross would be a meaningless blunder, and the death of the Son of God would be the greatest outrage recorded in the pages of history, sacred or secular! BUT—"All have sinned and come short of the glory of God" (Rom. 3:23). Therefore the cross was God's exhibition of the vilest and worst in the heart of unregenerate men, as well as His exhibition of the best in the heart of a compassionate, longsuffering God toward hell-deserving sinners. God met His own requirements in the shed blood of His Son on the cruel cross planted on Golgotha. The religions of the world demand blood

*from* their devotees and followers—blood to be offered in appeasement of their gods, whereas the singular fact of Christianity is that by the grace of God *blood flows FROM GOD to the sinner.* God was in Christ, reconciling the world unto Himself (II Cor. 5:19).

Since God did not act apart from Christ, it must follow that Christ's action is God's action. Before the world was, before there was a sinner to save, God in His omniscience saw the need for a Saviour—and He *provided* a Saviour. In I Peter 1:18—20 we read, "Forasmuch as ye know that ye were not redeemed with corruptible things, as silver and gold, from your vain conversation received by tradition from your fathers; but *with the precious BLOOD OF CHRIST,* as of a lamb without blemish and without spot: *who verily was foreordained BEFORE THE FOUNDATION OF THE WORLD, but was manifest in these last times for you.*"

There is but *ONE true Church.* Certainly local churches are scriptural, they are in the plan of God. It pleased Him to establish (through the Apostle Paul) churches throughout Asia Minor, and it pleases the Lord today to establish local churches through the preaching of the Gospel of His grace. *But all true local churches are members of the ONE true Church.* There are several outstanding denominational groups, but *all born again believers within those denominations* are members of the one true Church. Just as there is "one Lord, one faith, one baptism, one God and Father of all, who is above all, and through all, and in you all" (Eph. 4:5, 6), so is there but one true Church.

Jesus is the head and foundation of the Church, He is the Saviour of the body, and all born again believers are *members* of His body—"of His flesh and of His bones" (Eph. 5:30). The moment a person *believes* and is born of the Spirit, that person becomes a member of the body of Christ, added to the body through the baptism of the Holy Spirit:

"For as the body is one, and hath many members, and all the members of that one body, being many, are one body: *so also is Christ.* For by one Spirit are we all baptized into one body, whether we be Jews or Gentiles, whether we bond or free; and have been all made to drink into one Spirit. For the body is not one member, but many" (I Cor. 12:12—14).

Every saved person is a member of the New Testament Church, the body of Christ, united to the body through the baptism of the Holy Spirit the very moment he believes. The New Testament Church belongs to God as His purchased possession. The Greek word here translated "purchased" means to acquire or gain something, either through paying a purchase price or by labor. The noun derived from this verb is used several times in the New Testament, always denoting *acquisition.* For example, in I Thessalonians 5:9 it is rendered "obtain": "For God hath not appointed us to wrath, *but TO OBTAIN salvation* by our Lord Jesus Christ."

The same word is used again in II Thessalonians 2:14: "Whereunto He called you by our Gospel, *to the OBTAINING of the glory of our Lord Jesus Christ."* The Church is often referred to as having been bought with a price (I Cor. 6:20; 7:23; II Pet. 2:1), and that purchase price was *God's own blood* shed on Calvary in the Person of the Lord Jesus Christ, our Saviour.

Verse 29: *"For I know this, that after my departing shall grievous wolves enter in among you, not sparing the flock."*

*"I know this . . . ."* Not only did Paul preach and work under the inspiration of the Holy Spirit who could teach him all things; in this particular instance his knowledge of human nature, plus his experience with the dangers to which believers were exposed, convinced him, gave him absolute assurance, of what would happen in the church at Ephesus after he left that area.

*"Grievous wolves"* would enter into the flock, sparing none of them. The Greek word here translated *"grievous"* means "strong, mighty, dangerous." Those who would attack the church would be energized by the devil himself. In the comparison Paul makes here we see a wolf pouncing on a lamb without the protection of the shepherd. The lamb would, of course, be devoured, and the same would be true in the church at Ephesus. The "grievous wolves" who would come among the believers would not destroy the soul and bring damnation on them, but they would certainly play havoc with the "lambs," the babes in Christ, by destroying their confidence, their joy, their fruitfulness, and their testimony.

Since believers, members of the Church of God, are referred to as "the flock," *wolves* would be a natural symbol of the *enemies* of the flock—false teachers, hypocrites, dangerous men who would bring in lying, damnable heresies and attempt to frustrate the grace of God— and the *program* of God—in the local assembly. In Matthew 7:15 Jesus told His disciples, "Beware of false prophets, which come to you *in sheep's clothing,* but inwardly they are *ravening wolves!"* In Matthew 10:16 He warned them, "Behold, I send you forth *as sheep in the midst of wolves:* be ye therefore wise as serpents, and harmless as doves."

The scope of these verses spoken by our Lord goes far beyond the personal ministry of the twelve apostles. In a general sense it covers even the ministers of the Gospel during this present Day of Grace. Jesus spoke of the enemies of the Gospel during the Church Age, whereas Paul spoke of the enemies of the Gospel who were attacking during his ministry—that is, the Jews who traveled from place to place demanding that believers submit to the rituals of the Law of Moses. Immediately upon hearing of Paul's departure from a city or an area, they came from Jerusalem and by disputing in favor of the law versus Christianity they sought to

destroy the local assembly and hinder its soul-winning program.

Such "wolves in sheep's clothing" are still operating today in assemblies where the pure Gospel of the grace of God is preached. The devil does not worry about the congregation pastored by a liberal or modernist because he knows those people are "religious" but lost. But you can rest assured that when *God's* man delivers *God's message,* the wolves will enter and seek to destroy the flock!

Verse 30: *"Also of your own selves shall men arise, speaking perverse things, to draw away disciples after them."*

This announcement probably shocked the Ephesian elders. *Surely* not from *among themselves* would these troublemakers arise! But that was exactly what Paul meant. From their own congregation there would be some who *professed* to be Christians but were actually wolves in disguise. These men would be members of the local assembly, but they would speak perverse things, distracted doctrines.

You see, the devil knows he can do more damage from within than from without. He can work more effectively through people who are already members of a church, men who profess to be leaders and teachers of the Gospel, but who actually pervert the true doctrines of the Word, preaching just enough Gospel to cover the falsehood they preach. Such preaching will lead astray those who are not truly born again and led by the Holy Spirit. People who have simply been *convicted* of sin but have not been *converted* unto salvation through the miracle of the new birth are often members of a local assembly, and they are easily led astray by teachers who pervert the Gospel. When these people become calloused through error, it is almost impossible to reach them with the true message of salvation.

John the Beloved wrote of one such perverter of the true doctrines of the faith. In III John 9, 10 we read, "I wrote unto the church: but *Diotrephes,* who loveth to have the preeminence among them, receiveth us not. Wherefore, if I come, I will remember his deeds which he doeth, prating against us with malicious words: and not content therewith, neither doth he himself receive the brethren, and forbiddeth them that would, and casteth them out of the church."

Paul wrote to Timothy, "This thou knowest—that all they which are in Asia be turned away from me; of whom are *Phygellus* and *Hermogenes*" (II Tim. 1:15).

In I Timothy 1:20 Paul spoke of *"Hymenaeus* and *Alexander;* whom I have delivered unto Satan, that they may learn not to blaspheme!"

Such men as are mentioned here—and we still have them in our local assemblies today—are not led of the Holy Spirit but are under the influence of personal ambition, love of power and popularity. They seek to draw men after them because they covet the praise of men rather than the approval of God. Therefore they bring about divisions in the church, disturb the peace, and hinder the spiritual growth and prosperity of the entire assembly.

Paul declared to the Corinthian church, "Such are false apostles, deceitful workers, transforming themselves into the apostles of Christ. And no marvel; for Satan himself is transformed into an angel of light. Therefore it is no great thing if his ministers also be transformed as the ministers of righteousness; whose end shall be according to their works" (II Cor. 11:13—15).

We find Peter's warning in II Peter 2:1—3: "There were false prophets also among the people, even as there shall be false teachers among you, who privily shall bring in damnable heresies, even denying the Lord that bought them and bring upon themselves swift destruction. And many shall follow their pernicious ways; by

reason of whom the way of truth shall be evil spoken of. And through covetousness shall they with feigned words make merchandise of you: whose judgment now of a long time lingereth not, and their damnation slumbereth not."

John also warns against those who call themselves Christians but are not born again. He wrote, "Little children, . . . as ye have heard that antichrist shall come, even now are there many antichrists; whereby we know that it is the last time. They went out from us, but they were not of us; for if they had been of us, they would no doubt have continued with us: but they went out, that they might be made manifest that they were not all of us" (I John 2:18, 19).

These "antichrists" of whom John speaks were members of a *local church,* not the body of Christ. They were operating inside the assembly, but John is careful to tell us, *"They were not OF us."* Today some people might refer to these men as "backsliders," but they were not backsliders in the true sense. They had united with the local assembly, they joined in name, but they were never born into the family of God. Therefore in heart and experience they were never members of the true Church. Such people can be very effective "wolves" because they work *within* the assembly, even though they are not *OF* it except by profession.

Verse 31:   *"Therefore watch, and remember, that by the space of three years I ceased not to warn every one night and day with tears."*

*"Therefore"*—that is, in view of the dangers which faced the church at Ephesus and the attacks of Satan that would be hurled against it from without—*"watch, and remember."* *Peter* gives a similar warning: "Be sober, be vigilant; because your adversary the devil, as a roaring lion, walketh about, seeking whom he may devour" (I Pet. 5:8). The Ephesian elders were not to

forget Paul's warning. They were to remember not only the admonitions he gave them at this particular time, but "that *by the space of three years I ceased not to warn every one night and day.*"

Paul stayed longer in Ephesus than in any of the other locations where he preached or established churches. He spoke in the synagogue for three months (Acts 19:8), and when opposition there hindered his work he moved into the school of Tyrannus where he taught "by the space of two years" (Acts 19:10). But he also taught in homes, or wherever a group gathered who hungered and thirsted after righteousness. Thus was his ministry in Ephesus prolonged, and he spent three whole years there—preaching, teaching, admonishing, counseling.

The statement that he preached *"night and day"* of course does not mean that he preached for twenty-four hours daily for three years. Common sense tells us better. It simply means that for the three years Paul spent in the city of Ephesus he preached in the daytime, he preached at night, and he counseled with believers in all things that were profitable unto them. In other words, he applied the instruction he gave young Timothy when he told him to "preach the Word, be instant in season, out of season; reprove, rebuke, exhort with all longsuffering and doctrine" (II Tim. 4:2).

His mention of warning *"every one"* indicates to me that Paul's ministry in Ephesus included Jews, Greeks, rich men, poor men, bondmen and free men. He preached to all classes of people—and it certainly seems reasonable that he also instructed each *individual* who sought him privately. As Jesus taught in the home of Mary, Martha, and Lazarus, I believe Paul taught wherever even one person needed the Gospel—and I can easily believe that he took time to instruct new Christians in the walk of the believer!

The fact that Paul taught *"with tears"* expresses his

love and deep concern for the people in Ephesus. This
man had a love for *people*—saved and unsaved. He
yearned after his own kinsmen after the flesh, longing
to see them saved, willing to be "accursed from Christ"
if such sacrifice on his part could bring salvation to
his people (Rom. 9:2, 3). But just as he longed to see
sinners saved, he also carried a burden for those who
were converted under his preaching, taking care that
the "babes in Christ" should grow in grace "unto a
perfect man, unto the measure of the stature of the fulness of Christ" (Eph. 4:13). His writings to the churches
are filled with encouragement, understanding, instructions in the Christian walk, and warnings against turning
again "to the weak and beggarly elements" to which
they had been in bondage (Gal. 4:9). In II Corinthians
11:23—28, as Paul enumerated the trials, persecutions, and
afflictions he had endured for the sake of the Gospel,
he ended the account in these words: "Beside those
things that are *without*, that which cometh upon me
*daily, THE CARE OF ALL THE CHURCHES.*" No
wonder he preached *"with tears"!* The Psalmist wrote,
"He that goeth forth and weepeth, bearing precious
seed, shall doubtless come again with rejoicing, bringing
his sheaves with him" (Psalm 126:6). This was true of
the life and ministry of the Apostle Paul.

Verse 32: *"And now, brethren, I commend you to
God, and to the word of His grace, which is able to
build you up, and to give you an inheritance among
all them which are sanctified."*

*"Brethren, I commend you to God."* When human
strength fails, God is able to sustain. Paul would not
again return to this area. He had already told these
men that they would see his face no more (v. 25), and
he now committed them to the faithful care and keeping
of Him "who is able to keep us from falling, and to
present us faultless before the presence of His glory with

exceeding joy" (Jude 24).

"*. . . and to the Word of His grace,*" the precious, powerful Word of the living God, His promises of mercy, strength, power, and protection, "*which is able to build you up.*" The Word of God is the milk, bread, meat, and living water that feeds the believer, causing him to grow and become strong in the Lord. The Word of God is not dead formalism; it is life-giving power—the power of God unto salvation to all who believe (Rom. 1:16); and the power of God that saves us is able to keep and protect us. "For the weapons of our warfare are not carnal, but *mighty THROUGH GOD* to the pulling down of strongholds" (II Cor. 10:4).

"*. . . which is able to build you up.*" This language is suggestive of building a house, completing it step by step, slowly and through much labor. Therefore, the Word of God is able to build the Christian. As we read and feed upon the Word we are built up in the faith, in grace, in strength. The Word of God is able to confirm and establish believers in the midst of any dangers we may face.

"*. . . and to give you an inheritance*"—children, heirs of God, joint-heirs with Christ and with all the saints in the eternal blessings reserved for the children of God. Such an inheritance God has clearly and assuredly promised to His children. In Matthew 19:29 Jesus declared, "Every one that hath forsaken houses, or brethren, or sisters, or father, or mother, or wife, or children, or lands, for my name's sake, shall receive *an hundredfold,* and shall *inherit everlasting life.*"

In Mark 10:21 Jesus said to the rich young ruler, "One thing thou lackest:   go thy way, sell whatsoever thou hast, and give to the poor, *and thou shalt have treasure in heaven:*   and come, take up the cross, and follow me."

Revelation 21:7 promises, "He that overcometh shall *inherit ALL things;* and I will be his God, and he shall

be my son."

In I Peter 1:3—5 we find these blessed and assuring words: "Blessed be the God and Father of our Lord Jesus Christ, which according to His abundant mercy hath begotten us again unto a lively hope by the resurrection of Jesus Christ from the dead, *to an inheritance incorruptible, and undefiled, and that fadeth not away, RESERVED IN HEAVEN FOR YOU*, who are kept by the power of God through faith unto salvation ready to be revealed in the last time."

"*. . . among all which are sanctified.*" To be sanctified means to be set apart, therefore all born again believers are sanctified, set apart unto God. The moment we are born again we are taken out of the family of the devil and placed over into the family of God. We are translated from the kingdom of darkness into the kingdom of light. We are sanctified *positionally* the split second we believe; we are sanctified *experimentally* day by day as we study the Word of God. Christ is "made unto us . . . sanctification, and redemption: that, according as it is written, He that glorieth, let him glory in the Lord" (I Cor. 1:30, 31).

Verses 33 and 34: "*I have coveted no man's silver, or gold, or apparel. Yea, ye yourselves know, that these hands have ministered unto my necessities, and to them that were with me.*"

Paul did not preach "for filthy lucre's sake." He coveted no man's earthly possessions. Here he reminded the Ephesian elders that he had not made their money or their property the object of his living among them. He said to the Corinthians, "I seek not *your's*, but *YOU*" (II Cor. 12:14), and the same was true in Ephesus —or wherever Paul preached. He entered a community and lived among its people for one purpose—to preach the Gospel, to proclaim Christ and Him crucified.

When Saul of Tarsus was converted and became Paul

the apostle, "straightway he preached Christ . . . that He is the Son of God" (Acts 9:20). From that day forward he made the primary object of his life the preaching of the Gospel of the grace of God, and he could have legitimately demanded support from his ministry, from those among whom he labored so untiringly; but he did not. In I Corinthians 9:13—15 he testified, "Do ye not know that they which minister about holy things live of the things of the temple? and they which wait at the altar are partakers with the altar? *Even so hath the Lord ordained that they which preach the Gospel should LIVE of the Gospel.* But I have used none of these things: neither have I written these things, that it should be so done unto me: for it were better for me to die, than that any man should make my glorying void!"

If Paul had been selfish, he also had ample *opportunity* to receive gain, because the early believers committed their property to the disposal of the apostles. This is made plain in Acts 4:34, 35 where we read: "Neither was there any among them that lacked: for as many as were possessors of lands or houses *sold them, and brought the prices of the things that were sold, and laid them down at the apostles' feet: and distribution was made unto every man according as he had need."*

There *were* teachers in Paul's day who made merchandise of the souls of men. Even when Jesus came on the scene the temple was filled with money changers, those who sold animals to be offered as sacrifices. We have the same problem today, although there are no men in the churches selling animals or changing money for gain. Nevertheless, there are "religious racketeers," religion has become "big business" throughout the world, and many men today are making merchandise of the souls of their fellowmen.

I trust no one will misunderstand me—most assuredly I believe God's minister should be taken care of, I believe

the laborer is worthy of his hire. But I also believe that God is able and willing to supply the needs of His faithful servants. I can truthfully say that through more than a quarter of a century of preaching the Gospel and living by faith, my every need has been supplied. I have not had everything I *wanted,* there are many things I would have liked to have; but God knew those things were not best for me, therefore He withheld them from me. But He has faithfully supplied those things that were necessary, He has abundantly taken care of my needs.

Paul was a tentmaker by trade (Acts 18:3), and he chose to labor with his hands in order to support himself in the ministry lest he be accused of preaching for monetary gain rather than to the glory of God. In Thessalonica he labored "night and day," that he should not be "chargeable" (indebted) to those to whom he preached the Gospel (I Thess. 2:9).

To the Philippians he testified, "What things were gain to me, those I counted loss for Christ. Yea, doubtless, and I count all things but loss for the excellency of the knowledge of Christ Jesus my Lord: for whom I have suffered the loss of all things, and do count them but dung, that I may win Christ" (Phil. 3:7, 8). Paul's concern for the things of Christ transcended all thought of things material. He entered a community or city with the determination to lift up the blood-stained banner and declare the Gospel of the grace of God—or, as he expressed it to the Corinthians, *to know nothing among them, "save Jesus Christ, and Him crucified"* (I Cor. 2:2).

We might think it strange, according to customs of today, that Paul would say he had coveted no man's *apparel.* In those days, changes of raiment formed an important part of a man's property, and many times his apparel was worth almost as much as the rest of his earthly possessions combined. There were not many

extremely wealthy people, and those who were very poor often had only one change of raiment. Therefore it was not unusual for the poor to envy the rich man's apparel— but not so with Paul. He said, "I have learned, in whatsoever state I am, therewith to be content. I know both how to be abased, and I know how to abound: every where and in all things I am instructed both to be full and to be hungry, both to abound and to suffer need." Then he added triumphantly, *"I can do ALL THINGS through Christ which strengtheneth me!"* (Phil. 4:11—13).

*"Ye yourselves KNOW . . . ."* Paul had lived and labored among the Ephesians for three years, and they knew from personal observation what his manner of life had been.

*"These hands have ministered unto my necessities."* Tentmaking was rough work. The tents were woven in strips, the material was usually goats' hair, and the strips were then sewn together into the proper size. I can easily imagine that Paul's hands were rough and calloused—not at all like the scholar he was, but as the hands of a rugged day-laborer might be. Even today, in an age when most churches are able to support the man who pastors their congregation, no minister of God should feel himself above manual labor. The man who goes into the unevangelized mission field will of necessity find himself not only preaching the Word, but *building*— under adverse conditions, amid multiplied hardships, laboring with his hands in order to have an opportunity to preach the Gospel to those who have never heard the message of God's boundless love and grace.

The man who pastors a small church or a church in some of the slums of our great cities will also meet with necessity that will require him to labor with his hands and with his back, as well as in the harvest of souls by preaching the Word. Certainly it is no dishonor for a minister to expend physical labor in carrying out his

ministry, but it *is* dishonorable for a congregation to *force* a pastor to such occupation when the members are able to support him and allow him to give full time to ministering the Word and caring for the spiritual needs of his people. In order to feed the flock, the under-shepherd must first be fed; and time must be allowed for a minister to study, pray, and be filled with nourishment from God's Word.

Not only did Paul himself labor in order to provide his own livelihood, he also mentions *"them that were with me."* We know that Paul had various companions on his missionary journeys, and they, too, worked for their own support rather than be dependent upon those to whom they ministered. In I Corinthians 9:4—6 he speaks of his right to eat and drink, "to lead about a sister, a wife, as well as other apostles, and as the brethren of the Lord, and Cephas—*or I only and BARNABAS,* have not we power to forbear working?"

In Paul's second letter to the Thessalonians he reminded them that he and his companions "behaved not ourselves disorderly among you; *neither did we eat any man's bread for nought; but wrought with labour and travail night and day, that we might not be chargeable to any of you*—not because we have not power, but to make ourselves an ensample unto you to follow us" (II Thess. 3:7—9).

In I Corinthians 4:9—13, Paul also speaks in the plural, showing that not only he, but others of the apostles, worked for their support even while they ministered. He wrote, "I think that God hath set forth *us the apostles* last, as it were appointed to death: for *we* are made a spectacle unto the world, and to angels, and to men. *We* are fools for Christ's sake . . . *we* are weak . . . *we* are despised. Even unto this present hour *we* both hunger, and thirst, and are naked, and are buffeted, and have no certain dwellingplace; *AND LABOUR, WORKING WITH OUR OWN HANDS:* being reviled,

*we* bless; being persecuted, *we* suffer it: being defamed, *we* intreat: *we* are made as the filth of the world, and are the offscouring of all things unto this day!"

Beloved, can we today conceive of what the Gospel meant to these men, that they would by choice endure such hardships in order to *preach* the Gospel? This was not because they had *no right* to be supported in the ministry, but that they might be examples before those to whom they preached, and that God might have the glory. How much we make of a bit of hardship or deprivation today, when Paul and those who were with him in his labors endured so much, sacrificed so much, and took glory in it, that the Lord Jesus Christ might have pre-eminence over all things!

Verse 35:   *"I have shewed you all things, how that so labouring ye ought to support the weak, and to remember the words of the Lord Jesus, how He said, It is more blessed to give than to receive."*

*"I have SHEWED you all things . . . ."* Not by word only, but by *living example* as well, Paul taught the young churches.   He not only *told* them how to live as Christians should, he also *showed* them what an exemplary Christian life should be.   *"All things"* of course means all things beneficial to their spiritual life, all pure doctrine.   He refused to dodge an issue lest he hurt someone's feelings. He preached pure grace in the midst of the Judaisers. He declared the whole counsel of God in the presence of kings. He had but one message—the message of God's grace—and he preached it without apology.

*"So labouring, ye ought to support the weak"*—meaning, "You who are able to work with your hands should labor to provide the needs of those in the assembly who are sick or feeble, those who are unable to care for themselves."   Then Paul reminded them of the words of the Lord Jesus:

". . . how He said, *It is more blessed to give than to receive.*" This is a reference to the words of Jesus in Luke 14:12—14 when He said, "When thou makest a dinner or a supper, call not thy friends, nor thy brethren, neither thy kinsmen, nor thy rich neighbours; lest they also bid thee again, and a recompence be made thee. But when thou makest a feast, call the poor, the maimed, the lame, the blind: and thou shalt be blessed; for they cannot recompense thee: for thou shalt be recompensed at the resurrection of the just."

This passage does not contain a *word-for-word* expression of what Paul said to the Ephesian elders, but the teaching is the same—and as John the Beloved explained, "There are also many other things which Jesus did, the which, if they should be written every one, I suppose that *even the world itself could not contain the books that should be written*" (John 21:25). So Paul reminds his hearers of the lesson Jesus taught—the fact that it is more blessed to give than to receive. This is still true. Spiritually-minded believers get more joy from giving or doing *for* others than they find in *receiving from others.*

After all, this is in keeping with the life of Jesus and the very purpose for which He came into the world. He came "not to be ministered unto, but to minister, and *to give His life* a ransom for many" (Matt. 20:28). He gave His back to the smiters, His cheeks to them that plucked off the hair, and hid not His face from shame and spitting (Isa. 50:6). This He did in order to give pardon to the guilty sinner, comfort to the mourner, and rest to the heavy laden. He gave His tears to weep over Jerusalem (Matt. 23:37), and to sin-benighted souls today His invitation is still, "Come unto me, all ye that labour and are heavy laden, *and I will GIVE you rest!*" (Matt. 11:28). Paul walked so closely with Jesus, longing even to know *"the fellowship of His sufferings"* (Phil. 3:10), small wonder that he referred to the words of his

Lord in giving final instructions to these men upon whom rested the task of overseeing the work of the church in Ephesus.

Verse 36: *"And when he had thus spoken, he kneeled down, and prayed with them all."*

According to the Scriptures, *kneeling* seems to be the preferred posture for praying. I realize that there are many times when we cannot kneel, and I thank God that we can pray while we are standing, walking, riding in an airplane or an automobile—even from a bed of sickness and pain God hears His saints when they pray; but kneeling does indicate humility and reverence toward God.

*Solomon* knelt before the congregation of Israel when he prayed the prayer of dedication for the temple (II Chron. 6:13).

Three times a day *Daniel* knelt and prayed—not in some secret place, not in the dark hours of the night, but before his open window, facing toward the holy city Jerusalem, in plain view of those who plotted to take his life as penalty for praying to the one true God. (Read Daniel chapter 6.)

*Stephen,* the first Christian martyr, knelt as the stones thrown by his accusers beat the life from his body, "and cried with a loud voice, Lord, lay not this sin to their charge. And when he had said this, he fell asleep" (Acts 7:60).

*Peter* knelt as he prayed that life be restored to Tabitha (Acts 9:40).

Notice the attitudes of prayer the Lord Jesus assumed when He prayed in the Garden of Gethsemane, under the burden of the sin of the world: Matthew tells us that He *"fell on his face,* and prayed" (Matt. 26:39). Mark tells us that He *"fell on the ground,* and prayed" (Mark 14:35). Luke tells us that He withdrew from the disciples "about a stone's cast, and *kneeled down,* and

prayed" (Luke 22:41).

Son of God—very God in flesh, holding all power
in heaven and on earth—bowed in an agony of prayer,
face downward on the ground, kneeling and praying so
urgently that "His sweat was as it were great drops
of blood falling down to the ground." Who are *we*,
that we should not kneel in prayer when opportunity
permits? Paul declares emphatically, "God also hath
highly exalted Him (Jesus), and given Him a name which
is above every name: that *at the name of Jesus EVERY
KNEE should bow*, of things in heaven, and things in
earth, and things under the earth; and that every tongue
should confess that Jesus Christ is Lord, to the glory
of God the Father" (Phil. 2:9—11).

Also in Romans 14:11 Paul wrote, "As I live, saith the
Lord, *EVERY KNEE shall bow to me, and every tongue
shall confess to God!*"

I repeat—it is not necessary to *kneel* in order for our
prayers to be heard of God, but when opportunity permits, we should afford Him that respect and reverence.

Verses 37 and 38: *"And they all wept sore, and fell
on Paul's neck, and kissed him, sorrowing most of all
for the words which he spake, that they should see his
face no more.   And they accompanied him unto the
ship."*

*"They all wept sore."* It was from the Apostle Paul
that these men had first heard the message of salvation
and learned that they were among the "whosoever will"
invited to partake of the water of life freely.   Not only
had he brought them the message of eternal life through
God's grace in sending His Son to die for a world lost
in sin, but he had tarried with them—in their city, in
their homes—for three years, helping them to become
*established* in the faith, instructing them in the things
of God and in the affairs of the church over which they
would be presiding.   This alone would have bound them

to the apostle with bonds of love too strong to break without tears; but when we add to those circumstances the overpowering personality of this man, his unbending determination to preach only Christ crucified, his self-sacrificing example and his loving concern for his converts, we need not wonder that "they all wept sore" when the time came to bid Paul goodbye, knowing that he would be returning to them no more!

As for Paul, tears were not unfamiliar to him. We might say that he watered the seed of the Word with his tears as he delivered it. Writing to the church at Corinth he said, "Out of much affliction and anguish of heart I wrote unto you *with MANY TEARS;* not that ye should be grieved, but *that ye might know the LOVE which I have more abundantly unto you*" (II Cor. 2:4). Thus he wept in love for those whom he had won to Christ.

In Philippians 3:18, 19 he wrote, "For many walk, of whom I have told you often, *and now tell you even WEEPING, that they are the enemies of the cross of Christ:* whose end is destruction, whose God is their belly, and whose glory is in their shame, who mind earthly things."

Paul's weeping, as mentioned at various times throughout his ministry, was not a sign of weakness, but rather of strength. He did not weep because of the beatings, imprisonments, hunger, cold, deprivation, illness, or physical afflictions of any kind. He wept under the burden he carried on behalf of the Gospel—a burden for his own brethren, the Jews; a burden for his ordained ministry to the Gentiles, to all sinners; a burden for the welfare of his converts and the young churches he had established under the leadership of the Holy Spirit. Perhaps more than any of the other apostles, Paul had a vision of the true meaning of the cross of Christ in relation to this Dispensation of Grace, the Church Age; and he worked with honest and enlightened zeal to

accomplish what he could in the brief time allotted to him.

The elders *"fell on Paul's neck, and kissed him."* This was not unusual in that day and in that country. The kiss was a common form of greeting among members of the same sex, a common token of love for born again believers toward each other. Paul admonished the believers in Rome, "Salute one another with *an holy kiss.* The churches of Christ salute you" (Rom. 16:16). At the end of his first letter to the Corinthian church he said, "All the brethren greet you. Greet ye one another with *an holy kiss*" (I Cor. 16:20).

*"Sorrowing most of all for the words which he spake."* These "words which he spake" and which were causing such sorrow to the elders are found in verse 25. Paul made known to them the fact that he was going to Jerusalem where the only certainty that awaited him was the *uncertainty* about what might befall him there. He further testified that he was not moved or deterred by any of the dangers that lay ahead, that he intended to finish his course "with joy," fulfilling the ministry God had given him. And then he said, *"Behold, I know that ye all, among whom I have gone preaching the kingdom of God, SHALL SEE MY FACE NO MORE."*

This was no missionary journey on which Paul was embarking, it was not another of his travels to re-visit the young churches and eventually come again to Ephesus. This was their last goodbye to the man who had brought them light and life, and they understood that they would see him no more until they should meet with him in the world beyond, for which he had helped them to prepare. For this farewell, then, they sorrowed "most of all."

*"And they accompanied him unto the ship."* The chapter ends on a sad note. Paul set sail from Miletus on the next lap of his journey toward Jerusalem, his soul filled with a consuming love for his countrymen

and a burning passion to win them to Christianity. Therefore the bonds and afflictions which awaited him in the Holy City meant nothing to him, and his spirit drove him on toward his goal. Events that befell him on that journey and after he reached Jerusalem are penned by Luke in the next chapter—in amazing clarity.